Dangers Unclaimed

BOOK ONE IN THE UNTOLD DANGERS SERIES

AMBER BAYLEY

Dangers Unclaimed

Copyright © 2023 by Amber Bayley

All rights reserved.

No part of this book may be reproduced in any form or by any electronic or mechanical means, including information storage and retrieval systems, without written permission from the author, except for the use of brief quotations in a book review.

This book is a work of fiction. Names, characters, places, and incidents are products of the authors imagination or are used fictitiously. Any resemblance to actual persons, living or dead; events; or locations is entirely coincidental.

ISBN: 978-1-7394998-3-9 (eBook)

ISBN: 978-1-7394998-4-6 (paperback)

Cover design by Amber Bayley © 2023

Edited by Kelly George at Polished Proofreading & Copy-editing

Proofread by Holly Ballard

Contents

Content Warnings

Dangers Unclaimed is an adult, dark fantasy romance that contains strong language, explicit sex, and content some might find distressing, including child abduction, violence, death/murder, dubious consent, consensual and non-consensual biting, rough play and humiliation, degradation, domination, threatening behaviour, coercion, mentions of suicide, strangulation, stalking, mentions of emotional abuse and gaslighting, minor alcohol abuse, mentions of depression, death of a parent, mentions of childhood abuse by a parent, child endangerment, and gore.

For those who love Greek mythology and 80's movies,
but can't help thinking: you know what's missing?

Dinosaurs and demon dicks.

AMBER BAYLEY

Dangers Unclaimed

The Claimed and the Bound

One born, one made,
Fates forever entwined.
Twin souls,
Light and shadow.

Only the innocence of love,
Offered pure, will prove true.

To break the curse, reverse the cycle.
To keep the kingdom, claim the crown.
To be victorious, win the heart.
To find peace, search for meaning.

The father shifting the son a burden.
The mother sacrificing the daughter to darkness.
Both will suffer the consequences,
Until two halves become a whole.

Fail, and the beast will unleash its wrath.

CHAPTER I

Hardships

RAVEN

Growing up has always instilled more fear in me than death itself. While the girls in my class clambered to be Wendy in the school play, I was fighting the boys to be Peter Pan. He never had to grow up. He never had parents burden him with the pressures of looming adulthood.

Before I even hit puberty, I came to understand that society had different expectations for the maturity of girls compared to boys. Along with a long list of other narrow, ridiculous boundaries. Girls faced ridicule for enjoying dolls and fairy tales beyond the age of twelve. Whereas boys could play video games without judgement well into middle age.

Unfortunately, my mum often reinforced these higher patriarchal standards at home, too. She was my harshest critic. She blamed me for my dad disappearing when I was five. On my thirteenth birthday, she donated all my books, toys, and trinkets to charity, saying I was a young adult now and shouldn't be playing with such childish things.

A year later, I discovered the remnants of her childhood hidden in boxes in the attic. I plucked out a little red leather-bound book—a play of some kind—and took it to my room to read.

When Mum discovered me with it, she snatched the book from my hands and told me I was a spoiled brat for looking through her things and taking them without asking.

Fed up and defensive, I shouted I hated my life and wished I could live in one of the many fairy tales she'd stolen away from me. Her biting reply has stuck with me: 'You need to grow up fast, Raven. Clinging onto fairy tales and fantasies will be your ruin. Trust me, I learnt that the hard way.'

Mum never elaborated on what she meant by that. She rarely talked to me about her past. We barely had a relationship beyond the minimum required. In her defence, she worked two jobs to provide for me and my little brother, Robin. I was eight when he was born—conceived through a drunken one-night-stand. I'm twenty-three now, which means he must be fifteen.

God, I should know that. I'm a terrible half-sister.

Anyway, there were times when Mum would wistfully reveal her desire to move back to the States—the country to which she was born. She moved across an ocean to be with my dad in her early twenties, and he couldn't stand to make it five years for her sacrifice.

A mature woman's voice startles me out of my stupor. 'Raven, is that you?'

Gingerly emerging from my hiding place behind a maze of neatly trimmed hedges, I plaster on a smile, unsure if it's appropriate.

The woman is in her mid-fifties—short, blonde, and hard to place. She's one of Mum's work colleagues—Amanda, I think her name is. I met her in passing years ago.

'Hi—yes. Sorry, I just needed a minute,' I say, letting my melancholy show through.

Amanda's eyes shine, her face softening. 'Oh, sweetheart. I know it's such a distressing day for you and your brother. Losing a mother is tough at any age, but her death is truly tragic. She was still so young.' She reaches out to squeeze my arm in comfort. 'If you need anything at all, I'm here. I'm so sorry for your loss. Your mother was such a good friend to me.'

That leaves a bitter taste in my mouth, but I press my lips together to stop them from twitching. 'Thank you. That's kind of you,' I reply, going through the motions of polite funeral conversation. I'll be repeating this line about a hundred times today.

Amanda looks around, searching. Her leathery, tan face creases with concern. 'Where's Robin? I haven't seen him yet.'

Fiddling with a long lock of my wavy black hair, I mutter, 'I'm not sure. He's been staying with one of his friends since... it happened. They were going to drop him off.' Guilt nips at me; I haven't seen my little brother in over three years.

At eighteen, I moved to Edinburgh to attend university. I hardly ever returned to my quaint English hometown and only visited the first two years for the Christmas holidays. I skipped the last three, preferring to hang out with my ex's family in their stately home. I booked into a hotel for the Christmases I *did* travel down for, so I had an excuse to leave early in the evening. Mum never admitted to missing me, and Robin didn't seem to care either—too busy gaming with his school friends to notice my absence. With him being so much younger than me, we were never close.

Still, that's no excuse for my lack of effort in reaching out to him in the wake of our mother's death. It's been a week since she lost her life when she ran into oncoming traffic for some unfathomable reason. The police ruled it an accident, since she didn't leave a suicide note and showed no signs of self-destructive behaviour in the lead-up.

As Mum was walking a country road on the way to her afternoon yoga class, apparently something—most likely an animal—spooked her into losing all sense of road safety.

I was at work when the police called, informing me of her critical state in the hospital. At first, I could only collect myself enough to book a plane ticket. However, as soon as I arrived at the airport, I received the second call.

Boarding a plane to face that reality was something I couldn't stomach, so I rushed back to my flat and chose my favourite comfort read to escape into: *A Maze of Birds and Beasts* by S.L.D Hog. (A pen name, I assume, as I can't find further information on the author).

The book is about a teenage girl thrown into a maze by an evil king who claims to love her. She rises to whatever challenges the King throws, making friends with the beasts tasked to lead her astray. Ultimately, she defeats the King, escaping to her own world again, leaving her innocence behind in payment for her freedom.

Whenever I finish it, I always experience this pang of disappointment in her choice to leave. I'm a sucker for enemies-to-lovers. Unfortunately, that trope was never fulfilled. Though it had potential—that deliciously angsty tension between the characters sates me enough to still count it among my favourite reads.

I can't remember much after I fell asleep that night. Ignoring calls and messages, I think I went about the next day as usual: getting dressed, eating breakfast, taking a bus to the digital marketing office where I work, and chatting with colleagues on my lunch break. I kept the fact that my mum had just died to myself. It wasn't until Robin's friend's mother rang my office directly—letting me know he was staying with them—that I remembered I even *had* a brother.

A brother who's a teenage orphan now.

After that, I stepped up and sorted Mum's funeral, seeing as I couldn't expect a fifteen-year-old to do it. It still took me a few days to muster the courage to fly down, opting to handle the arrangements by phone and email.

I arrived late last night and checked into the airport hotel, making the excuse of being too tired to drive.

Again, Amanda pulls me from my thoughts. 'Shall we head inside? The service will start soon.'

As my thoughts cloud over, I nod, then numbly follow her towards the crematorium, wishing I could have stayed hidden inside that little maze of hedges all day.

A rustle from the tree above draws my focus up. Two onyx eyes, set inside a heart-shaped face of feathers, stare down at me—a barn owl. A fucking barn owl. I've never seen a wild owl in the light of day before. I've heard them cooing at night, especially as a child. There always seemed to be one which made its presence known near my childhood home. However, I don't recall ever seeing it. Mum hated owls with a passion. She played music late into the evening to drown out its insistent hooting.

Refusing to break eye contact with me, the owl clacks its beak, and a chill creeps over my skin, leaving goosebumps in its tracks.

With a shudder, I break first, rushing to catch up with Amanda.

I need no more reminders of my fucked-up childhood. Not today. I already resent my mum enough as it is.

Robin never turned up. He didn't attend his own mother's funeral.

Lucky son of a bitch.

Bad joke, Raven. Definitely in poor taste, considering.

The wake was at the local community centre. Only twenty people were in attendance; mainly work colleagues. Mum has no living relatives except a younger brother I've never met. To the best of my knowledge, he still lives in America. I doubt he even knows she's passed. I'd call him if I knew his number.

Driving down these dark country roads is unsettling. Or maybe I'm simply dreading returning to the home I was always so desperate to leave. I still can't believe I'll be living here for the foreseeable future. For Robin's sake. I can't expect him to come live with me in my studio flat in Edinburgh. He's settled in school and likes his friends. Being uprooted now, after this traumatic week, will only cause him more pain.

Robin was closer to Mum than I was. She always favoured him. It's a universal truth that mothers treat their daughters differently from their sons, expecting more from them while coddling their precious, infallible boys. Another reason Robin and I aren't close. He never had to grow up as quickly as I did. Mum never shouted at him for reading books and playing with toys. The insufferable brat got to cling to his innocence for as long as he wanted.

Spotting the semi-detached house, the last rays of the setting sun glinting off the windows, I sigh. The idea of living out of two suitcases for several weeks makes this situation more unpalatable. I've only had a matter of days to decide how to handle the daunting responsibility of looking after a teenage boy. I haven't managed to make any concrete plans; I haven't yet quit my job or informed my landlord of my inevitable move. I'm reluctant to accept my new reality; I'm holding onto the hope that I don't have to give up everything I've worked for these past five years to move back into my childhood home and be the sole guardian of my annoying little brother until he's eighteen.

Others struggle through worse hardships than these, but I like to wallow in my self-pity.

Pulling into the driveway, I notice the front door is ajar, disco lights flickering through the gap, music blaring. I scramble out of my rental car and rush to the porch. And when I push through the door, the scene before me leaves me gobsmacked.

There are empty bottles of wine; some are broken—their sharp shards scattered over the wooden floor of the hallway and living room. There are also crushed beer cans, empty pizza boxes, and too many teenagers to count.

Robin chose to host a fucking house party instead of attending his own mother's funeral. What the fuck is wrong with him? Is that a normal grief response? I'm not one to judge, I guess.

Disbelief still unhooking my jaw, I drift through to the kitchen, dodging drunk teens and over-amorous couples. I find Robin talking to a blonde girl by the fridge, his shoulder-length brown hair concealing his face from view, but I recognise the T-shirt—my dad's Ziggy Stardust one he forgot to take with him when he scarpered.

'Robin! What the fuck?!' I shout out over the loud music.

Robin twists sharply to face me and pales.

Did he not expect me to come here tonight?

His shocked expression quickly turns to stone. 'What? It's just a party. I threw Mum my own wake. I'm pretty sure mine's been more fun.'

I stomp over to him and snatch the beer can from his hand. 'You're a child. You shouldn't be drinking.'

Scowling, Robin folds his arms. 'I'm nearly sixteen.'

'That's still not eighteen.' I pour his beer down the sink. 'Tell everyone to go home. I'm surprised the neighbours haven't called the police yet.'

'They're on holiday,' he says in a flat tone. 'Anyway, who are you to come in here telling me what to do? Just because Mum's dead doesn't mean you get to boss me around.' His apple-green eyes flare with defiance. I've been his guardian for all of two minutes, and he's already challenging my authority.

'I signed the papers on the way home. I'm officially the boss of you for the next three years, so get used to it. Now, tell your friends to fuck off, or I will, and I'll make sure to embarrass you completely in the process,' I threaten, throwing him the black bin liner I retrieved from the kitchen drawer while speaking the order. 'And before you go to bed, this house better be spotless because there's no way I'm cleaning up after you.'

'You know what...' Robin chucks the bin liner back at me, red seeping into his cheeks and forehead. 'You sound just like her.'

The jibe stings, but I set my jaw. 'I'm going upstairs to shower and unpack. Send these dickheads home and clean this place up. You have an hour.' I thrust the bin liner back into his hands. 'Do it, you little shit.' I finally acknowledge the girl standing by his side, an awkward look on her face. 'No offence.' She gives me a tight smile before I storm out of the room, heading back to the car to collect my suitcases.

A little cold in only a form-fitting black dress and blazer, I hurry to unload the car, then lock it when both suitcases are out. Dragging them behind me, one handle in each hand, I wrestle back towards the front door, which is now closed. I haven't seen anyone leave yet.

I retrieve the key from my purse and try it in the lock, but the door doesn't open.

What the fuck?!

I bang on the door with an open palm. 'Robin. Let me in. Right now!'

'Go back to Scotland. I don't need you here. I've never needed you here!' Robin bellows through the door, his voice thick with resentment.

This comment is another blow; '*Never needed you here*' sounds like he may have but refuses to admit it.

'Open the door, Robin. It's been a hard day. I don't want to fight with you,' I urge in a less aggressive tone, though my anger still simmers.

A hoot of an owl makes me jump. I whirl around, searching the breeze-blown trees.

Nothing but darkness meets my suspicious gaze.

Another chill rakes down my spine at the sensation of being watched, even if it is only a bird.

Anxiety is a hot needle in my gut. I furiously continue banging on the door and ring the bell repeatedly, but Robin only turns the music up to drown me out.

Boiling over, I abandon my suitcases and stalk around to the back of the house. When I find the gate locked, I kick off my heels and scale the low fence. I jump down into the flower bed on the other side and my bare feet slide in mud. Luckily, I noticed the kitchen window was open when I was in there. If not for that, I would have left to stay at another hotel for the night.

I creep up to the open window, the harsh sound of electro-pop making me want to cover my ears with my hands. Peeking into the kitchen, I spot Robin in the same position with his female friend, as if my interruption had never happened. Blood rages through my veins. I grip the windowsill and climb in.

Knives and forks clatter to the tiles as I scramble over the sink. Robin looks up, eyes widening when he sees me coming for him. He spins to dart out of the kitchen, leaving his friend to face me alone.

'You better fucking run!' I yell, hearing him hurry up the stairs to hide in his room.

Out of breath, I turn to his friend. 'Did you know that little Robbie wet the bed until he was seven?'

He can't say I didn't warn him.

Chapter 2

I Wish

RAVEN

For hours, Robin has been hiding in his room behind a locked door. After shouting through the door at him without reply until my throat was raw, I gave in, and cleaned up his mess myself. The whole time I was kneeling on the floor, picking up broken bottle shards, I relished the knowledge that my embarrassing tales of his childhood would likely haunt him throughout the rest of his school years.

Bone-achingly tired, I peel off my little black funeral dress and slip on a pink silk camisole with matching shorts. The house is still warm from all the angsty bodies, along with the lingering smell of sweat, spilt beer, and stale pizza.

With a resentful sigh, I slide into my old bed and stare at the white, nondescript ceiling.

It's so strange coming back to my childhood bedroom. It's been over five years since I stayed the night, although it feels like ten.

Mum hasn't touched this room. When I moved out, I thought she'd immediately make this her office or yoga room. She didn't. Everything is exactly how I left it, from the lilac walls to the picture collage of me with all my old school friends. The light pine furniture is sitting empty and unused. The wardrobe is bare. I guess they'll all be filled with my things soon enough. The inevitability of it makes me want to groan. My fragile heart splinters: whatever's left inside seems desperate to flee the various cages which now surround it.

Equally desperate words spring to my mind—a silent plea: *I wish I didn't have to stay in this house. I wish I didn't have to look after my arsehole of a brother for the next three years. I wish someone could take over his guardianship so I can live my life the way I want—the way I never got to when I barely existed under this roof.*

I wish I didn't feel so alone.

My whole life, loneliness has lingered. Not through lack of company. I had a fair number of friends growing up, but not any I could tell my deepest, darkest secrets. None that I could truly be myself with. On the outside, I'm this smiley, happy, people-pleaser. While on the inside, I'm hollow. My shiny shell is the only thing keeping me from drifting off into oblivion.

A heaviness sinks onto my chest, making it hard for me to breathe. A sob chokes out of me, and I twist to bury my face into the pillow, suffocating the guttural sounds of my hopelessness.

My mum's gone. My brother hates me. My few fickle friends all live at the other end of the country. And now I'm shackled with a kind of burdening responsibility I never envisioned for myself.

Raising a child wasn't something I had planned. My lifelong ambitions have always revolved around exploring the world and falling in love time and time again. With places. With people. I don't want to be trapped here in this nothing town, in a boring job, arguing with a rebellious teen until I'm at least twenty-six. I crave adventure. Not that I was living to my fullest in Edinburgh, but at least I had the freedom to be selfish and savour the dreams of a child-free/carefree existence for a little longer.

Tears drying on my face and pillow, I curl up, now desperate for the relief of sleep.

Tomorrow, I have a load of paperwork to sort through. There's still so much I must do. Plus, I need to talk seriously with Robin about his behaviour and the rules he will have to follow if this house is ever to be harmonious.

Surprisingly, it doesn't take long for me to be lured into slumber.

Into dreams long forgotten.

As I step through a smoky mist, rainbow shimmers and sparkling lights warp around me. There's no white ceiling, only a dizzying night sky. Its stars are drops of silver swirling into deep indigo, obscured by a mystical sheen.

After I survey my surroundings, the conclusion I come to is that I'm inside a giant, translucent dome—*trapped*.

Impossible. This must be a dream.

A shiver dances over me, all the hairs on my arms standing on end when I notice an eerie figure taking shape ahead of me. Its body is that of a man, though pearlescent wings sprout from his back. The mist is camouflaging his features, but I discern that his hair is a shock of white—long enough to slick back on top, short enough not to be bothersome.

My name is a whisper in the dreamy air, echoing around me as the winged man stalks closer, the mist parting for him.

Fear striking me, I stumble away. My back hits the wall of the dome before I regain control of my unsteady legs. The wall isn't as hard and unyielding as glass; it's bouncy and almost slick in texture.

Am I inside a fucking bubble?

I push against it. Though malleable, it doesn't burst. I try to kick a foot at it, yet it only absorbs the force of my strike, rippling.

'It's a futile effort, love. You will only tire yourself out,' a velvety male voice purrs.

Spinning back to face the beastly man, I find he's no beast at all. His beauty is pure ecstasy and absolute pain in equal measure. The angles of his face are sharp—high cheekbones, straight nose, defined jaw. His irises shimmer silver, glowing as bright as his white-feathered wings. His skin is just as pale and gleaming, his rosy lips standing out, pouty and full.

His beauty is a curse to those fortunate enough to behold him.

I'm immediately under his spell, unable to reply because my mouth only hangs off its hinges.

Judging by the upward curve of his lips and his slight head tilt, my shocked expression amuses him. 'Every time... One of these days, you *will* remember me, starling.' He sighs, adjusting the lapels of his silken brocade jacket.

He's wearing all black, the collar of his silver buttoned shirt high on his graceful neck. He resembles an angel prince from a fairy tale, all-powerful and commanding. The name he called me—*starling*—sparks something. Recognition, maybe?

'My name is Raven,' I say after a long minute of him studying me, his face broodingly calm.

'I know your name,' he replies.

I frown at him. 'Then why did you call me starling?'

The man looms closer, his presence becoming a tangible thing. 'It's what I've always called you. You may think you've grown out of it, but you'll always be more a starling than a raven to me.'

With nowhere to go, I hold my hand up in warning. 'Stay back. Don't come any closer.'

He pauses, a crease forming in between his darker eyebrows. 'You'll fare better showing me the respect I deserve. You're talking to no mere man; I am a king. I wish you would remember *that* at least.' His tone is sharper than before.

'Where am I? Is this a dream?' I look down at myself; I'm still wearing the same silk camisole and shorts I went to bed in.

Peering back up at the man, I discover his eyes have also fallen to assess my body—silver flares, reducing his irises to molten heat. With my cheeks rosy, I quickly fold my arms over my chest, hiding my erect nipples.

His gaze whips up to meet mine, lips hooking into a devilish smirk. 'It is a dream of sorts. We have been meeting here for several years. Ever since we turned thirteen.'

I scoff in protest. 'What? No, we haven't. I don't know you. I've never seen you before.'

'Oh, starling. How many times do we have to go through this? I'm starting to lose my patience.' He rubs at his temple. 'Whenever you're feeling a little lost and alone, you materialise here, your mind calling out to me—*begging* for attention.'

'I've never begged for anything,' I rebut, taking that as an insult.

'Not verbally... yet.' His heated look to me is all arrogance and sin.

After swallowing hard, I deflect with more questions. 'What's your name? What are you?'

His wings jostle. 'I have many names. I'm the King of Birds and Beasts. The Harbinger of Death and Destruction. A God Among Tricksters and Thieves. The Demon of Your Dreams.' His voice has smoothed out. It's almost lyrical, like a deadly melody meant to hypnotise me.

Shivering, I bite my cheek, fighting against this invisible pull drawing me towards him. 'So, you're no angel?'

With humour lighting his eyes, he shakes his head. 'Neither are you, love.'

'What do I call you?'

'What you've always called me...' He pauses as if he expects me to somehow know the answer. When I continue staring at him blankly, he finishes his sentence after a dejected sigh. 'Julius.'

'Okay, *Julius*, I want to wake up now. Can you help me?' I ask a little reluctantly, my tone contemptuous.

His gaze thins. 'You're not usually this insufferable. It seems your brother has riled you more than I expected. It's lucky I granted you my favour so soon. Your bitterness would have only burrowed deeper and deeper, festering until it killed what little is left of your internal fire.'

'What are you talking about? How do you know I have a brother?'

Julius rolls his eyes. 'These pointless questions won't get us anywhere. Why don't you ask me for my help again? How I *love* to hear how much you need me,' he drawls, his wings folding closer to his body.

Heat licks my lower belly like his teasing words were a lit match. 'I *need* answers!' I shout, losing patience. 'So, stop fucking with me!'

Face like thunder, Julius prowls towards me with cat-like grace, and I gasp, flattening against the bubble wall.

When the dream demon is only inches from me, he roughly takes my chin in his hand to angle my face up.

Glaring down at me, Julius grits out, 'What you *need* is a good spanking, and that is exactly what you will get if you continue speaking to me in that manner. Do you understand?'

I nod meekly, fear icing my heart. Yet that fire in my belly seems to spread lower at his threat. My thighs clench against my will, and he notices the move, a smug smile on his lips.

His bruising grip becomes a sensual caress along my jaw, his thumb skimming over my lips. 'I've never dared to come this close to you,' he whispers, his attention still on my mouth. 'But then, you've never dared to shout at me before.' His hand lowers to my throat, fingers wrapping around, the pressure light yet dominating. My breath catches, watching his eyes darken to thin rings of silver. 'I'm not sure I hate it as much as I should.' His admittance seems to surprise him more than it does me.

'Let go of me,' I demand, yanking on his wrist, but it doesn't budge.

'Are you sure? It seems you're also of two minds. One wants to fight against me, the other desiring my touch, both rough and tender.'

His other hand snakes around my waist to my lower back, and in one swift thrust, my body is against his, our hips now flush. His scent is luxurious, with crisp notes of fresh pear and spiced lavender. I want to inhale him and keep him trapped in my lungs forever. But, when something hardens between us, air snags in the throat he's still holding, and my mind reduces to static electricity while my skin tingles with heat.

'It's been five years since you last called on me.' His mouth drops to my ear. 'And how I've missed you.' As his heavier breaths warm the shell of my ear, I quiver against him, and his responding sigh is practically a groan.

'I don't even know you. We shouldn't... *You* shouldn't be touching me like this,' I utter, my voice breathy and weak. 'I don't have sex dreams.'

Julius laughs, the sound lacking the warmth of humour. 'I should hope not. Unless your unconscious mind thinks only of me.' He grips my chin again, face hardening. 'You were a virgin when you left me. Has that changed?'

Desire morphs into anger in an instant. 'Excuse me?!' Lip curling in disgust, I push against his chest, and he steps away. 'That's—that's none of your fucking business.'

Julius' jaw clenches tight, thinly veiling his fury. 'Who took it?' His staccato voice promises death.

'*Who* are *you* to ask me that? You're just some weird sleep paralysis demon that my mind has conjured up to deal with stress.' I manoeuvre past him to rush away, hoping to find an exit. The mist thickens to an undefined wall of smoke, obscuring my path within a few seconds.

'Demon or no, I have a claim on your soul. You said so once yourself.'

I throw an anxious glance over my shoulder. Julius hasn't come after me, albeit his voice still sounds too close for comfort. 'Ha. I would never say anything of the sort. I don't believe in demons. Or souls, for that matter.'

'If you don't believe in souls, then why do you mind so much if I want to possess yours?' he queries, his tempting form now lost to the mist.

'Because nobody can own any part of me, theoretically or otherwise,' I throw back, still searching for a way out of this beautifully constructed nightmare.

Julius' chuckle is rich and seductive. 'My poor, dear starling, theoretically, I already have you in all ways imaginable. Most of those theories involve you naked and screaming my name.'

I come to a juddering halt, my heart racing ahead of me. Taking a huskier breath, I get out, 'Stop it! I want to go home. Let me out of here so I can wake up.'

Julius doesn't answer. A dread-inducing silence fills the space the mist has yet to invade.

'Julius? Did you hear me? I wish to go home. *Now*!' I call out, my skin prickling with awareness. I spin around, but he's nowhere in sight. 'Where are you?'

My breaths come quicker as a slow minute rolls on, the mist now so thick and grey that I can't see past the end of my nose.

'You know what, fuck you!' I yell up to the distorted stars, still visible as the blanketing mist lacks a ceiling.

Arms cage me from behind, and I scream, my legs lifting to kick out.

'Your mouth has become so incredibly dirty, my wilful little bird. If you want to fuck me so badly, you only have to say '*please*',' Julius murmurs against my cheek, his hand sliding under my camisole. His tormenting touch burns a pleasurable path across my stomach.

Before he can reach my breast, I elbow him in the ribs, and he grunts out a breath, releasing me.

'You'll be punished for that,' he warns, his wings stretching out before they vanish, leaving him looking frighteningly human.

Once again, the mist recedes, only enough to see him.

'I wish to leave. Let me go home,' I repeat, matching his glare.

'I've granted you enough wishes for tonight. I'm no genie,' Julius grumbles, straightening his jacket.

Confused, I respond with, 'Granted me wishes? What wishes?'

At that, a mischievous grin spreads across the dream demon's face. 'Oh, love, now we're getting somewhere.'

CHAPTER 3

Favour

RAVEN

My eyes thin to slits. 'You better start telling me what's going on.'

'Or what?' Julius cocks his head to regard me, his slow perusal of my body bringing more heat to the surface of my skin. 'What, sweet starling, will you do to me?' His tone is flirtatious again.

'I...' Unable to come up with a threat that won't sound completely ridiculous, I shut my mouth before embarrassing myself further.

'Hmm, disappointing but wise,' he says, slipping a hand into his trouser pocket. 'Now, back to your previous question regarding the wishes you made tonight.'

Before he can continue, I interject, 'I made no wishes.'

'Yes, you did. You made three. Well, four, to be precise, but I consider two to be one and the same.' He pulls a piece of parchment from his pocket and reads aloud. '*I wish I didn't have to stay in this house. I wish I didn't have to look after my arsehole of a brother for the next three years. I wish someone could take over his guardianship so I can live my life the way I want—the way I never got to when I barely existed under this roof. I wish I didn't feel so alone.*' He looks up, focusing back on me. 'Sound familiar?'

My heart drops to my stomach. I swallow before replying, 'I—I didn't... they were only thoughts. I was upset.'

'Those *thoughts* of yours were *very* loud and demanding, reaching me across the Veil. You wanted more than anything for them to be granted. You wished for someone to take the responsibility of your brother away. You wished you didn't have to stay in your mother's house. And you wished you didn't have to be alone anymore. Correct?'

I shake my head, but what he's relaying is all true. I did wish that—*do* wish that. Still, hearing this demon repeat my innermost thoughts—my *darkest* thoughts—back to me now makes me want to deny them. Mostly because there's a strange kind of terror seeping in at the prospect of my wishes being granted, especially if *he's* the genie.

Julius watches me through a colder lens. 'Don't lie to me. I know your mind better than you seem to. I know all your secrets. Your dreams. Your nightmares.' He steps towards me, his hand coming up to tuck a lock of hair behind my ear. 'Your deepest desires.' He trails his cool fingers down the column of my neck, then my arm. My skin pebbles at his light, reverent caress. 'Your darkest fantasies,' he murmurs, mouth skimming my cheekbone.

When did I stop breathing?

Julius lifts my chin to capture my gaze. He's a lot taller than I am, by at least a foot. 'You have my favour, love. There's not much I would deny you. Not when your soul calls to mine for aid.' He closes the gap, his lips a hairsbreadth from mine. 'That's why I granted all of your wishes tonight.'

Gasping, I wrench myself away from him. 'What do you mean? What have you done?'

'I've given you your heart's desire. I've done you a favour. You should be thanking me,' Julius answers, his reverence quickly reverting to displeasure.

'Where's my brother? What have you done with him?!' My questions are sharp and urgent, panic surging through my veins, turning them to ice.

Julius' expression is a mask of indifference once again. 'Robin is no longer your responsibility. He is now mine. I've already taken him to my castle. He shall be my pet. But don't worry. I will treat him kindly. As long as he behaves.'

With my mind whirling as fast as the stars above, I wobble on my suddenly shaky legs. Julius reaches for me, but I jerk back as if his fingers are knives meant to cut out my heart. 'No. No! Stay away!' Julius' lips purse at my outburst. His hands drop to his sides. 'No. This isn't happening. This is a dream. I'll wake up, and Robin will be asleep in his bed.'

Julius ignores my ramblings of disbelief. 'As for the second and third wish, I offer you the same: Come with me to my kingdom. Offer me your soul, and I will cherish it for as long as we both shall live. You and I are connected, starling. It's our curse to share. I don't want to lose you again.' He holds out his hand, palm up. 'Come with me. Be mine.'

I glare at his hand. 'I'd rather die.'

Julius snatches his hand back as if I've scalded him. 'Be careful what you ask for. To you, I've been generous—uncharacteristically kind. But I can also be cruel, ruthless, and spiteful.'

At breaking point, I cover my eyes with my hands, my throat on fire, tears welling, and I chant, 'Wake up. Wake up. Wake yourself up, Raven. This can't be real. Wake up!'

With a start, I wake to darkness. My eyelids fling open. Sitting bolt upright, my lungs work overtime as my addled mind catches up with my body.

Remembering my traumatising dream, I whip my covers off and leap out of bed. I race towards my bedroom door to yank it open. I trip over my own feet and fall out onto the landing. One knee splits open when it bashes against the wood floor. In pain and winded, I crawl towards Robin's bedroom, down the hallway.

'Robin!' I call, banging loudly on his door. I try turning the handle, but it's still locked. 'Robin, if you don't open this door right now, I'm breaking it down.'

When he doesn't answer, I grab the wooden chair that stands in the corner by the bookcase I was never allowed to peruse.

'Please. I'm scared. I need to check you're all right.'

For another ten seconds, I wait, the silence torture, before I bring the chair leg down on the door handle. 'Robin! *Please*, answer me. Tell me you're okay.'

Taking it up a notch, I swing the chair at the door. The loud crashing sound would be enough to wake the neighbours if they weren't on holiday.

Tears streaming, I continue smashing the chair to pieces, the door not bending to my will. I've only managed to dent and splinter the wood.

After the wasted effort, I collapse down, exhausted.

In a pleading voice, I beg, 'Tell me you're here. I need to know you're here. I'm sorry. I'm sorry I haven't done the same for you; I haven't been here. I should have called more. I should have visited more. I'm so sorry. *Please*, answer me.'

A few agonising seconds pass before the door lock clicks. Filled with relief, I pull myself up and twist the handle. The door creaks open, the darkness beckoning me in.

'Robin?' His name comes out as a strangled whisper, fear gripping my throat. Tentatively, I step over the threshold, the hairs on my neck standing on end.

I flick his light switch on and off, but nothing happens. The lights are out. My expelled breaths cloud in front of my face, the air in here unusually icy.

A slither of moonlight shines through his curtain-less window. I follow that dim beam to the empty bed. Robin isn't in it. The covers have been thrown to the floor, pillows askew.

'Robin?!' I say with more urgency, rushing over to check under the bed, the wardrobe.

There's no sign of him.

He's not here. But if he's not here, then who unlocked his door?

I shudder, panic flaring again.

Robin must have snuck out to stay with a friend. That has to be it. That has to be where he is. It's the only rational explanation. Even trying to convince myself of this, the dream demon's words echo in my ears. '*Robin is no longer your responsibility. He is now mine. I've taken him to my castle. He shall be my pet.*'

Searching the room for clues, my eyes snag on what looks to be a mobile phone on Robin's bedside table. Taking it in my hands, the screen lights up. The screensaver is a picture of Robin and the girl he was talking to in the kitchen earlier. That must be his girlfriend. There's no way a teenager would leave without their phone. It's practically attached to their hand at all times. Which means he either forgot it. *Unlikely.* Or he didn't leave of his own volition.

No. It was only a dream—a nightmare. *Robin left without his phone and is staying with a friend. He'll be back. He's fine. He's not been captured by a dream demon and taken to be kept as a pet in his castle. You didn't wish away his soul. Julius was purely a figment of your imagination.*

I jump in fright at a tap on the window. Spinning around, I lock eyes with a barn owl waiting outside the window's ledge. It spreads its wings before it pecks at the glass until a crack appears.

Moving backwards on instinct, a scream rips from my throat as I fall onto Robin's empty bed. I scramble off and dash out of the room, the darkness making it difficult to find my way back to my bedroom.

When I reach my room, I slam the door, lock it, and quickly pull the curtains shut. Hyperventilating, I slide down the wall and curl into a ball, wishing this was all a dream and I'll wake up for real this time to find my brother safe in his bed.

With my eyes squeezed shut, I whisper to myself—to Julius. 'I wish I had my brother back. I wish he were here with me. I wish he were back in his bed, safe and sound. I wish I were a better sister.' I sob into my hands. 'Please, Julius. Give him back to me. I'll do anything.'

Sleep. The word is a soft murmur in my head—a temptation.

Too scared to move, I stop crying. Stop wishing.

Dream. Another murmur, this one is more a command.

Julius must not be able to effectively communicate with me while I'm awake. Shit. How will I ever be able to fall back to sleep now with my emotions running so high?

That's when I remember I put anti-anxiety pills in my handbag yesterday. I can't fly without them. In haste, I retrieve them from my purse and swallow two dry.

When they've settled in my churning stomach, I crawl into bed and close my eyes, willing my mind to shut off, but it continues to race.

Fuck!

Shivering, I lift the duvet over my head and try to deepen my breaths, counting slowly.

I reach over a thousand before I...

CHAPTER 4

Play Fair

'Finally,' Julius huffs before I even crack an eye to take him in. 'I have a kingdom to run, you know. Time is a precious thing. You will learn that soon enough.'

He's leaning against a half-crumbled pillar, his wings still absent, his moonlight hair more ruffled than before. It's as if he's repeatedly run his fingers through it in frustration.

This dreamscape hasn't changed shape, only darkened, the rainbow shimmers and stars changing to tumultuous thunderclouds. Maybe his foul mood has tainted the air, its mystical quality poisoned by the toxicity of his demonic presence.

His audacity dissolves any tolerance I have left. I charge up to him, shouting, 'Give me my brother back, you bastard!'

My anger doesn't surprise Julius because he's quick to meet me in a single stride, forcing me to stammer a step before he grabs at my throat. He twists to slam me up against the pillar.

Shock has me gasping harsher than the wind he knocked out of me. I've never been manhandled so viciously. My ex, Albie, may have been a gaslighter, but he barely touched me. Even when I asked for rough play during sex, he never delivered, preferring to use a timid touch. Too timid to satisfy me. The lack of orgasms was one of the reasons our relationship fizzled. Well, I guess that was *my* reason. He always got off, no matter what.

'Ten minutes ago, you were weeping like a baby on your bedroom floor, begging me to reconsider, saying you will do *anything*.' Julius' eyes are black now, soulless, and full of malicious intent. 'Don't take me for a lovesick fool. I'm not above inflicting pain to get what I want from you.'

His fingers apply pressure on my neck, restricting airflow. I thrash, fear igniting my survival instinct. He doesn't react to my attempts to scratch or kick him. Against this wicked creature, I'm as weak as an insect. I may as well be a fly buzzing around a lion—more a nuisance than a threat. I've had dreams like this before, where my punches have no force—no strength behind them. Julius doesn't seem to have that problem. His strength is all too real.

Is it possible to die in a dream?

I don't particularly want to test that theory right now. So, when black spots start eating away at my vision, I choke out, 'Please.'

As soon as the polite word rasps past my lips, Julius lets me go, and I drop to the cracked marble floor at his feet, gulping down lungful after lungful of life-affirming air.

Julius looks down his nose at me. 'Manners cost nothing.'

Repressing the urge to spit a string of swear words at him, I bite my tongue and go to stand.

He places a hand on my head, forcing me back to my knees. 'You'll need to stay in that position to beg, love.' His smirk is fiendish. He's enjoying this—breaking me down.

Julius *must* be a demon to relish this cruelty. Though, to be fair, most men aren't any better, especially when they're in a position of power. And when it comes to women, there's not much men *won't* do while trying to exert their will.

I'll have to display my dominance as women have mastered in the face of an insecure man since the dawn of time: through quiet determination, perseverance, and cunning.

'What do I have to do to get my brother back?' I ask, meeting his eye with steely resolve.

Julius pretends to mull it over for a long, drawn-out beat before replying, 'There are only two options I will consider.' He twirls a lock of my hair between his fingers. 'On a separate note, seeing you kneeling before me is one of the most satisfying sights, I have to say. Especially in that silky slip of a thing you're wearing. Your night clothes have never been so... *titillating* before. I'm not complaining. Although it does make it *harder* for me to concentrate.' His focus drifts to the gap between my thinly covered breasts. My nipples pinch at his attention despite my feigned disgust.

Why is my body reacting to this demonic arsehole so acutely?

I'm horrified at myself when I realise too late that my gaze has dropped to his crotch, noticing the hard outline of his cock through his trousers. Unfortunately, his arousal only amplifies my own. But I fight it, determined not to show weakness. I can't let him think I'll accept being treated like this. I'm no dainty flower he can pluck.

If anything, I'm a fucking Venus flytrap.

A little sweetness will lure him in, and before he knows it, I'll have him exactly where I want him. 'Please, continue. What are my options?'

Julius narrows his eyes, clearly suspicious of my change of tack. 'Option one is simple: offer me your soul in exchange for Robin's. All you have to say is, *'Julius DiMinos, I wish for my soul to be yours and yours alone'*. And just like that, your brother will be returned to your world unharmed, with no memory of what has occurred tonight. As for you, my wilful little bird, you will come with me to my kingdom and live by my side until the Shadows claim us. I promise to treat you well. Despite my harshness tonight, I care for you more than you know. Some will even call you Queen. In time, I may allow you to not only *live* by my side, but to rule by it.'

Bargaining for my theoretical soul shouldn't worry me, as I've never believed in such a thing. However, the mere thought of offering even a fictional part of myself has dread building a well of lost opportunities and broken dreams in my chest. If I go along with this farce—accepting the exchange—I could be proved wrong and end up trapped in some diabolical castle for the rest of my life. Maybe even beyond that.

I can't comprehend that kind of meaningless existence. 'What's the second option?'

Julius frowns with a flicker of surprise, seemingly disappointed in my eagerness to dismiss the first. 'Option two is not for the faint of heart. It's a dangerous mission, even for the most fearsome of creatures. To reach a soul you wish to free, you must journey to my castle by foot through a complicated maze of birds and beasts. I'll provide you with no assistance and no assurance of survival. Those who venture into my maze often never find their way out. Upon starting, you'll have three days. Your brother will remain safe until then—his soul untainted. Fail, and not only will I keep *his* soul, but I'll also collect *yours*.'

Unnerved, I swallow the lump in my throat, my mouth too dry to respond. *A Maze of Birds and Beasts* is the name of my favourite book. This can't be happening. But if this *is* real, then it's no coincidence.

Was that book meant for me?

I remember finding it on a park bench at thirteen years old after Mum forbade me from reading books that weren't educational. I took it home and hid it behind my wardrobe for years, only reading it at night when I knew Mum was asleep. All this time, was it a warning? A guide to defeating an evil king and navigating a maze full of monsters and magic?

No. Don't be ridiculous, Raven. It was a work of fiction—a fantasy. Just like this dream. Just like your 'immortal soul'. It's utter bollocks.

Even so, the first option doesn't appeal to me despite my lack of belief in the terms. It would be giving up, and I like to think I'm better than that. Defying Julius will bring me more pleasure than going down without a fight.

Julius must read this on my face because he adds, 'Choose wisely. I don't wish to see you harmed. Of course, having your soul bound to that delicious body is the ideal scenario. Regardless, if it must break for me to claim, so be it. The danger to your life is your burden to bear, not mine. I *will* have you, even in pieces. It's inevitable, love. The maze is no place for a mortal. You won't last the night.'

Defiantly, I stand, annoyed that I'm not tall enough to come face-to-face with him. I catch the corner of his mouth hitch up before he bites down on it. 'If you thought for a second that I would hand over my soul without a fight, you clearly don't know me.'

'Oh, I know you,' Julius says, cupping my cheek. And for some inexplicable reason, I'm entranced enough to let him, resisting the compulsion to lean into his touch. 'But I had hope... I had *hoped* you would remember.'

'Remember what?'

'Your dreams. Your desires.' He presses himself against me as if seeking my warmth. 'Which were once aligned with my own.'

'I doubt that very much,' I refute, leaning away. 'I choose the maze.'

Julius recoils, his jaw working. 'Then you choose death.'

Folding my arms, I raise my chin and say, 'We'll see about that.'

With a click of his fingers, Julius transports us to a dark, empty plain on the borders of his maze, spanning the entire horizon. The starless sky is a cloudy black, thunder cracking in the distance. The walls of the maze are tall, grey, corporeal shadows. It's unlike anything I've seen before.

A sulphuric smell burns my nostrils. 'Where are we?' My voice comes out hushed, the wind whipping my hair back from my face, my body already chilled to the core. I wrap my arms around myself, feeling more naked than ever before, despite my useless clothes. They're covering me enough to maintain dignity but not enough to save me from hypothermia.

'This is the Underworld, love.'

The casual way he says that makes me want to punch him.

The Underworld?! *For fuck's sake. Really*?

Julius passes me a knowing glance, guessing my thoughts. 'You can still change your mind, you know. However, as soon as you step into that maze, I can't help you.'

'Can you hinder me?' I question, wondering what the fine print of this deal is. 'What's stopping you from killing me as soon as I step a foot inside?'

A flicker of annoyance crosses his face. 'No. I'm bound to my castle for the duration, prevented from causing you harm. It matters not; the maze will throw plenty of dangers at you. I need not interfere.'

'Can I change into something more appropriate?' I'm shivering now, my teeth clenched to stop them from chattering. '*Please*?'

Eyebrow cocked, Julius looks me over before he answers, 'I will allow you shoes since you asked so nicely.' With a motion of his hand, white trainers materialise on the dirt in front of me.

I rush to shove them on my feet before they disappear. 'Just shoes? Come on. I'm practically naked. Can't you materialise a coat while you're at it?' I've always been in the habit of pushing my luck.

Julius expels a loud breath as though dealing with a greedy child asking for another helping of pudding. 'You're in no position to demand such frivolous things from me.'

'Frivolous?! It's fucking freezing! Making me travel through a 'deadly maze' in just this isn't fair. I won't stand any sort of chance,' I argue, not letting it lie. This is life or death. I won't survive the night dressed the way I am.

'Are you forgetting that this is the Underworld? We don't play fair down here. Your world is no better, either.'

I turn to him, my expression pleading.

We stare each other down for an extended beat before he sighs, his focus shifting back to the maze ahead. 'Fine. Think of it as a sign of good faith.'

With a little flourish, Julius waves a hand in my direction. A pair of dark grey, fleece-lined leggings, a long-sleeved cream top, and a thin but waterproof grey jacket appear folded at my feet. Warmth returns to my limbs, just looking at them.

'Thank you. I appreciate it,' I force out, remembering the manners that soften him.

Expression flat, Julius nods. 'See. I'm not always cruel. But don't push your luck any further. My generous mood is wavering.'

As I begin to pull my leggings over my silk shorts, he captures my wrist to stop me.

'What?' I ask curtly.

'Those nice warm clothes in exchange for the ones you're wearing. It's only *fair*.' His tone is a taunt, but it also conveys salacious mischief.

'I have nothing on underneath,' I mumble, heat creeping into the apples of my cheeks.

'I know.' Julius' smile is devious as his gaze tracks down my body again. He holds his hand out expectantly. 'You'd better hurry. Like you said, it's fucking freezing.'

My grey eyes scan the desolate plain, checking no one else is around. As far as I can tell, it's just us out here. If not, the malignant dark will be my ally. 'Urgh, fine. Turn around,' I demand, using a spinning finger to reinforce the command.

A derisive laugh breezes past Julius' lips. 'Demons are not known for their chivalry, love.' He motions for me to pass over my clothes with two beckoning fingers—a dirty innuendo if I've ever seen one.

Swearing, I spin around instead, giving him my back. Face red with anger, as well as embarrassment, I get the worst over with first. With a swift tug on the leg trim, my shorts drop to my feet, and I kick them behind me. I throw a scowl at Julius over my shoulder, but his attention is exactly where you'd expect—my bare arse. He licks his parted lips, lust glazing his blown-wide eyes. His fists clench at his sides as if he's fighting the urge to touch me.

My neck snaps back into place; the sight of him affected by the sight of me is causing the heat from my cheeks to spread, dragging low. The heaviness between my legs is sudden and jarring.

Before this heady feeling overtakes me, I yank the leggings on, thankful they're almost black. Hopefully, they won't show any damp patches.

Heart pounding and lungs stalling, I take my camisole off next; my nipples are sharp, aching points. Before I can pull the cream top on, the tickle of feather-light fingertips sliding across my bare shoulder freezes me in place.

Julius sweeps the waves of my raven hair over one shoulder, and I gasp. Chills chase his slow, tormenting touch as he traces my spine down to my tailbone. Clutching the cream material to my chest—hiding my breasts—I remain still, counting each quick, shallow breath.

A moment later, the wet tease of his tongue is at the nape of my neck. I shiver, my eyes fluttering closed—my senses narrowing to his tiny yet extremely stimulating ministrations.

'You're too innocent to be sin incarnate,' Julius whispers against the sensitive skin below my ear as he holds my hips in place. Unconsciously, I arch my back, my arse skimming his erection. He hisses—a wince of restraint. 'This deadly dance is unnecessary. Agree to be mine, and I'll have you any way you wish.'

His abnormally sharp canines scrape my shoulder before he kisses the curve of my neck, while his right-hand glides down past my naval to cup my vagina through the leggings.

Surprise alone has me lurching forward, my mind appalled by the hesitation of my treacherous body—ripping it away from his unsolicited, yet jolt-inducing groping before the unthinkable happens.

This demon stole your brother's soul and is vying to damn yours, too, I think, berating myself. *And you're letting him seduce you?*

Angrier at myself, I hastily sling my new top on, creating a much-needed barrier between us. 'Did I say you could touch me? Fucking creep.' I focus on the darkness ahead, not turning back to face him. I worry he'll see the truth in my flushed skin, which is still aflame.

'I won't apologise for listening to your body. It's practically begging for me to claim it,' Julius drawls, the husk in his voice sending another pang of desire straight to my clit. 'But... next time, I'll wait for your permission.' His sincerity startles me.

Shrugging on my jacket, I throw back, 'There won't be a next time. You'll *never* get my permission, *demon*. You make my skin crawl.' It's a lie, and I know he knows it.

With my arms protectively crossed over my chest, I muster the courage to face him. His hands are firmly in his pockets, his stance rigid, his eyes razor sharp and cutting.

'Keep telling yourself that and perhaps you'll start to believe it. However, you may find yourself stuck down here. Lies are the foundation of all lost souls.'

Change the subject, Raven. Stay focused on your task. You're here to save Robin. Don't let this arrogant monster crawl under your skin.

'How will I keep track of the time?'

Julius shrugs, clearly losing interest. 'I suppose you'll have to guess.'

Huffing, I reframe. 'Is there a sun that I can use in the day?'

'Down here, darkness is eternal. There will be no sun to keep time, as time is both an illusion and the measure of all things. It can't be tracked or kept, only lost.'

'I hate riddles,' I mutter, grinding my teeth.

Julius looks to the maze again, his expression contemplative. 'The truth is no riddle. It's easy to find, for those of us who aren't afraid to search within.'

I place my hands on my hips. 'What do you mean by that?'

Julius takes another step towards me, his expression softening. Though flustered, I stand my ground, unsure what he'll do next. His proximity continues to feed the inferno blazing through my veins. 'You'll soon see, my wilful little bird.' He zips up my jacket for me. 'Your time starts now.'

CHAPTER 5

Only a Taste

RAVEN

With my heart in my throat, I race towards the maze entrance, my mind lagging. I didn't ask enough questions. I have no idea what awaits me inside. If I'm going by my favourite book, the creatures that stalk the maze are callous, bloodthirsty predators, searching for their next meal or plaything.

Senselessly, I didn't even try to barter for a weapon. I'm an unarmed mortal woman with no food, water, tools, or clue in which direction to turn.

I'm completely fucked.

But I couldn't have accepted defeat so soon. This option was the only way to save both mine and Robin's souls. This way, we have a chance to return home together.

When I glance back, Julius is gone. He told me he'd be confined to his castle for the next three days, restricted, and unable to cause me harm. That doesn't mean he can't instruct another to kill me on his behalf. There's plenty of room for loopholes in this already unbalanced deal.

In hindsight, I should have demanded to see some paperwork. But, as Julius said, I was in no position to demand anything from him. He had—*still has*—all the power. He's a demon king, hell-bent on owning my soul.

Why me? I'm ashamed to admit that his rapt attention and determined pursuit make me feel almost... *special*.

Julius talked to me as if we'd known each other for years. He mentioned numerous times that I've dreamt of him before—that I forget every exchange. Dreams have always been elusive mysteries for me. I used to believe I didn't have them—that all my mind conjured up in sleep was blank space because I could never recall much else upon waking.

It's been five years, Julius said, since the last time my soul apparently called out to him. I've been living in Edinburgh all that time. Maybe our connection has something to do with my childhood home. Otherwise, he could have reached me last night at the hotel, or the two Christmases I travelled down for. And I'm sure the owl has something to do with this. He could have possessed it to keep tabs on me, as he seems unable to walk in his corporeal form in my world. But then, who stole Robin out of his bed? Is my body really here, or is it lying empty, my mind the only thing in danger?

Again, I should have asked more questions.

Reaching the entrance of the maze, my neck has to crank back to take it all in. The giant iron gate is closed and opaque. How the fuck will I be able to open *that*? It looks like it weighs a tonne. Hopefully, there's a smaller door hidden somewhere.

I start searching, pressing my palms to the icy iron to locate a crack or handle. There doesn't seem to be any. Groaning in frustration, I attempt to pull on the bar connected to the main gate. It must slide along, but I'm not strong enough to budge it. Or it could be locked. Julius only said my time starts now, directing me to the gate. He never told me how to open it.

The tricky bastard.

My time is ticking down. If I can't find a way in, it's already over.

Grunting like a wild beast, I tug on the bar with all my might. Still, it doesn't even slide an inch.

For fuck's sake!

'Julius! How the fuck am I supposed to get inside if this fucking gate won't open?!' I scream to the thunderous sky, thin veins of lightning my only light source.

I'm not expecting him to answer; I'm sure he's now bound to his castle. Can he hear me, though? Is he watching my every move somehow? He is a demon with unimaginable powers I can't even fathom. Maybe he's all-knowing, like a god?

Not giving up, I place my palms flat on the rough walls of the maze, finding that it's stone-like. Black vines run through cracks, sprouting dark violet flowers in some spots—they're probably poisonous.

This is the Underworld, Raven. Assume everything will try to kill you, I tell myself, not daring to touch the suspicious blooms.

I'll have to keep my wits about me; always be wary and on guard. I can't trust anyone but myself. Thinking about it, I likely won't be able to trust my own eyes and ears. Surely malicious spirits are eager to lead me astray, using my senses against me.

I can't risk walking too far away from the gate because I may never find it again. It's too dark to see how far the maze spans. It could go on for miles in both directions. This is the only way in. There must be something I'm missing.

I take a step back, now calm enough to assess. There are groves in the iron, although I doubt I'll be able to climb to the top without falling to my premature death. That's exactly what Julius wants—for me to fail before I even begin. In death, he can claim my soul. He did mention he'd rather I didn't break my connection to this body of mine.

What will he do with my soul if there's no body attached? Will he house it in another? Or keep me trapped in a lamp like a genie?

I'd rather not find out.

I must stay alive at all costs, even if my time runs out. Alive, I have the means to escape. Dead... well, there's no coming back from that. I'll never be able to return to the land of the living as a soulless corpse.

'Open sesame?' I try, feeling silly as soon as the words leave my mouth.

A deep chuckle makes me jump in fright. '*Open sesame*?' Julius repeats in a mocking tone. He's casually leaning against the maze wall to my left, examining his nails. 'What next? Alakazam?'

Burning with embarrassment, I grind my teeth before I ask, 'How do I get inside, then?'

He finally spares me a glance. 'Do you know Ancient Greek, by any chance?'

'Of course, I don't. Anyway, I thought you left. I thought you were bound to your castle for the next three days.'

Julius' mouth twitches in satisfaction. 'Your time may have started, but you have yet to set a foot inside the maze. I'm able to come and go as I please until then.'

'As you so *kindly* pointed out, the option stated that I'm to journey through your maze by foot. So, I have to be allowed inside it for the deal to be valid,' I remind him, finding a loophole in my favour.

Julius pushes off the wall and slinks towards me. 'Ah, you see, you would have me there, except, in the next breath, I stipulated I will be under no obligation to provide any assistance or assurance.' When he reaches me, he taps my nose condescendingly. 'Do not think you can use my words against me. By my will, I could leave you here until your time runs out.'

The injustice of this has my eyes aching with unshed tears. He tricked me. He worded it perfectly, and I trusted him—a fucking *demon*—to be fair and honest. *That's what you get for dealing with the Devil*, I think, scolding myself.

'What do you want in exchange for my entry into the maze? I've already given you the clothes off my back. What more do you want?' I question, knowing that he wouldn't have bothered to return if he wasn't after something. He could have simply left me out here.

It's a full minute before Julius answers. The whole while, he observes me, his expression impassive. It's a wonder how I manage to keep my cool; I'm not a patient person at the best of times. 'A kiss,' he says, maintaining eye contact. 'A kiss in exchange for your entry into the maze.'

Blinking, I stare at him in disbelief. He could have asked for anything—my firstborn child, my future, my body—more than a single kiss. He was in a prime position to win my soul on a technicality. Instead, he's giving me another chance for one little kiss? He didn't say it had to be on the lips. A peck on the cheek is all he'll get from me.

As if he can read that thought on my face, Julius continues before I can accept those vague terms. 'One kiss on the mouth. And you have to mean it. I want to feel your desire for me. You've been trying to contain it.' His next step closer isn't as sure as his others. Is he nervous? I watch his throat bob on a hard swallow. 'Let it out, starling. Just this once.'

'If I kiss you, you'll open this gate so I can enter the maze to start my quest?' I ask to clarify the terms. I'm not making the same mistake twice.

Julius' smile seems genuine. '*Quest*? I like that. And yes. Those are my terms. Do you accept?' He's close enough for me to touch—to kiss.

'I accept,' I breathe, my lungs suddenly uncooperative, my focus dropping to his mouth in preparation. I wonder what he tastes like. Will this kiss be the death of me? Will his lips be a cold-steel trap? Will his saliva contain a paralysing venom? Will his tongue be sharp enough to cut me to pieces?

Will I enjoy it?

'Tick tock,' Julius goads with a flash of his eyebrows. He's a statue, staring down at me, his eyes gleaming with delight and something darker. Something wickedly sensual.

Of course, he's expecting *me* to make the first move. I shouted at him only ten minutes ago for touching me intimately without verbal consent. This is payback.

'You're a tree. I can't reach you unless you stoop,' I complain, building the courage to do this.

'If I'm a tree, then climb me,' Julius replies, unbending.

Rolling my eyes, I grip his shoulders before I launch myself at him, hoping he'll catch me. He does, eagerly. My legs wrap around his waist as his arms prop them up, his large hands gripping my arse. His fingers dig in—squeezing—and a breath winces out of me. Not because it hurts, but because I'm trying hard to repress the moan that's creeping up my throat.

We momentarily scan each other's faces, searching for weakness. We're both breathing too hard to hide our undeniable attraction. That's all part of the deal, though. I have to *mean* it—unleash this pent-up desire.

It's only one little kiss. What harm could it do? I've kissed a fair few men before now. Most of the time, it's an underwhelming experience. I'm sure this will be no different. Julius may be beautiful on the outside—a true work of art—but he's rotten to the core. He's a vile, disgusting creature of the night.

Before I can talk myself out of it, I lean in and press my lips to his. They're soft and pillowy. Warm and delicious. My mouth slants, timid at first. I trace the tip of my tongue along the seam of his lips, and he parts them to allow me entry.

The kiss deepens when his tongue meets mine. He tastes of strawberries and wine. His smell is nearly as intoxicating.

We exchange a soft sound between us, his groan answering the moan that slipped from me.

Before I know what's happening, my back is pressed against the gate, his erection grinding up against my throbbing centre. The layers of clothing separating our skin feel like no barrier at all, though I also find myself wishing them away.

Julius nips at my bottom lip, hips rolling to give me the friction I need to build. Another moan from me snaps the rest of his restraint. His throaty growl is primal—feral and full of carnal greed. I'm trapped between his hard body and the unyielding iron gate, his hips grinding me to mush. My hands are in his hair, my fingers gripping at the base of his skull. My mind is all matter, lost to a lavishing lust.

This is the epitome of sin: sick, twisted, depraved, and utterly addictive. Pleasure, as I've never known it, winds through me, sizzling and scalding every nerve ending.

This one kiss is my undoing. After this, I will crave it—*him*—forever more.

I've been corrupted. Defiled. Debased.

Yet, I can't find it within myself to care.

I fucking *revel* in it.

Head twirling with dizziness, I break away, needing to catch my breath. Julius' head dips, burying his face into the crook of my neck. He inhales sharply, taking in my scent.

'Fuck,' he whispers, his grip on my arse tightening. This time, my wince is one of pain. 'Fuck,' he repeats, his voice filled with what I can only assume is regret. 'This was a mistake.'

With that, Julius drops me to my feet and steps back. With two fingers, he rubs his mouth as if hoping to wipe that kiss from his memory as well as his lips.

I do the same, scrubbing my swollen, tingling skin. The scorching ache between my legs persists, begging to be eased. I ignore it. 'There—you got what you wanted. Now, open the gate and let me through,' I command. Unfortunately, my voice isn't as unaffected as I had hoped; it's a dead giveaway.

'For the love of souls, starling. Do you think I got what I wanted? That was only a taste—a tease. What I want is to rip those clothes off your body and fuck you raw so you come all over my cock, again and again until our lungs give out,' Julius grits out, suddenly angry.

I'm angry now, too, his dirty words implanting dangerously tempting images. 'You just said it was a mistake!'

'It *was* a mistake! Now, nothing else will ever be able to hold my attention again. Now, you have no chance of escaping me. I will see to it that you fail this *quest*. I will not be able to help myself,' he admits unashamedly.

'What the fuck? We had a deal!' I rage, pushing against his chest, but he's unmovable.

'Pneuma,' Julius utters, and the gate grinds open enough for me to slip through. 'There—deal upheld. But mark my words, wilful little bird... your soul, body, *and* heart will be mine in three days.'

'Don't count on it,' I retort, giving him my back. Feigning confidence, I stride up to the gap in the gate with my head held high.

'I can practically hear your pussy purring for me, love,' he taunts, darkened eyes glinting in undeserved triumph. 'The scent of your arousal is so overpowering, I can taste it, and it's the *sweetest* thing. I can't wait to slip my tongue inside you to taste more.'

The suggestive lick of his lips has my vagina clenching at the mere idea.

Exaggerating the movement, I plant a foot over the threshold, finally inside the maze. 'Go back to your castle, demon. I'll meet you there soon.'

CHAPTER 6

The Maze

RAVEN

Each eerie path seems more hopeless than the last. There's dead end after dead end, the maze walls narrowing to make them appear longer than they are. The air is thicker inside than out, the smell of sulphur thankfully muted.

Luckily, it's not as dark or cold as expected. The walls themselves have a luminescent glow which lights my way through. Unfortunately, my path is also peppered with roots and rocks, making the uneven ground hazardous. Running is not an option unless I want to chance the very likely risk of falling every few metres.

There must be a way to track the time. Or does time work differently in the Underworld? It already feels as though I've walked for hours when, in all likelihood, it's been mere minutes.

The maze is spooky in its silence. I don't know whether or not it's a good omen; this lack of noise—lack of audible warning. A dangerous beast could be lurking around the next bend and I wouldn't know until it was too late to hide. Not that there are many places for me to take refuge.

These paths are open—devoid of much besides me and the acidic air.

With my feet busy treading the obscure trail, my mind wanders back to the kiss I shared with Julius. Easily, it was the best, most erotic kiss of my life. Someone who can kiss like that is no angel. Reminiscing alone is working me up again. The ghost of his eager lips, his wicked tongue, those greedy hands, his grinding hips... his very hard and *very* insistent co—

Raven! For fuck's sake. Stop!

Needing a moment to cool down, I lean forward, using the wall to steady myself. I want to bash my head against it. Maybe that will rid me of this unwelcome desire. I can't let myself melt into submission, even in my mind's darkest, most salacious corners. Julius is not only dangerous; he's inhuman. He's an immortal predator—a soul-sucking demon who tricked me into a bargain I couldn't get out of. That kiss was practically coerced. He knew I couldn't refuse without damning both my brother and me. Even that slither of insecurity I glimpsed was probably all an act to soften me.

Nevertheless, I can't help the way Julius made me feel. Controlling my body's reaction was an impossible task. I can barely regulate it now, after the fact. The way my vagina continues to pine for the missed opportunity is pathetic. To be fair, it has seen no action for nearly a year, and Julius is the most beautiful being ever to show interest, so I don't blame its excitement.

Albie, my ex, has been my one and only sexual partner. I lost my virginity to him at nineteen, once we'd been dating for four months.

I've kissed more men *and* women in the last six months than my entire life.

Since the breakup, I've been making up for lost time by finally sowing my wild oats in a purely oral sense. I haven't been sexually attracted to anyone enough to share more than saliva with them. Until now, that is. Julius has thoroughly implanted the all-consuming idea of sex into every fibre of my being. As I carefully traverse this maze, it's all I'm thinking about.

A screech echoes through the winding, unlearnable maze. The sound is piercing despite its distance.

Frozen by fear, the desire fizzles, my body turning to cold stone.

I was wrong. The silence was a comfort compared to this.

I'm still trembling when I reach a new portion of the maze. The dreadful calls of the 'residents' continue to unsettle my steps. If it's not some bird-like screech slicing the frigid air, it's a grumbling groan of some mysterious beast rattling the hard earth beneath the flimsy soles of my uncomfortable trainers.

This new section of branching paths is shorter and narrower. Hopefully, evading any monsters I bump into on my travels will be easier. When needed, I can be swift and nimble.

Back-pedalling from another dead end, I take the next twist, and my eyes alight onto an enormous mass of dark indigo feathers, a second before my mind catches up with my over-enthusiastic feet.

As soon as my disorientated brain registers the giant, bird-like creature for the danger it is, I go still, praying my footfalls weren't loud enough to garner its attention. Luckily, it's faced away from me.

Slowly, I inch backwards, my body poised to run the second I'm caught in its sights. I breathe an inaudible sigh of relief when I'm safely around the corner, able to peek at the creature without making my presence known.

It's ostrich-like: tall, with clawed, flightless wings for arms and a long, thick neck. However, as it twists its head in my direction, I find it's scarily similar to the type of dinosaurs that haunted my childhood nightmares after watching films like *Jurassic Park*. Theropods, I think they're called. Spielberg took creative liberties with the design of Velociraptors, but these demonic creatures are not far off them.

With shiny blue-black feathers covering its sturdy body, its face looks naked in comparison. However, its beaky snout is the most horrifying thing about it. The end is slightly curved and pointed—a sharp tip to complement its rows of yellowing teeth. Its beady eyes are the deepest amber, yet cold and calculating, lacking all warmth. Its tail is long, mostly feathers. Its hands and larger three-toed feet all end in hooked claws.

I shrink back when it chirps, hiding my peeping eye in case it spots me.

Usually, birdsong is calming—a treat for my ears. This creature's song only promises a grisly death.

Before it can suspect my lingering presence, I slink off, hurrying to take the next available route. Hopefully, it will lead me far away from this unimaginable danger so I can continue without consequence.

However, I soon realise that every action in this maze brings consequences not even the best of us can avoid.

Because danger always follows...

Chapter 7

Tactics

Julius

Cock still hard and throbbing, I pace my throne room, the taste of Raven's desire lasting on my tongue, the smell of her arousal mingling with my every breath.

This is torture, as I've never known it.

I come to a standstill, head lifting to admire the elegantly painted ceiling, hoping the faux, silver-flecked night sky will calm me. My blood is rushing like a wild river on the run. How can I tolerate being trapped inside my castle for three days while that infuriatingly fragile, yet surprisingly resourceful girl—*woman*—chooses to be live bait instead of my queen?

I said Raven's mortality was not my burden, but the more I envisage her being torn to pieces by the dromaeosaurids, trampled into the earth by cyclopes, or worse: that fiery heart of hers eaten by sirens or...

Don't think of him. Thinking of him too often will awaken his wrath. Then your little starling will be lost, even to you.

The wild and wicked creatures trapped inside my maze act as a deterrent for those who wish to oppose my will and rule. Most have been there for centuries. The dromaeosaurids are long-extinct creatures I crafted into being when I came to rule, replacing the lesser terror birds there before. *Jurassic Park* is my favourite film for a few reasons: the obvious being that dinosaurs were not only cool, but unmistakably terrifying; any mortal would piss themselves even encountering the smaller Velociraptor. My maze's other deterrents are typical mythical beasts bred by the same demons who created the kingdom I inherited.

Still on edge, though my erection thankfully easing, I force myself to sit on my obsidian throne, the black velvet padding softening the overall harshness of the piece. With the dark grey stone floor and silver-accented wall panels, the room is fit for a king in this layer of the Underworld.

The mortals fail to realise that 'Hell' and 'the Underworld' differ. Firstly, Hell is an exaggerated myth. The Underworld is where all untethered souls pass through. Some are forced to stay—the Collected.

I'm one of many self-proclaimed kings. We have less egotistical titles—The Keepers of Lost Souls or eudaemons. Mortals call us demons, which we have adopted over time.

There are two ways in which I can obtain a soul. One: a soul is lost through a bargain or bet. And two: a mortal has unfinished business they're unable to let go of after death. They usually drift on the spiritual plain for years before their soul fades. Then, when a soul is weak enough, a keeper may capture it without barter or payment.

When it comes to Raven's soul... I have never needed or desired one as much as hers. It's been calling to me since we both turned thirteen. I'm a child to most immortals, a king at only twenty-three. It's unheard of. Few inherit their titles like I did—through a generational curse. A curse which can only be broken by the same mortal line who created it. That's where Raven comes in.

My little starling doesn't know that her lineage can be traced back to ancient Greece. An untold number of women in her familial line have been linked by everything, except blood, to the generations of the males in mine.

Raven and I are twin souls, born in the exact same moment in time. It was a good omen—something the curse mentions specifically. And because of that coincidence, my father believed I would finally end our curse.

Claiming Raven's soul and re-joining it with mine is my last-ditch attempt to break the cycle. It's the only way I can think to rid myself of the unthinkable fate the previous generations of males in my family have suffered before me, spanning thousands of years.

I was prepared to play fair—offering Raven the two options I usually give the souls I covet—standing by the rules which bind me as a keeper. Unlike what mortals may believe, even demons have a code of honour. Some might dare to say *morality*.

My morality and honour went out of the window when I tasted Raven tonight. Now, I have no intention of playing by the rules regarding her. I've been envisioning our first kiss since we were fifteen. Around the time her curves took shape, that annoying little girl who kept pulling me into her dreams, seeking an end to her loneliness, turned into someone I couldn't expel from my mind, no matter how hard I tried.

After a while, I started to look forward to our time together, though she never remembered our interactions. I had to spend the first hour of the dream explaining our connection. Every. Single. Time.

At first, this effort was tedious. It still is. Nevertheless, it was worth the dull and repetitive introduction by the end of the nights we shared. We would spend hours simply talking. There was a time when our understanding of each other surpassed our understanding of ourselves. Our souls have always been a mirror; our hearts are clearer when reflected through the other's eyes.

Then, my wilful little bird decided to fly the nest; she left for university. I hadn't realised it would be an issue for us until the shout of her soul had withered to a mere echo. I've tried for five years to invade her dreams to no avail.

After tonight, I'm almost certain her childhood home was the catalyst. I sensed her soul's presence when she stepped through the front door. Waiting for her to fall asleep was beyond frustrating. Using that fucking owl to watch her, the whole time unable to communicate, was demeaning. Possession is draining, even when it's a simple-minded creature. I don't know how my father kept it up all those years.

The five years apart has only strengthened my desire for Raven. Seeing her again tonight has thoroughly solidified my plans.

I must have her. She *will* be mine.

Our souls can't be parted again, especially after that kiss sealed our bond. Perhaps I should have told her that the rumours are true—kissing a demon of my sort is practically marking your soul as theirs.

Now, I'll be able to physically feel her emotions when they're strong enough as though they're my own. Also, I'll be able to track her even if she returns to the mortal lands. She's officially marked. This means that no other demon—except one who shall not be named—can collect her soul if she dies in my maze.

Again, the thought of Raven succumbing to death has my throat constricting and my undead, immortal heart aching. How I obtain her soul should not bother me; it ends up in my hands whether she lives or dies. Her only way out of my clutches is if she defies the odds and accomplishes the impossible—if she completes her '*quest*'. Only one other mortal has ever done it, and she had assistance. Raven is alone, facing the unbound dangers without so much as a weapon. She's defenceless against the monsters which lurk. Her fresh, untainted blood is an irresistible lure.

Swallowing down my unease, I reach for my call bell and ring it. The power of the chimes works its magic, and before I can take my next breath, my second in command—Dato—materialises before me, his inky-feathered, harpy wings ruffling with indignance. I must have called on him at an inconvenient time.

Dato is dressed in his usual black armoured suit. As my Commander of Defence, the protective garb is often necessary. Demons are known for their sinful greed. And my kingdom is great; a treasure many in the Underworld covet. Harpyiai are not as difficult to destroy as one such as myself. Injury can kill them, and they don't heal as fast as vrykolakas or lycanthropes.

Running a hand through the silken strands of his onyx hair, Dato speaks, 'You rang, My King?' His tone is dry, his angular, hooded eyes narrow, conveying his ire.

'Yes. I have a task for you,' I start, ignoring his insolence. Out of my three commanders, I would consider Dato a friend, whereas Hex and Lorcan grate on my nerves more often than not. Despite our familiarity, Dato is still in my service; his soul is mine for the keeping for at least another thirty years. 'A mortal girl is journeying through my maze, hoping to retrieve her brother's soul, which she inadvertently wished away.'

'Yeah, say no more. It shouldn't take long to hunt her down. I'll send Hex. He's been dying for a taste of mortal blood. Or if you think she deserves a quick death, I'll send Lorcan.' Dato's casual approach speaks volumes of my past tactics.

I shake my head. 'Dato, for this particular mortal, your task is the opposite. I want you to make sure she stays alive.'

Dato's eyebrows flick up. 'You want me to *protect* the mortal? The mortal currently trying to beat you in a bargain for two souls. The mortal journeying through one of the most dangerous mazes in all plains of existence. *That's* my task?'

'Yes,' I say, unwilling to elaborate. Not even Dato knows about my history with Raven or the connection of our twin souls. Though I suppose he might guess she's the mortal I need to obtain above all others now that I've singled her out for protection.

The particulars of my family's curse are heavily guarded secrets. Lesser demons would likely exploit the situation if the details were widely known.

'Obviously, we can't allow her to complete the maze. I would simply prefer for her *not* to perish while trying. I want you to scare her away without causing her irrevocable harm. Or, if all else fails, befriend her in the hopes of leading her astray.'

'Scare or befriend?' Dato's confusion is plain to see. 'Julius, are you okay?' he asks, brow creasing with worry.

I wave off his misplaced concern. 'Her name is Raven Aria Adaway. She's twenty-three years old. Her brother, Robin, is currently asleep in my main living chamber. Before you depart, instruct a servant to ready a room for him on the same floor.'

Forehead still lined, Dato's wings bristle. Unlike me, he can't wish them away. 'Wait, there's a mortal here in the castle? Sleeping in *your* living chamber? Why is he not in the dungeon?'

'Because he's my guest. As part of the bargain, I promised he would be treated well.'

'Is this a new tactic you're trying out? Catch more souls with honey or something?' he questions, scratching his head.

'Or something.' I purse my lips to keep them from revealing more.

'Shall I enlist Hex and Lorcan? I'm sure this unusual... *task* will be enough to cure their chronic boredom for a week or two.'

'I'll allow it as long as you rein in their behaviour. A pretty, mortal girl is a walking meal to the likes of those two.' Tension building, I massage my temple to ease the strain. 'Remember, do *not* gravely injure her. A few minor cuts or bruises are acceptable. But try to handle her with care. I want her in one piece at the end of this,' I stress.

Dato bows his head. 'My King, I will see to it the girl survives and remains intact.' He pivots on his heel, making his leave.

'And Dato,' I call out, remembering another crucial point. He rotates his head to receive further instruction. 'If one of you dares to fuck her, I will tear out the offender's treasonous heart and crush it in my palm. Do you hear me?'

Amusement huffs out of him. 'Our cold, black hearts have never bled for mortals, Julius.' His expression drops to one of disgust at the mere prospect. 'And I assure you, they never will.'

On that note, Dato marches out of the door, shoulders set, his midnight-blue tail twitching in agitation, the feathers on the end spikier than usual.

Chapter 8

Hunting Party

Dato

After giving the order to rehouse the mortal child to one of Julius' many soulless servants, I make my way to the castle's top-floor balcony. I could take flight from the ground, but launch requires more effort. Jumping from a greater height—trusting the wind to catch my wings—allows me to soar more efficiently. Plus, it's super fucking badass to jump from a building without fear.

Stepping up onto the balustrades, I take a moment to survey the eternally dark, dismal landscape of Julius' kingdom—Vyrinthos. The horrors of the Vyrinthos maze stretch as far as the eye can see. Beyond the castle grounds is the wall-protected city of Galbrek, where lesser demons—who once sold their soul to the DiMinos line—live without threat from the creatures who run wild on the other side of the stone barrier.

As a harpy, I have the means to pass over the maze; the thunderous sky is my faithful friend. There's an enchantment which restricts others from the same luxury. If anyone else tried to fly over the maze, they'd be struck down in a flash of lightning.

With my far-seeing eyes on the infinitely stormy horizon, I step off into empty air, the thrilling lurch in my stomach a rush I've come to savour. Spreading my wings, the wind embraces them. I glide for a full minute before I have to use the muscles in my back to flap.

Knowing Hex and Lorcan, they'll be preparing for their end-of-the-week hunt. I bank to the left, my sights on their favourite hangout spot—a hut beside the river Melas. Its black waters have a glossy sheen from this height.

As the only safe water source in the maze, it lures every creature needing refreshment. It's a great place to hunt, as usually our prey is weakened by thirst.

A minute later, I touch down with light feet on the stony bank, my wings tucking in closer to my body. Confident no creature is creeping around this part of the maze, seeing as my superior eyesight didn't catch a flicker of movement before landing, I stride towards the grey stone hut without scanning my surroundings. This area's ashy, bare-branched trees can't conceal much, anyway.

Before I can knock, Hex shouts, 'Dato, you're losing your touch. I could hear you from a mile away.'

I open the door to see Hex and Lorcan playing cards at the small wooden table. A few chairs and a worn leather sofa are the only other furniture inside, apart from the large cabinet in the corner, which is always stocked full of alcohol.

Lorcan, like usual, is shirtless. His tanned skin has a thin, shining layer of sweat which coats his muscular torso, the monochrome tattoos covering his arms and chest highlighted. He must have recently come in from a run.

As a lycanthrope (with the ability to change form), Lorcan wears as little as possible. Because clothes, as he likes to say, are a nuisance. Luckily, we're spared from seeing his cock on the regular because his lower half doesn't shift as much as his top half. The stretchy material of his baggy joggers often remains intact after the transformation is complete.

Stretching his thick arms, Lorcan stands. He ties the top half of his long, chestnut hair into a bun. 'Are you coming on the hunt with us tonight?' he asks me in his gruff voice, patting down his short beard.

'Of course, but this hunt will have to be a little different from the usual,' I mention casually, a teasing smirk on my face. 'A short while ago, Julius summoned me to the castle. He's *bound* to approve of our antics tonight despite being unable to join.'

This draws Hex's attention. He knows by now what I mean by that. His reddish-brown eyes snap to me, glinting. His pupils enlarge: hunger activated. 'Oh, do share, my friend. What's waiting for us in the maze tonight?'

'A mortal girl, twenty-three,' I answer, and as soon as the word *mortal* leaves my mouth, Hex's fangs pop out, his fawn skin crinkling around his eyes as he hisses in excitement. Nothing quenches a vrykolakas' thirst as much as a mortal's blood.

Hex leans forward, his long fingers gripping the edge of the table. 'Is she hot? Can we play with our food first?'

His eagerness is catching. A low purr of longing resonates from Lorcan's throat. 'I thought I caught the scent of perfume on the way here. I assumed one of the servants must have got their grubby little hands on a bottle.'

Hex is standing now, running his fingers through his dark brown waves. 'You didn't answer my question, Dato. Have you seen her? *Is she hot*? I haven't fucked a mortal in so long.' The front laces of his white shirt are tied one second, but with incredible speed, he loosens them in a blur of movement.

'Unfortunately, this mortal is off-limits in that regard. You must dull your powers of seduction, Hex,' I say sternly, pointing a finger at him in warning. He baulks, mouth dropping open to protest, but I'm quick to add, 'Our task is to preserve her life for the next three days.'

Hex scowls. 'Preserve her life? Are you fucking kidding me?'

'Julius wants her alive? Why? Surely, he doesn't want her to complete the maze,' Lorcan chimes in, equally as frowny.

I shrug. 'For some unexplained reason, he wants her in one piece by the end of this. We're to either scare her out of the maze or gain her trust enough to throw her off course.'

Snorting with displeasure, Hex drops back into his seat. 'I'm out. Sounds tedious. If I can't fuck her or kill her, then what's the point?' He returns to shuffling the deck of cards, ready to deal the next hand.

'We have orders. And it's not like we can't have fun with her in other ways. We're just not allowed to fatally wound her or let her get eaten. Come on; it beats sitting around here, waiting for the prey to come to us.' When I see that neither seems as interested as I thought they would be, I sweeten the deal. 'The first to catch her gets to decide what to do with her.'

They both perk up at that, and I raise an eyebrow, tickled by how easy it is to incite their baser instincts. They love a good bet as much as keeper demons do.

'What about her blood? Is that off-limits, too?' Hex enquires, dropping the cards to the table again. Mouth watering, he licks his lips. 'And are we permitted to make our own bargains with her?'

'All Julius said was, '*If any one of you dares to fuck her, I'll rip your hearts out*', blardy, blardy, blah. You know how dramatic he can be,' I reply, pushing off the wall. 'Minor injuries are acceptable. How else are we supposed to scare her away?'

Lorcan and Hex share a look, a silent exchange to gauge whether the other will take my bait.

A wolfish smile spreads across Lorcan's face. 'You know I can't say no to a hunting party.'

Hex runs his tongue over his sharp, needle-point fangs. 'I don't care who gets to her first. Her blood is *mine*.'

With all of us poised to start, I pronounce, 'On the count of three...'

CHAPTER 9

Rock Bottom

RAVEN

Heart pounding out of my chest, I cover my mouth to stifle my panting breaths as I press my back against the maze wall. I've been running to evade this raptor for ten minutes now, taking turn after turn, praying I come across a good enough hiding place to rest for a short while.

This little alcove is the best I've found. It should shield me from view if the raptor passes. However, if the relentless predator stalks down here, then I might as well be fucking birdseed at this point.

In hindsight—e.g., on the verge of becoming a meal—I should have taken the deal Julius offered me at the start. At least then, I would have stayed alive, even if my theoretical soul was eternally his. It also would have guaranteed Robin's release. Granted, he would have been alone without me there to be his guardian, but he'd be safe. Free. Even if he ends up in foster care, that's better than being a caged pet in the Underworld, right?

I could have bartered for certain freedoms if I humoured Julius by expressing more interest in his first option. He mentioned I had his favour and there's not much he would deny me. Except for giving me my brother back without conditions attached, of course. *Dick*.

Anyway, I should have tried harder to set my own conditions—visiting my brother back in our world, for example. I don't know how possible that would be without a soul. Julius can't seem to leave the Underworld, even with his superhu...demonic powers.

In *A Maze of Birds and Beasts*, the protagonist sacrifices her innocence to complete the maze and beat the King. Was that a metaphor for her soul? I always assumed it had to do with her feeling like she had grown as a person by the end—overcoming her childishness to learn from her previous mistakes in life.

That's why I related to her character so much. I was also forced to abandon my innocence before I was ready to. But my tempestuous relationship with my mum pushed me to become a more resilient, independent person who had the strength to move to the other side of the country on their own. It's partly why I rejected Julius' first offer before I thought it through; I can't stand the idea of someone else dictating my life again. *I* want to be in control of it.

Also, I don't need to be made a queen. I'm pretty fucking powerful in my own right. And I certainly don't need some fucking '*king*' ruling over me.

Hyped-up on my own self-confidence, I decide that hiding won't save me. The raptor will eventually be able to zero in on me by smell alone, and I highly doubt I can outrun or evade it for much longer. I need to arm myself to deter it from picking a fight with me in the first place.

To start, I tiptoe out from the alcove's deluded safety, treading carefully to not alert the raptor of my whereabouts before I can find something to use as a defence.

There are several rocks scattered in my path that I could throw. Unfortunately, none are big or sharp enough to do significant damage.

A searching screech slices through my resolve, and I whip around to see the raptor at the other end of the path, with me equally in its sights. It yaps again, excited to have finally found its prey—*me*.

Fuck. You need to run! *You definitely need to run*! My inner voice is desperate, but it's not until the raptor springs forward in attack mode that my body finally listens.

I race to the next junction and veer left, hoping I haven't fucked myself over by choosing another dead end. If I have, the name is quite fitting; Death will be eager to meet me at the end of it.

While running, I scan the ground in case there's something I can use against it. A handful of small stones and twigs will not do much to stop those hooked claws from dicing me up like an onion. I imagine being ripped apart and eaten alive is probably one of the worst, and most painful, ways to die.

Fucking great.

Being Julius' little pet for all eternity looks pretty damn cushty right about now. Going by how he edged me earlier, I could have at least got some orgasms out of the arrangement.

Facing the very real prospect of death has me wondering if I can change my answer and make use of mine and Julius' connection to soul-call him, or whatever I've done in my dreams to summon him in the past. Will he take pity on me and save me from being eaten? He warned me that my survival was not his burden to bear. He'll claim my soul, regardless. But then, in his words, he won't have my '*delicious body*'—this raptor will.

Fuck it. There's no harm in trying.

Julius, if you can hear me, I'm about to be dead meat. So, I've changed my mind: Option one sounds better; I'll take that.

Nope. Nothing. He doesn't come.

And I was wrong. Even admitting defeat in my head has caused my pride significant harm.

I throw a glance over my shoulder. The raptor skids into view, taking the same sharp left I did. There will be no escaping it now. It not only has me in its sights, but it also has my scent and the sound of my thumping footfalls to go by.

Adrenaline alone carries my overworked body to the next fork in the maze. I go right this time, then right again at the next available opportunity, aiming to confuse it. In my head, a half-baked plan rises out of the chaos: If I double back, maybe my pursuer will keep going around and around in a circle, chasing the ghost of my scent. Then, I might be able to slip away undetected if I'm *incredibly* lucky.

My optimistic plan is dashed when I come across a wide, deep pit in the middle of the path. I say 'come across' as if I didn't nearly run straight into the thing. Thankfully, I managed to stop the momentum of my legs in time.

The excited chirps of the raptor are louder—closer. However, there is no way around this chasm; the shadows are so dark I can't see the bottom. This is practically a dead end. I have nowhere to go from here, and any second now, the raptor will appear at the mouth of this path, its own mouth watering at the thought of feasting on my tender flesh.

Shaking uncontrollably, I pivot to face the grisly fate coming to claim me. Its snout is the first thing that comes into view, a few larger teeth overlapping its closed, beaky lips. Its head rotates in my direction, and its beady eyes narrow their focus, locking me in as a target. Bile surges up my throat, but I swallow it down.

There's a moment of silence, the raptor's head tilting to regard me. It's probably wondering why I'm not running. Maybe it doesn't have the awareness to realise what I nearly didn't either.

Maybe there *is* hope after all.

Slowly, I inch backwards, and the subtle movement makes the raptor twitch, its jaws snapping as though it can already taste me. When I risk the next tentative step, it loses its patience and launches itself into a sprint, its shiny blueish-black feathers fluttering as it moves with a hunter's grace.

That's it. The faster, the better.

When the raptor is ten meters away, its powerful legs push off the ground, propelling its whole body into the air. Apparently, it doesn't need wings to fly. Spielberg was accurate in that respect: raptors are impressive jumpers.

But so am I.

At the very last second, I throw myself at the wall, halfway over the pit. The impact winds me. But, before gravity does its job, I scramble to find purchase and tightly grip the mass of black vines I spied a moment ago, trusting that they're strong enough to hold my weight. They aren't for long: the vines breaking and pulling free from the wall.

To stop my descent, I jam my foot into a divot in the stone, using that to lessen the load. I reach for another cluster of vines to further distribute my weight. The whole time I'm trying not to fall to my death, the raptor is snapping its jaws inches away from my face. Its claws make a swishing sound as it swipes at me, its little feathered arms too short to reach.

It seems unwilling to step too close to the edge of the pit. But that might change the hungrier it becomes.

Needing to chance it, I reach for more winding vines, my left trainer seeking another foothold. I've never been rock-climbing, and it shows; I'm shit at this.

All four of my limbs are shaking, and I'm panting. The strenuous task of moving across this wall to the other side of the pit seems unachievable.

Hold on, a small voice echoes back to me. It's so faint I almost miss it. Was that my voice or Julius'? Nah, it couldn't be him. My mind is my own. For the time being, anyway.

Even if I shimmy my way to the other side, who's to say the raptor can't make the jump? Judging by the Olympic-level display I just witnessed, it could do it if it's willing to risk an injury. All this effort could be for nought; I'm only delaying the inevitable.

But at least you're not giving up without a fight.

Groaning with the effort, I cling on, my muscles screaming at me to let go.

Don't let go.

The raptor snorts an aggravated breath, moving closer to the edge. When it leans across to catch me between its teeth, I snatch my hand back in the nick of time.

As a consequence of my jolt and lapse in focus, the vine I'm grasping in my other hand rips away from the wall, and I swing down with a frightened cry. My nails break against the rough stone as my fingers frantically search for another divot to cling to, but it's no use. The vine frays to nothing before I can find the support I need, and a scream gets caught in my throat as I plummet down into the bottomless pit.

I soon discover I'm wrong when pain shoots up my legs as they hit muddy ground. I land on my side; any remaining oxygen is punched out of my body. Cursing this place and Julius, I writhe in agony for a minute, too stunned to think.

When I can breathe again, I look up to see the raptor toeing the cusp, pacing, and snorting its displeasure. It could jump down, but I doubt it's senseless enough to risk it. I'm only down here because I had no choice but to chance it. I'm surprised the fall didn't kill me. Luckily, the ground was softer than the paths I'd been treading. My ankles hurt, though I don't suspect they're broken. Not that it matters when I'm stuck down here with no way of escape. Plus, the raptor is still up there, waiting.

Is it any better than dying down here in the mud? Being eaten would be quicker. It's more painful, but dehydration will be equally torturous to endure.

Julius, if you're listening, I'd appreciate you sending someone to help me out of here. Can we make another deal… please?

In this time of crisis, I humour myself, waiting for his telepathic whisper. But my panicking mind is too loud to discern anything which isn't *I'm going to die. I'm going to die a slow, miserable death.*

I give in to my fear and cry, thick tears rolling down my mud-splattered cheeks. I failed spectacularly. I didn't even make it through the night. And now, I'm not the only one damned. Robin is, too.

Dirt rains down on my head as the raptor's pacing loosens the compact earth. Its chirps and yaps are whiny, yet it doesn't want to give up its dinner pursuit.

I hug my aching legs to my chest, massaging all the areas that hurt—from my twisted ankles to my knocked knees—while I continue wallowing. I've hit rock bottom here. It's hard to imagine a bleaker set of circumstances.

It's a long moment before I realise the raptor has stopped pacing. Not only that, but it's also gone completely silent.

Looking up to search, I note that its prowling shadow has also disappeared. I force myself to stand, wincing as my ankles wobble, the pain radiating through my battered body.

Then my ears catch light footsteps approaching the edge.

Cupping my hands around my mouth, I call up to the sky, 'Hello? Julius, is that you?'

Pathetically, my heart skips a beat, and I find myself hoping it *is* him.

In a blur, an unfamiliar man is suddenly sitting casually on top of the maze wall, high above. He looks down at me and his head tilts. A puzzled frown touches his face before it disappears a moment later. His hair isn't long, but shaggy—dark brown, almost black. His skin is as fair as daylight, yet it's the opposite of warm. He's wearing the sort of white shirt medieval nobles have on in films: billowy with laces at the collar. He's objectively handsome. Very handsome compared to most men. His expression turns appraising as he continues assessing me.

'It's your lucky day, darling. I'm much better looking,' the man says, his smile revealing two lengthening teeth.

Vampire fangs.

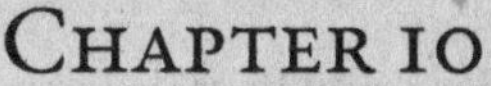

Chapter 10

Deal-breaker

Raven

'I s there something the matter? I know I'm stunning, but I'm sure you can manage a hello. It's only polite,' the vampire says, humour lighting his dark eyes.

When I don't answer, he jumps down from the wall into an effortless crouch right on the edge of the pit. He reminds me of a cat playing with a mouse. The mouse being me.

'You're giving me the silent treatment already? You should thank me. I scared away the big bad Deinonychus for you,' he claims, resting his elbows on his knees. 'He was still hoping to make a meal out of you.'

'And you're not?' I challenge, hobbling out of the light to hide in the shadows. 'You're a vampire, right?'

He shrugs a shoulder. 'I prefer vrykolaka. But call me what you wish.'

'Do you have a name?'

His lips twitch up. 'Hex. What's yours?'

'Nice to meet you, Hex. I'm Raven,' I answer more sweetly, hoping that if I'm pleasant enough, I can talk my way out of this. Like Julius, Hex is still male. Which means my feminine wiles can easily manipulate him.

Hex breathes a laugh. 'Oh, this will be fun. I can already tell.'

Ignoring that comment, I continue playing nice. 'As you can see, I'm kinda stuck down here. Could you help me out, by any chance?' I ask, then I remember my manners. 'Please?'

I'm taking a risk here; Hex could be as dangerous as the raptor. His charm could be an act meant to put me at ease and make me assume I'm safe when I'm not.

Pretending to think on it, Hex hums before he says, 'I could.'

'Okay. Well. *Will you*?' I force a smile, trying not to let my impatience show.

Hex inspects his nails, feigning disinterest. 'Maybe. Depends.'

I fold my arms under my bust and huff out, 'On what?'

'On what I get out of it.' Dropping to a sitting position, his legs dangle. He leans back as if relaxing on a tropical beach, carefree.

Through gritted teeth, I ask, 'I'm guessing you want to make a deal?'

'We *are* in the Underworld. And I *am* a demon.'

'I thought you were a vampire.'

'One and the same around here,' he tells me with a flash of his eyebrows.

From what I've learnt in my previous dealings with Julius, the deal's wording matters most, not the intention. 'Okay, if I agree to make a deal, will you help me out of this pit and let me go safely on my merry way?'

Surprise flashes in Hex's eyes, a knowing grin spreading from ear to ear. 'Are you trying to con a demon out of a deal with the promise of a deal you have no intention of making?'

'I don't know what you mean,' I lie. That was exactly what I was hoping to do. I made sure to say, '*If I agree to make a deal...*' I didn't specify that I *would* make a deal or whom I'd make a deal with.

Hex mockingly claps his hands. 'Clever girl. A younger demon might have fallen for that one.'

I blow out a resigned sigh. 'Fine. What do you want in exchange?'

'I want your blood, deal-breaker,' Hex answers, although I had already guessed as much.

'And you promise not to kill me in the process? Or anytime afterwards?'

With his hand on his heart, he vows, 'I have no plans to kill you, darling. So yes, I promise not to suck you dry. Though you're more than welcome to suck *me* dry.'

I roll my eyes at his vulgarity, then take a moment to think on it, knowing I have little choice if I want to get out of this literal hellhole. 'I guess losing a little blood is not the end of the world.' I step to the centre, so he has a full view of me again. 'Well... are you going to help me out of this pit?'

Hex's menacing fangs catch the light. Even with his mouth closed, they hook over his lips. He licks one of them. 'Sure, I'll help you out... as soon as you agree to let me bite you anytime I want, any*where* I want. Say those exact words, and you have yourself a deal.'

I scoff. 'No. One bite to the neck, like in the films. Take it or leave it.' The idea of being this vampire's blood bank for the next three days makes me want to vomit.

Hex's expression hardens, his lazy grin disappearing. 'You do know that I don't have to offer *any* deal to take what I want from you, right? I could quite easily jump down and bite you anywhere I please. I could drain you of your blood right here and now.'

Fear ripples down my spine at his threat, but I square my shoulders and raise my chin in defiance. 'Then why haven't you? Why offer me a deal at all?'

Hex's smile is quick to return. 'Because, deep down, my dear, I'm a gentleman at heart. I may not have a soul, but still have my old-fashioned values. And it seems my Achilles heel is a damsel in distress.'

My eyes narrow with suspicion. 'Did Julius send you to help me?'

'Not directly,' he admits. 'But you're lucky I found you before Lorcan or Dato did. I'm the nice one. They would have handled this a hell of a lot differently.'

My stomach drops at the news. 'There's more of you?'

'Don't worry, my darling deal-breaker. I'm the only one who will be vying for your blood. Although I'm sure the others would be equally as keen to take a bite out of you.' His voice is a silky purr, as seducing as Julius'.

'So, if you've been ordered to help me, then I don't need to make a deal with you.'

Hex frowns, realising I've talked him into a corner. '*Help* isn't exactly the word the King used, but your optimism is cute. I could leave you to rot in here until your time is up, giving you just enough water to survive.'

And there was me foolishly thinking for a second that Julius cared for my welfare. 'I'm not agreeing to your terms. It's too much for not enough,' I say in a bitter tone, suspecting I'm losing any advantage he may have allowed me at the start.

Hex hisses out an exasperated sigh. 'All right. Think of it this way... if you consent to be my blood source while you're inside the maze, then I'll be more inclined to stay by your side. You saw how the Deinonychus fled when I showed up. With me around, you won't have to worry about them.'

A little glimmer of hope shines through this shit show of a situation. 'You'll protect me?'

'If you agree to my terms, I'll protect your life the best I can against the beasts which roam the maze,' Hex answers carefully, and I notice he was precise with his wording. If Julius ordered it, Hex would kill me without hesitation. Technically, Julius doesn't roam the maze; he lives easily at his castle in the centre.

Taking another minute to mull over my limited options, and checking that I haven't missed a trick, I come to the only feasible solution. 'Urgh, fine. I agree to let you bite me anytime and anywhere you wish. All I ask is that you give me a little warning first, okay? I'm a little squeamish when it comes to blood.'

'Sorry, I'll make no such concession. Taking you by surprise will be the best part. Like all predators, being hand-fed sucks all the fun out of feeding time. Pun intended.'

Before I can protest, he's already jumping down to meet me. Fear seizing my limbs, I stumble back until I hit the muddy wall. But the vampire follows, on the prowl.

'The deal is done,' Hex reminds me, my fear amusing him. He offers me his hand, but when I don't immediately take it, he adds, 'I thought you wanted out of this godforsaken pit.'

I hesitate a moment longer before I reach out to touch my palm to his. His skin isn't as cold as I was expecting it to be.

As Hex's fingers enclose, he yanks me to him, leaving no space between our bodies. A breath stutters out of me when his head dips so our noses touch. My scandalised reaction makes him chuckle.

When his mouth lowers to my neck, I gasp, my back arching in reflex. I'm not sure if it bends to escape or push closer. He smells sweet: hints of burnt sugar and cinnamon—a lure.

'Hmm. If you like that, wait until my teeth sink into you. Right here.' He presses a kiss to the skin between my neck and shoulder. 'You'll be begging for me *not* to stop.' His innuendo brings heat to the surface of my skin.

Why do these demons have to be so fucking sexy? It's incredibly unfair. Evil creatures are supposed to be repulsive. Not able to seduce me with a few murmured words and soft touches.

We're standing in the pit one second, and the next, we're whooshing upwards. My insides get left behind, the nauseating lurch taking me by surprise.

Back on the path, Hex keeps his arms locked around my waist, holding me upright. At first, I think he's being considerate, but then, without warning, he bites exactly where he marked me with a kiss.

The sting of his fangs is like two twin flames sliding in to scorch my veins. I cry out, trying to push him off me, but he's too strong. His greedy growl is my only admonishment. He doesn't hit me in retaliation; he only continues sucking on my neck.

Struggling is only causing me more pain, so I try to quit squirming. Going against my fighting instinct is like holding myself underwater without a lungful of air. My legs want to kick. My arms want to flail. But I force myself to relax, and something unexpected happens as soon as I do.

I start to enjoy it. I enjoy it *too* much.

I feel the pull of his fangs and the flick of his tongue on a completely unrelated part of my anatomy. A pounding heat between my legs has my winces morphing into moans. Responding to the change, Hex's possessive growl softens to a reverent purr, and his grip on me loosens. The hand cradling my neck slides down to cup my breast, and when he finds my nipple hard, he stops drinking my blood.

'Fuck, I thought I'd turned it off,' he says, breathing heavily.

'Turned what off?' I enquire, my chest heaving into his palm, desperate for another squeeze.

'Never mind. It's too late now. Just enjoy it.'

When Hex goes back to feeding from me, the sensation intensifies. Chasing it, I rub myself against him without shame, pleasure building from the super-charged air. He's hard, yet he's no longer touching me in any way that could be perceived as sexual. His hands are back on my neck and shoulder, as though fucking me is of no interest to him.

This pisses me off.

So, high on endorphins, my hand travels down his lean stomach, then lower, to paw his erection through his trousers.

In a flash of speed, my back hits the wall, and Hex is groaning into my neck, taking longer drags of my blood as I continue to stroke him, up and down.

Hex sneaks paranoid glances over his shoulder to check we're not being watched before his hand returns to my breast, his thumb flicking over the stiff peak of my nipple. I arch into him, a needy whine in my throat.

'Fuck me.' The demand falls out of my mouth without care, my mind completely lost.

Rolling my nipple between his fingers, the material of my top a bunching barrier, Hex licks up the column of my throat to whisper in my ear, 'I wish I could. But I can't.'

When I hook my leg over his hip to grind against him, he winces as if denying himself me is the hardest thing he's ever done.

'You're going to get me killed,' Hex grits out, but he doesn't stop me. He checks our surroundings again. 'Hold still, darling. I know what will send you over the edge.'

His mouth is at my neck again, on the other side. His fresh bite delivers surprising pleasure with the pain, and I jolt, yelping. All it takes is a small pinch of my nipple to shudder into a powerful orgasm. With Hex holding my head to his chest, my cries of release are muffled.

Hex uses the flat of his tongue to mop up the blood pooling in the dip of my collarbone as I come down, my breaths evening out.

Lust clouding his black eyes, he licks his red-stained lips. 'That's a good girl. I knew you'd beg,' he drawls, a cocky smirk making him look more fiendish.

Coming to my senses, I slap the smirk right off his face. 'You did something to me!'

'Yeah, I made you come,' Hex retorts, pinning my arms to my sides so I can't strike him again.

'No. Your bite... it... it—'

'Made you so horny that you begged me to fuck you?' he finishes, his smugness returning. 'You know, I've never had anyone slap me for making them come before.'

My fists clench in his grip. 'I should have punched you.'

'Trust me, darling, that would hurt you a lot more than it would me.'

I glare at him, ignoring the tingling aftershocks of my orgasm. 'Next time, turn off whatever made it so...'

'Pleasurable? You'd prefer it to hurt?'

'Stop finishing my sentences!' I screech, sounding childish now. 'And yes, I'd rather that than mind control.'

Hex laughs. 'Mind control? All my venom did was heighten the desire already circulating through your veins. If you weren't interested, you wouldn't have tried to jack me off in the middle of it. *I* should be the one feeling violated.'

'Oh, fuck off!' I break his hold with a sharp twist, but he locks me back a second later, slotting his knee between my legs.

'Don't you mean fuck *me*?' he breathes against my neck, sending chills racing down my spine as his lips graze the sore spot of the first bite.

A fresh wave of wetness pools where the tingles of my desire are strongest. Despite my better judgment, I incline my head, inviting another bite.

'What the fuck, Hex?!' a new male voice demands, rough and deep.

Jumping back, Hex is quick to put space between us. 'What? I found her first!' His tone is defensive.

A shirtless man (is he a man or a demon? It's hard to tell), with half his long, chestnut hair in a bun, is striding towards us with a heavy frown and bare feet. His well-defined muscles gleam with sweat, his warm-toned skin covered in black and grey tattoos. He's more ruggedly handsome than clean-shaven Hex, but there's no denying his equal appeal. A few scars enhance the roughness of his overall appearance. Two thin slices through his right eyebrow drag down over the top of his cheek, missing his eye. But the most noticeable scars are the three white claw marks scratched onto his left pectoral muscle.

Still a little turned on, I bite my bottom lip while I admire his burly physique.

Hex's venom really did a number on me.

'I can smell her orgasm from here. Dato told you to rein it in,' the man chastises, shoving Hex further away from me with a feral snarl.

'I tried,' Hex defends, shoving him back. And his answering growl is possessive, like I'm some carcass worth fighting over. 'It's not my fault her body is more responsive than most.'

My face flushes at how they speak about me as if I'm not right in front of them. 'Who the fuck are you?' I demand from the shirtless man.

The shirtless man rotates his head to look me over, from the bite marks on my neck to my trainers. His gaze lifts to my still-stiff nipples, visible under my thin top. His nostrils flare as though catching a whiff of something delicious. He squeezes his hazel eyes shut before shaking his head.

He forces his attention back to Hex. 'I knew you'd think with your fangs and fuck everything up.'

'Calm down. I only made a little deal for her blood. That's all,' Hex replies with a sneer, eyes rolling.

'That better be all you did.' A third male voice descends from the sky.

I look up to see a man (or, more accurately, a demon) with wings like Julius', but black with a blue sheen, hovering above us. Tucking them in to land, he perches on top of the maze wall with a stern expression. He appears just as pissed off as the shirtless guy and just as hot. However, his beauty is all clean, soft lines, and smooth, medium-beige skin. And, even without wings, I imagine he'd look majestic in his armoured uniform.

Then his tail whips out, swishing about his feet. It should put me off, but it doesn't.

'I'm guessing this is Dato and Lorcan. Who's who?' I ask Hex, fed up with being ignored.

Hex points to the winged demon on the wall. 'That's Dato. And this beast is Lorcan,' he tells me, poking Lorcan in the chest.

Lorcan bats his hand away with another warning snarl.

All three of them have a similar way of speaking. Like Julius, Hex and Dato's accent is more classically English, whereas Lorcan has a faint lilt to his voice, which is hard to place. If I had to guess, perhaps a hint of Scottish? Which means he might not have lived his whole life in the Underworld. I wonder if any of them have resided in my world for a time. Or they could have been born there and turned into a demon later on.

Demons. They're *demons*. That's the only detail about them that should matter.

With these *demons* on all sides, my heckles rise. Julius sent them to what? Escort me through the maze so I don't get eaten? Unlikely. There's no way I will be naïve enough to trust them. Even Hex. He only promised to keep me alive, not help me navigate the maze. If I stay with them, they'll make sure I never reach the castle. I need to separate myself as soon as possible.

'Well, this has been fun,' I say in a falsely chipper tone, slowly backing away. 'But I better be going; the clock's ticking.'

As soon as I whirl around to make a frenzied dash, Lorcan grabs me by the hair, fist tight.

'Let go!' I shriek as he pushes my face against the wall to subdue me. I look to Hex to intervene, but he only purses his lips, watching on without concern.

'If you even *think* about running from us again, I will tie your pretty hair around my wrist and drag you along by it,' Lorcan warns, yanking my head back until I cry.

With angry tears in my eyes, I glower at Hex with all the disdain I can muster. 'We had a deal! You're supposed to protect me from harm.'

Hex shrugs nonchalantly. 'I said I'll protect your life, and right now, it's not in danger. Lorcan's only doing his alpha shit. You'll get used to it.'

'Some friendly advice, mortal... never try to run from a lycanthrope. You won't make it very far,' Dato imparts, jumping down to us. 'That's enough, Lorc. I think she's learnt her lesson.'

Unceremoniously, I'm thrown to the ground, my hair released from Lorcan's punishing grip. Wincing, I massage the sore part of my scalp. 'I never stood a fucking chance in here, did I?'

'Nope,' Dato replies, flashing me an unsympathetic grin.

CHAPTER II

Idle Rage

JULIUS

Regret has never tasted so bitter yet so tantalisingly sweet.

When I felt my starling's desire lighting up her blood, flowing as a sensual spectre through mine, I simultaneously wanted to fuck my fist while punching the other through a wall.

Without having to summon Dato, I know Raven has been found. Fucking Hex and his fucking bloodlust venom. I should have been more specific. At the time, I was too worked up to pay enough attention to the wording of my commands. As a demon, if you leave something unsaid, it can cost you dearly. We are tricksters and scoundrels, eager to use and abuse loopholes when and where we find them.

Never expect a demon to work inside the rules, for they will find any crack, however small, to break free of them. I should have known better than to trust even my most trusted. Despite our... *ally*-ship, Dato would salivate at any opportunity to push an undefined boundary. It's in our nature to surrender to our selfish greed, which is why friendships in the Underworld are fragile.

What I should have told Dato was that if they touched her in *any* way sexually, I would rip their hearts out. I merely said if any of them *fucked* her. That slip-up leaves room for many things related to, though not in breach of, sex. Like Hex pumping Raven with enough of his venom to make her come so hard, she made *me* tremble with the mere echo of it.

Raven's first demonic orgasm wasn't by my hand. Imagining her clinging to Hex, riding out her climax as he sucked the blood from her neck. Her wet and moaning any name that wasn't mine...

Fucking Hex! I'll tear him to pieces and feed him to the dromaeosaurid.

Filled with idle rage, I use my pent-up telekinetic energy to send a table flying into the wall with a roar. My crystal decanter of whiskey shatters, its glittering shards clinking as they skitter across the stone floor.

It doesn't help that I'm so fucking turned on at the same time as being the most enraged I've felt in years. Her pleasure pulsed as if it were my own, edging me to no satisfying end.

Taking calming breaths, I rearrange my hard, aching cock. If I could leave this castle, the first thing I'd do is hunt her down and fuck her in front of the lot of them. Show them exactly who she belongs to. I'll have her coming again and again while they watch, full of envy. Her body and soul are mine. I've marked her with my kiss. It's inevitable.

They can't have her.

I storm up to my dais to snatch the call bell. I must update the restrictions before they realise my mistake and take advantage.

Its musical chimes ring in my ears as I shake the gold bell in an overly aggressive fashion. And when Dato doesn't materialise within the first ten pretty clangs, I lose my temper and chuck it across the room. With a mangled jingle, it breaks apart on impact.

Fuck. I've just broken the one thing I can use to draw Dato's attention. Now, I'll have to wait for him to fly back here in his own time. Patience is a virtue, and as a demon *and* a king, my interest in sin surmounts.

Berating myself for losing control, I drop down onto my throne with a grunt. I can't stand being a prisoner in my own fucking castle. If I left, the deal would be immediately void, which means Raven would win by default; her and her brother's souls would be their own. No matter how impatient or irritatingly idle I feel these next three days, giving in to the temptation to see her in person is *not* an option I can even *think* to indulge. Her soul is worth waiting for. And her soft, sinful body will be worth the frustration of mine.

As I sit and relive how her hips ground against mine during our kiss... her vanilla scent, her breathy moans, the tentative flicks of her tongue... I yield to the only temptation I know won't break our deal.

I unbutton my trousers, the image of Raven naked, with her back to me, burning hot in my mind's eye. Breath heavy in my throat, I start stroking my cock as soon as it's free. I use my spit to lubricate my palm while I work it up and down the shaft, gripping the end with a tug as I imagine her mouth around it.

Pleasure spikes not even a minute in, and I'm a second away from release when there's a knock on the throne room door.

Muttering obscenities, I hastily tuck myself back into my trousers, more frustrated now than ever. 'Dato, that better be you.'

The door creaks open, and it's not Dato; one of my servants is timidly standing in the doorway, wringing his hands. 'Sorry to disturb you, My King. There's been an issue with the boy.'

'What boy?' My tone is full of impatience and unexpended tension.

'Robin. The mortal boy, staying in the castle. He's awake,' he tells me, staring at the floor, as subservient as always.

If I could, I'd pin him with an indignant look. 'Yes, and?'

Nervously, he chews on his lips before replying, 'And... he's escaped his room.'

Fucking mortals. I would say they're more trouble than they're worth, but that would be a lie.

Down here, they're worth the risk of having your heart ripped out.

If Hex, Dato, and Lorcan aren't careful, that *risk* will become a reality.

CHAPTER 12

Obsession

HEX

My mouth won't stop watering. The rich, metallic tang of the mortal still clings to my taste buds. Her power runs through my undead veins like electric heat—a zap of pure, undiluted life.

I'm desperate for another bite of that raven-haired, quick-witted deal-breaker. Mortal women are uncommon delicacies in the maze. Men aren't as precious with their souls, especially when power is the prize.

If a man had been in the same situation, I found Raven—vulnerable and trapped inside that pit, with no escape—I wouldn't have hesitated to make him my meal. Nevertheless, I would have injected my venom one and the same. It doesn't take much for men to beg me to fuck them, either. I was only surprised Raven responded so eagerly because I'd turned the metaphorical tap off; only traces leaked out. Then, as soon as I hit her with it, full force, she came in an instant. It was fucking ecstasy. Her blood was brimming with endorphins. The rush was nearly enough to tip me over the edge.

As long as Dato and Lorcan keep their mouths shut, Julius need not know. He only said we couldn't fuck her; he left the rest in murky waters. And I will happily bathe in those waters. The filthier, the better.

Julius may be a keeper king, but he can't kill demons without just cause. Otherwise, no others will sell their souls into service if they believe him so petty.

If he'd worded his command better, I'd be bound, knowing if I went against the restrictions explicitly set, he would be within his right to rip out my heart.

But Julius failed to affirm any boundary except one. Well, two: I can't kill her, either. Not that I want to. When I found her first, I had the choice to scare or seduce. Of course, I chose to seduce. She's fucking delectable. Killing her would be a waste; mortals taste far sweeter when their life-blood pumps.

Both Dato and Lorcan would have tried to scare her out of the maze first. There's not much befriending her could offer them with sex off the table. For me, a deal for her blood sounded more fun. I have bitten without consent in the past, but times change. And, when it comes to females especially, I prefer to barter for their permission, even if the deal isn't exactly fair.

Now that I've had a taste, it's nearly impossible not to crave another. Even at this early stage, there's no denying the markings of an obsession. Vrykolakas have been known to form blood bonds with the mortals they feed off. It's rare to occur after only one bite. Still, with the way I can't stop my eyes from wandering to her as she walks slightly ahead, a few steps behind Lorcan, with Dato circling the skies above, and taking into consideration how my fangs ache to sink into her skin again, after only an hour out of it, the evidence is indisputable.

To be fair, I've already bitten her twice. The second certainly wasn't necessary. Yet I couldn't seem to help myself. The fight in her blood must be potent for me to lose my head. I've never felt so out of control before. I'm acting like a freshly turned vrykolaka—consumed by bloodlust—a slave to their basic instincts to feed and fuck.

Making her come with only my mouth at her neck and a few tweaks of a nipple has over-inflated my ego. It's also implanted very dirty ideas inside my head. Ideas that could get the heart excavated from my chest.

Fingers click in front of my nose. 'Hello? Did you hear me?' Raven asks, the annoyance plain on her face.

'No. I'm not in the habit of listening to nonsense,' I tease, knowing exactly what she said regardless of whether I heard it or not. She's been saying the same fucking thing since we started 'escorting' her, i.e., taking her around and around in a circle. '*Where are we going? And when will you let me take the lead?*'

'All of you are such huge dicks. This is so unfair,' she complains in a petulant tone, stomping as she walks. Her attitude is adorable and way too endearing.

I can't resist a smile. 'You're right about that... we do have huge dicks. Thanks for noticing.'

Raven shakes her head, her jaw clenched, nostrils flaring. 'This is going against my deal. Julius wasn't allowed to interfere.'

'The King isn't here to interfere.' Lorcan's response is clipped.

'But he sent you to fuck with me,' she counters, raising her voice. 'That is, by definition, interfering.'

'Unfortunately, fucking you is something we're *not* allowed to do. It doesn't mean we can't have fun, though,' I tell her, exaggerating my smile so my fangs show. They haven't retracted since I caught the scent of her blood. Again, another sign of obsession.

'Hex, you open your mouth too much. Just shut up and ignore her,' Lorcan castigates, throwing me a look of contempt over his shoulder.

'You think you can dictate my turns and ignore me for three days?' Raven laughs without humour. 'You can try. But I'll try harder. I promise you that.'

Her fighting spirit is refreshing. Usually, mortals aren't so resilient when facing such disappointing odds. Not only has she survived a Deinonychus attack, but she's held her own in a deal with me and continues to grate on our every nerve, knowing we can't kill her. I assume she believes that if she pushes her luck enough, we'll cast her off and let her be.

Lorcan might. He has zero tolerance for anything remotely annoying. Dato wouldn't quit, but he'd keep his distance, watching her from afar. As for me, I'm secretly loving every barbed comment and jibe. Her persistent moaning makes me want to shove my cock down her throat. Taming her is threatening to become a new fantasy of mine. And, if she keeps this up, I will fucking ravage her the next time I let my fangs think for me.

When Raven starts singing Britney Spears at the top of her lungs, I lose my composure and cover my mouth to hold my laughter prisoner. Lorcan isn't as pleased. On the third repeated verse, he catches her by the throat and slams her against the wall. Half-chocked, she continues singing—the sound raspy.

There's no holding in my laugh anymore.

Lorcan's face flushes red with anger. 'Sing one more note, and I'll squeeze on your vocal cords until they fray, songbird,' he threatens, his nose inches from hers.

Raven, playing with fire, lifts to kiss the tip of it. Lorcan jumps back as if she delivered a knock-out punch.

'Big, tough werewolf scared of a little kiss?' she mocks, and my mouth hangs open at her bravery.

Lorcan blinks at her for a beat, as stunned as I am. Then, speechless, he swiftly marches away, his scowl vicious.

In all my years, I've never seen anyone disarmed so quickly by an innocent peck on the nose. Raven managed to rile Lorcan's wrath yet get away unscathed. That's a first.

Dato swoops down to land. 'The river Melas starts only a five-minute walk from here. You'll need to stop for water, mortal.'

'Is it poisonous?' Raven asks, licking her dry lips as though even the thought of water is easing her thirst.

'It's not toxic to mortals, no. But I'm sure it's not what you're used to. Its side effects are only minor,' Dato answers, choosing to tail us by foot.

'What are the side effects?' she demands, stopping to face Dato.

Dato crosses his arms over his chest plate. 'The side effects are better than dying of dehydration. That's what they are.'

Raven looks to me to elaborate, her expression expectant.

With a sigh, I give in to her, not as petty as Dato. 'The river Melas rouses the seven deadly sins. Whoever drinks from the black waters suffers their greatest deviance. It will lure a sin or two from your heart. Any desires you've been repressing will become harder to deny.'

Raven's forehead crinkles. 'That's it? The water won't harm me physically?'

I shake my head, surprised she's not more wary of my warning. 'Sometimes, the power of the mind is far stronger than the shell in which it resides. That's why Julius craves your soul more than he does your body. Although your body is also a prize worth coveting, I must say.'

'Hex.' Dato uses my name as a warning.

In exasperation, I snap, 'What?'

'Stop flirting with the mortal,' he replies, pushing on my head as he continues past us towards Lorcan.

Raven and I exchange a look, her stormy grey eyes scrutinising. 'You weren't lying when you said you were the nice one,' she says before she leans in to kiss my cheek. 'Thank you for warning me.' With that, she spins on her heel and rushes to catch up with Dato and Lorcan.

Something strange happens to my face—it heats. I'm fucking blushing like a damn schoolgirl. What the fuck is wrong with me?

She's what's wrong, Hex. You've let a mortal girl burrow under your skin in only an hour of knowing her. After one fucking feed.

I'm officially obsessed.

This means I'll likely end up heartless in less than three days.

CHAPTER 13

Secret Sins

RAVEN

Relief unclenches my heart when the narrow, winding paths of the maze end. This new section has greenery. Technically, it's not green; the foliage grows in shades of grey. From the tall, uniform hedges that replace the stone walls, to the muddy grass lining the banks of the black waters of river Melas.

The open space has me breathing more deeply, the tension in my shoulders easing slightly. I walk straight past Dato and Lorcan, aiming for the river, desperate for a testing sip. My throat has been uncomfortably dry since entering the maze. I haven't drunk anything since the funeral. Usually, I drink a glass of water before bed, but I was too tired and distracted—cleaning up Robin's mess—to properly take care of myself.

Before I stray too far, Lorcan grabs my elbow and whirls me back to face him. 'Don't scurry off, songbird. Stay within Hex's sight. If you don't, I will hunt you down and crush that flighty spirit of yours.'

'You've already done that,' I bite back, ripping away from him.

I hurry down the bank. Then, kneeling at the river's edge, I cup a handful of the opaque water and bring it to my chapped lips.

At first, I take cautious sips, Hex's warning in the forefront of my mind. But, when I feel no different, my thirst gets the better of me, and I proceed to guzzle down handful after handful.

This part of the river isn't wide or fast-flowing. The urge to wade in to wash the sweat and mud off me is replacing all caution. I peer over my shoulder. Dato has taken off again, keeping watch from the skies. Lorcan is prowling the borders like the territorial animal he clearly is. While Hex is watching me, perched on top of a wall, mere metres away.

My eyes greedily roam the vampire's form. The laces at his collar are loose, showing off his toned chest. In this light, his skin isn't as pale as I thought. Or maybe my blood has brought some colour to the surface. I've noticed his pupils aren't as all-encompassing either; a thin ring of red-tinted brown surrounds them. I'm guessing they change depending on his hunger.

My neck throbs at the memory of his ravenous kiss. Another area of my body throbs in tandem.

Collecting a breath, I shrug off my jacket. I'll just go for a quick dip and keep my clothes on. They need to be washed, anyway.

Walking into the slow, rolling river, I hear Hex shout, 'Hey, deal-breaker! What are you doing?'

'I'm freshening up,' I call back, splashing my hands along the surface as I sink in up to my hips.

I check behind me to see that Hex is no longer sitting on the wall. He's moved closer, casually pacing the bank, whistling.

'Do many women take on this maze?' I ask.

'There have been a few in my fifty years here. But I'm sure you won't be surprised to hear it's mostly mortal men on a quest for power or wealth,' Hex answers.

Fifty years?! I wonder how old Hex really is. I know Julius is only twenty-three, the same age as me. I would think that's very young for a demon.

'Did any of them make it to the castle?'

'Only one,' he replies, his tone hesitant.

'A woman?' I guess, washing my face of mud-splatter.

'Of course. Men typically aren't smart enough to survive the first night.'

'What was her prize?'

'Her freedom. I think her soul was already promised before she was born,' Hex divulges, but he soon swears under his breath as though he let slip something he shouldn't have.

I stop rubbing the mud stain out of my top to look his way. 'What kind of parent sells their unborn child's soul like that?'

Hex shrugs. 'I don't know. Someone who thought they wouldn't have a kid in the first place? Or someone desperate to save their soul?'

Wrinkling my nose unsympathetically, I turn back to the water. 'Did you meet this soul-promised woman?'

'I did.'

'Did you make the same deal with her?' For some unfathomable reason, the thought of Hex biting this other woman makes me want to slap him again. 'Did you bite her?'

Hex chuckles. 'Why? Are you jealous?'

'No,' I'm quick to reply. 'But... did you?'

'Yes, I drank her blood. Once. If it makes you feel any better, she didn't enjoy it as much as you did,' he tells me, still laughing.

My cheeks fill with fire. Why am I jealous of some woman who became a vampire's meal long before I did?

'Are you enjoying your bath?' Hex enquires, changing the subject. 'Envy looks good on you, by the way.'

Shit. Of course. The water is making me feel this way, drawing out my most secret sins.

Wanting to wash the sweat and grime from my hair, I bend to dip my head, my heavy locks cascading down to caress the delicate waves. I work the cool liquid through my strands with wet fingers, starting at my scalp. My clothes weigh down my actions. Their sodden texture is making me want to vomit.

I wring out my hair, and before I can think twice about it, I pull up my top and throw it towards the bank. Hex sucks in an audible breath.

With my back to him, he can't see my breasts, so what's the harm? And, with my lower half submerged in these practically opaque waters, it wouldn't matter if I whipped off these leggings, either.

My hips shimmy as I drag the material of my leggings down my thighs. I cast them aside, too. Now, I'm as naked as sin, standing in the calm waters of an underworld river, a vampire's eyes boring into my back.

I splash my bare chest with water. Droplets trickle down between my breasts, the tickle of them making me giggle. I bite my bottom lip, wishing my teeth were as sharp as Hex's.

Skin sensitised, my hands move of their own accord, my fingers running down my neck and chest. I skim my nipples, and my sharp intake of breath elicits a groan from the bank. The fact that Hex is watching me, enjoying the show, turns me on more. One of my wayward hands slides low over my stomach, then dips below the swaying waves.

My eyes fall closed when my fingers brush over my clit. I breathe a moan, and I hear Hex sigh the word '*fuck*'.

Opening them again, they catch on movement ahead, on the other side of the river.

Lorcan.

He emerges from a cluster of dead trees. And, when his gaze finds me, he stills.

A fire sparks in his hazel eyes, turning them to liquid gold.

However, I'm leapt upon from behind when Lorcan takes that first sure step towards me. There's a sharp pain at my neck, and strong arms come around my waist, drawing me against a hard body—Hex. A possessive growl rips from his throat, warning Lorcan off. Before I can make sense of the situation, pleasure fills my veins, and I arch into the vampire.

The fact that I'm naked, with one demon claiming me with a bite while another watches on, somehow doesn't faze me. I fail to realise I've started frantically rubbing my clit. It's not until Hex stills my arm that it registers.

'Slower,' Hex rasps, his fingers trailing to my elbow. He glides that same hand across my chest to fondle my breast.

Moaning my approval, my head lolls back, resting on Hex's shoulder as he continues to lap up the blood from the bite he delivered. I watch Lorcan watching us. His erection is obvious in his loose joggers. His jaw is tight, eyes locked on my writhing body, nostrils flaring.

Lust is a heavenly sin, I think, satisfaction radiating through me. I wouldn't be surprised if I was glowing right now.

If I play this right, these demons will be eating out of the palm of my hand by tomorrow, and firmly on my side by the time we reach the Demon King's castle.

Boldly, I beckon Lorcan closer, eyes half-lidded. Reacting to this, Hex's grip on me tightens, silently telling me he'd rather not share. Lorcan doesn't pay attention to him. He's looking at me. So, he comes; his stride is confident, determined—his predatory focus singular.

Hex cups both of my breasts, pressing me against him, the urgency of his erection a call to action. I reach around my hip to stroke it through his trousers, and he gyrates into my open palm. His moans of appreciation vibrate through the skin he penetrated at my neck.

Lorcan, golden gaze blazing, wades into the river to reach us. He stops before me, and I swallow thickly, worried I've read him wrong. But, when he lifts my chin with a tender touch, my heart leaps. His earthy scent is grounding; the deep tones of cut wood and ash are more masculine in their dominance.

'I'll offer you a deal,' Lorcan says, his voice rough as bark. 'Let me make you come the way *I* want...' His eyes touch on Hex for a second, his sneer disdainful. 'And I promise to stop bruising this pretty, porcelain skin of yours.' His thumb brushes my lower lip. 'Don't be under any illusion, though. I will continue to lead, but I'll do it with mercy.'

Lost to lust, I whisper, 'Deal.'

This is a good start to my plan. Not only do I get another orgasm out of it, but I also get the assurance of a gentler touch from this beast of a demon. I'm happy to make this type of deal any day of the week.

'Hex,' Lorcan says to draw his attention. 'Lift her legs.'

Hex takes less than a second to comply; I'm hauled out of the water before I can blink. My legs are then spread wide, Hex hooking an arm under each of my knees, bearing my centre to Lorcan in all its glistening glory. Being completely exposed like this makes my head swim. Or maybe it's the blood loss.

Gasping, I reach around to grab a handful of Hex's hair and tug hard. He hisses a curse in my ear. He deserves some punishment; I told him not to hit me with his venom again. As it turns out, he doesn't need the river to bring out his jealous side. I should be more annoyed, but his weakness only makes me giddy. I already have power over him. Now, I need to gain some ground with the other two. Starting with Lorcan.

We both watch as Lorcan lowers to his knees, the water coming up to his broad shoulders. His mouth moves to the inside of my right thigh, and the teasing touch of his lips has my vagina clenching around nothing.

Hex practically folds me in half to reach my nipples, plucking them as his forearms hold me up on display.

I whine, desperate for Lorcan to stop torturing me with barely-there kisses, his beard tickling my sensitive skin. 'More,' I demand, but this only earns me a nip of reproach.

'Beg for my tongue, and I'll consider it,' Lorcan replies, his tone wickedly low.

Forgoing pride, I do just that. 'Please, Lorcan. Please, fuck me with your tongue. I need it.'

Lorcan's dark chuckle sends chills racing over my damp skin.

'Don't fuck her with it or your fingers,' Hex interjects. 'We need to toe the line, not cross it.'

Lorcan nods his understanding, then leans in, his bulky fingers holding me open for a long, savouring lick. A cry leaves my lips, pleasure twinging deep inside me.

Hex kisses along my jaw. 'Look at you, begging your second demon of the night to fuck you. Such a greedy girl. Do you like being our plaything?'

'Yes,' I wince out, the tip of Lorcan's tongue circling my clit. Combined with Hex's titillating ministrations, it's almost too much to bear. But Hex doesn't know that I'm the one toying with them—using their attraction to me to my advantage.

With a hard swipe of his tongue, Lorcan has me shouting his name. Hex, not wanting to be left out, pinches my nipples hard until I say his name as a plea for mercy.

'I'm going to bite these next time,' Hex warns, smoothing over the hurt he caused with a gentler caress.

Lorcan lifts his head from the juncture of my thighs to speak. 'If you come without permission, I will force you down on all fours and spank you until your arse is raw. Do you understand?'

I nod my head, too overwhelmed to form words. His threat sounds like a temptation. Part of me wants to defy him to test his wrath.

'Are you ready to come for us, deal-breaker?' Hex asks, kissing my neck. His tongue teases the third bite mark, and I become a trembling mess in his arms.

Again, I nod, turning my head to seek a real kiss. Hex is happy to oblige, his tongue coaxing my mouth open. I taste the iron from my blood, but it doesn't bother me. Not when his kiss is this savagely sweet.

Lorcan sucks on my clit, and I buck my hips, crying into Hex. My toes curl as they have me clinging to the edge for dear life, waiting for permission.

When Lorcan's tongue starts to roll faster and faster, I break the kiss to plead for release. 'I can't hold it any longer,' I warn them, gritting my teeth against this pounding, searing heat flowing like a tidal wave through me. 'Oh, God, please let me come!'

Hex makes a noise of amusement. 'You have my permission. Does she have yours, Lorc?'

'Hmm, she does,' Lorcan drawls. 'Now, sing for us, songbird.'

With one more pointed drag of his tongue, Lorcan has me coming so hard that stars flash in my vision. He and Hex continue playing with me as I ride it out, sending fresh pangs through my already overstimulated body. A feral scream tears from my throat, my nipples and clit becoming hyper-sensitive to their lighter yet persistent handling.

Using the flat of his tongue, Lorcan laps up the product of my orgasm, and a satisfied growl vibrates against my inflamed skin. 'So fucking sweet.'

'Please, I've had enough. I can't take anymore,' I whimper, my heart pounding out of my chest, my stomach aching in the most wonderful way. I'm so light-headed I think I might pass out.

'What if I want you to give us another? I think we deserve it for all the shit you gave *us* on the way here,' Lorcan says, his fire-gold eyes glinting with mischief.

Hex nibbles my ear. 'I think you can handle one more. You're stronger than this. You can take what we give you. Isn't that right?'

I find myself nodding along in my dazed state, even though the muscles in my centre are still spasming.

However, before they can start another round of their exquisite torment, Dato lands beside us with a heavy splash. He knocks Lorcan away with a hard swipe of his wing, then he snatches me out of Hex's arms to cradle me in his, while simultaneously sending a swift kick into Hex's gut. Hex falls back into the water, spluttering obscenities.

Lorcan lurches to his feet, his growl fierce. Dato uses his wings as a protective cocoon.

'Have you both lost your fucking minds? What part of off-limits did you not understand? Julius will have your heads for this!' Dato shouts at them.

Hex drags himself up, completely drenched. 'Come on, Dato. Don't tell me you haven't been itching to use those glaring loopholes Julius permitted. You're only upset because you missed out on the fun.'

'The two of you are so fucking dead. Do you think Julius will look past this as some mistake on his part? She's clearly not just any ordinary mortal, you oblivious fuckwits. He needs her soul pure. You both should know this.' With a huff, Dato storms away from them, with me still naked and trembling in his arms.

'They didn't force me. I wanted it,' I make known, the effects of lust wearing off as my skin dries.

'Then Julius might think to kill you, too,' Dato replies, climbing the bank, his tail swishing behind him, showing his irritation.

As soon as we reach the grass, Dato sets me down. Shivering, I wrap my arms around myself, my nakedness now shameful, especially in front of Dato, who seems to only despise me for it.

He keeps his wings around us like a shield. 'Pass me her clothes.' His order is thrown over his shoulder.

Hex is beside us in a flash, handing Dato my wet clothes. I'll fucking freeze to death with them on. I didn't think enough about the consequences when the river lured me in.

'Arms up, mortal,' Dato commands, and I catch the little waver in his voice. Maybe he isn't as unaffected by my body as much as he wants me to believe.

I hesitate, face flaming. But after I gulp down my embarrassment, I do as he requests. I notice his throat working when my body is fully exposed to him. He tries to keep his eyes off me while he slides the soaked material of my top over my head and down my torso to cover my breasts. However, the material is now see-through, so it's not much help.

'I knew you'd be trouble as soon as I saw you,' Dato mutters, dropping into a crouch to help me put on my leggings.

At that moment, something warm and velvety wraps around my calf. Peering down, I find that it's Dato's tail, the inky feathers at the tip soft against my skin. My shiver is *not* one of disgust. When he realises his tail is attached to me, he quickly swipes it away as though it has a mind of its own.

Liking the blush highlighting his high cheekbones, I use Dato's muscular shoulders to keep myself stable. 'I had hoped you were watching us,' I whisper, my admission surprising us both.

Blinking his shock, Dato looks up. He scans my face for deception. His gaze drops to my bare legs, and his fingers purposely trace the backs of my thighs to my buttocks as he drags the stubborn material up to cover the most intimate part of me. 'If I had free rein... I would have done more than watch.'

My clit twinges at his admission, engorging again.

Fucking hell. How on earth can my still-throbbing vagina crave more after the two mind-blowing orgasms it's already had tonight. I've never been this horny before. Maybe it's the air down here, or Hex's venom circulates longer than necessary.

Dato's wings release me as soon as I'm dressed, and he's quick to slink off, not sparing me a backward glance.

'We need to get her to the Hearth of Hergal before she freezes,' he says, running to take flight.

The restless, storm-swollen sky is clearly Dato's favourite place to hide.

CHAPTER 14

Tantrum

JULIUS

After spending the last half an hour scouring the castle, searching for Robin, I reach the walk-in freezer door. One of the cooks said he heard a noise coming from inside. I doubt the Velociraptor carcasses from yesterday's hunt have risen from the dead to knock over the spice rack. It must be the clumsiness of a mortal boy.

I politely knock and announce my presence to not shock the kid into pissing himself. 'Oh, Robin, out of all the places you could have hidden after escaping a very warm, comfortable room, you chose to lock yourself inside a freezer which only opens from the outside? Obviously, brains don't run in the family.'

When he doesn't answer, I open the door and step inside. A plucked wing of a dead creature whizzes past my head. It lands against the wall with a splat. Rotating back, I find Robin arming himself with another.

I sharpen my look at him. 'Really? Do you think you can fight me off with uncooked meat? Perhaps if you'd picked up one of the severed Utahraptor legs but a Velociraptor wing? Even as a snack, they're unsubstantial. As a weapon, it's truly pathetic. Chose better next time, kid.'

'Let me go! You can't keep me here!' Robin shouts, raising his fist of meat as though I should take that as a legitimate threat.

I let out an exasperated sigh. 'I don't plan on keeping you in the freezer. That was your own doing.'

'You know what I mean, arsehole!' He chucks the meat at me, but I use my powers to stop its momentum mid-flight. I send it hurtling back his way, and he ducks just in time.

I smooth down the lines of my jacket. 'I'm not in the mood for childish games. Go back to your room and stay there. I won't tell you again.'

'What do you want with me?' Robin demands, his glare now more one of confusion than anger.

'It's not *you* I want. I'm waiting for your sister. Like you, she's a stubborn brat who'd risk everything on a whim. She had the chance to save your soul, yet she chose to defy me. You'll likely both be mine to claim once these three days are up,' I explain mildly. '*But*, if you behave yourself and cease this little *tantrum*, I may generously allow you to live your life as your own until it expires.'

Robin blinks at me, his mouth agape. 'What the fuck *are* you?'

'You're too young to use that sort of foul language. It's unbecoming. Now, off to bed with you before I stop playing nice and drag you to the dungeons myself.'

'This has to be a nightmare,' Robin says, squeezing his eyes shut. 'I'm dreaming.'

'What is it with you mortals and not believing your five senses?' I use my power to fling another wing in his direction. It slaps him across the cheek with a wet clop.

'Ow, what was that for?' Robin whines, wiping his face with his sleeve.

'You felt that, right? Hence, you're very much awake. Although one could argue the Underworld is a living nightmare, so I'll leave that up to you to decide.'

Robin looks like a deer in the headlights when he stammers out, 'The—the Underworld? I'm in Hell? Am—am I dead?'

Blowing out my frustration, I massage the bridge of my nose. 'Urgh, I should have given you more sleep tonic. I don't have the patience to deal with this right now,' I mutter, more to myself than him. 'Look, Robin—you're alive, you're awake, and you're unharmed. You're not eternally damned... just yet. You have less than three days until Raven's time runs out on her *quest*. I will let you roam the castle grounds if you promise to stay inside the safety of the central wall. What lies beyond it will not hesitate to kill you. And before you get your hopes up, there's no escaping; there's only death. You wouldn't last an hour, given your choice of weaponry.' I point to the goop, still clinging to where the wing hit the wall.

Robin stares, wide-eyed, at me for what must be a full minute.

Noticing how his T-shirt vibrates, I realise he's shivering with cold. Sometimes, I forget mortals tend to be more sensitive to their environment than demons. I step aside, leaving the doorway clear.

'Go on. I'll have one of my servants draw you a warm bath upstairs. If your bedroom is not to your liking, choose another. Just not mine.'

Robin goes to comply but then hesitates, not trusting my kindness.

I slip my hands into my trouser pockets, the cold creeping up on me. 'Take my kindness while it lasts, kid. I may not be so accommodating as time ticks on. It depends on how your sister fares in my maze.'

With a downturned face, Robin gives up on the fight he knows he can't win, and stomps past me.

I catch him by the shoulder. 'You didn't ask after your sister. Not even once. As a brother, you're not worth the risk to her life, whereas her soul is worth a hundred of yours. A *thousand*.' With a shove, I release him, then watch him storm out of the kitchen, guilt hunching his shoulders.

On the way back to the throne room, I imagine scenarios of what my starling could be doing right now. Or, more specifically, *who* she could be doing.

These flare-ups of jealousy aren't unusual. The first bout started after she told me of her first kiss at sixteen. I proceeded to tear her dream world apart, throwing my first teenage tantrum.

Before that, I'd always been strictly punished for showing the barest glimpse of emotion. Only when it comes to Raven do I temporarily lose control of myself. She has forced things out of me that I've worked hard to repress since I was old enough to discern my feelings.

Mercifully, Raven promptly forgot my jealous rage as soon as she woke from the dream. Sometimes, her memory loss benefited me, especially on those nights I confided things I wouldn't have uttered aloud to anyone I thought might remember. With her, I allowed myself a certain amount of vulnerability. Mainly because I knew she wouldn't retain information long enough to hurt me with it. Secrets become ammunition over time, no matter who holds those truths.

Truth is a weapon, and power eventually corrupts even the purest of souls—that weapon becoming easier and easier to wield.

After Raven left for university, and I could no longer keep her under my watchful eye, my imagination ran wild. Weekends were the worst. I'd drink myself to sleep, imagining her in another student's bed after a fun night out. It was unlikely, but I had hoped she'd return the virgin she left as. Though, unlike the males in my line before me, virginity does not equal purity in my eyes. It only riles me to know another, lesser male, touched her in the way I desire to.

The same can be said for the feelings I'm experiencing tonight. The thought of Hex, or any other demon, taking her pleasure as their own makes me want to burn my kingdom to ash.

My fists clench at my sides, and I try to shake the rage-inducing images out of my head. In this moment, my jealousy is too potent—unnatural.

Perhaps these emotions are amplified. They may be feeding off a second source—Raven. My commanders could have taken her to the river Melas to quench her thirst. If so, I must prepare for the other sins to abuse our connection.

Dread rots me from the inside. I hadn't anticipated this when I originally devised the idea to send three attractive male demons in pursuit of my beautiful prize. Of course, she'd have to drink from the river eventually. Then they'd be there, right in front of her, when greed, gluttony, envy, pride, and worst of all—*lust*—were the sins she'd be most drawn by. Perhaps wrath if pushed too far. But never sloth. She's too determined for that sin to take root.

Usually, only two or three sins have their time to shine when the host has drunk or bathed in the black waters. Envy has already ensnared her; I can sense it. I only hope her pride is stronger than her need for intimacy after being alone for so many years.

I will soon find out.

Changing course, I head for my bedchamber, hoping for the best, though preparing for the worst. No one will be brave enough to disturb me in my private rooms. If there were an emergency, they'd sound the alarm.

A few minutes later, I'm pacing before my four-poster bed, the elegant opulence of the jewel-toned room doing little to comfort me.

When I think Raven must have beaten the odds and only experienced one sin, my blood starts to heat, making its way to my cock to lengthen it.

Curse the fucking Shadows! Anything would have been better than lust.

Lungs heavier, I perch on my bed, trying to absorb as much of the sin as possible to lessen the effects on my starling. The idea sprouting roots, I lean back against my midnight-blue pillows, unbutton my shirt and trousers, and then strip them off until I'm lying on the bed in only my briefs.

Cock now impossibly rigid, I take it out of my underwear to start stroking myself. For a smoother glide, I use the lubricant from my bedside dresser instead of spit. I also use my vivid imagination to my benefit, along with my memories of Raven. Of the times she's looked particularly sexy.

Late in our teens, she started showing up at night in only a baggy, long-line T-shirt and knickers. I lost count of the times I've fisted myself to those memories of her over the years since.

A sharp pang of pleasure hits me, coaxing a groan from deep within my chest. *Fuck.* That's not a good sign. Either she's touching herself, like I am, or... I don't dare think about the alternative. I like my room; I'd prefer it not to be smashed to pieces.

More pulses have me writhing on my bed, my legs tangling in the sheets. I squeeze the end of my cock, hoping some pain will counteract the utter ecstasy threatening to finish me so soon.

Surely, this supersedes what she can do to herself. She must have help. Someone—probably Hex—is fanning her flames. Most likely with his venom. Fucking vrykolakas can never resist the ego boost of making their meal orgasm. They get high off the rush of endorphins. And Raven, corrupted by lust, would be a tasty treat not many could abstain from.

The next jolt takes me by surprise. It's so powerful it rouses my telekinetic energy—my whole bed lifting off the floor as I come with a roar. Warm wetness coats my hands and stomach, then quickly cools. I'm shaking so hard my teeth chatter. All I can do is breathe through it. My gasps are fast and shallow. I blink away the cloud of lust misting my vision as I reach for tissues.

While I'm cleaning myself up, lust sparks anew, and I freeze. No fucking way are they starting up again.

My jealous rage resurfacing, I spring to my feet and rush to my window to open it.

I'm halfway out the window, my wings itching to materialise, when I remember the deal would be null and void if I move another inch outside. I lurch back, my skin tingling. I can't allow my male ego to ruin this chance. Everything I've ever wanted is within reach. I only have to wait two and a half more days.

Let Hex, Lorcan, and Dato have their fun with her.

It will be the last pleasure they'll ever know.

CHAPTER 15

Weakness

LORCAN

The temptation to continue licking my lips—reliving the succulent taste of that deviant, little seductress—has me salivating like a rabid dog. As a lycanthrope, seizing the opportunity to dominate is pathological. The scent of her arousal was too enticing, too stimulating. I couldn't deny my need to make her come on my terms. I *knew* when she first showed that delicate power of hers—daring to run from me—a deal between us was bound to happen.

Earlier, finding out Hex had done the same stirred my alpha instinct to compete to be the best sexual option. Lycanthropes and vrykolakas are both territorial creatures.

When there's been a desirable female in our midst, Hex and I have butted heads more than I can count. If the female is willing, we share—our tryst in the river is not unusual. Except, it's never happened with a mortal before. Mortals aren't typically that fearless in the face of demons.

I may be an alpha, but I'm also a pack animal. Hex, Dato, and even Julius, I consider under my protection. They're the closest I have to family, seeing as my half-Scottish, half-Turkish family died long before I was turned.

When it comes down to it, I would never allow a female to come between us. On the other hand, *this* female feels different. Maybe her mortality and innocence makes her all the more desirable. There's also an element of danger to her, especially as Julius has already staked his claim, which is very unusual for him.

Don't get me wrong, as a keeper demon, claiming souls is Julius' passion—his purpose. Yet, the songbird is special. She's not only important to whatever his family's curse is, he's protecting her fragile body from harm in a maze designed to kill intruders. Furthermore, he's made her off-limits in a sexual sense. In all my years in the DiMinos' service, I have never seen Julius even *look* a female's way. All this time, I thought he was either gay or asexual. For him to lay claim to a mortal woman's pussy like that is... interesting.

Toeing that line, as Hex put it, will likely cause us some trouble later down the road. Still, I'm not worried; Hex and I can hold our own against Julius. Dato won't want to get involved. He and Julius are practically brothers, seeing as they grew up together.

Hex and I are older than both of them. Our service—our *souls*—were Julius' to inherit when he reached the ripe old age of eighteen. Nobody would think it, but Hex is the oldest of us by over a century. Vrykolakas can live for hundreds of years if not staked in the heart or starved of blood. Lycanthropes can live to well over two hundred, but we age in a similar way to mortals. Harpyiai, like Dato, have similar lifespans to my kind. Keeper demons can live eternally if they so wish. Collecting souls preserves their life force and makes them ageless. Although they can still be killed, or cursed in the DiMinos' case.

Julius' family curse is a well-kept secret. All we know is that it has something to do with a line of mortal women dating back thousands of years. Rumour has it that a scorned witch was the first to bind a DiMinos king and his successors.

We never found out what happened to Julius' father. He was ruling over his kingdom one day, and the next... *poof*—disappeared.

Julius took his crown at only eighteen. He is the youngest demon king in history. To be fair, all DiMinos kings have been relatively young compared to other rulers in the Underworld. The curse is the reason; they all end up disappearing before their fifties. Compared to other keeper demons (who sometimes rule for hundreds of years), half a century is still considered an adolescent period.

Looking to my right, I catch the shuddering tremor that wracks Raven's lithe body. She may appear dainty, but she has more than a good handful of meat in all the best places. I appreciate the fullness of the female form. For how I like to fuck, I need some handholds. If they're too thin, I'd run the risk of breaking them. Hex isn't as fussy; he will fuck anything remotely human in shape as long as he can bite it. Dato is the worst; he's extremely picky with his sexual partners. He'll sometimes dip his toes into the wider pool of bisexuality, like Hex, but he mainly goes for the types of females he knows he can't get. He's pined after a few who had set their sights on Julius, ignoring the likes of me, Hex, and Dato. I assume it's because he has an inferiority complex when it comes to Julius, which brings out some of Dato's competitive spirit. It didn't seem to matter to Julius; he was never quite as taken with those females as he is with this mortal.

I act when our little songbird's legs tremble hard enough for her to wobble. Without asking for her permission (I rarely do—alpha, remember?) I sweep her off her feet and carry her like the damsel in distress she refuses to be.

Raven pushes against my chest. 'I—I don't ne—ed you t' car—ry meee,' she forces out, her chattering teeth making it hard for her to speak.

I slide her a look to the contrary. 'Until that sentence can come out of your pretty mouth coherently, you, my sweet songbird, will be caged in my arms.'

'I di—dn't peg youuu for the... chiv—alrous type,' she comments through violent shivers. Despite her initial reluctance, she clings to me, her hands an unbreakable loop around my neck.

'I'm not. You have Hex for that. You're just slowing me down. We'll get there faster this way,' I argue, not ready to admit that carrying her brings me great satisfaction. I'm lycanthrope; we love holding onto what we want, like a dog with a bone. We're a possessive lot. Most demons are.

'What happen—ed earlier...' she starts, looking embarrassed, 'It was the eff—ects of... the river.' She bites her bottom lip, holding back her truth.

I snort a laugh. 'If that's what you want to believe...'

Her jaw sets. 'It's not happening... again.'

'Sure it won't,' I say, unconvinced. Even when she's denying her desire, I can smell the tart sweetness ripening on her. Simply being in my arms is turning her on.

'I... It—'

Before she can reply, the chilling chirps of a group of Velociraptors cause her to stop, her body shifting away from the threatening chatter, her arms tightening around my neck. A little noise of fear squeaks out of her.

'Don't fret, my darling deal-breaker,' Hex says, instantly blurring to our side. 'They won't come near you with us around, like I said earlier.'

Raven scrutinises the five hog-sized dinosaurs trailing us. Their rough skin is dull green while their plumage is a contrastingly vibrant shade of rust. 'They *are* smaller than Spielberg depicted. The one that was hunting me was a lot bigger and scarier.'

Hex snickers. 'The one you need to worry about is the Utahraptor. They're not as easily discouraged by our presence.'

'What else do I have to worry about in here?' she asks, her voice a little steadier. 'Please don't tell me Julius has a pet T-Rex.'

A laugh unexpectedly huffs out of me before I can contain it. 'No. There's only the dromaeosaurid. They've always been Julius' favourite. Although other creatures will be just as happy to hunt you down for your flesh. Some will for the thrill alone.'

Raven arches an eyebrow. 'Are *you* on that list?'

Suppressing a smile, I reply, 'Of course. All three of us are.'

'What about Julius? You all work for him, right?'

I nod. 'Dato is his First Commander in all things, mainly defence. I'm the Commander of Beasts because I can transform, which allows me to communicate with them in the ways most demons can't.'

'And I'm the Commander of Souls, seeing as I'm fast enough to catch them,' Hex chimes in, not wanting to be left out. 'Unfortunately, I can't control them once they're caught. That's Julius' speciality.'

Raven's forehead creases in confusion. 'How do you catch a soul? Aren't they like... ethereal or something? Ghostly?'

'Julius creates these orbs, which I use to contain them,' Hex answers proudly, thriving off her interest.

Raven's shivering hasn't improved much since I picked her up. Hypothermia must be setting in by now. 'Those wet clothes aren't helping you keep warm,' I mention, changing the subject. Hex and I aren't as affected by the cold as a mortal body would be. Our wet clothes won't chill our bones like hers will.

'Yeah, you should definitely take them off.' The devious glint in Hex's eye twinkles.

'I think I'll manage until we reach this hearth place. Who is it home to again?' Raven enquires, snuggling against my bare chest for warmth.

The action has me warming, too. Strange. It doesn't seem to be a sexual reaction. My dick isn't hardening.

'Hergal; he helps maintain the maze. A lesser demon,' Hex tells her, side-eyeing me, likely envious of my position. An odd reaction from him, too; Hex has never cared to snuggle with the walking blood-bags he entertains.

I peer down at Raven as I continue walking with her in my arms. 'Hergal is a cyclops. Have you ever heard of their kind?'

She lifts her head, her eyes wide. 'A *cyclops*?! Like Goliath?'

'Common misconception,' Hex says, shaking his head. 'Cyclopes are average-sized, with only slightly superior strength to that of mortal men. The only things the Greeks got right about them was that they're one-eyed and thick as shit.'

Dato flies into view, making to land. When he does, he gives me a perplexed look, noticing Raven.

I clear my throat before I mumble, 'Her legs were trembling like a newborn fawn.' I hope my explanation is enough to cover my ever-growing weakness for her.

Dato's judgemental gaze narrows, but he doesn't question me. 'Thank the Shadows that Hergal doesn't seem to be at his hearth tonight. But it means we'll have to break in.'

'What if he comes back? Won't he be pissed?' Raven questions in alarm.

'Probably,' Dato answers honestly, shrugging.

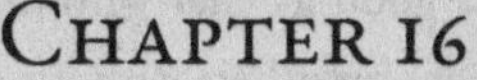

CHAPTER 16

The Hearth of Hergal

RAVEN

The Hearth of Hergal is a simple wooden structure, like one of those rustic cabins, tucked away in a remote forest. Except, this forest is sparse, grey, and eternally night-cloaked.

'You can put me down now,' I say to Lorcan, twisting in his arms.

'I don't answer to you, songbird. Our deal was for mercy, not obedience. I'll put you down when and where I damn well please,' he bites back, his top lip curling into a snarl.

I clamp my mouth shut. Arguing with Lorcan isn't going to endear me to him. That tactic might work with Hex; he seems to enjoy the pushback.

What I've deduced thus far is that Hex likes flattery and banter. Simple ego boosts and verbal sparring has worked to keep his interest. Whereas Lorcan prefers his conquests to be more subservient; someone he can dominate and look after. A woman he can serve in his own wolfish way without the appearance of weakness on his part. At the end of the day, a wolf is just a bigger, wilder dog. They're loyal, but they're also proud. Taming him will be a more arduous task.

But I'm always up for a challenge.

Dato is the demon I haven't quite yet figured out. I only caught that brief glimpse of heat in his eyes when I admitted to hoping he'd watched us in the river. He's more reserved than the other demons I've met so far, keeping his thoughts and feelings to himself. He's quick to chastise the other two, which means he's the responsible one. If I had to guess, I'd say Dato wants someone who can understand him; a good listener who puts his needs above theirs. I imagine he's the one to do that for others without much in return.

Lorcan carries me up to the door of the wooden 'house', then drops my legs so I can stand, yet his arm remains secure around my waist in case of collapse.

Dato's wings tuck close to his body when he joins us on the rickety porch. 'Hex, the orb?'

Hex pulls out a small, greenish glass-like orb from his trouser pocket. It easily fits in the palm of his hand. He passes it to Dato, who presses his lips against the smooth surface and utters a short sentence in an unfamiliar language. The glass starts to glow, a low hum emitting from it.

'What is it?' I ask, in awe.

With his primary focus on the glowing orb, Dato answers, 'It's a tool we use to ward off enchantments. We can't break the door without first breaking the spell which protects it from damage.'

When the greenish glow dims, Dato nods to Lorcan, who proceeds to kick the wooden door open. Hex whizzes past us, and a second later, he's made himself comfortable in a tattered leather armchair, pouring something that looks suspiciously like home-brewed beer.

Dato breezes in, striding straight to the iron fireplace to light it. Lorcan gives me a little shove inside, then closes the door to shut us in, the busted hinges making it sit a little skewed. He slides the bolt across the top to keep it closed.

When Lorcan is sure I can't easily escape, he leaves to check out the only other room off the living area. I'm guessing it's Hergal's bedroom.

'Is there a bathroom?' I ask, surveying the room, taking in the small, rustic kitchenette in the corner. There's no dining table. That's sad. Hergal must not have regular guests. The dank, musty smell of the place likely prevents visitors from staying long.

Hex shakes his head. 'Sorry to disappoint, but nature is Hergal's bathroom. I can escort you to the nearest bush if you're desperate?'

'I'm fine for now,' I say, thankful I don't feel the need yet.

Hex pats his lap. 'Come—sit. Do you want a drink?' He offers me his glass of brown, alcoholic dishwater.

I stay standing but take the glass from him to sniff it; the alcohol is pungent. 'Is this supposed to be beer?'

Hex chuckles. 'Beer? That's child's play, darling. This is homemade whiskey. Bark flavour, I believe.' When he notices my expression of distaste, he adds, 'It's not as bad as it sounds. It just has a woody taste to it.'

Pleasantly surprised, I raise my eyebrows. 'Wood-flavoured moonshine?'

Intrigued to try it, I take a sip. The liquid fire gets caught in my throat, searing it. I splutter and cough, which only makes Dato and Hex laugh.

'In an hour, you'll be downing it,' Hex predicts, giving me a cheeky wink as I pass him back the glass.

Lorcan walks in with a dirty, grey, *gigantic*, moth-eaten T-shirt in his hands. He throws it at me, and I catch it. 'Put that on. Your clothes will need to dry by the fire.'

The T-shirt smells like a damp armpit. I make a face of disgust. 'I'm not wearing this.'

'It's that or nothing. I think it's safe to assume none of us would take issue with the second option,' Lorcan replies, leaning against the wall opposite me with his arms folded.

At present, I'm not in a subservient mood. '*Or...* I stay in what I've got on and stand by the fire until I'm dry.'

Lorcan leaves the wall to prowl closer, his eyes darkening. I stiffen, refusing to back away.

Standing toe-to-toe with me, he grunts, 'Strip, or I'll do it for you.'

I look to Hex, who's trying not to show his glee while lazily sipping his drink. Then I glance Dato's way; he's pretending not to listen, his attention on the newly sparked fire.

When I'm brave enough to meet Lorcan's eyes, I find them glowing gold, as though he already expects what I'm about to say next, and the idea excites him.

Maybe I don't have to be subservient to Lorcan but strong enough to bend against his will without breaking. I reckon Lorcan likes a challenge as much as I do, so long as he wins.

I know what I have to do—what he secretly *wants* me to do.

So, leaning into his space, I say with conviction, '*Make me*, beastie boy.'

Lorcan's nostrils flare, the gold in his irises brightening, and my heart thrums at the prospect of being prey to something I *want* catching me.

The second I start to move back, Lorcan's calloused hands dart out to seize me. Then, only a moment later, I'm on the floor with him on top of me. I put up a good struggle and manage to keep my leggings on for a full minute before he yanks them down far enough to slip my feet out.

As we roll around on the dust-caked rug, Hex watches on, his head tilting left and right, his hand cupping his erection through his trousers. Dato has also turned his attention to us. He's more subtle, stealing glances over his shoulder, his face unreadable. Yet his tail is twirling, revealing his excitement.

Lorcan flips me onto my front and presses my head down while he lifts my top to expose my arse. He swats it a little harder than I anticipated, and I call him a perverted bastard despite my toes curling at the sharp yet satisfying sensation.

'Don't pretend your pussy isn't pounding, songbird. If you didn't want this, you wouldn't have asked me to make you do it,' Lorcan rumbles before another yank of my top has it locking my arms up above my head, my bare breasts squashed under me. Lorcan straddles my arse, his erection right between my cheeks, and I gasp before realising he's still wearing his joggers. 'Now, give up the struggle before you hurt yourself. You're too weak as it is.' His hand slides up my spine, and I shiver with want.

I'm a fucking heathen for enjoying this.

With one more pull, I'm freed from the last stitch of my damp clothing, leaving me completely naked beneath him. I tuck my arms in to hide my side boob. 'Give me the T-shirt,' I demand, out of breath.

'Get it yourself,' Lorcan replies, releasing me to stand. He drops into the nearest chair, ready to enjoy the show.

They've already seen you naked, Raven, I remind myself, the flashback of what they did to my body at the river providing an echo of that past orgasm. This feels a little different, though. I'm not under the influence of sin. The lust circulating my veins is all my creation.

Face burning, nipples erect, vagina aching, I scramble up, all three demons ogling my naked form. I grab the grubby T-shirt, which has somehow found its way into Hex's hands, and hastily pull it on to cover myself.

After, I throw each of them a hateful glare.

Hex is the only one who can't mask his amusement. 'That hateful scowl of yours is adorable,' he remarks, offering me his glass again.

This time, when I accept, I take a big gulp. The burn I thought might distract me away from lust only enhancing it. 'Fuck. That's strong.'

'Strong enough to be your excuse?' Hex asks, giving me another knowing wink. Again, he taps his lap, desperate for me to sit on it.

Turning my nose up, I walk away with his glass, and he grumbles his annoyance under his breath. But, on further inspection, I realise that, with Dato now occupying the last armchair, there's nowhere for me to rest my feet.

So, stubbornly, I plant my arse down on the floor by the fireplace to sulk.

After only half an hour and a polished-off glass of moonshine later, I'm away with the fairies. I wonder if they exist, too.

Loose-lipped, I'm delighting the demons with stories from my university days—club nights, lectures, breaking down my degree in the social sciences for them, and my sexual conquest—all one of them. They don't seem as enthralled to hear what my ex used to do in our relationship as they did about my drunken kiss with my housemate, Rebecca, in our first year.

Albie wasn't *that* bad. In fact, he regularly declared himself a nice guy. Yet his 'niceness' was frequently used as an excuse to shame me from the things he didn't think were good for me. He used phrases like: '*I'm only trying to help you be a better partner to me*', and '*I do so much for you, don't you want to do this one thing to make me happy?*'

'This guy actually said he was put off by you pursuing him?' Hex questions, looking confounded.

Leaning my weight back on my arms, my legs now prickling with heat from the fire, I reply, 'Yep. His exact words were: '*Women shouldn't initiate sex. It's emasculating for a man and unnatural*'.'

Lorcan snorts. 'Sounds like the sort of thing a guy with no ability to please a woman would say.'

Appearing even more bewildered, Hex scratches his head. 'Isn't that the dream? That your girlfriend wants to fuck you?'

I shrug. 'Not for Albie, apparently. It wasn't solely that... even though I had to wait for *him* to initiate, I also wasn't allowed to use toys on myself. He said it classed as cheating.'

Hex chokes on his drink. 'Myth and mercy, you can't be serious.'

'No joke. When he found my vibrator, he took the batteries out and didn't speak to me for two weeks. I had to apologise and throw it out before he forgave me.'

'You should have told him the truth, mortal... You should have told him your vibrator was a bigger man than he could ever be,' Dato delivers, and we all chuckle, the moonshine making us giddy from the fumes alone.

I lie back, my head resting on my arms, the cyclops' old T-shirt riding up my thighs, bearing my centre to the fire's radiant heat. Dato's on my left, his gaze locked on my bent legs. He's the only one who hasn't tasted the cyclops' home-brew tonight. Adding to my suspicion that he's stuck in this responsible, self-sacrificing role.

It's time to test the waters with him.

Fidgeting, I say, 'This floor is so uncomfortable.'

'I offered you my lap, remember?' Hex reminds me, still a little bitter.

But it's not *his* lap I want to sit on.

'You're too far away from the fire. And I'm still a little cold,' I lie, pouting. My attention returns to Dato. 'Can I sit on *your* lap instead?' My voice is all innocence.

Dato's eyebrows shoot up in surprise, his tail going shock-still. 'Erm...' He glances at the other two, unsure if he heard me right. Or maybe he's suspicious of my intent.

I wave a hand as though he should forget I even asked. 'Don't worry. Albie never let me sit on his lap, either,' I mention in a casual tone, hoping the conflation rouses the response I'm after.

Dato's eye twitches, clearly hating that I've lumped him in with the guy we've been taking the piss out of for the past half an hour. Without a word, he beckons me to him with two fingers.

A thrill zips through me at my little triumph.

Keeping my expression mild, I jump to my feet and pad the small distance towards Dato. The other two are so silent I wouldn't be surprised to find out they're actually holding their breath.

I stop in front of Dato, swaying a little. He holds my wrist to steady me, then pulls me onto his lap, sweeping an arm under my legs to hook them over his so I'm lounging instead of sitting rigid.

'More comfortable now?' Dato asks me, spreading his legs so my arse can fit in the gap. His smell is airier than the others, like a winter's breeze, with notes of frozen sage and wild rain.

'Very,' I say, the alcohol making me bold enough to rest my head against his shoulder.

He tenses. 'What are you doing?'

'She's a snuggler,' Lorcan answers for me, humour in his voice.

Dato's wings come around us like a comfort blanket, and I hum a little contented sigh, wriggling to get myself 'comfortable', when really, my motivation is to turn him on.

It works—Dato's chest rises and falls erratically while a hard bulge forms against my hip.

'Stop squirming,' Dato commands, his hand landing on my bare thigh to inhibit its movement. His other arm is a sling around my shoulders, providing support.

'Sorry, it's weird not having any underwear on. And this T-shirt is so itchy.' I make sure to remind him of my near-nakedness. 'So, tell me, Dato... what's your story?'

CHAPTER 17

Vulnerability

'What's my *story*? I'm not some fairytale princess,' Dato says, rolling his eyes. 'Anyway, just because you're mouthing off about your pathetic little life doesn't mean the rest of us are as willing to share.'

'Oh, come on. How does being a demon work? Were you born a harpy, or did you turn into one when you lost your soul?' I pry, not put off by his jibe.

'Harpyiai can't be *made* like vrykolakas and lycanthropes. We're *born* into our wings. The Underworld is all I've ever known,' Dato divulges as though he's proud of this fact.

'Dato likes to brag about being a full-blooded demon. It's the only interesting thing about him,' Hex says from across the room.

Dato casts Hex a scathing look. 'And the only interesting thing about Hex is his uncanny ability to make everyone he meets want to punch him in the dick.'

Lorcan and I snicker while Hex gives a conceding shrug.

'That's not the only thing most want to do with my dick,' Hex claims, his gaze falling on me. 'Some even beg for it. Right, deal-breaker?'

My body is already hot from the alcohol and fire combined, but Hex's reminder makes the flush in my face sizzle with added embarrassment. I ignore the comment, hopefully driving him up the wall; Hex is the biggest attention seeker out of the three of them.

I peer up at Dato through my lashes, then start playing with the ridge of his breastplate. 'You've never been to my world?'

'No. I don't need to. All demons know what the mortal lands are like. We can watch you through various means. We grow up consuming your media. From what I've seen, it can be equally as brutal as this world. Though, down here, we're bound to our rules. On the other hand, Mortals seem to relish breaking them.' Dato bats my hand away, then shifts to remove his breastplate, revealing the black, long-sleeved top underneath.

Did he do that so he could feel my touch?

Emboldened, I slide my palm up Dato's sternum. All the hard muscles in his stomach and chest tense. His tail snakes around my ankle as he sucks in a breath and holds it, waiting for my next move. The room has gone achingly silent.

'The only rules worth following are the ones you set yourself. The rest…' My fingers trail back down to trace the grooves of his stomach. 'Can be moulded to fit our journeys.'

Dato studies my face. 'What *aren't* you willing to do to get to the castle?'

'That's not the question you should be asking,' I tell him, moving to take his hand in mine. He lets me, his gaze dropping to where I'm gliding his palm up my thigh. 'What you should be asking is what I'll let *you* do to get me there.'

Opening my legs wider, I place his hand at the juncture of my thighs; I'm wet and ready for him to enter. He squeezes his eyes shut and groans out another held breath.

Dato can't seem to help himself. He drags a finger through my wetness, then cups me there. 'Fucking mazes. Why are you so wet already?' he queries, his insecurity on show.

Does he not know how fucking hot he is?

'Because I want you. I want all three of you,' I admit in a sultry tone, my chest heaving as he starts circling my clit with his thumb. The fucked up thing is… that wasn't a lie; I *do* want to play around with all three of them. I'm not purely seducing them to save my brother and me. If our souls weren't on the line, I'd be doing this for the hell of it because I *wanted* to.

Dato suddenly withdraws his hand, sitting up straighter. His tail unwinds itself from my ankle and drops to the floor. 'Liar. All you want is our help. You're only offering yourself to us out of fear—desperation.'

Before Dato can throw me off, I rush to straddle him. He's hard even though he's fighting this. 'If that's the case, then fear has never felt so good,' I murmur, moving my hips to grind against the bulge in his trousers. I pull my T-shirt off and throw it behind me. His wings are still around us, preventing Hex and Lorcan from seeing what I'm doing to him.

This is Dato's semi-private show.

As Dato watches me writhe on him, naked and flushed, he reaches up to squeeze my breast. He licks his lips. 'What do you expect out of this, mortal? Do you think fucking us will do you any favours? You think we'll... what? Fall in love with you? We're three of the most powerful demons in Vyrinthos. We can get an easy lay any day of the week. You're nothing special.' He drops his hand, his eyes now as hard as his cock.

I cease all movement, aiming a glare at him instead.

Hex huffs out a disbelieving laugh. 'Dato, you need to work on your dirty talk. You can't insult the poor girl while she's fucking you dry.'

'Well, you can. But not like that,' Lorcan inputs, sounding amused. 'I'm sure our songbird wouldn't mind *some* mild degradation. Isn't that right, you little slut?' His tone is playful, not as cutting as Dato's was.

Dato's gaze rakes down my naked torso, his jaw clenching. From his attitude, he's pissed off with *himself* for wanting me and pissed off at *me* because he believes I only want him to help me reach the castle. Or maybe he's trying to put me off because he's worried about taking advantage of my situation.

Hex was wrong. *Dato's* the nice one.

Sighing, my hands come to rest on Dato's shoulders. I look him in the eye to get my next point across. They're a pretty walnut colour. 'Yes, I want your help. Okay? You got me. But you know what I want more, though? I want to piss Julius off for all he's done trying to claim me. And you know what I want more than even that? I want to finally be the kind of person who does whatever the fuck they want. And right now, putting all this Underworld bullshit aside, I just want to enjoy this buzz and get fucked by three hot demons.'

Of course, part of this is manipulation; I'm trying to sneak my way onto Dato's good side.

Nevertheless, there's also a lot of truth to what I'm saying; I'm tired of being a responsible adult. I've never been allowed to explore my deepest fantasies and desires. First, my mum forced me to grow up too fast for reasons she never disclosed. Then Albie extinguished my sexual appetite to make himself feel more like a man. Now, I have a fifteen-year-old kid I need to rescue from the depths of a hellish kingdom run by a demon king who wants to keep me in a gilded cage, soulless. This might be my last and only chance to taste freedom. Because what I experienced at the river between Hex and Lorcan was the most alive I've ever felt, even as their unofficial prisoner.

A big part of this is real. Too real.

Dato grips my hips, encouraging me to continue grinding on him. I oblige, moving cautiously. 'First, Hex made you come, then Lorcan. Do you want to know how *I'd* make you moan my name? Is that it? Is that what you want?'

'Yes, I want to know,' I breathe, my need mounting with the curiosity alone. The friction helping, too.

With his dark eyes glazed, Dato leans forward to capture my mouth with his. I'm a little surprised. Hex only kissed me earlier because I initiated it.

Dato sweeps his hands through my hair as the end of his tail brushes lightly up my spine. He holds me close while he kisses the hell out of me. I should have known Dato was the type to make sex personal. He clearly needs intimacy to connect to his desire, unlike Hex and Lorcan.

I give as good as I get, teasing him with my tongue as I continue riding him over his clothes.

'That's it, songbird. Fuck Dato's mouth with your tongue, like the little slut you are,' Lorcan says, voice like gravel.

I glance Lorcan's way, not breaking the kiss; he's rubbing himself over his joggers, watching me move on Dato. His smile to me is wolfish, his eyes pure gold.

'Dato, move your fucking wings out of the way. We want to watch,' Hex snips, tone impatient—eager.

A rush of air sweeps across my exposed back as Dato's wings retract, draping over the sides of the armchair.

Dato leans back in his seat and his thumb finds my clit again. 'Do you like being watched? Do you like their eyes on you while you writhe in my lap, wishing I'd fuck you?'

'Yes, I like it. I've never felt this desired before,' I answer, showing a little vulnerability. Dato seems to respond to honesty.

'You've never felt wanted before, have you? No one has let you take control.'

'No,' I grit out, pleasure rolling over me as Dato's thumb speeds up. I circle my hips, assisting.

'Then use me, mortal. Take your own pleasure. Show us how much you want it,' Dato encourages, leaving me bereft of his touch again.

I let out a whine of protest, and the three demons chuckle.

'You heard him. Make *yourself* come while we watch,' Hex urges me, and when I look over my shoulder, I catch him stroking himself, his trousers loose around his hips. Even from this distance, it's impressive.

'Use me,' Dato repeats, grabbing my arse to line me up with his concealed erection.

Feeling empowered to take what I want, I pick up the pace, sliding up and down his restricted length, the friction of his trousers causing enough bite not to need his hands down there. So, I take those idle appendages and place them on my breasts. He plays with them, kneading and tweaking my nipples while his tail vibrates behind him.

I moan Dato's name, and he groans, urging me on. When he peers up at me, something akin to adoration in his eyes, the need to kiss him again is overwhelming. So, I do because he's letting me take control.

My orgasm is a slow, languorous, rippling current, drawn out and luxurious as it washes over me. My moans of release are lost in Dato's mouth, and we don't stop kissing until those small cries of pleasure develop into great heaving sobs.

Overcome with emotion—which for some reason hit me harder than my orgasm—I bury my face into Dato's neck and wail.

'Oh, fuck. What's wrong with her? Is she hurt?' I hear Hex ask; his voice is close now.

'Shhh, it's okay, Raven. You're okay,' Dato whispers, stroking my hair as Hex rubs my back. 'I think she's just tired and overwhelmed. It's been a long night for her.'

'I'm sorry,' I whimper, trying to get a grip of myself.

'Hey.' Lorcan cups my face, and I open my eyes to find him crouching down behind Dato, face-to-face with me. 'You don't need to apologise to us. We get it.' He uses a tissue to dab away the wetness around my eyes. I can only assume he had other ideas for this tissue before I started bawling—ruining our fun.

'Come on, mortal. Time for bed,' Dato says, sweeping my legs up as he stands with me.

He carries me into Hergal's bedroom, which consists of a single mattress on a black iron bed frame. The room has only a little chest of drawers to accompany it.

Dato lowers me onto the bed. Hex already used his speed to pull the cover back for me. Then Lorcan redresses me in the cyclops' tent-like T-shirt—I had forgotten I was still naked.

Even though the T-shirt and bed smell like old sweat and mould, I appreciate the cosy warmth and snuggle up, tucking my knees into my stomach as I lay on my side, the straw-like pillow bearable to rest my head on.

'You should feel better after a few hours' sleep,' Dato says, tucking me in. 'We'll be in the other room.' His tail darts down to caress my face, and he snatches it back a second later, seeming annoyed at its mindless action.

'Call if you need anything,' Hex adds, giving me a tight-lipped smile before all three of them step out of the room. They leave the door ajar.

What the fuck just happened?

One minute, I was dry-humping Dato to orgasm. The next, I was crying my eyes out. Then I was put to bed like a lost little kid in need of coddling.

And all three of them showed me empathy. *Demons.* Those evil, soulless creatures have treated me with more compassion and understanding in the last five minutes than anyone has in my entire life.

That's fucking sad to admit.

Emotionally and physically drained, I hug myself while my tears dry. Am I simply overwhelmed with worry? Was that what made me break? Or was it that I finally felt seen for the first time? That at last, I was encouraged to live my fantasy: to practice being the bold, unapologetic person I've always wished to be. The kind of person who can own their desires and not be shamed for purely wanting more than they've been forced to accept before.

I don't know. But Dato's right: I'm exhausted, and sleep should do me good.

So, I do it—I force myself into slumber. Because it's about time I take control of myself and do what the fuck makes me feel good.

CHAPTER 18

Bad Brother

ROBIN

The absence of sunlight doesn't necessarily mean that darkness prevails, not in the Underworld, apparently. There seems to be some otherworldly sheen which provides enough illumination under the stormy night sky to distinguish its haunting beauty. Even the leafless trees glow ghostly pale.

I don't *feel* dead. I know that Julius guy told me I wasn't, but this situation is too surreal to stop questioning my mortality.

I rest my chin on my hands while I stare out, searching the grey-walled horizon for an end to the maze my sister is currently travelling through to reach me. The bedroom I decided on has a small balcony I'm using to oversee the demon city where I'm being held captive.

What I miss most is my phone. It's fucking boring wasting time offline. I don't know how to live without it—how to communicate, or even how to experience a moment without the distraction of a screen to record it.

Shit. Do I miss an inanimate object more than I miss my mum? Nah. But maybe I'm just more reliant on technology than I was on a parent. I stopped needing Mum to do everything for me a few years ago. She worked so much that I barely saw her. It didn't particularly affect our relationship; I knew she would always be there if I *did* need anything.

Unlike Raven, who I haven't seen since Christmas day three years ago.

Sure, she used to send me the odd text now and then, asking how I was, but our conversations were brief and shallow. I can't remember the last time we learnt anything new about each other. Even before she moved out, our sibling bond was more of a fraying tether, made of the weakest thread.

I've always been able to sense Raven's resentment towards me. Mum often scolded her, always berating her for one thing or another. I think Mum took her frustrations out on Raven. Whereas, with me, Mum was softer—more lenient.

I'm guessing that's why Raven stayed away. It's still shitty to blame me for how Mum treated her, though. Being an eleven-year-old, it's not like I could have done much about it.

At fifteen, I don't feel like a kid anymore. Can anyone really cling to childhood innocence for long in this day and age? Especially now that I don't have a parent to instil a sense of comfort in which to grow at a steadier pace. No matter what Raven is to me now—sister or guardian—she's not my mother. I'm on my own.

Maybe this is how Raven has always felt.

My stomach aches with guilt. Raven is putting herself in danger to save me, and I didn't even think to ask that demon if she was okay. Am I a bad brother as much as she's a bad sister? She's a lot older than me, yeah. But it's not like I made her life at home with us any easier.

Admittedly, I was a little shit. I probably still am. Sometimes, I'd rub Mum's favour in Raven's face. And while she would do the chores set out for her, I'd neglect mine to play video games or slob about the house.

All right, I could have been more considerate. I could have acknowledged the unfairness. Instead, I relished Raven's misfortune of being a girl. Having those gender stereotypes shoved down her throat by her own mother must have been hard to stomach. For me, I basked in my privilege, wilfully ignoring the dimming light in my sister's eyes year after year.

Clearly, I'm being punished for my sins now. Here. In *the Underworld*—my literal soul on the line.

Is it too late to atone?

If what Julius says is true, then a deadly trap lies beyond this city's border; one very few escape unharmed. What if Raven dies trying to save me, and I never get to tell her I'm sorry?

Raven isn't innocent; she left me and never tried hard to stay in contact. With Mum working so much, I was chronically alone. I have friends, but over the past three years, there's been this sister-shaped hole in my heart which longed to be filled with that sibling banter and affection I'd see in other households.

My hobbies helped me cope with loneliness, especially gaming and poetry writing. Still, without my sister around to make fun of me for them, it makes them seem reductive. I used to enjoy our verbal sparring matches as a child. Raven used to grow frustrated when I purposely used unnecessarily long and complicated words I knew she wouldn't understand, and then she'd tease me for being an English boffin.

Despite the nostalgia, I can't easily forget that Raven waited a week before returning for Mum's funeral. I had to stay with a friend, holding back tears until that friend and his family had fallen asleep each night.

We both made mistakes that may never be rectified now we're caught up in this fantastical situation.

I'm stuck in a city of demons, for fuck's sake; I'm screwed. And Raven's position is even more precarious than mine.

Should I risk my life to search for her? She's risking hers for me.

Even with my fifteen-year-old male bravado, I admit I'm not naturally brave. The thought of scaling the city wall to enter a maze of monsters turns my stomach. Anyway, what could I do to protect her? I spend most of my time in the virtual world, where it's never truly game over. I can only use a keyboard or pen with any real skill.

The only thing I can do is wait around, hoping Raven can fight against the odds.

Or...

Maybe there *is* something I can do to help our situation right here in the castle.

'What do you want, kid? I'm busy,' Julius slurs when I find him lounging with a bottle of red wine in his throne room. There's not a glass in sight. His white-blonde hair is more dishevelled than it was a few hours ago. His jacket is crumpled on the floor, his shirt wine-stained and open at the collar. He looks like he's been dragged through a hedge, his silver eyes red-rimmed and worn.

'Nothing. I'm just bored,' I say, shuffling my feet. This was a ridiculous idea. He's obviously in a terrible mood. The broken table and shattered glass on the floor are indication enough that I must tread carefully here.

Sighing, Julius runs a hand over his face. 'I'm your captor, not your entertainment.'

'Do you have a games room, a library, or something?'

'Yes. I said you had free roam. Go find it yourself.' He waves me off, then takes a generous swig of wine. 'There are board games and a pool table somewhere.'

'I can't play those sorts of games by myself,' I complain, lingering at the doorway.

Julius looks up at me, his forehead creasing. 'What are you asking for? Do you want me to command one of my staff to babysit you? You want someone to hold your hand? They've got work to do. Go away and stop bothering me with your childish whims.'

On the verge of giving up, I go to leave, then hesitate. This guy might be saying he wants to be left alone, but I know first-hand that's often a lie you tell yourself when, inside, you're sick and tired of the loneliness.

I slide my hands into my jogger pockets. 'I've never played pool before.'

Julius takes another gulp of wine. 'And I should care... why?'

Shrugging a shoulder, I reply, 'Just thought, you know... maybe you could teach me.'

Silence.

Julius' annoyed expression morphs into a truly puzzled one when it computes. 'You want me to teach you how to play pool? *Me*? The demon who captured you and is forcing your sister to risk her life in my maze to save both your souls from eternal damnation.'

'Yeah. Like I said, I'm bored.'

The demon squints at me. 'Why are you under the impression that I'd have any interest in wasting my time doing something so mindlessly dull and tedious?

Don't you think I have better things to do than hang out with a moody teenager?'

'From the looks of things... no. It doesn't seem like you have anything better to do.'

The barest hint of a smile touches Julius' lips. 'You have some nerve, kid. Perhaps you and Raven *do* have some common traits, after all.'

'Do you know if she's okay?' I ask, my gaze fixed on my socks.

After a pause, Julius grumbles, 'She's more than okay, unfortunately.' He places the bottle of wine on the side table beside his throne. 'Her life will be preserved if that's what you're worried about. She's well-guarded.'

My insides calm their squirming. 'So... you're not going to let her die?'

Julius shakes his head. 'Like you, I don't wish to see her come to any harm despite our differences.'

'You don't want her harmed, yet you want to cleave out her soul so you can keep her prisoner for the rest of her life?'

Julius' eyes narrow on me again. 'You don't understand our ways. Being in my service is no prison sentence; it's an honour most clamber to trade for. My layer of the Underworld is considered a pleasurable place to reside compared to others. I'll treat Raven like a queen as soon as she allows herself to be mine.'

'I don't know my sister well enough to say whether she would want that. All I know is that she's never been treated with the respect she deserves. Not by me *or* Mum.' I fiddle with the hem of my T-shirt. 'Is there any way I can contact her?'

'No. Communication is out of the question.' Julius' voice is stern. When he takes in the disappointment in my expression, he continues, '*But*, we may be able to *see* her. Although I'd need your assistance to channel the power to do so.'

I look up to see a cunning smile spread across the demon's angelic face, making him appear more devilish. 'What would I have to do?'

Julius rises from his throne and strides towards me, his steps wavering a little from too much wine. 'Come with me, kid.' He passes by, walking out the door, expecting me to follow. 'Afterwards, I'll promise to play pool with you.'

Keen to put my plan into action, I follow him.

Chapter 19

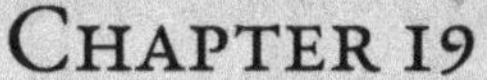

Rise and Shine

RAVEN

'*What do we usually talk about when I'm here?*' I ask the white-blonde dream demon, resting my back against a cream and gold stone pillar. Julius shifts his weight on the edge of a cracked water fountain opposite. The shallow surface of liquid shines as bright as the bubble-like walls of this dome we're stuck under. 'We talk about your life: what you get up to at school, your friends, your work. You also complain about your mother and brother to me.'

'And you remember it all while I forget? Why?'

'It's difficult for mortals to retain information they don't comprehend. Once you wake, like most dreams, this won't be converted to memory,' he explains, swirling the water with his index finger absent-mindedly. 'Believe me, starling, I wish you could remember.'

My expression hardens. 'Can you stop calling me that?'

'No,' he says unapologetically.

Glaring at him, I slide down the pillar, then cross my legs to sit at the base of it. 'And what do you talk to me about?'

Julius' silver eyes lift to meet mine, and I repress a shiver. 'Things I wouldn't dare tell any other.' He doesn't elaborate.

'How long do these... 'meetings' usually last?'

'For however long you are asleep,' he answers, no hint of impatience in his voice. Although I'm sure that if what he tells me is true, he answers these same questions every time we interact. 'We usually get six or seven hours together at least.'

'If I'm with you the whole time I'm asleep, won't I still be tired in the morning?'

Julius shakes his head. 'Your mind and body still recharge, even when your subconscious is active.'

'Okay. Well... is this a regular thing? Do I appear here every night?' I ask, still curious to know the specifics.

'It depends on your mood. Sometimes, your soul calls to me nightly, for weeks on end. And other times, it's months before I sense the tug to this place.' He looks down at his shiny black boots, contemplative. 'I think your soul seeks mine when it's feeling particularly lonely—when you're overwhelmed with life and need someone to confide in.'

My face grows hot to the touch. I didn't realise I was so pathetic as to create a whole dream world, all for me to have someone—a hot, sleep-paralysis demon—to talk to.

'What's the matter, love? Did you have a bad day?' Julius enquires, his eyes soft yet still somehow intense, as though he can see right through to the core of who I am without needing me to speak.

I lower my gaze, watching my fingers pinch at the hem of my long-line T-shirt. When I first fell into this dreamscape, Julius eyed my legs like he wanted to take a bite out of them. The heat in his stare still simmers, his attention snagging on my bare skin whenever he thinks I'm not looking.

Apparently, we're the same age—sixteen. Though he looks more like a man than the boys at my school. The black, formfitting suit he wears is unlike any I've seen. It's something an evil prince in a fairytale would commit untold sin in. He's also over six-foot, and his shoulders are too broad for a teen. His beauty is too well-formed. I've never seen a teenage boy so finely crafted. He's too gorgeous to be real. He can only belong in my dreams.

For a second, I thought I saw a flash of white wings when he first emerged from the mist. He laughed when I asked if he was an angel.

'There are no angels,' he'd said. 'Being a saint is an impossible feat, even for the divine.'

'Where has your mind wandered to?' Julius' voice snaps me out of my musings.

'I'm thinking over everything you've told me,' I reply, tucking my legs beneath my T-shirt and stretching it.

There's a weighted silence before Julius' empathetic sigh drifts through the space between us. 'Why does your soul cry, starling? Talk to me.'

'My brother…' I start, unsure whether I should humour this beautiful figment of my imagination.

'What did that brat do now?' Julius coaxes, a touch of anger in his tone—anger on my behalf.

My mouth twitches up in a weary smile.

Julius spends the next hour listening intently as I wring every worry and insecurity out of myself. He nods his head, eyes conveying his understanding, and he doesn't seem to zone out once while I detail all the tiny arguments my little brother and I have daily. I work up to the reason I believe I'm especially melancholy tonight.

'He told me he might have been the mistake, but I'm the child our mum regrets having,' I utter, wrapping my arms around my legs, trying to hold myself together.

In the silence that follows, I peek up at Julius. He's watching the still water sparkle, his forehead heavy.

'Don't listen to him. He only wanted to hurt you. I can't imagine anyone regretting having you in their life. You are a gift,' he tells me in earnest.

I chew on my bottom lip, his words warming me inside and out. I can't speak, my eyes and throat closing—burning.

'Did you hear me, love? You are a gift,' Julius repeats, making sure that statement has an impact. 'You are starlight, hope beyond darkness. You are pure joy while being the most decadent pain. You make those you know and meet want to emulate your effortless presence and charm, yet they also resent you for it. You make all that matters around you insignificant. Time and space bends for you.' He gestures widely to the captured slice of space inside our dreamscape as if I'm its true creator. 'For the love of souls, starling, you make me want to carve out my heart just to show you how it bleeds for you and you alone.'

At that, my head snaps up to take him in. His face is open—raw—and full of reverence. I open my mouth to tell him to stop, but no words come out.

Julius continues, his silver eyes liquid. 'You make me want to grind our worlds to dust so we can dance together on their ashes—the only two souls in existence. As that's how I feel when I'm with you.'

Gobsmacked, I stammer, 'I—I...'

Julius rushes to stand. He turns his back on me. 'Don't say anything,' he says, his voice pitched low. 'Let me believe for tonight that you feel the same—that you don't forget me every time.'

The heaviness of guilt slumps my shoulders and presses against my chest. 'I'm sorry,' I whisper, meaning it.

Julius hangs his head and sighs. 'I think it's time you woke up.'

And, before I can answer, he walks away into the swirling mist.

A loud clap of thunder overhead shatters our shared dream into a thousand tiny pieces.

The bubble bursts like it would glass.

I wake with a start.

Reddish-brown eyes greet me.

'Rise and shine, deal-breaker. Did you sleep well?' Hex asks, staring down at me. He's shirtless, his head propped on one elbow. The bed is too narrow for the both of us, so every part of me is pressed against him. I can't complain; all that lean muscle is a lovely sight to wake up to. 'You moan in your sleep. Did you know? It's a turn-on.'

'I was dreaming,' I say defensively, pushing him away to give myself space. He doesn't budge. My palm lingers on his toned chest, his soft skin a tempting contrast.

'How are you feeling?'

If I didn't know any better, I'd think there was genuine concern in his voice.

'Never worse. There's no part of me that doesn't ache, and I smell like a mouldy mole rat,' I grumble, rubbing my eyes.

Hex sweeps some frizzy strands of hair away from my face. 'There's nothing I can do about the smell, unfortunately. Nothing yet, anyway. But I can help ease your pain if you'd let me.'

My eyes narrow to slits. 'Why wouldn't I let you?'

'Because it will require you to drink a few drops of my blood,' he answers, flashing me a knowing grin.

'Ew, no.' It's purely a gut reaction; the idea of drinking anyone's blood is repulsive to me.

Hex laughs. The crinkles around his eyes and the slight dimple in his left cheek steal my attention. 'It tastes better than you think. A vrykolaka's blood is sweet. It's highly coveted for its flavour and healing properties.'

'Can it heal anything? Like a mortal wound or a terminal disease?' I probe, more intrigued than my stomach is willing to tolerate.

'In small doses, it can heal minor ailments. In larger quantities, it can turn you into a vrykolaka.'

My nose scrunches, rejecting that fate. 'Why would anyone risk it?'

Quickly, Hex's face falls. 'You think being a vrykolaka is a curse? It's anything but. I've lived over a century in the never ageing body of a twenty-seven-year-old. I have inhuman speed and increased strength.' He traces the curve of my lips, his gaze caught there. 'It's a blessing.'

'But you're stuck down here, soulless. A slave to a tyrannical king,' I remind him obstinately.

Amusement lifts the corners of his mouth. 'You have a very low opinion of Julius. He's the reason we're here, protecting you from harm.'

'He's also the reason *I'm* here, full stop,' I retort, my tone dry. I've been actively trying to rid my mind of the Demon King. My subconscious is stubbornly rebelling against those wishes, throwing that dream at me out of nowhere. Was it truly a dream or a memory? Whatever it was, I hope it fucking fades back into obscurity. I don't even want to remember his name, let alone any nice thing he's said to my past sleeping self.

'You make me want to carve out my heart just to show you how it bleeds for you and you alone.'

For fuck's sake, brain. Enough!

'I can see why he wants to keep you alive now.' Hex's fingers dance softly over the bite marks he left on my neck, bringing me back to the present. A shiver of need has me exhaling sharply, my muscles tightening. 'You are extremely precious. If I could, I would have you all to myself.'

'Who said I'd let you?' I challenge, liking how he falters, his gaze colliding with mine, his pupils dilating to black. 'What makes you think I even want you as part of the group?'

'Oh, deal-breaker, you are playing a *very* dangerous game,' Hex says a second before he grabs the neck of my T-shirt and rips it with enough force to expose my right breast to him.

I shriek, trying to roll away, but his teeth clamp down around my nipple before I escape. The pain is immediate and breathtaking. But as quickly as it comes, it fades, replaced by a wave of pleasure so intense my hips spring off the bed before slamming back down again.

Hex drinks deep, his tongue lashing my hardened nipple. Moaning, I grasp a handful of his hair. Not to yank him away but to keep him close.

Flushing with desire, I relish my quickened heartbeat as it throbs between my legs, the adrenaline of being caught prey intensifying the heady sensation.

'You're mine, anytime I want, any*where* I want,' Hex rasps, my blood coating his lips.

His fingers find my clit, and with a single touch, I come with a cry of pure ecstasy. He delights in the rush of wetness he finds, sliding his fingers up and down, then around and around, dangerously close to the place he's unable to penetrate.

Hex's groan is one of frustration. 'By the blood, I want to fuck you more than I want to draw my next breath.'

Now that he's finished with my nipple, the cold air stings it. 'Fuck, Hex. Why there? It's going to rub against my clothes.'

His answering smile is wicked. 'It won't hurt as much as it will leave you aching to be filled. Every brush against my mark will have you moaning my name.'

'Are you looking to get slapped again?' I threaten, elbowing him away so I can sit up. I cover myself with what remains of Hergal's T-shirt. Hex is right: even the faintest touch of the fabric against my bitten breast sends shockwaves reverberating through my system. 'For fuck's sake! I can't move around like this.' When Hex snickers, I kick him. 'You fucking arrogant vamp!'

Catching my shoulder, Hex forces me back into a lying position beside him. 'Calm down. I said I'd help.' He lifts his thumb to one of his lengthened fangs and applies pressure until black blood swells. 'Here.' He offers his pricked thumb to me, a strangely tempting onyx bead glistening on its tip.

Sardonically, I remark, 'I want to keep my mortality, thanks.'

'You would need at least a full pint to turn. And then you'd have to die to complete the transition. A few drops will be out of your system by lunchtime,' he reassures, bringing his thumb to my lips. 'Go on, suck it.' His dark eyes glint at that suggestive order.

I hesitate, thinking there must be a catch. Why does this vampire care about my suffering? He's supposed to make my life harder in this maze, so I quit or fail. Instead, he's not only seizing any opportunity to seduce me, he's also being almost sweet in his clear pursuit. 'What do *you* get out of this?'

Hex's eyebrows flash up in surprise as though he didn't even pose the question to himself. 'Er...'

'Why are you helping me?' I pry, my heart fluttering more than I should allow.

Scowling, Hex retracts his hand. 'I don't care for you if that's what you're implying. I just... like a blank canvas,' he argues, surveying the old bite marks on my neck. 'That's all this is.'

I study his face, the lie written in how his features tighten and tic. 'Fine,' I say, grabbing his hand. 'But if I turn into a vampire, the first thing I'm going to do with my super strength is rip your dick off.'

Hex's mouth twists into a crooked smirk. 'If you want my dick so much, I'll gladly give it to you.'

I enclose my lips around his thumb, accepting this small taste of immortality. The first drop that hits my tongue elicits a shudder, and I crave more. The flavour is sweet like honey yet as tart as a young raspberry. Lost to carnal greed, I lavishly suck on his offering, my eyes rolling to the back of my head.

Hex hisses a curse as if me feeding off him brings him the same pleasure. I grope his crouch, finding him hard.

'Fucking mazes, I want that mouth of yours around my cock.'

Finding myself all too eager to make that a reality, I fumble with the laces of his trousers. And when it's loose enough, my hand slips beneath, fingers grazing his smooth, warm length. Again, he swears under his breath, then withdraws his thumb from my mouth.

Hex rests his head on the single straw pillow when I sit up. He shifts so he's almost beneath me, this movement a whir of air.

'Are you ready to taste more of me?' he asks, hooking his thumbs inside the waistband of his trousers. He slides them down enough for his cock to spring free.

My jaw aches simply looking at it; it's thick and long. Fuck. How is that going to fit inside my mouth? He smiles at my hesitation, guessing my thoughts.

'You can take it, darling. Demons are above average in all things,' Hex informs me, arching an eyebrow, a smug smirk on his almost flush face. My blood has invigorated him; it's given his pallid, immortal skin a more human glow. 'Especially in this regard.'

With the lingering sweetness of his blood still tingling on my tongue, I spit on my palm before reaching for his intimidating length.

'Next time, spit directly on me,' Hex instructs, his jaw clenching in anticipation.

When our skin makes contact—the first fisted glide down his shaft—he grips my T-shirt and rips it at the seams so more of me is exposed.

'Suck it as greedily as you sucked my thumb,' he demands, squeezing my bitten breast.

When no pain comes, I look down at my chest to find his bite has healed. There's only pebbled pink skin where the puncture of his two pin-like fangs left a mark mere moments ago. His blood magic worked. 'It's gone already,' I say, astounded.

'Yeah, yeah, it's a miracle. Now, focus on the task at hand,' Hex replies, his cock twitching in eagerness.

'Hmm, maybe I'm no longer in the mood,' I tease, withdrawing my touch.

Hex groans, his eyes screwing shut. 'If you keep toying with me, I'll lose this gentlemanly facade. Then you'll really know what it is to be fucked,' he warns, pinching my nipple in admonishment.

Before I can throw out a witty response, the door swings open. Lorcan and Dato crowd the doorway, unsurprised to see us in our compromising position. Hex doesn't seem bothered at all, either.

'We were gone *five* minutes,' Dato says, clearly exasperated.

A mischievous grin spreads across Hex's face. 'I couldn't help myself. Do you guys want to join us?' His gaze slides from them to me. 'Three cocks are better than one, right?'

As I'm about to snap back at the presumption, Dato interjects, 'As much fun as that sounds, we've got to go; Hergal is on his way back. I'd rather not test his wrath with the fragile mortal around.'

'Fucking cyclopes, always ruining the fun,' Hex mutters bitterly, shimmying his trousers back over his hips.

Lorcan throws my now-dry clothes at me. 'Next time, songbird, wait for me, or you'll live to regret it.'

Swallowing hard, I ignore the thrill that supercharges my now-tainted blood.

CHAPTER 20

Shield

RAVEN

As I'm lacing my trainers, now back in the dry outfit Julius conjured for me, a tremor vibrates the mould-eaten wooden planks that somehow pass as a bedroom floor.

From his position on the bed, Hex has been watching me dress since Dato and Lorcan rushed back outside to distract Hergal. We're to sneak out before the cyclops comes too close.

'What was that?' I ask, my voice as shaky as the foundations of this hearth.

Hex stands, gesturing for me to do the same. 'Hergal's nearing. We need to leave before he sees you.'

I peer up at him from my crouch. 'That was an awfully heavy footfall. I thought you said cyclopes weren't much bigger than mortal men.'

Hex looks a little sheepish. 'Did I say that? Erm, well, they're not giants by any stretch of the imagination. The Greeks often overexaggerated.'

'But this hearth is normal-sized,' I state, noticing the ceiling isn't higher than average. 'How can Hergal fit in here if he's huge?'

'Well observed. But there's one thing we forgot to mention about Hergal: his form fits his temper. And, when he's calm, he's practically tiny. But... anger him...' Hex winces.

'Sooo, that tremor we felt...' I say, dread blooming.

'Is a bad omen, yes,' Hex finishes for me. 'Which is why you should hurry up so I can whisk you away before he finds out we've broken in.' Before I can stand on my own terms, he drags me up. 'You can tie your shoes later.'

In a flash, Hex sweeps me off my feet, and the cabin hazes as he speeds towards the broken front door with me in his arms.

'Why couldn't we sneak out the bedroom window?' I put to him, a little light-headed from the whirl of movement.

'Because we only broke the enchantment on the front door. It's our only way in and out,' Hex answers, checking that the coast is clear through the wonky crack between the door and its frame.

A knot of anxiety tightens in my stomach. 'What about Dato and Lorcan? Will they be okay?'

This makes Hex stare down at me, a strange expression on his face. Is it confusion? Surprise? Curiosity? Maybe a mix of the three.

'What?' I demand, uncomfortable under his assessing gaze.

'You care about their welfare?' Hex asks although it sounds more like a statement.

My eyes widen, then scrunch as I frown. 'No. No, of course I don't.'

A genuine smile breaks across Hex's face. 'Aw, you care about us already? How sweet.' His tone is mocking in its warmth.

'*Us*? I asked if Lorcan and Dato would be okay, not you,' I point out with a scoff, wanting to knock him down a peg or two.

Hex breathes a laugh, then does something I would never have expected: he leans down to kiss the tip of my nose. 'Precious.' His irises flare a little redder than usual before his image swiftly fades into the air around us.

We must be moving at an incredible speed because I'm suddenly weightless, and it feels as though my insides were all left behind where we stood a split second ago.

Thankfully, my eyes shut of their own accord, but I can tell when we come to a stop because my stomach snaps back into place, and I lurch out of Hex's arms to vomit last night's moonshine all over the grey grass, the crisper air doing nothing to help curb my motion sickness.

'Sorry, I forgot mortals have weak stomachs,' Hex says, passing me a hand-kerchief.

My throat is on fire as I wipe my mouth with the cotton square. When I notice it's bloodstained, I cringe. 'Is this what you use after you feed off people?'

'Yes. But I'm a very clean eater,' he replies defensively. 'That's all *your* blood, by the way. I wash it after every walking meal.'

I push myself to stand and round on him, my heart crumpling at his careless words. 'Is that how you see me? Am I just food to you?'

There's that look again—the bewildered curiosity. Hex steps closer, his head tilting. 'How do you *want* me to see you?' He takes the handkerchief from me to dab at the beads of sweat on my forehead before he pockets it. 'Because I care to know.'

His response throws me off. So, avoiding his surprisingly empathetic gaze, I retreat. 'Are we safe now?' I ask, changing the subject.

Surveying our surroundings, Hex says, 'No one is safe inside the maze. A great number of creatures will be able to sniff you out, especially now the contents of your stomach have been sprayed all over the ground.'

My face warms at the reminder. I need to freshen up. My plans rely on me being attractive enough to tempt three apathetic demons over to my side by any means necessary. I can't do that smelling like a sickly mole rat.

'I guess we should keep moving, then,' I bite out. And, before Hex can reply, I spin on my heel to stalk off.

Of course, my vexing vampire trails closely behind. And I'm ashamed to admit his company brings me tremendous comfort. The notion is so ridiculous—feeling safe with a bloodsucking demon.

Wait... when did Hex become *my* vampire?

It's not long before a niggling worry for Dato and Lorcan creeps up on me. If Hergal's rage makes him grow into a huge monster, could he have hurt them?

I glance over my shoulder at Hex as we take another turn through this woodier section of the maze; the trees are lined up on each side to structure the wild, winding paths.

So far, he's allowed me to dictate direction. Maybe he knows I'm going the wrong way, so my perceived freedom of choice here doesn't matter much. Or perhaps he's fairer than the other two, now we're alone.

Am I growing on Hex? Does he like me enough to help me on my quest to the heart of the maze? Will he betray his king for me? He's already close to dismissing the Demon King's order not to fuck me. If we'd had the chance to continue what we started in Hergal's bedroom, I'm pretty sure it wouldn't have ended at that blowjob. He said that if I wanted his dick, he would give it to me.

When I was drunk on his arousing venom after the first bite, I asked him to fuck me, and he found it hard to deny me even then, after only ten minutes of knowing me.

Would he deny me now if I were brave enough to ask again?

You'd think I'd be used to rejection by now; I grew up being resented. Then, when I started talking about university, Mum pushed me to apply to places hours away so I couldn't possibly continue living at home. Not that I had wanted to stay. But knowing she'd rather me long gone made the decision easier. It's probably one of the reasons I rarely came back to visit. Deep down, I knew Mum and Robin didn't want me. They seemed happier without me around. After that, there was Albie, who made a point to reject my advances, sexual or otherwise, and took pleasure in shaming me for craving affection.

I'm not sure I can handle embarrassing myself again. Even though my goal has been to use my sexuality to butter these demons up, manipulation and seduction are foreign concepts to me. I've never had to be so bold before. And surprisingly, I don't hate myself for it. In my defence, my body is the only thing I can offer them. It's the only thing I imagine they'd want from me, apart from my soul.

You can't offer them more than sex, anyway, Raven. They're a means to an end, I remind myself, tearing my eyes away from Hex to look ahead. *You don't actually like any of them. And you shouldn't like yourself around them.*

It's not only my soul I have to protect.

I need to shield my heart, too.

Chapter 21

A Thunder of Mud

Dato

'Hergal, can't we talk about this in a civilised manner?' I shout down at the twelve-foot, one-tonne, wrathful cyclops as I swoop over his head, leading his heavy, wooden club away from Lorcan on the ground.

Lorcan is in his lycanthrope form, at his most powerful. The bottom half of his body is still relatively normal—his legs only a fraction longer and hairier. Although his joggers conceal much of it. Thank the Shadows for that. I've seen his wolf cock on more than one occasion, and I'd rather not rouse my inferiority complex right now.

The muddy ground has been churned up by Lorcan's larger clawed feet. Not exactly paws, but close. His top half has been transformed from his hips to his crown. He's always been built like a fucking brick house, more muscular than me, Hex, and Julius, combined. However, in *this* form, he's a beast. Cords of pure muscle stack on top of each other and are coated in a velvety blanket of dark russet-brown fur; his tattoos are barely visible beneath.

Lifting his elongated snout to the sky, Lorcan's fierce gold eyes find me. His head is pure wolf, from the leathery black nose and sharp canines to the pointed ears which twitch at any slight sound.

Hex has his super speed, I have my sharp sight, and Lorcan has his heightened hearing and smell. Together, we're a deadly team. That's why I'm not too worried about Hergal, even if Hex isn't here to help. Lorcan and I can handle a one-eyed, giant baby throwing a tantrum any day of the week.

Red-faced, Hergal bellows his rage, swiping at me with the club. I dodge his attack, but my right wing senses the swoosh of air trailing the blow.

'I will smash you! No one steals from me,' Hergal grunts, his empty hand reaching up, hoping to catch me. He misses, but only by a feather.

'We didn't steal anything, you big buffoon! We needed shelter for a couple of hours, that's all,' I throw back, omitting the fact that not only is his favourite T-shirt ripped to shreds, thanks to a lust-clouded Hex, but also his moonshine supply has dwindled to a few drops. Again, mostly thanks to Hex.

'You broke spell, then broke door,' the cyclops reminds me, his booming voice rattling my eardrums.

Another forceful swing of his club hits empty air.

'I already apologised—twice. What more do you want?'

'Fix what broken,' Hergal demands. And with an earth-shattering thump, he brings the club down to the ground, mud flying nearly as high as I am. By the looks of it, the tremors rocket up Lorcan's usually sturdy body. He very nearly loses his balance.

Spotting the opportunity, Hergal lifts his giant barefoot, preparing to squash Lorcan. Thankfully, Lorcan is too swift for him. He dives out of the way before Hergal stomps, and then he whirls to sink his teeth into the flash of the cyclops' massive calf—almost twice the size of a tree trunk.

Hergal yowls in pain, shaking his leg to throw Lorcan off. Holding firm, Lorcan uses his long claws to shred into Hergal's rough, pinkish skin, his grey, fraying shorts cutting off at the knee. Cyclopes have thick skin, so even Lorcan's sharp claws don't draw that much blood.

Hergal reaches down and tries to pry Lorcan off his leg. 'No bite! Let go!'

'Put down the club and leave us be,' I counter, dropping to loop my legs around Hergal's head. The cyclops has no hair to cling to, so my hands slip as they try to grasp a firm hold of his bald head. 'When we've completed our mission, I'll ask Julius to send someone to fix whatever you want.'

Shaking his head vigorously, attempting to dislodge me, Hergal says, 'No. Now. Fix Now!'

I use my wings to bash his face from both sides, and he groans, lifting his club, ready to bat me off.

'We don't have time, you fuckwit! We have more important things to do,' I tell him through gritted teeth, ducking when the club comes around his head. If he's not careful, he's going to knock himself out.

Actually, that's not a bad idea, I think, shifting my weight so I'm straddling his left shoulder. I use my right wing to obscure his vision. And, when he swings up with the club again, I backflip off him at the last second, dragging his head to the side with me, right in the line of his strike. The club connects with his forehead. It sends him sprawling back.

When I land on my feet, I jump out of the way as Hergal comes crashing to the ground. The earth quakes beneath him. There's mud everywhere. Even my wings are thick with the blackish sludge, dulling my usually shiny plumage.

Lorcan springs on Hergal's chest, and his claws poke into the cyclops' throat to keep him pinned.

'Stay down, cloppy,' Lorcan warns, brave enough to continue the goading which got us into this mess in the first place.

We were supposed to distract Hergal. I thought Lorcan knew to start with a polite conversation. Instead, he opened with the line, '*Hey, Hergie, have you put on weight since the last time I saw you*?' I swear Lorcan is always on the hunt for a fight. Maybe I should have left *him* with the mortal. Though Raven seems more comfortable with Hex out of the three of us.

Plus, I expect Lorcan is still a little pissed about missing out on the morning activities they indulged in while he and I were on patrol. If I left the wolf alone with her, he'd try to even the score with Hex. The competitive arse. Am I the only one who doesn't let my dick dictate my every action?

Wiping the mud off my face with my sleeve, I stride up to Hergal, who's busy moaning in pain, his huge, chunky hand rubbing his forehead. 'Right. Are we done here? Will you let us carry on with our mission in peace?'

'I smelled mortal. I want taste,' Hergal comes out with.

Oh, that's why he won't give in; he caught a whiff of Raven and got excited. His interest in her isn't sexual. He doesn't want to taste her pussy; he wants to take a bite out of her in the literal sense. Cyclopes love the taste of human flesh.

'Sorry. This one is off-limits. No eating. King's orders,' I make clear to him.

Mud-caked, my wings fan out, and my tail swipes the backs of them to fling most of the muck off.

Hergal roars, not liking my answer. 'I will hunt mortal!'

'No. No, you won't,' I say mildly.

'I will,' the cyclops persists, a defiant growl in his throat.

Lorcan growls back, his claws digging into Hergal's neck. The cyclops stiffens, his one brown, oval eye moving to the wolf on his chest. 'If you even lay your greedy little eye on our songbird, I'll cut it out and feed it to you. Do you hear me?'

Hergal's face turns purple, his fresh wave of anger having nowhere to go now he's at his fullest size.

The ground quakes anew, and Hergal smiles, knowing his luck is about to change. Lorcan and I share a fleeting look that conveys '*oh, shit*' without having to speak the words out loud.

I check my left, just in time to see a rock bigger than my head hurtling straight for me. Reflexes still sharp, I manage to duck, but it clips my wing, and I wince as I roll to the ground. More mud clings to my feathers, weighing them down.

When a rock comes for Lorcan, he dives off Hergal and lands in a more graceful crouch beside me.

Bounding out of the trees comes two of Hergal's cyclops companions: Durk and Munty. They're already growing in size. Seeing their buddy lying in the mud must have set them off.

For the love of souls, one pissed-off cyclops is hard enough to deal with. But three... I don't like those odds. Especially as Hex isn't here. Lorcan and I are also running low on energy. Only the mortal got any sleep last night.

'Dato, what do you want to do? Shall we try our luck with them?' Lorcan asks, more optimistic than I am.

I use him to pull myself up to stand, my injured wing twitching. 'You think we can take on all three?'

'Sure, we've beaten worse odds,' he reminds me, flashing a wolfish grin—all sharp white teeth. Despite being used to seeing him this way, Lorcan's vicious lycanthrope form still unsettles me sometimes.

Hergal stirs, sitting up. He reaches for his club as his friends approach, revenge in their singular eyes. Unlike Hergal, both Durk and Munty have hair.

Durk's is a shoulder-length brown wave. Whereas Munty has short, mousey wisps. Yet their faces are as round and slab-like as his. It's as though their features were beaten out of a boulder.

Merely looking at the three full-sized cyclopes—their skin as tough as dried leather, their skulls as hard as stone—tires me. If we stay, this fight will get brutal and bloody. Lorcan and I will be lucky to come away with all our bones intact. Cyclopes have been known to pull off a harpy's wings in a brawl. It can take weeks to grow a full set of working wings back. I'd rather not risk the damage.

'Is the mortal worth this fuss?' I voice the question, guilt already nipping me for even thinking of abandoning the task Julius set us—thinking of abandoning *her*.

Lorcan throws me a scowl. 'You think I want to fight for *her*?' He laughs dryly. 'Come on, Dato. You know me better than that. I'd fight them for the thrill alone.'

Lorcan's not lying; he probably would. But I've noticed his golden eyes shining brighter since we met Raven. He can deny it, but deep down, there's also worry. He knows these brutes will hunt her down if we leave now, their stomachs growling for mortal flesh. Hex is strong but won't stand a chance against all three without us.

We back up as Durk and Munty help Hergal to his feet. I spread my injured wing to test its strength. 'Lorc, I can fly us out of here,' I wince out, the pain sharp yet bearable.

Lorcan snorts his displeasure. 'You know I don't like the skies. Wolves are built to feel the ground beneath their claws.'

'If we don't fly out of here now, we won't get the head start we need to catch up with Hex and Raven before these twats do,' I implore, dragging him towards a clearer, sturdier patch of ground, where I can better take off from.

'Fine,' Lorcan relents, his form shifting slowly back to his more human-like appearance—his fur receding into his skin, his snout shrinking. He moves to the front of me, then hesitates. 'Are you sure you're strong enough to take my weight? Your wings aren't looking their best, birdman.'

'I've flown in worse condition. Just come here,' I urge him, keeping my eyes on the three cyclopes as they turn to face us, their fists clenched around the handles of their clubs—ready for battle.

I'm weighted forward when Lorcan jumps into my arms, knees nearly buckling from the strain. 'Fucking mazes, have you eaten a whole Utahraptor today? I swear you weren't this heavy the last time we did this.'

'The last time we did this, I was practically a pup,' Lorcan snarls, circling an arm around my neck, the pressure tighter than necessary.

'We rip your wings off!' Hergal threatens, finally understanding that I'm about to take to the skies, where they can't follow.

The three cyclopes charge, their heavy footfalls a thunder of mud, the vibrations destabilising me.

I push off the ground before I topple over. My wings flap a storm, pain shooting through the injured one and down my spine. Growling, I use every ounce of strength to lift us into the air. There's nothing Lorcan can do to help me except stay still while I fight to get us airborne.

The cyclopes barrel towards us, but I'm high enough to soar over their heads. Their hands outstretch, eager to snatch us out of the sky. They don't succeed.

Sweat soaking my brow, I aim higher in case they think to throw more rocks our way. Lorcan clings on, his eyes closed. He hates heights. Hex loves me flying him around, though I don't often allow it. I can't remember the last time I took Lorcan on a flight with me. It probably *was* when we were a lot younger.

Lorcan is about a decade older than I am, bitten by his now-dead alpha around thirty years ago when he was a skinny fourteen-year-old. Technically, he's in his mid-forties, but his body is that of a thirty-year-old, at most. Same as Hex and me. However, unlike Hex, Lorcan and I both age. Albeit, we do so at a slower pace than mortals. As soon as Julius hits twenty-five, his body won't age, either.

'I hope you're concentrating on staying in the fucking sky, Dato,' Lorcan remarks, squinting at me, still afraid to open his eyes fully.

'I'm keeping my mind busy, so I don't think about the pain,' I reply honestly, my left wing aching and on the verge of seizing already.

'Are they following?' Lorcan enquires, his eyes pressing shut again.

I shoot a glance towards the ground, the paths of the maze shadowed lines from up here. However, my superior eyesight can catch details others can't.

Below, I spot a pack of Velociraptors ripping into the carcass of some smaller prey. Up ahead, the paths look clear, although the trees are thicker and fuller, which makes it harder to distinguish what lurks underneath the dusty clusters of leaves. Behind us, the three cyclopes have their heads tilted to the sky, taking turns in the maze to mimic our flight path.

'Fuck. They're hot on my tail,' I say, beating my wings harder and faster. Pain is a lash against my back, hot and slicing.

'Can't you fly faster?' Lorcan pushes, braving a glance downwards.

'I'm fucking trying!' I snap, my jaw clenched tight. 'Can you pick up the mortal's scent from up here?'

Lorcan's nose twitches as he sniffs the rushing streams of air. 'You're going in the right direction. It's getting stronger.'

'At least Hex is still on board with the plan to lead her away from the castle. They're still moving more east than north.'

Admittedly, a small part of me worried Hex might go rogue if left alone too long with the mortal. She's proved to be very cunning: using her charm and those fucking perfect tits to bamboozle us, especially Hex. My moment of folly last night—kissing her—touching what belongs to my king—won't be repeated. No matter how much I enjoyed having her riding me dry while she moaned my name.

And she kissed me. She kissed me like she wanted to.

'Dato, you're losing height!'

I snap out of my dazed state, unsure if pain or lust were the cause. 'Huh?'

Lorcan catches a glimpse of something over my shoulder. His eyes widen before he shouts, 'Look out!'

Unable to heed his warning in time, the projectile slams into my back, and we go careening out of the sky into the winding lines of canopy below.

CHAPTER 22

Hold On Tight

Hex

'What did you guys talk about when I was asleep?' Raven pries, glancing at me as we meander down another wrong turn in the maze.

The longer we walk without any sign of Dato and Lorcan, the more nervous energy buzzes through me, making my skin prickle with dread. I scan the dark grey blanket that is the afternoon sky, searching for a flash of midnight-blue wings.

Nothing.

Raven bumps my arm with hers. 'Did you conspire against me the whole time?'

'Yes,' I answer honestly. And when she pouts, I continue, 'We also went into very graphic detail about all the things we'd do to you if we were allowed to fuck you.'

With a gasp of faux outrage, she pinches me. 'The only person who can decide that is *me*, you know. Fuck the Demon King and his perceived claim on my soul. He doesn't own it yet. Anyway, even if he *did* win my soul, I never agreed to give him my body along with it. It will always be mine to fuck whomever I please, and it certainly won't be fucking him.' There's vehemence behind her words. And I'm sure she thinks she means it. Still, despite her protests, her heartbeat always skips whenever Julius is mentioned.

It's actually starting to grate on me. Jealousy is not an emotion I'm used to.

'Trust me, without debauchery, the Underworld can quickly become a very dull place. I'm sure you'll be begging the King to warm your bed after a decade of chastity,' I tell her solemnly. The idea of handing Raven over to Julius is becoming as unappealing to me as it is to her.

'I'll just fuck everybody *but* him,' she comes back with, her footfalls more pronounced beside me. Riling her is proving to be a fun way to dwindle her time.

'Says the girl who has only fucked one person in her entire life.'

Raven chucks me a glare. 'I'm only twenty-three.'

'Exactly. You're too young and inexperienced to be making such claims. Stop trying to be who you're not, darling.'

At the brief pause, I check over my shoulder to see she's stopped a few paces behind. I pivot back, the wounded look on her face making my smirk slip.

'Maybe I'm trying to be the person I've never been allowed to be. Have you thought of that?' Raven challenges, her grey eyes misting. 'My whole life, I've been stifled yet all the while neglected. Do you know what that's like? Strictly controlled but discarded at every opportunity by those who were supposed to love you?'

My stomach clenches around guilt. 'I do. And I'm sorry. I was only messing with you.'

Raven doesn't reply; she carries on walking, her head tipped to conceal the pain she flashed me.

'You know Julius would murder anyone you'd even *think* about fucking instead of him,' I say to ease the tension, casually putting an arm around her shoulders; the urge to comfort her is overwhelming.

'I'll have to make it a long list, then. The less demons around, the better,' she responds, her tone icy. 'You'll be at the top of it.'

I guess that means I'm not forgiven.

Unable to help myself, I laugh. 'I hope Julius never breaks that spirit of yours, darling.'

'He won't,' she promises. 'Nobody will.'

Both our heads snap up at a roar of thunder. No, not thunder; thunder isn't accompanied by a great quiver in the earth.

I whip around, my fangs automatically lengthening at the promise of a threat. 'Shit.'

'What was that?' Raven asks in a hushed voice, moving closer to me, seeking solace. Her hand slips into mine, and my stomach fucking flips. I'm going soft. Myth and mercy, I'm a bloody demon. Hand-holding is for sentimental mortals.

Despite my internalised rejection, my hand tightens around hers, unwilling to let go. The feel of her dainty, little hand in mine—so soft and smooth—is too good to deny myself.

'Dato and Lorcan should have found us by now,' I mention, studying the sky again while my thumb tenderly strokes the back of her hand.

The next rumble dislodges the dirt around the trunks of the trees on either side of us. My sensitive ears pick up the increased rhythm of Raven's heart. She's scared.

If I were her, I would be, too.

Hold on, my own heart is also beating more forcefully. Am I scared *for* her?

'Jump on my back. We need to move swiftly,' I instruct, bending forward, signalling for her to mount me.

Raven's eyes widen as her brow pinches. 'I—I can't handle your speed. I'll be sick on you.'

'You think I care about bodily fluids? For the love of souls, I live off blood.'

With an impatient huff, I grab her legs and force her onto my back. At first, she gasps but then wraps her slender arms around my neck to stabilise herself.

'Dig your nails in if you want me to stop,' I tell her, gripping under her knees. 'Now, hold on tight.'

CHAPTER 23

Recharge

JULIUS

The Harvest Hall is a place I only visit when I need to recharge my power. It can be an unnerving experience for those who have never been near a harvested soul. The room is unremarkable: its walls are dull black, its floor polished stone. It's the contents of the hall which elicit gasps from visitors.

After I disable the safety enchantments, unlock the seal, and open the heavy door for Robin, I guide him through by the shoulders, then lock us inside the elongated room.

The first podium catches Robin's eye immediately; the bright glow of the recently captured soul is hard to miss. I don't expect the kid to know what he's gaping at. The soul is contained inside a clear, spherical orb mounted on top of a harvesting stand of enchanted silver, as it's the most conductive metal. He's simply staring at a fancy light installation for all he knows.

'Is this where you keep all your souls? Or just the new ones,' Robin queries, surpassing all my earlier expectations. Perhaps this kid isn't as dense as he looks.

'They're newly harvested. They dim after a month or so; their energy wanes over time,' I explain, watching him step up to take a closer look. 'Don't touch the orb; you could get a shock. Only keeper demons can manipulate the energy of a soul. Other demons have no use for them, though they are collected and viewed as more of a status symbol in the Underworld. They can be traded as currency. Any soul, even an old one, would fetch a high price at market.'

His head swivels back to regard me. 'What do *you* use them for?'

'I can withdraw energy from them to enhance my powers. The fresher, the better.'

Concern flashes across Robin's face. 'Does it kill the soul? You sucking all its energy out?'

'No. A soul cannot die. It only fades. I transfer its *excess* energy. It takes a significant amount for a soul to pass through the Veil, and on its journey, it collects more. The energy I manipulate is mostly that of the Veil.'

'But you could drain a soul if you wanted?'

I shrug a shoulder. 'I could, although that would be unwise. If a soul is drained too quickly, it becomes useless after only a few transfers. Think of it as a rechargeable battery; if you use it too often without allowing time for a full charge, it will drain quicker each time. If you're patient and take good care of it, it maintains its charge more efficiently.'

'Our immortal souls are *batteries* to you?' His tone is desert dry.

Rolling my eyes, I move to the other side of the ornate silver stand opposite him. 'It was only an analogy. Don't be so sensitive.'

'If you're the only demon here who can transfer its energy, what do you need *me* for?' Robin asks, his eyes thinning with suspicion.

'You're my strongest connection to Raven; you share the same blood. And I will need a little of it to home in on her,' I answer, opening my palm out expectantly.

Eyeing my hand with scepticism, Robin responds with, 'You can't find her in your own maze without my blood? Not very powerful, are you?'

I should be insulted. I should threaten him for his lack of respect. Instead, my mouth curls up, his attitude reminding me of his sister more and more. 'I'm bound to my castle with powerful magic. At present, my powers are limited. Creating an invisible window is difficult enough at the best of times. Without your blood, we won't be able to see her.' I withdraw my hand. 'Have you changed your mind? Do you not care to see how your sister is faring on her quest to rescue you?'

My words settle on his shoulders like a heavy weight, and he exhales—deflating. He doesn't answer. He simply offers his hand, palm up. I flatten it out before I cut across its centre with my thumbnail, which I sharpened with magic. He winces, reflexes telling him to withdraw, but I keep a tight hold of his wrist.

'Ow, I thought you were only going to prick a finger,' Robin complains, watching as I tilt his hand over the orb, his blood dripping onto its surface.

'I imagine your sister is currently at the mercy of an insatiable vampire, and you're moaning about one little cut,' I mutter, unable to hide my resentment. I fail to mention that her pain is certainly offset by the immense pleasure Hex is pumping through her blood with every injection of venom. I'm sure, as a brother, he'd rather not hear of such things.

'Stand here,' I instruct, pointing to the space beside me. 'I might need more from you.'

When I release his hand, Robin does as I ask. He keeps his palm open, allowing a small trickle of blood to seep from the superficial wound. It pools between his fleshy pads, which he uses as a makeshift cup so not an ounce drips to the floor.

'Now, be quiet. I need to concentrate,' I say, inching closer to the orb.

'I wasn't even talking,' he mumbles, looking offended.

'Hush.'

Closing my eyes, I hover my hands over the contained soul. This close, the buzz of its energy is a constant hum. When my skin makes contact with the smooth surface, slick with Robin's blood, every muscle in my body contracts as power crackles through my veins like lightning. It's instantly revitalising.

I suck in a breath, needing it to clear my power-drunk mind to control the intoxicating influx of energy. Steadier, I condense it down to a flicker, transferring some back into the orb, allowing only a slow seep instead of a gush.

In my mind, I form the window and picture Raven through it. My power listens, sculpting it into reality. Robin gasps.

I open my eyes to find the window from my imagination floating in the air before us. It's cloudy: a bubble of time and space, not yet clear enough to see through. The magic of the eudaemon deal is working against my intrusion.

To push through, I extract more energy from the orb, using it to enhance the picture—demisting it. My skin glows. The bright light behind my eyes shines a torch on the hazy images inside the bubble-like window.

Robin looks between me and the window, his mouth hanging open in awe. 'Fucking hell, this is the coolest shit I've ever seen.'

'If Hell was real, you'd be damned for that foul use of language,' I comment, still working to clear the image. And to my surprise, the kid snickers.

Both distracted, what's now clearly presented to us doesn't register for an extended beat.

But, when it does, I lose all sense of control.

Chapter 24

The Well of Eternal Winter

RAVEN

As soon as my nails bite into Hex's shoulders, he stops. He drops my legs, and I dive to the ground to throw up for the second time today. With my stomach already emptied, only bile spews.

Chivalrously holding my hair back for me as I wretch, Hex says, 'We're not far from the Well of Eternal Winter. There, you can wash your mouth out and rehydrate.'

'I can't take another minute at that speed. I can't even think straight anymore. Everything is in slow motion,' I complain, the ground whirling beneath my splayed hands.

'All right, I'll slow down. I promise.'

Before I can argue, Hex scoops me up in his arms and takes off running again. This time, though, he's moving at a mortal speed. Still, the jiggling motion of his hurried steps continues to rattle the contents of my stomach. Well, what's left of it. If I'm sick again, I wouldn't be surprised if I coughed up part of my small intestine.

About ten minutes later, we arrive at a large stone well in the middle of our path. Around it sits a thin layer of ice, and above it hangs a low white cloud which rains down fluffy snowflakes. It's as if this well has its own atmosphere, unaffected by its environment.

'The Well of Eternal Winter; most freeze from the inside out as soon as the water touches their tongue,' Hex informs, setting me beside it on a small seat carved from the same stone. It's fucking cold; the frost is creeping through my leggings.

I cut him with a look. 'And you expect *me* to drink it? I thought you didn't want me dead?'

Chuckling, Hex pulls out an orb from his pocket. It appears to be the same one from Hergal's hearth. 'It's enchanted. All I have to do is break it. I've drunk from this well countless times. You'll be fine.'

'Can you test it before I drink?' I request, still cautious.

With an expression of lingering mirth, Hex nods, then pulls on the rope until the bucket is at the top. 'Personally, I don't hold much magic. I can only perform a couple of minor spells. One of those spells happens to be a refreshing charm.' He places the bucket of water down at his feet.

'What does that do?'

Holding the glowing orb in both hands over the bucket, Hex murmurs words in that demonic language I can't understand. When he's finished, and the orb light dims, he looks back up at me. 'It makes water all-cleansing. So, if you drink even a sip, it will rehydrate you, but it also refreshes your breath and washes away any toxins your body may be holding on to.'

He passes me a tiny cup made of ice that was resting on the well's lip. This well was designed to lure poor, unsuspecting victims in to quench their thirst, not knowing a single drop could freeze them solid.

'I thought you were going to test it first,' I remind him, not even daring to fill the cup. 'I don't want to be anywhere near that bucket until I know it's safe.'

Smiling as though my distrust of him is the cutest thing, Hex bends and plunges his hand into the bucket of water. Some of it splashes out, and I lurch back. He brings water, cupped in his palm, to his lips to sip.

'As I said… refreshing.' He winks at me. It's a challenge; he wants to see if I trust him enough to take him at his word.

After a moment's hesitation, I sigh. 'If I became a statue of ice, would you still think I'm hot?' I ask jokingly, dropping the cup to the water's surface. There are tiny crystalline icicles at the bottom of the bucket. That doesn't bring peace to my mind.

'Of course. You would be the hottest piece of ice that ever existed,' Hex answers, his tone feigning seriousness.

I dip the cup under, making sure not to let any droplets touch my skin.

'Afraid to get your fingers wet, darling? I promise you, there's no greater joy in life.' His comment is an obvious innuendo, so I pin him with a sharpened glare, and he snickers.

Slowly, I lift the cup to my lips, my gaze flitting back up to check Hex's expression. He's still finding my caution extremely amusing.

'Fuck it,' I say before I chuck the cup's contents back. The water is a chilling winter breeze as it rushes down my throat. When I open my mouth again, a cloud of iced breath hits the warmer air. 'Wow. That *is* refreshing.'

The cup's kiss has made my fingers and lips numb. I set it back down on the well.

'As I said.' Hex's hands settle on his narrow hips. 'You'll learn to trust me eventually.'

Thirst now quenched and breath smelling of winter mint, I stand, reinvigorated. 'What now?'

Hex smirks, the type that makes me feel a little uneasy in its wickedness. 'Now... *Now*, you strip.'

Clutching my non-existent pearls, I exclaim, 'What?!'

Hex's eyes become black pools of sin again. 'Take. Off. Your. Clothes. You should be used to being naked by now.'

'Why?' I demand, stepping back from him, the memory of Lorcan forcibly stripping me last night resurfacing. However, instead of making my skin crawl, it does the opposite; an electric current charges through my blood, bringing heat to the surface.

Hex must notice the change because his smile widens. 'Because you reek of Hergal, and that rotten scent will lead him straight here. We need to wash his stench off you before he finds us.'

'Oh,' is all I say. I wasn't actually expecting him to have a valid reason.

Chin tilted down—all predator—Hex stalks closer until he's standing less than a metre from me. 'We don't have time to indulge your modesty. You need to strip naked so I can wash you.'

I raise an eyebrow. 'And why exactly can't I wash myself?'

Flashing me his lengthening fangs, Hex replies, 'Because I said so.'

A shiver of want has me exhaling a shaky breath. 'If you bite me, we both know we'll waste more time here than necessary.'

'*Waste*?' he repeats the word, looking insulted. 'Nothing I do is a waste of time. I'm very, *very* precise, especially when it comes to what my mouth can do to you.'

He lifts my chin, staring down into my eyes. My stomach flips at the blatant desire I find sizzling in his fire-flecked, onyx gaze.

Hex leans in, and just when I think he's about to sink his teeth into me, his fangs retract a second before he kisses me. He innocuously slips my jacket off while his mouth moves on mine. It's not a vicious clash of tongues like ours this morning; it's soft, sweet, and brief.

Even so, we're both breathless by the time he withdraws. Without another word, he pulls my top over my head, exposing my torso to the icy air.

I cover my breasts with my hands and quip, 'Can we at least do this away from the mini slice of winter?' I point to the snow cloud above us, the tiny flakes soaking into our hair as soon as they land.

'We can't take the bucket too far from the well,' Hex says, tugging my leggings down to my ankles.

Flushing with a mixture of embarrassment and lust, I cross my legs, trying to hide my vagina from view.

Hex reaches around to slap my arse, making me yelp. 'I told you: I won't indulge your modesty.' He rips my hands away from my breasts. 'It's not like I haven't seen it all before. You forget so easily that I was nibbling on this nipple less than two hours ago,' he remarks, twisting said nipple.

With a wincing giggle, I bat his grabby hands away. 'Stop playing around! You said we don't have time. Just tip the bucket over my head already.'

To draw me flush against him, Hex loops an arm around my naked waist. He's already as hard as stone. 'I don't hear any thunder, do you?' He starts nuzzling my neck, fangs scraping my skin without sinking in.

'Come on. I'm cold,' I moan, in both senses of the word. My hands lift to his chest, intending to force him away, but instead, I grasp at the fabric of his white shirt.

'Myth and mercy, you have no idea how badly I want to bite you right now,' Hex murmurs into my skin while he gropes my arse. 'How desperate I am to slide my cock deep inside you while I feast on your blood.'

His admission of need only increases my own. The fact that he's fully dressed while I'm vulnerable and naked also adds fuel to the fire sparking in my lower belly.

'Are you going to wash me or not?'

He presses a smile into my neck. 'If I had the time, I'd wash every inch of you by hand... twice.' He steps back, reaching down for the bucket.

The mischievous glint in Hex's gaze lets me know what's coming. I squeeze my eyes shut and brace myself.

A beat later, I'm hit with a torrent of liquid ice, and I can't help my high-pitched shriek.

Freezing, though thankfully not frozen solid, I hop from foot to foot, wrapping my arms around myself as shivers wrack my now magically cleansed body. 'You bastard!'

Hex laughs at me, clearly pleased with himself. But when my teeth start to chatter, he's quick to lean me against his body for warmth. 'I've got you,' he promises, pulling the shirt from his back.

With surprising tenderness, Hex uses his shirt to dry me while maintaining eye contact. This moment feels more intimate than it should. Intimacy is not something I'm used to. Yet it's something I've always craved.

I swallow, my *lack* of unease disconcerting yet empowering. 'I want you, Hex. I want you to fuck me.' The words come out hushed but unbidden.

He should know as well as I do that I have no excuse to fall back on this time. His venom has been cleansed from my system entirely; his charmed water saw to that. This is all me: overcome by my desire to be completely his, if only for a short time.

Hex's eyes widen for a fraction of a second before they fall, heavy-lidded to my lips.

His mouth crashes against mine like a breaking wave, brutal in the face of its undoing.

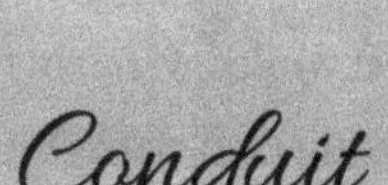

CHAPTER 25

Conduit

ROBIN

Luckily, Raven is pressed so closely against the guy she's kissing in the bubble that I don't glimpse any parts of her a brother should *never* see.

Gagging, I cover my eyes. 'What the fuck?! Why would you show me this?'

When Julius doesn't respond, I swivel to face him.

A moment ago, he was exuding light. Now, that light has fallen captive to shadows. His usually silver eyes have delved to the deepest black, the whites eaten up by the starless night. In addition, his expression might as well be cut from stone—hard and sharp.

Murderous.

From the looks of things, this real-time clip we're viewing of my sister and this guy—whom I can only assume Julius knows—is not what he was expecting to see, either.

A flicker of fear has me swallowing hard. I have no idea what this demon is capable of if wronged. He wants my sister to be his queen, and he's now watching her make out with someone else. Naked.

Urgh, gross. But it didn't look like she was in any danger. It seemed consensual. I can't be sure, though. It's a little out of character for her, but maybe she's changed since she left home.

From the little I know of her personal life, she's only ever had one boyfriend. So, finding out she's practically on the verge of shagging some random bloke she's only just met in the middle of a dangerous Underworld maze is kind of shocking.

My heart crawls up my throat while I watch in frozen terror as Julius' shadows surge. I'm not going to check what's happening through the window; I don't want to be scarred for life. Anyway, I can tell from the harsh lines on Julius' face that it's... *progressing*.

'Hex is *dead*. He's fucking dead,' Julius growls, so low I almost don't hear him over the crackle of his power.

'Close the window. We're intruding on something we shouldn't,' I manage to get out, my voice mousey.

'I will rip his fucking heart from his chest!' Julius roars, shadows rolling off him in waves. His palpable fury makes me blanch, and when I try to creep away, he catches me by the elbow to yank me back. 'Where do you think you're going?'

His shadows engulf us both, and I choke on them—their fumes burning my lungs.

'Let me go!' I shout, struggling against his hold.

'I need more from you,' Julius grits out, snatching my bloodied hand and slapping it down on the orb under his.

Sparks fly, and a painful tremor races up my arm. A scream explodes from my throat, set off by the war raging inside my chest.

His grip crushing, Julius declares, 'Your sister also needs to be punished.'

The storm of shadows whirls around us in a loop of pure chaos while Julius uses me and my blood as a conduit to steal more energy, wielding that power for something I can't decipher. The window is long gone, yet the absence of it hasn't calmed him.

Time is an endless wave of pain, crashing into me without a break.

Weakened, my knees buckle, but Julius keeps me on my feet.

A terrifying thought sinks its claws into my brain.

He won't stop.

My death will be her punishment.

CHAPTER 26

Ruined

RAVEN

Hex's fingers knot in my hair as his tongue slides against mine. His other hand still massages my arse, grinding my centre against the hardened space between his hips.

Lips puffy, Hex leans away, his dark eyes scanning my face. 'You've ruined me, deal-breaker. One-hundred and fifty-three years, I've lasted. I've survived a war, being turned, losing my soul, fighting demons, and yet here I am, dying to fuck one mortal girl after only twelve hours of knowing her,' he muses, laughing at himself. 'I wish we had more time. The things I'd do to you.'

His hand slides around my hip, then slips between my legs. I tip my head back and moan, his skilful fingers teasing my clit to heady heights.

'This time, I won't bite you. I want to show you that I can put the work in.' His teasing touch becomes a taunt, his fingers looping tight circles around that sensitive spot at inhuman speed, practically vibrating. 'A bit of manual labour can be character building.'

Building quickly in a different way, I writhe against him. My teeth clench as I fight a cry.

'Don't fight it. I need you to come before Hergal does,' Hex jokes, pressing harder and impossibly faster.

My release is almost painful. I thrash, my body unable to hold this wild pleasure inside me.

Hex slows his torture, his mouth at my neck, but he keeps to his word and doesn't bite. However, his body is vibrating with the need to. It must take a lot of willpower not to succumb to his bloodlust in circumstances like this, especially as his hunger seems tied to his sexual appetite. That's been the case with us, anyway. It might be different with others he's fed from.

Maybe I *have* ruined him.

'I apologise in advance; this will only take a minute,' he warns, sweeping my legs out from under me and guiding my back down so I'm lying flat beneath him. 'I promise, under different circumstances, I can last all night long.'

The ground is cold, but at least he's not laid me on the sheet of ice, only metres away. 'If you can't last, just be honest about it,' I say, goading him into a verbal sparring match.

Quiet sex is boring. That's how it used to be with Albie. It was always awkward because he never responded when I attempted to vocalise my arousal or talk dirty. Often, the only sound was the neighbour's muffled dialogue from the flat upstairs.

With a spark of mischief lighting his eyes, Hex moulds his hand around my throat as he undoes the laces of his trousers. 'Pushing a demon's buttons when he has you caged naked beneath him is not something most would dare do.'

'Maybe I prefer this cage compared to others.' I take his face in my hands, drawing him down to kiss at will. I'm addicted to the sweet taste of him.

Groaning, Hex opens my legs wider, slotting himself between them. After more fumbling with his trousers, his smooth cock slides up my centre, coating itself in my arousal.

My heart is the roar of thunder that's missing in the earth from Hergal's pursuit. We have time for this. I don't think it would matter if we didn't. I can't imagine stopping; my desire to be filled is too great.

I spoke too soon.

Fate tempted, the ground starts shaking, and we both go rigid, staring wide-eyed at each other. A violent jolt unbalances the earth around us, and Hex's supporting arm gives out. His weight comes crashing down on me as the Underworld spins on its axis.

Darkness falls heavy, and suddenly Hex rolls off me, clawing at his head, his eyes screwing shut. He's crying out as if in pain.

I reach for Hex, repeatedly calling his name, truly afraid for him.

Dark clouds swirl overhead. Lightning streaks across the sky with a loud, terrifying clap. The clouds morph into shadows, which swoop down to the ground, their curling tendrils like haunting spectres in the night, creeping towards us.

This can't be Hergal. This is something worse.

This is terrible, malicious magic.

CHAPTER 27

The Devil

'Julius, stop! *Please*,' I beg, the orb scalding my palm. Its light is flickering just as precariously as my heart; it's on the cusp of giving out completely. The Demon King ignores me, one arm still holding up my weight.

For a second, consciousness slips away, the respite from pain welcome.

'I don't want to die.' The desperately hopeless words get stuck in my throat, but I think Julius must catch them regardless because he's suddenly hauling me away from the orb.

The Shadows cease their furious storm, sinking to the ground as I do. They disappear through the cracks in the stone. The pain recedes, too, leaving a hollow ache in my temples and chest. My palm throbs, the skin a deep pink from the burn.

Julius drops me to the ground. It's only a short distance, but I still grunt at the bump to my hip.

While I catch my breath, Julius returns to the silver stand. The fresh soul, which was luminous and bright only a few minutes ago, is now barely a dull glow. He—*we*—drained it. He drained *me*.

'You nearly killed me,' I throw at Julius, holding my wounded hand close to my chest as though I can protect it from any more abuse.

'You're alive, aren't you?' he retorts, his expression now blank.

Still panting, I prop myself up using my elbows. 'What did you do?'

'Nothing that wasn't deserved,' he answers vaguely, running his hands over the orb. It shines a little brighter. It's clear he's trying to restore some of the energy he stole before it's too late.

'Did you hurt my sister?' I demand. If I'm not dead, what punishment did he seek for her?

'I haven't hurt her. Not physically, at least.' Julius' tone is still dangerously low. The whites have returned to his eyes, the silver of his irises thin but present.

'She doesn't belong to you. Neither of us do. Just let us go home,' I try, tears I didn't notice forming start running freely down my cheeks.

Rage boiling back over, Julius' razor-sharp gaze cuts to me. 'I don't give a fuck if she does or doesn't. The point is she *will*. Whether she wants to or not is no longer my concern. She can never escape me again.'

'What if she completes the maze? You have to keep to your end of the bargain,' I remind him, but my stomach roils, apprehension snaking its way through.

'She won't complete the maze,' he says with certainty. 'I've now made sure of it.'

My heart drops to the pit of hopelessness forming inside me. 'You fucking arsehole. What did you do?!'

'You'll find out soon enough.' Julius uses his power to open the heavy door to the hall. 'Now, get the fuck out of my sight.'

'I can't walk, you dick. I'm too weak.'

Julius doesn't bother sparing me a glance when he replies, 'Then crawl.' He continues tending to the flickering soul, wiping my blood off the glass with his sleeve.

With great difficulty, I drag myself to my feet, using the wall for support. I stagger over to the open door, then turn back, anger and disgust swelling my chest.

'You're the Devil,' I spit out at him.

That gets the Demon King's attention. He lifts his chin, glowering through his dark lashes. He's truly menacing. I don't know why I thought I could ever befriend him. The guy isn't just evil, he's unhinged—delusional.

In a low voice, Julius says, 'No. I'm not the Devil. But if he *were* real,' —A shadow passes over his eyes— 'I'd be his worst nightmare.'

With those parting words, he flicks his wrist, and the door slams in my face, sending me reeling back.

My arse hits the floor, and everything goes black.

CHAPTER 28

Fast Forward

HEX

I must have passed out from the pain because a few light slaps across my cheek rouses me awake.

'Hex, please. Wake up!' Raven's voice is a shaky rasp, emotion a destabiliser. When my eyelids flutter open, she sighs in relief.

'Thank fuck. I thought your brain had been melted,' she tells me, wiping her face, eyes red and puffy.

Has she been crying over me?

My head throbs as Raven helps me up to a sitting position. 'How long was I out for?'

'Only a couple of minutes. What the fuck happened?' Raven demands, resting her arse on her heels.

Her clothes are back on, hiding her delectable body once again. Curse the Shadows. Do I believe Julius decided to have a meltdown right as I was about to fuck his pre-claimed mortal by chance? No. It couldn't have been a coincidence. Which means, somehow, he *knows*. He knows I was about to disobey his order.

Perhaps the interference was needed. I lost my head for a minute there, which will likely result in me losing my heart in more ways than one.

Fucking this mortal is probably the most self-destructing thing I could think to do, and undoubtedly the hardest impulse to deny. Never in my extended lifetime have I craved sinking my cock into something more so than my fangs. Feeding is usually my primary focus—the activity which supersedes all else. But with Raven, lust is overtaking blood.

Is my darling deal-breaker worth the risk to my immortal life?

Before this incident, I thought I'd get away with it. But now, even if I don't end up fucking her, I'm still fucked regardless. Unless I can convince Julius that I'm still loyal to him. For that to work, I'd have to screw Raven over in the less pleasurable sense.

'Hex?' Raven prompts, losing her patience.

I blink at her, my mind still in disarray from the dark magic display. 'That was Julius calling on the Shadows to fast forward time.'

Her mouth parts, forehead scrunching in confusion. 'Fast forward time? What does that mean?'

Arching an eyebrow, I say dryly, 'You need me to translate the English language for you?'

She shakes her head in denial, the ramifications too much for her to accept. 'No, no, no. That's not possible. Time can't be controlled, right?'

'Controlled, no. Manipulated... Time is relative, my dear. And in the Underworld, it can be harnessed with enough power. Though it doesn't come without consequence.'

I dust myself off and stand, then pull my shirt back on. Raven swiftly follows me up. Feeling around my crotch, I realise the laces of my trousers are already tied. She must have graciously tucked my cock inside and done them up for me when I was unconscious. What a fucking angel.

Comfortable enough, I continue, 'That's why I'm still alive; Julius likely ran out of power. He could very well be dead. The Shadows usually take more than they give.'

Raven appears stricken, and I'm unsure if it's due to her predicament or the possibility of Julius' death. Surely, she'd be happy to know he's gone—the threat vanquished—her and her brother's soul won by default.

'Do you know how much time I've lost?' she asks, her eyes wide and sparkling.

Swiping dust from her chin with my thumb, I answer, 'I'm sorry, darling. I can't be sure. Though it looks to be over a day.'

Raven crumples at that, but I catch her before she hits the ground. A sob stutters out of her mouth, and she buries her face into my chest, gripping my shirt like it's her anchor—like *I'm* her anchor.

An unfamiliar sensation grips my heart just as desperately—guilt. And something else I can't quite put my finger on. It's not pleasant. It's fucking uncomfortable. But also... oddly warming.

'I thought he would play fair. I thought I stood a chance. That fucking cheating arsehole!' Raven cries, frustration seeping through her shock and dismay.

'We demons never play fair.' I peer down and lift her chin. Her bleary eyes take a second to focus on me. 'Especially when the prize is this precious. I can't say I wouldn't also be tempted to move time and space for you.'

Raven's tear-stained face smooths a little, yet her hopeless anguish is still plain to see. 'I could have less than a day to save my brother.'

It unsettles me how my heart clenches as though I, in some way, care. I don't know her brother; his life and his soul are of little importance to me. Raven, however, is quickly becoming a life I not only want to protect for my king but a soul I may decide to deny him.

At the end of the day, will it be a choice at all?

If this mortal keeps treating me like I'm her only hope—her light in the shadows—then the selfish part of me could do something selfless for her.

If I defy Julius by helping Raven complete the maze, I may not escape his wrath and end up heartless. On the other hand, if I let Julius claim her soul for his own, my heart might break, anyway. The only thing I could gain from helping her would be her heart in return. But there's a flaw in that: even if she *does* fall for me, she'd still leave the Underworld. I've got over fifty years of service left to the DiMinos line, and it's not as if I could cross the Veil without great power. This situation is a lose-lose for me.

Not helping, I lose her. Helping, I lose her.

The only sensible option is the one where I keep my heart in my chest. I'll have to live with the cracks this mortal is causing.

Raven's breathing calms, her cries reducing to heavy sighs. 'I don't know what I would do without you here, Hex.' She cups my cheek. 'Thank you for keeping me on my feet. For keeping me steady.' Her voice is barely there—a whisper of vulnerability.

Fucking mazes, forget cracking; by the time she's done with me, Julius will have to pluck out pieces of my heart using a microscope.

It takes all of my remaining strength not to kiss her. I can't risk it now I know Julius could be watching.

The ground grumbles beneath us, and our expressions tighten again. A roar in the distance has the nearby Velociraptors chirping anxiously.

'We need to move. Hergal's caught up, and by the sounds of it, he's not in the best mood.' Grabbing her hand, I drag her into a run. I don't have the energy to use my super speed; Julius zapped all my power when he targeted me.

In hindsight, I shouldn't have wasted time comforting her. Instead, I should have bitten her to regain some strength. I'm too weak to protect her to the best of my abilities.

Let's hope I won't need to.

CHAPTER 29

Sanctuary

RAVEN

My wrist is raw from Hex's tugging when we find the next fork in the maze. This section is less dense, the outlining trees thicker yet sparse. It's hardly a maze at all. It makes the direction all the more ambiguous.

The whole time we've been racing away from the sinister, earth-shattering steps of the cyclops, I've been panicking internally. Not only because I'm being hunted yet again, but because I could only be a few hours away from failing this quest. Robin's soul, as well as my own, are on the cusp of being as far out of reach as this fucking Underworld castle.

Still, despite hating Juli—the Demon King for everything he's put me through, when Hex floated the idea that the Shadows could have taken his life as payment, it affected me in a way I wasn't expecting. I should be wishing him dead. Instead, my heart fucking *sank*. The thought of that bastard's light being snuffed out makes me feel physically sick. It's a reaction I cannot control for some inexplicable reason.

My body and my mind are opposing forces when it comes to the Demon King. It's as if something rooted deep inside me has latched onto the very idea of him. Perhaps it's the bond he talked about; our souls must recognise each other in some twisted way. Whereas the logical part of me hopes I can disregard everything I'm feeling towards a demon I barely know, (consciously, at least) and pray that he's dead.

Another gravelly roar tells us our pursuer is closing in. Hex is still too weak to carry me at super speed, so we've lagged. My lacklustre thighs cannot keep up with a vampire's inhuman pace.

Only a moment later, I trip on the root of a tree. Hex isn't fast enough to catch me on this occasion before I come crashing down to the hard ground. I nearly cause him to fall back on top of me.

'Shit.' Hex bends to haul me up. 'Are you all right?'

Pushing myself to walk, pain shoots up my left leg, and I swallow a yelp. 'I can't run like this. I can barely walk.' I'm on the verge of tears again, hopelessness creeping back in to clog my throat and burn my eyes.

Without having to ask, Hex scoops me up and runs for the both of us. He attempts to use his vampire speed but can only manage short bursts before it fizzles out. After only a minute, he's gasping from the exertion.

'You can't keep this up,' I voice, and the resigned look on his face confirms it. 'You're not strong enough to fight him either, are you?'

Hex closes his eyes. 'I'm sorry, darling. For the next few hours, I'm practically mortal.'

I wipe the sweat from his forehead for him. 'There has to be something we can do.'

Slowing, Hex assesses our surroundings, searching for something. 'The only thing we can do now is to hide someplace a cyclops can't fit while full of rage.'

'Can't we try to climb a tree?' I look up. There are some leaves on these trees. Maybe not enough to cover us, but it's better than being out in the open like this.

Hex places me back on my remaining sturdy foot and says, 'No. We want to be low to the ground, not at his eye level. Plus, the trees here are equally as deadly. Even the thickest branches will fail you. They're meant to; everything in this maze is built to lure you to premature death.'

'We could bury ourselves,' I suggest, using my fingernails to claw into the ground, testing it.

Nope, hard as rock.

'We don't have the time to dig, anyway,' he says dismissively, pulling me back up to stand.

'Then *where*, Hex? Where the fuck can we hide?!' My frustration is getting the better of me. I take a second to huff it out before I add, 'I'm sorry. I know you're trying. I'd be dead already if it weren't for you.'

Something flashes in Hex's dark eyes. With a tight jaw, he gulps. 'No need to inflate my ego, darling. And anyway, even if I weren't here to help, I'm sure you would have found a way to stay alive all on your own. I wouldn't be surprised if you manage to sweet talk your way out of Hergal's mouth if caught.'

'Let's stick to the plan of *not* getting caught, though,' I reply, my grateful smile more of a grimace.

The cyclops' heavy steps continue to shadow us as Hex moves with me in his arms as fast as he can. The frequent vibrations unsteady us. Hex looks as though his legs might buckle soon; he's shaking as violently as the ground.

When I think he can't walk another step, he breathes out, 'There.' He nods in the direction of a small grove of trees. The biggest in the centre has a thin slash in its bark. 'It appears to be hollowed out. Hamadryads sometimes use this part of the maze to build temporary hideouts.'

'What's a hamadryad? Are they dangerous? Could they be lurking around?' I question him, the knots in my belly multiplying.

Hex heads for the hollowed-out tree. 'Wood nymphs. They're practically harmless by day, though vicious as soon as night falls. They know me well enough, so we should be fine if we come across one.'

'When you say they know you, do you mean...?'

'I might have fucked a few nymphs in my time, yes.'

Jealousy is a snake in my gut—poisonous and slithering. 'What do they look like?'

Hex's lips quirk up. 'Not as hot as you, if that's what you're asking.'

'That wasn't my question,' I refute, looking away so he can't see my flush-stained cheeks. But it's how I wanted him to answer.

'Some are fairly attractive, as long as you don't mind a little rough skin. They're called wood nymphs for more than the obvious. They're incredibly hard to feed from, let alone fuck. I prefer water nymphs. But they're more difficult to catch... too slippery.'

'Too wet for you, huh?' I jest, playfully poking his chest.

Hex's chuckle is strained. I'm surprised he's still standing; he's so exhausted. 'There's no such thing as too wet. You'll learn that with me.'

I'm smiling like a giddy schoolgirl when we reach the hollow tree. Hex drops me to my feet, half collapsing, his chest heaving. Returning the favour, I support his weight, dragging him with me through the gap in the trunk.

Inside, it's dark and narrow, the scent musky and dank, like rotting wood. It's a tight fit; we both have to press together, chest to chest.

It's the worst place to hide if you're claustrophobic. Which, unfortunately, I am.

My breaths come in short, quick, staccato bursts, and my mind blanks. Blood rushes to my head, my ears roaring louder than Hergal.

Heart racing, I push back against the wood, trying to create the illusion of space. It's no use. My system is drowning in adrenaline—trapped with nowhere to go, just like us.

Hex takes my face in his hands. 'What's wrong?'

'Claustrophobic,' I manage between gasps of air. 'Panic attack.'

The smashing sound of giant footsteps surrounds us, and the vibrations rocket through my bones.

Too close. He's too close. Everything is too close.

'You need to be quieter. They'll hear you,' Hex whispers, stroking my hair to calm me.

'*They'll*? There's more than one?!' This news only reinforces my panic attack.

'Sounds like three.'

Fuck. That's it. We're dead. We're dead!

'I can't breathe,' I choke out, my chest tight, my throat closing.

Pushing my hair back from my face, Hex murmurs, 'Yes, you can. You can control it. I'm right here with you. You're not alone in this. Breathe with me, all right?'

He touches his lips to mine, mouth open. His exhale rushes through, and I suck in what he offers without thought. The unexpected move shocks me out of my accelerated rhythm.

'That's a good girl. Take what I give you.'

His fingers rake through my hair, massaging my scalp. Tingles rush down my spine and spread far and wide, settling low in my belly.

Hex gulps air and breathes into another open-mouthed kiss, my lungs filling again. It's jarring, but it seems to be doing the trick, confusing my body and distracting my mind.

Hex leans back to study me. 'Better?'

I nod, my tummy doing these weird backflips. 'That's, without doubt, the most bizarre kiss I've ever experienced. But not the worst.'

'Just wait until my mouth finds your pussy. Remember, I'm a biter,' he says wickedly. I can't see much of his face in this light, but I can picture the smirk.

'Your fangs are going nowhere near my vagina,' I state, cringing.

'That's what they all say... at first.' The smoke in his tone warms my blood.

'Why haven't you fed off me? Wouldn't my blood help rebuild your strength?' The question has been on the tip of my tongue for a while. I worried that asking it might invite a bite.

A beat passes.

'It's not worth the risk. Hergal is too close. The smell of your blood will act as a lure. The cleansing charm would have worked to rid you of enough of your scent to make it harder for a predator to track you down,' he explains.

After that, the booming presence of three searching cyclopes keeps us quiet. The entire time, Hex uses soft touches to reassure me. And, after a while, I relax, the small space not as stifling. Surprisingly, it's starting to feel like a sanctuary of sorts.

In here, with Hex holding onto me like I'm the most precious thing in the Underworld, I'm safe.

At that realisation, my heart skips a few beats.

Am I falling for this demon?

I can't; it's unthinkable. Yeah, he's helping me now, but only because he's following his king's orders. He's not helping me where it counts. I suspect he's still hindering me when it comes to the maze. Earlier, I must have been going in the wrong direction for him to allow me free rein.

Hex is still my enemy. He's not my friend and definitely not some-one—some*thing*—I can fall in love with.

'Is there a reason you don't like small spaces?' Hex pries, the booming becoming background noise once again.

Avoiding the question, I ask my own. 'Have they passed us?'

'Sounds like it,' he answers. 'We'll stay hidden for a little longer, just in case.'

We fall silent again.

It's a minute before Hex repeats his earlier line of inquiry. And when I only sigh, he pushes, 'Come on. You can tell me. I promise not to think any less of you.'

Shutting my eyes, I sigh again; the details are a crushing weight on my shoulders. Maybe speaking them will ease the pressure which has plagued me since childhood.

I rest my head against the bark and draw strength from the darkness behind my eyelids. 'When I was young, my mum would lock me in the downstairs cupboard for hours. She called it the Oubliette. She wouldn't only reserve it for when I was naughty. Sometimes, she'd throw me in there for no reason. It happened a lot in the year following my dad's departure from our lives. She struggled to cope, and the Oubliette was a place to put me when she felt overwhelmed.'

Hex sighs in understanding. 'I'm sorry you had to go through that. I'm not surprised it had a lasting effect on you. No child should be treated in such a way.'

'Hmm. By the time Robin was born, she had stopped doing it. I brought the Oubliette up years later, and she denied it completely. She said I must have been dreaming because she'd never do such a thing.'

Hex's grip tightens on my waist. 'Really? She gaslit you into believing you made it up?'

'Yep. But I'm not sure she meant to,' I say, shivering at the resurgence of painful memories. 'I think she blocked a lot out. She was always staring into space, her mind wandering to far off places. I reckon something happened in her childhood that traumatised her.'

After that, Hex is stoically and uncharacteristically quiet for a long time. His fingertips smooth over my curves and edges in that silence.

'It wasn't your fault, Raven. You were a child. You were innocent,' he comes out with, his thumb tracing the shape of my mouth. 'You *are* innocent. And beautiful. And funny. And smart. And charming. You don't deserve any of this.' His lips replace his thumb—a chaste kiss which has me gasping. 'By the blood, I wish I could keep you.'

'Maybe you can. Maybe I'll let you,' I find myself replying, unsure if I mean it. In this moment, I think I do.

Hex steals another kiss, this one lingering. 'I can't.' His response is a pain-filled exhalation. He moves, leaving me bereft of his warmth—slipping out of my grasp through the slit in the trunk. 'Let's go. Before the giant fuckwits think to retrace their steps.'

What surprises me most is my disappointment.

Part of me wishes we could have stayed trapped in that moment forever.

Blinking back tears, I come out of hiding, ready to follow Hex's lead and only let my heart *wish* to feel.

CHAPTER 30

Target

Julius

The fresh soul's glow eventually dulls to grey. I took too much too quickly; my loss of control rendered it useless. It's simply a shell encased in glass with no energy left to power it. It can still be traded, but its value has been severely reduced.

Usually, a soul can last me years. Decades potentially. Once a week, I come here to recharge, transferring from either a new soul or an older one I haven't drawn from in a while. I've never depleted a soul so thoroughly before.

The gravity of what I've done slowly starts to sink in. Shame follows swiftly behind. I called on the Shadows to manipulate time for my own gain. Not even my father would have resorted to those extremes. Soon, the Shadows will expect payment. Simply wielding that amount of power has left me as depleted as this poor, abused soul.

At some point in the near future, I'll find out the cost. It's not evident yet. This means my payment will likely be time taken to make up for the loss I caused everyone else. Demons from all layers of the Underworld will not be best pleased with me. With this, I've painted an even bigger target on my back.

And then there's Robin.

In my frenzy of fury, I nearly killed the kid. Part of the deal I made with Raven was to keep her brother safe while he was in my care. Instead, I used him as a buffer to harness more power, leaving him weak.

You're *weak, Julius. Depleting a soul. Using a child. Dealing with the Shadows. All because you were jealous of a vrykolaka. Pathetic.* It's not my voice inside my head; it's my father's. It's always him.

Seeing Hex holding my starling—her naked, him kissing her, touching her in the way I've always dreamed—flipped a switch inside me, releasing something darker than the Shadows that came after.

The Shadows only come to those on the precipice of a considerably wicked sin. If I don't pull myself back and regain control, I'll end up evoking the curse more rapidly than its natural cycle intends. Then I'll end up exactly like *him*, past the point of no return. Thus, the DiMinos line will finish with me, and subsequently, the Underworld will follow suit.

When I need more time, I decide to wish it away.

My reasoning was skewed, clouded by jealousy and rage. Raven rejected the possibility of ruling by my side one day to risk her life in my deadly maze. Yet she gives her body freely to a demon she's only recently met? There's no logic in that. Why him and not me? I'm a king. I'm the demon who knows her soul inside and out. She may not remember me, but deep down, she must sense our connection. How could she disregard that—*me*—so easily?

Perhaps Raven has resorted to offering more than just her blood to Hex, with the aim of progressing in the maze. Admittedly, I've left her with little choice. Or she could very well be using Hex to punish me for the situation I've forced her into. She knows I crave more than her soul; I made my attraction to her obvious.

Thinking on it now, I shouldn't have led with lust. Although my body has always responded strongly when she's nearby. At the time, I couldn't think straight. I'm still struggling after that kiss we shared. What I *should* have been clearer on was my desire for not only her soul and her body but *her* as a whole. Confessing my feelings and opening up to her may have softened her resolve.

With how I've handled things, I'd be lucky if she didn't hate me to her core. I'm sure Hex has already told her that her time is nearly up. That I bent the rules. That I cheated her. Like me, I expect she's livid.

No. She's not as wrathful as I am. She'd be more upset, her anger aimed inwards—eating her up from the inside.

If I weren't so drained of power, I'd be able to sense how she was feeling. Being unable... I'm not sure if it's a blessing or a curse.

It would be unwise to direct any more anger her way. I've already made it practically impossible for her to complete the maze. If I continue to punish her, she may never forgive me. Who I really should be punishing is Hex. He's the bastard who was about to betray me by stealing what's mine.

In the vrykolaka's defence, I know from first-hand experience how irresistible Raven is without her even trying to be. It's always been difficult to deny her what she desires. Still, I gave an order, and as his king, it was binding. The wording was off; I inadvertently left too much room to manoeuvre. Nevertheless, his intent was clear: he was about to fuck her.

That leaves us in a grey area. Technically, Hex hasn't broken any rules, as I stopped him before he could. Even so, I can argue for treasonous intent. It might be enough to justify his killing. And, if it's not, I'll deal with the consequences later.

Right now, I need to channel all my anger and resentment away from Raven, and the only way to do that is to aim it at Hex.

Another reason I have to kill Hex is that he's my competition. I can't have my wilful little starling falling in love with anyone except me. And the way they were looking at each other... *Fuck*. Just picturing them together in my head causes the darkness to rise inside me, tasting like bitter tar.

I must kill that fucking vrykolaka as soon as possible; he threatens my whole purpose.

Still seething, I regretfully accept this unfortunate soul in my collection can't be recharged. What's done is done. I step off the podium, my legs trembling from standing longer than my body is comfortable with after such an ordeal. I stumble twice on my way towards the door of the Harvest Hall.

What my body needs is a few hours' rest. Then, I can come back here to recharge more responsibly. By my estimations, Raven has about twelve hours left. She's lost over a day. Everyone in the Underworld has. They should all be feeling the effects by now: the headache, the disorientation. It won't be long until I'm inundated with messages from other demons demanding I explain my reasoning behind the skip.

Opening the door, I find Robin. The kid didn't make it far; he's sprawled out on the floor, unconscious. For the love of souls, when he tells Raven what I did, she'll despise me. It could take years for her to see past the things I've done to claim her. I don't have years to wait. The only way to rectify the situation is to make it up to the kid—befriend him. I must show his sister I'm not the monster she thinks I am.

A tiny part of me also feels guilty for causing the kid harm. He's not as bratty as I expected him to be. I think the whole *I-don't-care-about-anyone-except-my-self* attitude is mostly bravado. Not so dissimilar to me in that way.

Bending down, I place one arm under his legs and the other around his shoulders. With a groan of effort, I heave him up. My weakness is self-inflicted. His isn't. It's only right I start making amends by helping him off the floor I made him crawl across.

I'm wheezing by the time I reach Robin's room. I roll the kid onto his bed with a satisfied sigh, relieved to be rid of his weight. I could carry a full-grown man without breaking a sweat if I had my usual strength.

I cover the kid with a blanket and leave at the fastest pace I can manage without fainting, running low on time. Again, my own fault. I have less than twelve hours to rest, replenish my power, and plan my next move.

Although my target is already set—Hex. He will be dead by the end of the day. It's the only way to secure my claim on Raven when this is all done and dusted.

My wilful little starling will soon realise I'm her only option.

CHAPTER 31

Violence

RAVEN

'Where are we going?' I've been following Hex silently for five minutes, assuming Hergal and his one-eyed besties are still nearby.

Not turning to address me directly, Hex throws over his shoulder, 'We're going back to find Dato and Lorcan. They may need our help.'

I halt where I stand. 'No! I can't go back. I don't have the time to spare. I need to keep moving forward.'

Hex swivels to face me, his expression flat. 'Let's speak plainly, darling. You're not solving this maze. Going backwards will not hinder you in the slightest.'

'Why? Is it because we've been going in the wrong direction? Is that why you've been letting me lead? Because you know it hasn't made a difference?'

Lips pursing, Hex remains silent. That's answer enough.

I shove him. 'You fucking dickhead! I knew it!'

'What did you expect? That I'd suddenly assist you on this foolhardy quest simply because I'd given you a few orgasms?' Hex folds his arms, a snarky look on his face.

'I didn't expect your *assistance*, but I did believe that you respected me enough to allow me the choice when, in reality, it was all a ploy.'

Hex clicks his tongue. 'It's not my fault you were *choosing* wrong.'

'No. But what would you have done if I'd chosen right?' I put to him, needing to know where he stands before I fall.

There's a pause as Hex bites his cheek, avoiding my gaze.

'Would you have stopped me?' I push, inconspicuously inching away from him, already anticipating his answer.

He lets his arms hang back to his hips and sighs. 'Yes.'

His confession is a punch to the gut. Whether expected or not, it still hurts.

'How? Would you have used force? Would you have hurt me if I didn't comply?'

Pinching the bridge of his nose, Hex reluctantly answers, 'If you fight me, then we'd both be choosing violence. I prefer *not* to resort to manhandling. Unless that's what you're into.' His wink to me is half-hearted. He knows now is not the time to flirt.

My affronted look has his lips thinning. 'I'm not going back,' I state clearly—boldly.

Hex grumbles on an exhale, then drops his chin to his chest. 'Deal-breaker, please don't make me make you.'

'What if we make another deal instead?' I offer, also not wanting to resort to violence yet. I like Hex. I like him too much. The thought of burning the bridge we've built, rickety though it may be, fills me with apprehension. Without meaning to, Hex *has* been helping me. He's been a reassuring presence that I've latched onto. Increasingly, I've been looking to him for comfort and guidance.

With a subtle shake of his head, Hex says, 'There's nothing you could offer me. Nothing I couldn't have regardless.'

My mouth falls open at his arrogance. 'You think I'd fuck you by choice?' I scoff, needing to deflate his ego. 'I'm only tolerating your presence because of our deal. And if you don't at least let me figure this maze out for myself, then they'll be no more kisses, no more fucking around like we're something we're not. No more playing nice. You've served your purpose; you got me out of that pit. And I've already given you more than enough blood for the trouble.'

I step back again, hoping it's subtle. His attention flickers to my feet.

'We're at an impasse here, Hex. You want to check on your friends. I understand that. But *you* must understand I will do whatever it takes to save my brother. He's just a kid. And I'm running out of time.' Another small shuffle back. 'I need to keep going.'

Expressionless, Hex says, 'I'm not letting you go.'

I glower at him, a fire igniting in my chest. 'Well, I'm not going back willingly. I promise you, I will fight you every step of the way. And if I have to... I'll... I'll kill you.'

My eyes catch on a piece of splintered wood about ten metres away. I could use that to stake him in the heart. That's how you kill vampires, right? Anyway, with him weakened as he is, there's at least a small chance I could win in a physical fight.

Not liking that plan, my heart clenches painfully. But what choice do I have? He's refusing to allow me one.

Hex's face hardens. 'You're threatening to kill me now? Would you do it?'

'Wouldn't you?' I counter, my voice rising with my blood pressure. 'If your *precious* king ordered it, would you kill me and hand over my soul? You may as well be tearing my throat out right now; you're so set on helping him steal my life from me. My brother's life, too.'

Running a tongue over his teeth, Hex looks skyward. 'You're being dramatic. You'll both live. That's what I'm here to ensure. And when your fragile little body withers with time, Julius may even grant you immortality. Doesn't that sound compensable?'

'Being caged for all eternity is not living. I don't want to be like you,' I tell him, my lip curling with disgust. 'Hex, you may not have bars around you, but you *are* a prisoner. You're trapped in this maze, just like me.'

My next step back from the irked vampire doesn't go unnoticed.

'Take another step, and you'll regret it,' Hex warns, his tone more serious than I've ever heard.

I stand rigidly still for a long moment, wondering if I should run for it or use the splintered wood in my defence.

Hex follows my line of sight to the discarded piece of jagged wood. 'Don't even *think* about it,' he growls, his focus again narrowing on me. He tilts his head, assessing. 'You really *would* kill me, wouldn't you?' When I don't reply, he *tsks*. 'And there was me thinking we were friends.'

'Friends help each other out,' I snap back, and his jaw tics.

'What will it be, deal-breaker?' His eyes darken to bottomless black pits, his eyelashes heavy. 'Good girls get rewarded, bad girls get punished.'

Before I can actively decide, my feet are already pounding in the opposite direction to Hex, away from the only weapon I can use against him. My mind screams in frustration at my body's cowardice and my heart's hesitation.

In less than ten seconds, Hex catches me, and with embarrassing ease, I'm wrestled to the ground. I intend to elbow him in the ribs, but he thwarts me by pinning my arms down. With a feral cry, I start thrashing like a wild beast, bucking and kicking.

Flattening, Hex uses his weight to dig my hips into the dirt. 'You're only hurting yourself, darling. Stop fighting me.'

'Never!' I grunt out, continuing my struggle.

With a stroke of luck, one buck back bounces against his groin, making him lose his breath momentarily. His hand juts down to shield his cock, his reflexes telling him to protect it.

Twisting, I elbow him in the face. He tips forward, his other hand rushing to clutch his busted nose. Victorious, I fling him to the side and take off. This time, my mind is in control; I sprint towards the splintered wood. There's no way I can outlast him without a weapon.

However, I'm tackled again before I can reach it, the air being knocked out of me. We roll, Hex hooking onto my leg when I try to kick him away. We're facing each other now, him between my legs.

'If this is any indicator of how you'll be in bed, then count me in,' Hex drawls, his fangs lengthening, preparing to bite.

With one arm already subdued, I use the other to grasp the hair at his crown, tugging sharply. He winces out a curse. Securing the upper hand, I fling a knee up into his ribs, which dislodges him again.

On my hands and knees, I crawl towards the piece of wood, lungs burning for breath. Right as my fingers wrap around it, Hex drags me back by my foot, and then there's pressure on my inner thigh, just below the juncture.

Hex's fangs sink through my leggings, and I scream at the pain. He supplies me with no relief, no venom to soothe or satisfy.

Whipping around as best I can, I attempt to stab him with the piece of wood, but it's not sharp enough. It merely beats at his shoulder while he feeds from me—gaining his strength back with every ounce as my own energy drains equally as fast.

I bash him with the wood, calling him every derogatory name under the sun. Hot, thick tears of defeat roll down my flushed cheeks.

Hex snatches the wood from my hand on one flail and flings it far from my reach. His glare is so wicked I flinch. I can't tell if he wants to eat me in a good or bad way.

'You're hurting me,' I whimper, more hurt that he chose to cause me pain when he didn't have to.

Hex unhooks his fangs from my thigh, his mouth wet with my blood. 'You went for the wood.' He licks his lips, then adds, 'You hurt me first.'

'I won't give up,' I maintain, fists clenching, preparing to counterstrike.

Smirking, the devious glint in his eye returns. 'Oh, you want to go another round?'

With surprising force, I dive onto Hex, pushing him back into the dirt. My bitten thigh pulses with fire as I straddle his chest. And as hard as I can, I thump my fist into his jaw. A vicious growl erupts from his throat as he blocks my next punch.

Grasping tightly onto my wrists, Hex switches our position, flipping me onto my back. He crushes his forearm against my throat, settling his weight heavily between my legs.

Choking, I scramble to ease the pressure on my neck. I use my nails to claw at his arms, his chest—anywhere I can reach—my vision blackening.

Hex lowers to whisper into my ear. 'You can't fight me if you're unconscious.'

Airflow restricted, my chest gets tighter and tighter. 'Please, stop,' I croak.

Conflict is written in how his features tighten at my visible distress. And, before I black out, his forearm lifts from my throat.

I roll to my side, gasping. Black spots continue to smudge the outer edges of my vision.

With a gentler touch, Hex reaches for me. 'Come on, let's stop thi—'

Seizing the opportunity, I kick him in the stomach, and he tumbles back. Not knowing what else I can do, I stumble to my feet and leg it again.

When Hex pounces on me this time, he forces my face into the dirt, his full weight on my back. 'Such a naughty girl. You beg me for mercy, then pull a stunt like that...' He tuts. 'What am I going to do with you? Huh?' He doesn't sound bitter anymore; his tone is more playful, as though my continued attempts to fight him are turning him on.

My theory is backed up by the hard evidence pressing against my arse.

Despite my vicious resentment, my blood heats, gathering in one particularly sensitive area of my body.

Hex inhales sharply, then groans. 'Myth and mercy, your arousal smells so fucking good.'

My hips are thrust up without warning, head still held to the ground. Hex rubs his erection between my legs, and a moan slips out before I can contain it.

'I'll be kind and give you a safe word,' Hex says in a husky tone, his free hand snaking up my top to palm my left breast, as the other is inaccessible; it's crushed under me. He pinches my nipple, and I cry out. 'Birdie. That's your safe word. I'll only tell you once.'

Without waiting for me to acknowledge it, Hex yanks my leggings down over my hips, exposing my backside. And before I can protest, he spanks me—hard. Gritting my teeth against the sting of the blow, I whimper.

'I told you: bad girls get punished.' Hex spanks me again, a little lighter this time, but my skin still prickles at the searing slap.

I try to wriggle out of his hold, but he grips tighter onto the roots of my hair. The needle-hot prickles spread through my scalp. Of course, I heard the safe word he gave me, yet for some reason, I can't bring myself to utter it.

With my limited view of him, I only catch the shuffle of his hips. But I definitely *feel* the difference as the smooth head of his cock slides over my slick entrance from behind.

'Fuck, you love being punished, don't you, darling?' Hex asks rhetorically, finding out for himself how wet I am.

I answer him anyway with a breathy moan.

Hex's grip on my hip is bruising. 'Well, I'm just getting started.'

With renewed speed, he flips me onto my back and drags me down to him before I can blink. He rips my leggings the rest of the way down my legs, then proceeds to dive towards the juncture of my thighs with the grace of a leopard going for its prey.

Automatically, my legs want to close, but he uses his hands, bracketing my thighs and spreading them wide. My head rolls back as soon as his speedy tongue starts frantically flicking my clit. My back arches off the ground, the vibrations pulsing deep.

As my body throbs with desire, I peer down to watch him lap me up. His eyes are closed, savouring every lick. And when they open, they ensnare mine, and he grins, looking as menacing as the Devil himself.

There's no warning for what Hex does next; he latches onto my clit and sucks deeply, bringing blood to the surface. I realise his intention too late.

I scream when his fangs pierce the sensitive skin on each side of my clit, but I only suffer a moment of pain before his venom hits.

With a violent shudder, I come right there and then, so hard, my vision blackens again. Sounds I've never made before are pouring out of my mouth while Hex forces my hips down, still sucking greedily.

I'm tempted to use my safe word. It's too much. 'Stop! Please stop.'

He doesn't. And that only increases my pleasure.

Instead of using my safe word, I push against his head, trying to move him away from that sensitive area. He growls at me but concedes, focusing his attention further down.

'I've always wondered what would kill me in the end. And if it's this pretty pussy that does it, then so be it.' At his resignation, his two fingers enter me, sliding in as far as they can push. 'I can't think of a better way to go down than going down on you.'

With his long digits penetrating deep, Hex has well and truly disobeyed the Demon King's order. Uncaring, he fucks me with them, slow and steady, curling to hit the best spot.

He lightly swipes his tongue over my swollen clit again, his heavy breaths adding more heat to the oversensitive area. He's probably cleaning up any beads of blood left from his tiny puncture marks.

Building anew, I roll my hips in time to his measured rhythm. The crisp wind nips at my exposed skin, but like my vamp, I no longer give a fuck about outside forces.

Hex moves to hover over me, fingers still working to stimulate. He shifts my hips to line them up with his cock, and then his hand is back at my throat. 'Are you ready for your final punishment?' He pulls up my top to free my breasts, then bows to drag his teeth over a pebbled nipple. 'I'm going to pound you into the ground so hard, the walls of this maze will tremble along with you.'

At the mention of the maze, I rise out of my lust-clouded daze. And, right when Hex's cock is about to replace his fingers, I shout, 'Birdie! Birdie!'

Immediately, Hex releases my throat and leans back, looking confused. 'You do understand what a safe word is, right?'

I roll my top back down and half sit up, my arms supporting. 'Of course, I know. I'm not *that* inexperienced,' I mutter, a little miffed at his condescension. 'I only want to secure the terms of our new deal first.'

Hex's eyes narrow. 'You want to make a deal right now?'

'Yes.'

Blatantly trying to distract me, he strokes himself, and I blush because my gaze lingers too long, the irresistible sight making my vagina clench. 'What will you offer me? Make it good.'

Biting my puffy bottom lip, I finally raise my eyes to his. 'I'll let you fuck me however you like if you let me decide what paths to take in the maze without interference.'

It takes a split-second for Hex's face to drop into a frown. '*Let* me fuck you? At the Well of Eternal Winter, you said you wanted me.'

I shrug. 'Circumstances have changed since then. I've been *very* clear about that the last ten minutes.'

In a mere blink, Hex is standing, pulling up his trousers. 'No deal.' He starts walking away.

Did that hurt him? Maybe I was too convincing when I told him I wouldn't fuck him by choice. He must know I was lying. Right?

I jump up and chase after him, still naked from the waist down. I shiver against the cold. 'Why?'

When I grab the back of his shirt, Hex spins to slap my hand away. 'Because I don't fuck the unwilling.'

I huff a humourless laugh and come back with, 'No. You just threaten them with violence, bite them, then choke them half to death.' I prod his chest. 'Don't stand there and pretend you have any morals. You would cause me harm if ordered.' Welling up, I push him away. 'Our deal doesn't protect me from *you*!' I can't control the hiccup of emotion in my voice.

Hex groans in frustration, a tense hand jamming into his hair. Before he speaks, he meets my accusatory glare. 'Fuck orders and fuck our deal.' He rushes to close the gap, taking my face in his hands. 'I wouldn't let any harm come to you even if Julius demanded it. I couldn't. I've refused before, and I'll refuse again.' There's something in his tone which conveys the finality of that decision.

Hex won't hurt me beyond what he's already done; I believe that.

But my curiosity is piqued by his last statement. 'Refused *what* before?' When Hex drops his hands, I continue probing. 'Did the Demon King order you to kill me at first?'

Lowering his gaze, Hex mumbles his answer. 'No. Not Julius.' His head lifts again. 'Look, we haven't got time to argue about this. Dato and Lorcan could be seriously injured. If you want a deal, I'll give you one...' He sighs in defeat. 'Come back with me willingly, and after we find them, I promise not to stand in your way if you choose the correct path.' At my winning smile, he quickly adds, 'But I can't promise the same from Dato and Lorcan. You'll have to make your own deals with them.'

Elated, I offer him my hand to shake. 'Hex, you have yourself a willing participant.'

Ignoring my hand, he catches me by the collar and pulls me in for a hungry kiss. My arse still bare, he slaps it, and I yelp into his mouth.

He breaks the kiss to murmur, 'Go and cover that pretty pussy before I'm tempted to take another bite.' He kisses my smile. 'And before we head back, I'll give you a few drops of my blood so you can walk easier. After our *very* sexy tussle, I bet every inch of you is aching.'

I nod, back in a teasing mood. 'Hmm. Are you regretting giving me that safe word now?'

Hex chuckles. 'Oh, you're so lucky I did. You wouldn't have been able to walk straight again with the punishment I had planned for you.'

'According to our new deal, I only have to be willing. You never said I had to be a good girl,' I say seductively, raking my nails down his torso. 'Bad girls always take their punishments well.'

Wanting to catch the vamp by surprise, I bite down on his shoulder, drawing blood. His cock jerks at the audacity of me taking without asking—turning the tables on him. He lets me lick up his healing essence, the sound of his wincing hiss more pleasure than pain.

When I'm finished and healed, Hex rubs at his shoulder's bruised and broken skin. 'Such a violent little bird. You certainly give Velociraptors a run for their money.'

Time ticking, I race to get dressed, then follow my only hope back to find the other two demons I still have to deal with.

Wish me luck.

CHAPTER 32

Break Bread

Freshly baked bread is the mouth-watering aroma that lures me from a too-short sleep.

The last thing I remember was collapsing outside of the Harvest Hall after Julius nearly killed me. *Who the hell tucked me into bed, then?* I ask myself, rubbing my eyes.

Strangely, my hand doesn't hurt anymore. I check my palm and find the skin unburnt and unbroken. Did Julius use his magic to heal me? I'd be surprised. Maybe one of his servants helped me.

To test my strength, I stretch in bed. All my muscles ache, but it's not bad enough to keep me immobile.

My tummy growling with hunger, I slip out of bed and follow my nose. I haven't eaten anything since I was kidnapped over twelve hours ago. Although it's hard to decipher time in the Underworld. It doesn't seem to follow a system. The sky here is always dark, but when it's supposedly daytime, the inky canvas of night is painted with wisps of grey, lightening and brightening the whole picture.

The clock in the grand entrance hall displays the time, but the metal hands haven't ticked since I began watching. It must be broken; it's frozen at 11:57 a. m. If I remember correctly, I was taken from my bed at home around midnight.

This whole ordeal has felt a lot longer than twelve hours. It feels as though I've been stuck here for days.

I don't notice the woman behind me until she coughs to get my attention. Hand holding my heart in my chest, I spin to face her.

She's an older lady, probably in her mid-sixties; her white hair is neatly tucked into a long braid. The lines around her dark blue eyes make her chalky skin appear cracked. Fitting in with the other servants, her uniform is plain charcoal, with a white collar and apron.

'That clock is wrong. The skip disrupted its magic. Someone will have to redo the incantation,' the woman says, shaking her head as if it's a nuisance to even think about. 'It's mid-afternoon now.'

I glance at the clock again. 'What's a skip?'

'The time jump King Julius orchestrated,' she answers, giving me a funny look. 'I thought you were there. He told me to watch over you while you slept because he used you as a conduit, and worried you'd not feel too well when you woke up.'

'*Worried*?' I parrot in a sardonic tone. 'The arsehole nearly killed me. I'm sure he couldn't care less how I was feeling.'

The woman appears scandalised at my disrespect. 'Don't let the King hear you talking like that about him. He'll throw you in the dungeon. He's an extremely sensitive demon.'

'Right now, I don't really give a shit. All I want is some food; I'm starving,' I tell her, patting my empty belly to accentuate my point. 'The smell of bread woke me up.'

The woman frowns at my blasé attitude but nods in acceptance. 'If you want to eat, follow me to the dining hall. A late lunch is about to be served.'

She pivots and hurries away down a corridor. I rush to catch up.

'Hey, what's your name? Are you a demon, too?'

'All the soulless in the Underworld are demons, but not all of us have demonic forms. I was mortal once. I still would be if I hadn't sold my soul many years ago. Most, like the King, were born to the Underworld. Others were born mortal but were turned into something more powerful. And then there are people like me, or you, who lose their soul and can't return to our world without it,' she explains, somewhat sadly.

'I haven't lost my soul,' I refute defensively.

The woman side-eyes me, her eyebrow high. 'Yet.'

Ignoring her remark, I say, 'You didn't tell me your name.'

She holds her chin up when she answers, 'Marguerite.' Her French accent makes itself known with that introduction. It must have been a long time since she lived in France for her to lose it so thoroughly.

I follow Marguerite down a staircase and past the kitchens. 'So, why did you sell your soul? Or is that rude to ask down here?'

A small smile graces Marguerite's wrinkled lips. 'I gave up my soul to save my daughter. She had a terminal illness and deserved more years than she was fated. I had already lived enough years to be content to spend the rest of mine in service.'

'How many years have you worked here, then?'

Marguerite shrugs. 'I've lost count. My life is no longer a natural one.'

'You mean, you could be stuck as a servant in this castle *forever*?!' I can't hide the expression of horror from my face before she sees it.

Unexpectedly, she laughs. 'There's no such thing as forever, garçon. Everything has a beginning, a middle, and an end. Most of us can't see the end coming.' She flattens down her apron. 'One day, my time will be up. This shell I serve in will lose its usefulness, and only then will I be allowed to rest in peace.'

With a flash of my eyebrows, I reply, 'Wow, that's morbid. You're not really selling me on the life of the eternally damned, you know.'

Glancing across, Marguerite lets out another titter of laughter. 'I can see why he's warmed to you. He used to have that same dry humour.'

My face scrunches in confusion. 'Who?'

Marguerite doesn't answer my question. She directs me to walk through the door to the dining hall, holding it open for me. 'Try not to call him an arsehole again.'

Before I can repeat my question, she shoves me into the room and shuts the door behind me.

The dining hall is surprisingly quaint and understated compared to the in-your-face opulence the rest of the castle exhibits. There's one rectangular table, topped with white and grey marble, in the centre of the room. The walls are exposed grey stone. A collection of old paintings hangs above an in-built fireplace on the left side. The room is mostly lit by candles and silver lanterns, adding to the cosy ambience. The bread I smelt earlier is displayed in woven baskets at each end of the table. There are some plain crusty rolls and what looks to be some cheese loaves. Butter dishes sit beside them.

There are about ten chairs on each side of the table, and at the head, in a silver, throne-like seat, sits the white-haired Demon King, wine in hand. He gives me a forced, weary smile in greeting.

'Robin, I hope you're feeling better. Please, join me for this late lunch,' Julius starts politely, gesturing for me to take any seat I wish. 'We both need to rebuild our strength.'

'I'd rather eat alone,' I say, stubbornly standing where I am.

Julius' mouth presses into a hard line as though he's trying to keep from snapping back at me. After a tense beat, he tries again. 'I apologise for how I treated you earlier. I understand your reservations, but I promise you, from now on, I will do my best not to put you in harm's way. What you witnessed earlier... that was out of character for me. I usually treat my souls as precious gems. And, when yours and your sister's are in my possession, I will cherish them.'

'You're talking like it's a certainty. Raven still has two days left to get here. She will,' I state, confident that my sister's will is stronger than whatever she faces in the maze. There's something that niggles at the back of my mind, though. Didn't Marguerite mention a time jump earlier? She said what happened in the Harvest Hall had something to do with it.

Julius reaches across for a knife and then uses it to cut into a cheese loaf. 'Raven no longer has that much time. At the stroke of midnight tonight, the deal is won.' He doesn't look at me while he speaks, focusing on buttering his slice of bread. 'If you want to eat, now is the only time I will allow it. So... *sit*.' There's more force behind this, a bite to his tone.

But I bite back, 'Is that what you used me for? You cheated her out of time as punishment for not wanting you? Are you fucking for real?!'

'Sit down and lower your voice before I send you back to bed hungry,' Julius warns through gritted teeth.

When I spin on my heel and try to open the door, it doesn't budge. 'Let me out, then.'

There's a clang of cutlery, then Julius' exasperated exhale. 'Can you just sit down? Please? I'm trying extremely hard to be nice to you.'

I look over my shoulder and make a face at him in disbelief. 'This is you trying to be *nice*?'

'Yes. It's especially difficult with you,' he says under his breath, readjusting the knife he threw down on the table. 'I apologised and offered you food. What more do you want?'

'Erm, well, let's see...' I pretend to think about it. 'How about you let me and my sister go, then leave us the fuck alone?' My plan to befriend him earlier seems so juvenile now. I suspect I wouldn't have been able to keep it up for very long, even if the Harvest Hall incident hadn't happened. The guy is a complete dick, and I have just as little patience as he seems to.

'I can't do that, kid. There are reasons behind all this which you are not privy to. I need Raven's soul, and, unfortunately, I took advantage of a loophole, which means I could barter with your soul in exchange for hers. If she had taken the deal I offered her, you'd be having lunch at home right now. But, like you, your sister is a stubborn little thing. And here we are.'

I cross my arms tightly over my chest. 'Loophole?'

'I will explain as soon as you take a seat.'

Caving in because I'm too curious and hungry, I grab a roll and drop to his right in the middle seat. I tear through the crust with my fingers, then knife on some butter. If this arsehole wants to break bread, I'll eat every fucking crumb and spit it back in his face.

When I take my first bite, Julius continues, 'I can obtain a soul one of two ways; either I barter for them, or I capture those which are already lost.'

'Then how did you claim mine? I didn't get anything from it.'

'A child's soul is bartered differently. Up until the age of eighteen, it can only be inherited. A guardian, usually the parent, can offer a child up to save their own soul. Raven inherited your soul from your mother, which granted her the freedom to wish it away for someone else to claim.'

While chewing my mouthful of bread, I digest the information. As I process, two servants enter, carrying platters of meats and cheeses, along with fruits, scones, and teacakes. Jam and cream are placed down to accompany the offering. The servants leave after handing me a ready-made pot of tea.

I pour myself some into the china teacup. 'Raven wished away my soul? When?' I struggle to conceal the hurt from my voice.

Setting down his goblet, Julius answers, 'Only a few minutes before I stole you away. She didn't say the words, but she meant them. Another demon wouldn't have heard, but I did.'

'So, what you're telling me is... my sister *thought* me away? With the power of her mind?' I question dryly. 'Wow. Didn't know I was *that* difficult to live with.'

'Meeting you, it's not so hard to believe,' he remarks, avoiding the point.

'That was the loophole, then: only you could answer her unspoken wish because of your weird connection thingy? Are all wishes granted if you speak them?' I enquire, recalling all the times I wished my mum dead over the years. Did a demon hear me? Am I the reason she's gone?

'No. It's not usually that simple. A person would have to seek out a particular demon to enter a deal with. Normally, there are several hoops to jump first. But with Raven, I took advantage of our situation.' Julius sits back, looking a little contrite. He fiddles with the stem of his goblet when he adds, 'I'm sorry you were caught up in the middle of all this. It wasn't your soul I was after. I've never accepted payment in the form of offspring before. But... you were an opportunity I couldn't pass up.'

Losing my appetite, I drop the half-eaten roll to my plate and stare at it. 'She meant it? Wishing me away?'

Julius also stares down at his half-eaten bread. 'At the time, she did. But she was upset. Since then, I think she's more than proven that her wish was only a silent plea for help.' He takes a sip of wine. 'I can feel how much she cares for you and your well-being.'

He's probably full of shit, trying to get on my good side. But I find myself asking, 'You can feel that?'

Julius nods. '*We* might not share a connection, kid, but I can sense how much *she* means to *you* deep down as well.'

The tight knot in my chest loosens a little. 'She's my sister. Of course, I care about her.'

Meeting my eye, Julius queries, 'Have you ever told her that?'

Not as far as I remember. Surely, she *knows*, though. 'Family are obligated to care for one another.'

'It isn't love if it's in any way obligatory. What you describe is duty—loyalty.'

'How would *you* know the difference? Have you ever loved anyone except yourself?' I throw back, my mood petty.

Lips twitching, Julius regards me. 'No demon I know has ever protected a mortal's life before, let alone dealt with the Shadows to obtain them.'

'You're claiming to *love* Raven now?' I snort a laugh. 'See, that's where I think you're deluding yourself.' I pick up a cupcake and chuck it on my plate. 'Love can't be obligatory, I agree. But you know what else love can't be... it can't be obtained,' I deliver, peeling the paper case from the sponge.

For a thinly stretched beat, Julius remains thoughtfully quiet as I eat my cake.

'Enjoy my hospitality while it lasts. After midnight, you will be returned to your world, and you may live your life how you choose. I will only come to collect your soul upon your death.' He stands, picking up the whole bottle of wine instead of his goblet.

'And what about my sister? I'm not leaving without her,' I declare, rushing to my feet.

'You will. And Raven will stay with me. I promise you; I will care for her far better than you and your mother ever did.'

With that parting remark, he sweeps out of the room on a gust of wind that blows out half of the candles.

As my heart twists with guilt and frustration, I scream and throw my plate across the room.

CHAPTER 33

Personal

RAVEN

Despite being at full strength—thanks to vampire blood—I continue treating Hex as my personal steed. My arms and legs are firmly wrapped around him, mounted on his back as he rushes to retrace our steps through the maze at super speed.

'What's your top speed?' I'm talking into Hex's neck as my face has been buried there for the last half an hour, eyes scrunched shut. My body is still struggling to adjust to the intermittent whirs of movement.

Hex slows to give me a break. 'I've never measured it, but I reckon, on a *really* good day, perhaps over a hundred miles per hour.'

Stomach settling, I lift my head and open my eyes. 'Not *that* much faster than a cheetah, then,' I tease. For me, it *feels* like we're travelling no slower than the speed of light.

'When it comes to hunting, a cheetah's success rate is only around sixty per cent. As for *my* track record... I have *never* let my prey get away. Remember that the next time you think to run,' he warns, and I can hear the wicked smirk in his voice. I'm starting to think he *wants* me to try again so that he can catch me.

The idea shoots a thrill straight to my core, heating my entire body.

Maybe I want that, too.

'How did you become a vampire in the first place? And why aren't your kind more than folklore in my world?' I ask, more interested in his life story than I've shown so far.

'We don't have time for a full history lesson, so I'll give you a brief rundown,' Hex starts, jogging at a steady rhythm. 'Before the turn of the twentieth century, vrykolakas lived in the mortal lands without much fear. We could easily hide amongst you without being detected, until the advancements of mankind made it nearly impossible to continue. The same can be said for lycanthropes and such kind.'

'Are there still vampires and werewolves that live amongst mortals today?'

'If they're still lucky enough to possess their soul, then there's a small possibility. However, they would have to be extremely careful not to be discovered. From what I know, most demonic creatures returned to the Underworld by the end of the First World War. The risks were too high. We don't exclusively need to feed from mortals, so the Underworld was a far safer place to live and hunt.'

'When were *you* turned, though?' I pry, wanting to hear a more personal story than the one he's currently sharing.

Marching on, Hex takes a moment before responding, as though unsure of how much information he's willing to part with. 'It's not a very enthralling tale. But if you insist... I had recently turned twenty-seven, living in Victorian Britain as a butcher's son. My family also ran a small farm. One evening, I was out herding sheep, when there was a commotion; I thought a neighbour's dog was attacking. It was a woman—a female vrykolaka, I should say. In her bloodlust, she fed from me, but she decided to keep me when I was on the brink of death. Her companion had left for the Underworld several years before, and loneliness had crept up on her. For that reason, she turned me and then stole me away.' His tone is tinged with sadness. I'm guessing that means he had to leave his family behind.

After a sigh, he continues, 'In the years that followed, we became lovers. Then, the First World War hit Europe. By then, we were already tired of our circumstances—constantly on the move, hiding in society's shadow. After the Spanish Influenza subsided, we decided to travel through the Veil, choosing a layer of the Underworld with a large vrykolakas population. Not long later, we drifted apart, and I chose to finally leave her. Further down the line, I ran into trouble, so I came here seeking protection. I sold my soul to Julius' father, and nothing much has happened since then.'

The twisting in my gut forces my next question. 'Did you love her?'

Hex peers over his shoulder at me. 'No. But, at the time, I thought I did. There was too much resentment for love to blossom. She all but ended my life—made it so I could never be around my family, lest they find out their son was a bloodsucking demon. She could also be quite malicious. Our companionship was often tumultuous.'

I swallow down the lump in my throat. 'Do you still see her?'

Faintly, Hex shakes his head. 'She died a few years after I left her.'

Not caring if this is insensitive, I probe, 'How?'

Hex readjusts my position, hiking me up higher. 'She returned to the Veil of her own volition. By that point, she had lived well over three hundred years and was tired of it.'

'Do a lot of demons do that? End their immortality?'

'Not the majority. But what you can't understand—as a fragile mortal who will be lucky to live past ninety—is that immortality can be fucking tedious. After the first century, your body could well be at its peak, yet your mind may not. Sometimes, even the thought of eternity is tiring. Some would prefer to rest in peace.'

'Can demons find peace?'

Hex nods. 'If their soul is uncorrupted, they can.'

'What about *your* soul?' I know I'm probably overstepping, but I can't help myself. The thought of Hex never finding peace makes my heart constrict.

Luckily, Hex doesn't seem to take offence to my grilling. In fact, the muscles in his neck and shoulders soften, as though the more I ask, the more he's comfortable divulging. 'I will only find out the state of my soul when I come to claim it back. I still have fifty years of service before I know for sure. But I trusted the DiMinos line to take good care of it.'

'The Demon King just tried to kill you, I wouldn't be so sure,' I say, voice flat and wary.

Hex snickers, unperturbed. 'Julius may be hot-headed, but he's no fool. Purposely corrupting a soul is the biggest crime a keeper demon can commit.

If anything happened to mine, no lesser demon would ever entrust a soul to a DiMinos again.'

'Surely, killing you would be worse,' I argue, wondering why murder seems to be the lesser of evils down here.

'Ah, well, Julius could argue he had good reason. My eternal soul is worth much more than the shell I use to cart you around this maze.' He reaches back to squeeze my arse.

I slap his hand away. 'You offered!'

Hex breathes a laugh. 'I'm not complaining. Who wouldn't want your breasts pressed firmly against their back for an extended period?'

As a reprimand, I nip his nape, but that only makes him moan in appreciation, so I stop. 'You're twisted. Anyway, back to our conversation... How can a body function without a soul? You, Dato, and Lorcan all seem to have your own personalities. If you're a shell, how can you still think and feel?'

'A soul is more than a personality, my dear. It's this indescribable essence which is pure energy. It's limitless. Losing it doesn't affect brain or body function,' Hex explains.

Not understanding, I quiz, 'What *does* it affect, then? What does being soulless feel like?'

'It's hard to put into words how it feels exactly. It's like you have this missing piece, which you know is vital, yet you keep on living regardless, like breathing despite not having lungs. Without a soul, you can't rest. You can't enjoy the silence. Also, you're constantly running on empty; your energy is always drawn from this shallow pool. It's a strange existence. That's why it can only be tolerated for so long. *Too* long, and you start to fade away. That's how the Shadows are made: the soulless who never reclaimed their peace. If my soul were to be corrupted, I'd soon find myself turning to the Shadows for comfort, and they will eventually claim me as their own.'

'So... the Shadows are sentient. Are they evil?'

With a soft, patient expression, Hex shakes his head again. 'An untouched soul is limitless light, and the Shadows are its antithesis—darkness. Neither is good nor evil. Neither think nor feel. They're simply the purest forms of opposing energies. Both can be harnessed for nefarious purposes.'

Even though Hex explained it well, I still struggle to understand it all. 'Life was so much simpler yesterday,' I say wistfully, resting my chin on his shoulder. 'I'm still hoping this is all one *really* vivid dream.'

Snorting in amusement, Hex mutters, 'I've been hoping that since eighteen-ninety-seven.'

After another fifteen minutes of travelling, Hex and I come to a natural stop at a fork in the maze near the Hearth of Hergal. Hex believes the cyclopes won't think to track our scent back here, as we stuck to our original trail on return. Our whereabouts will hopefully be masked by our earlier scent already followed.

'Do you think Dato and Lorcan are dead?' I ask, jumping down from Hex's back. I can't deny the well of worry in the pit of my stomach, which surges when I think of Dato and Lorcan, bloodied and broken somewhere nearby. Like Julius, their suspected deaths should elate me.

They don't.

I'm in no way lighter. All I'm feeling right now is twinges of heartache.

'I'd be surprised. They're both well-trained and hard to kill,' Hex replies, and I let out a discreet sigh of relief. 'Saying that, three cyclopes together are a tough team to beat. They're bound to be injured. The fact that they haven't caught up with us by now makes me believe they're in a terrible state.'

I follow Hex, his fast pace attainable yet tiring. 'Can your blood heal them?'

'It can, but it depends on how severely they're hurt. It might take some time.'

At this, I baulk. If these fucking demons keep taking my time, I'll have none left for this miserable quest.

Halfway down a fairly open path, Hex halts, sniffing the air. 'I smell blood,' he says, his fangs lengthening automatically. 'They're close.'

Blood; that's not a good sign.

Needing speed, Hex snatches me up and carries me with him as he trusts his heightened senses. I clutch his shirt with both hands, my face smooshed against his chest.

'Fucking mazes,' Hex breathes, releasing my legs when we stop by a collection of tattered trees.

Following his gaze, my heart plummets to the ground as fast as the two broken heaps at our feet look to have done. Dato, both wings missing chunks, is unconscious and bleeding from the head, his angelic face pointed towards the sky he usually dominates. Whereas Lorcan—lying a few feet from him—seems to be awake, though dazed. His face is pressed to the dirt, all four limbs bent and broken. He's groaning, clearly in severe pain.

The sound churns my stomach, bile rising to my throat.

As he charges in, Hex opens a vein in his wrist, then swiftly forces his blood into Lorcan's mouth. Spluttering, Lorcan rejects it at first, but seconds later, his mouth parts for more.

With my arms wound around myself, I watch Hex turn his attention to Dato, prying his lips apart to revive the harpy with his blood. I hold my breath, noting the shallow movements of Dato's chest. It's lucky we arrived when we did; it appears he was on the verge of death.

Noticing the scattered branches and leaves around us, I look up. The trees above are as broken as their bodies are. They must have come crashing down on top of them—*through* them. It would have been worse if they hadn't; the trees slowed their descent.

Lorcan, now strong enough to keep his eyes open, rolls onto his back, grunting from the effort. He gulps down clean air, his short beard caked in mud.

I back up, still slightly intimidated by him, even though he's in no condition to do anything to me.

That's when the thought hits.

Right now, all three of my demon chaperones are weakened. Hex is giving so much of his blood away that he'll be relatively mortal again. That is until he feeds from me.

I shouldn't let him.

I'm surprised he hasn't bitten me yet to replenish. It's probably because he's too distracted—working to save his friends.

He's distracted, Raven. Take advantage of that, I implore internally, taking another step back. *Run now before he remembers you're here. Before they're all strong enough to stop you again.*

Despite knowing what I'm considering is best for Robin and me, I can't help but feel a little shitty leaving them now when they're in dire need of assistance. They could heal quicker if I let Hex drink his power back.

On the other hand, if I don't seize the opportunity to escape, I'm compromising myself. Hex has promised not to hinder me moving forward, but I still have Dato and Lorcan to contend with. They will continue to sabotage my quest using force. There's no way I can overpower them at full strength. I couldn't even win a fight against Hex when he was powerless.

The only thing I have going for me is my determination to reach my brother by any means necessary. And if I have to resort to leaving these demons to fight for their lives without my help, then that's what I have to do. It's not personal. It's the only way I can think to proceed.

With my mind made up but my heart heavy, I slip away, not turning back.

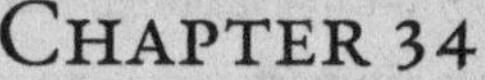

CHAPTER 34

Ladies In Waiting

RAVEN

To acquiesce my stitch, I fold almost in half. The air I gulp down scalds. I lean against a tree, eyes darting around—paranoia high.

It's not only three scorned demons I have to worry about: there's also a fuck tonne more murderous beasts prowling this maze. Beasts who can't be reasoned with. There will be no offering *them* sex to save my skin, quite literally.

With more oxygen circulating, I continue jogging to make up time. I have until the day is done to find the heart of the maze and the castle where my annoying little brother is being held as bait. It's already late afternoon. I hope Robin is giving the Demon King hell. It's the only instance where I've ever wished for him to *be* the little shit that he is.

Is Robin as scared as I am? Is he as worried about me as I am about him?

It's true I haven't been much of a sister to Robin in recent years, but I tried to be when we were young. When Mum worked late into the evenings, I always made dinner for us. I always made sure his lunch box was stocked for school the next day. I can't remember him ever saying thank you. What's worse is that I can't remember us ever telling each other *I love you*. Come to think of it, I'm hard-pressed to recall if *anyone* has uttered those words to me, and vice versa.

Another fucking sad thing to add to my list.

No wonder I'm so desperate for these demons to show me affection. I've relished the attention they've rained on me like I'm some dried-up daisy. Like I'm a starving man at an all-you-can-eat buffet. I'm a greedy little heathen who hasn't been focusing on what's important: saving mine and my brother's soul.

Yeah, I can argue that what I've done so far was all to lure Hex, Lorcan, and Dato into helping me instead of sabotaging my quest. But I also can't deny that I've enjoyed myself *immensely*. I've never had more than one orgasm in a day before. None of which weren't by my own hand.

And if it made the Demon King jealous... well... win-win.

The melodic trill of a female voice has me throwing myself behind a tree trunk to hide. Someone has started singing nearby. It's a beautiful sound, high and clear. After the first unintelligible verse, another female voice joins in.

Clutching my chest—trying to push my heart back into place—I step out from behind the tree and cautiously move towards the singers, on high alert. They may sound beautiful, but not all is what it appears to be in the Underworld.

I creep from tree to tree, trying to keep my path clear of twigs and crunchy, dry leaves. Maybe I'll have more luck seeking assistance from a female demon. They could be the harmless wood nymphs Hex mentioned earlier. He also said they become more vicious as soon as night falls. The sky still holds enough ash grey to count as day.

The language they sing in could be Ancient Greek or a demonic tongue, for all I know. Whatever it is, it's lovely to listen to; the words flow like a calm, winding river.

Catching a glimpse of white, I hang back, using grey bark as cover. I peer around the trunk to better see the alluring singers.

Two women in white nightgowns are prancing around a small stone fountain in a clearing. The taller of the two has long, curly red hair and skin as pale as the moon. The other has cropped black hair and mahogany brown skin.

On further inspection, there's something off about their complexions. They have this translucent glow as if they aren't fully corporeal. Neither appears to be much older than I am. Both are as stunningly beautiful as their song.

They hold hands and spin in a circle, their lulling melody turning to joyous laughter. Transfixed, I smile, wishing I could join them.

Who's to say I can't? They don't look very threatening. If anything, they're a breath of fresh air in a stifling place this solemn and unnerving.

Emboldened by my optimistic logic, I step into the clearing. 'H—Hello, I—erm... I heard you both singing. You have lovely voices, by the way... Anyway, I—I need some help finding the castle at the centre of the maze, and I was wondering if you'd be so kind as to point me in the right direction,' I utter, my voice shaking a little.

Their laughter dies in their throats when they turn to consider me with curious eyes and tilting heads. I stand very still, prepared to retreat if they make any sudden movements that might indicate an attack.

The one with mahogany brown skin glides towards me, her movements slow and steady, and I step back, holding my breath. 'Do not be afraid, dear one. We shall not harm you.'

'What are your names?' I ask, forcing friendliness.

'We cannot remember,' the red-headed one replies, touching her forehead as though that would help her recall.

'We are the Ladies In Waiting,' the first cuts back in, stepping closer again.

Resisting the urge to run, I stand my ground. 'Are you nymphs?'

Both laugh at my question, then shake their heads.

'Then what are you?'

'We are the Ladies In Waiting,' the first repeats, a confused look on her softly sculpted face.

'Okay,' I accept, not understanding what she means by that. I'm not versed in Greek Mythology. What other dangerous creatures are there? By all accounts, they look more like goddesses than demons. 'Can you help me?'

'We can only help if you join us,' the second answers, drifting over to the fountain in the middle. She cups her hands and dips them into the clear water. Then, she drinks, a satisfied hum on her tongue.

Unease washes over me for no apparent reason. Didn't I wish to join them a few minutes ago? 'All right. How do I join you? I don't know the words to your song, I'm afraid.'

They both smile wide.

'We can teach you. Come—take my hand,' the first coaxes, beckoning me closer, her palm outstretched.

Heart stalling, I hesitate, my instincts telling me something isn't quite right here. Accepting their 'help' might not be the wisest decision. Realistically, though, I don't have much choice in the matter. I'm too short on time to pass up any assistance in this maze.

So, I swallow my trepidation and touch hands with the first Lady In Waiting. Her deep umber skin is cold to the touch and as silky as air. I'm glad she's solid enough that my hand doesn't pass through.

'Do not worry, dear one, we shall take good care of you,' she promises, leading me towards the fountain where the other waits patiently.

The second Lady In Waiting smiles at me in a welcoming way. When I'm near enough, she trails her fingers down my arm and around my back as she sweeps behind me.

Picking up the black waves of my hair, she starts to plait it loosely, taking care not to snag any knots. The first moves around to face me. With a soft smile, she leans in to place a dainty kiss on my cheek.

'Beautiful,' she whispers, taking in my features.

I blink in surprise as a blush rises to the surface of my skin. 'Thank you.'

'She will make a lovely lady,' the second comments, her delicate, icy fingers fluttering at the base of my spine. And I shiver, my nipples peaking.

Why am I turned on right now?

'This one is not a lady: she is a queen,' the first refutes, tilting my chin higher.

'I'm just a girl,' I protest, laughing uncomfortably. 'I'm in this maze to save my brother. That's why I need directions to the castle.' I'm hoping the casual reminder prompts them to deliver on their promise.

'I thought you wanted to join us?' the second says, taking my hand, our fingers entwining.

'I did—I do,' I'm quick to respond, that nugget of unease dropping like lead in my stomach. 'I just... I'll be happy to stay for a song, but I really need someone to point me in the right direction.'

Both beauties are in front of me now, blocking my view of the fountain. The first leans in again, and my back straightens when her full lips whisper over mine.

'Are you thirsty, dear one?' she asks, her hands going to my hips.

'Erm, not really,' I answer, acutely aware of an unexpected heat pooling low in my belly.

The second squeezes my hand, her nails digging in a little. 'Drink. Then we will teach you how to sing our song,' she encourages, her hands roaming up my arm again to my shoulder.

Moving closer, she tilts my face towards hers to plant a more forceful kiss on my lips.

A shocked gasp manages to slip past our fused mouths, and I go to push her back, but then the first holds my arms in place.

'We promise to take care of you,' the first assures me, one hand unlocking from my wrist to slide up to my breast. 'We like you, dear one. You shall become one of us.'

My centre starts to throb, and my mind clouds. Wasn't I supposed to be doing something?

The second pulls back to allow me to breathe. 'Join us.'

While the first is still teasing my nipple and kissing my neck, the second pulls her gown over her head. She's naked underneath, her moonlit skin perfect in its heavenly glow. She lifts my hand to place it on her breast and, turning shy, I bite my lower lip, enjoying the feel of her nipple as it hardens under my touch.

Was this what I came here for? I swear I was searching for something.

'To sing with us, first, you must drink,' the first stipulates more strongly, edging me closer to the fountain.

'Is it fresh?' I ask, and something in the back of my mind flashes—a warning—a male voice reciting a charm to make water safe to drink. It's a faint memory of danger.

'Very fresh,' the second guarantees, gliding my hand down her stomach to the apex of her thighs. 'Drink and be one of us.' I expect heat where I touch her, but it's like my fingers dip inside a frosted lake.

Alarm bells ring as the first brings her cupped hands to my lips. Clear water glistens a little *too* brightly inside. 'Drink, and you will be able to sing our song.'

I try to withdraw my hand from the second, but her grip tightens, pushing to flatten my hand against her sex. 'Do you not like us?' she questions, her light eyes darkening with hurt. 'Do you not wish to sing with us anymore?'

My tongue is thick in my throat when I mumble, 'Of course, I like you. I—I'm just not thirsty.' The first is scrutinising me now, too. So, I add, 'You're both beautiful, and I'd love to sing with you. This is just... something I'm not used to.' I'm starting to think we have *very* different definitions of singing.

Why am I here? Is this a dream?

The first lifts her cupped hand to my lips again, her eyes locking onto mine. 'If you want our help, you will drink.' Her voice has become more stern—sinister.

'I don't want to,' I whisper, quiet as a mouse. And sucking my lips inward, I seal them between my teeth, so I can't be forced.

They both frown at me, and the second's grip on my wrist becomes crushing. She yanks me forward, my body smacking against her naked flesh. She hisses in my face, her eyes misting milky white.

The first grabs my plait and yanks my head back sharply.

'Let me go!' I cry, struggling between their sandwiching bodies.

The first reaches around to pry my mouth open for the other to pour water into. The second scoops a trickle of the liquid in her free hand.

However, before she can drop any into my mouth, I catch the first's finger between my teeth and bite down. She screeches, lurching back with her hand clutched close to her chest.

I wriggle out of the first's grasp and run for it, not knowing much except that I must escape this situation. I think my life depends on it. But, before I can reach the trees, I'm leapt upon from behind.

My face hits the grey grass with a dull thud, and I'm rolled onto my back. The second is suddenly crawling on top of me, clawing at my face. I attempt to hold her at bay by pushing her chin up and away.

We're both screaming. Her bare legs clench around my waist while she strives to hold my hands down. The first rushes over to assist, her hands cupped. They're determined to force that fucking water down my throat.

What will happen to me if they succeed?

Wildly bucking my hips, I aim to dislodge the naked redhead from her straddle position. The first bends down, her cupped hands hovering over my mouth. I twist my face away, mouth slamming shut.

The second wraps her hands around my throat and squeezes. My mouth instinctually wants to open to suck in more air, but I fight against the impulse.

'Open up, dear one,' the first orders, her voice no longer melodic. It has a harsher rasp to it. Deeper, too—like a woman possessed.

Panic rises in my chest. But with it, something else surfaces.

When my mouth opens, a bright light erupts from within, and the Ladies In Waiting both shriek in fear, shielding their faces with their arms. I push the second off me as I scramble to my feet, the light fading.

They both crawl back, eyes wide as they stare at me, their jaws slack.

'It is impossible,' the first whispers, something akin to horrified awe on her face.

'What's impossible?' I demand, my limbs tingly, my heart fluttering in my heaving chest.

'That way,' the second directs, pointing north. 'The castle... take the next path to the left, keep on straight until you come to a rocky outcrop, then choose the second right at the fork. After that, listen for the river Melas. It will lead you where you need to go.' She sounds breathless—stunned.

'The castle? What's at the castle?' I query, my mind still foggy.

'Your brother,' the second reminds, and it all clicks back into place.

On reflex, I rub at my forehead, confusion abating. How could I forget about Robin? Their seduction must have disorientated me. 'What did you do to me? What are you?'

'We are the Ladies In Waiting,' the first repeats, pushing to her feet. 'We only wanted you to join us. It is what you asked for.'

Scowling, I snap back, 'You said you wouldn't hurt me.'

'We made a grave mistake. Please, accept our apologies,' the second hurries to say, meeker than she was before I shot light at her from my mouth.

What the fuck *was* that, anyway?

The first's jaw tics as if she is flat against speaking an apology to me.

Turning to her companion, the second remarks, 'You were right before: she is not a lady. She is greater. And we are bound to bow.'

The first sends a narrow-eyed glare my way. 'Perhaps. It is not yet set in stone. We shall see what the Shadows do to oppose.'

I look between them. 'What are you talking about?'

'On your way, dear one,' the first replies, standing aside. 'You got what you came for. Now go.'

With caution, I heed her order and slip past, not giving them my back in case they pounce again.

'We hope to see you again, païs tou Theia,' the second says as I back away.

Who the fuck do they think I am exactly?

Not lingering any longer for answers they don't seem willing to give, I follow the second's directions and take the next path left.

Something inside is telling me that I'm going in the right direction.

Something warm and embracing.

I let it guide me.

CHAPTER 35

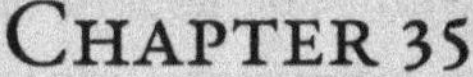

One Bird, Three Stones

RAVEN

Overhead, the perpetual storm clouds rumble their warning. A thickening mist rolls over the rocky maze walls, tumbling towards me.

This section combines the different segments I've traversed so far. The paths are structured and narrow, the ground uneven, but sporadic portions open to wider clearings. Cliffs surround the paths cut from their greyish stone, creating a valley in-between, where the maze runs in sharp, jaggedly carved turns.

There are no more trees. Though I can hear the distance sloshing of the river Melas. The red-headed Lady In Waiting told me to listen out for it. And heeding her advice, I take routes that only allow the sound to intensify.

I'm sweating; constant jogging has raised my body's temperature. I'm tempted to discard my jacket. Instead, I slip it off and wrap it around my waist, knotting the arms at the front. I wipe my damp forehead and continue, glad my hair is plaited away from my face.

It must be nearing the evening now. A few hours have passed since I left Hex to heal Dato and Lorcan. I wonder if they're okay. The sight of them bloody and broken in heaps on the ground—Lorcan in pain, Dato near death... makes me want to turn back, to check on them.

You can't go back, Raven. You can only keep moving forward. You should be happy to be rid of them. They were working against you. They're your enemy.

No matter how many times I remind myself of this, I still can't control how my insides roll up into a tight ball at the thought of them still injured.

I abandoned them in their time of need. Am I any better than a soulless demon? They risked their lives to protect me, and I couldn't even give up a little more time to stay and help them heal. There was a chance I could have convinced Dato and Lorcan to make the same deal Hex did with me.

But you couldn't afford to risk it. Too much is at stake.

To be fair to me, Hex is the soft touch. He's been the easiest to manipulate. Like me, he's somewhat desperate to be liked—loved even. Whereas Dato and Lorcan are more secretive about their insecurities. They've been harder to read and, thus, win over. Saying that, last night at Hergal's, I made a lot of progress with them both. Waking up this morning, I would have even gone as far as to say the four of us had made a tentative bond.

Then I went and broke it by running away.

What's worse than the guilt is the ache in my chest; I miss them. Especially Hex. He's been my emotional support here, always cracking inappropriate jokes and shamelessly flirting with me. I have no doubt that if those cyclopes *had* found us earlier, he would have fought them to the death, protecting me. Even weakened, he would have given them everything he had.

Shame has my face flushing hotter than exertion ever could. Choking on it, I fail to contain the overflow of tears. To collect myself, I pause to rub my sleeves over my eyes, struggling to dry them before more form.

You're so fucking weak. You're fooling yourself into thinking you mean anything to anyone. The Demon King ordered them to protect you. It was their job. They couldn't care less about you as a person. They'll be happy to see you caged and soulless until you fade to shadow.

My inner critic only pushes me to cry harder.

With my face in my hands, I let it all out. I want to scream, but that would be unwise—I'll lead every bird and beast in a ten-mile radius to me.

I force my anxious mind to revert to my favourite book. *What did the protagonist do at this point?* If I remember correctly, she had narrowly escaped the clutches of a gang of monstrous thieves by climbing up a cliff face. Similar to the cliffs bracketing this section of the maze. Unlike me right now—sad and alone—she had help from a turncoat. Someone a little like Hex.

In the book, the main turncoat is even described as a blood-hungry trickster, not to be trusted. Yet, despite deceiving her at the start, he never fails her at the heart of it. From the first meeting, he takes pity on her, then, dissatisfied with his king, he ends up saving her at numerous points in the story behind his king's back.

If only Hex weren't so fucking fond of the Demon King, then, by now, we'd be a proper team. Or maybe I'm still wishful thinking.

Shoving everything to the back of my mind, I carry on. My pace is more sluggish than before. The wariness has settled deep within my bones.

Footsteps. Behind me.

I spin around, my heart leaping to my mouth. They were faint, but I could tell they weren't the clawed clicks of raptor feet. These were human-like, which must mean a demon of some kind is on my tail.

The mist is too thick to see to the end of my path, so I sprint in the opposite direction without waiting to find out who's following, pushing my aching legs to work through panic and fatigue.

I race through the maze like my life depends on it. It likely does. But unfortunately, I can't keep that exhausting pace up for long.

I'm forced to spare a moment to recover and start hyperventilating. My head is swimming too much for me to see straight. I'm practically on the verge of collapse.

A low growl echoes down the path. Or did it? It could be coming from anywhere—the path adjacent, the way ahead—I can't be sure.

Fuck. *Fuck*!

The only thing I can do is push on. So, I grit my teeth and stumble the rest of the way down the path I'm already travelling. Blood is pounding in my ears. Making it more difficult to pick up on the current whereabouts of my pursuer.

A shadow passes overhead, and my stomach takes a dive.

Oh, no.

I don't just have one beast after me.

I suspect that I have three very angry demons taunting me, determined to hunt me down and enact their revenge.

One bird, three stones.

They're going to *pulverise* me.

It's all scare tactics: the footsteps, the growling, the flying overhead. They could have easily caught me by now, but they're choosing to fuck with me first.

Well, *fuck them*! I won't let them scare me into submission anymore. I know they can't truly hurt me.

Hex made me a promise. And, yeah, I left him. But I fulfilled my side of the bargain first; I willingly returned to find Dato and Lorcan with him. He never specified that I had to stay by his side afterwards. As a demon, he should have known better than to be vague.

Holding my head up high, I march on, moving as fast as possible without running. Now I know the right direction, they'll resort to violence to stop me. They'll have to keep me restrained because, at every opportunity, I'll go my own way.

I'm fighting back.

'Oh, little bird.' Hex's voice reverberates off the stone, creating an echo chamber. 'You think you can fly away from us that easily?'

His taunting tone sends a shudder through me. I'm in trouble. It's not down to *if* they catch me, but *when*.

Another question prolongs the quaking: how do they plan to punish me?

'I had to. Dato and Lorcan would have stopped me from progressing. Running was the only way I could reach the castle in time,' I call out in explanation, hoping he understands my reasoning. 'It wasn't anything against you, Hex. You're my favourite.'

At my admission, Hex gives an incredulous snicker. Then, the growler from earlier (Lorcan) makes his dominating presence heard. The sound is significantly more ferocious than the previous.

Maybe telling Hex he was my favourite wasn't the best move. Now, I've gone and pissed Lorcan and Dato off more. I had hoped Hex would intercede if they were too rough with me. A part of me also wanted Hex to know he wasn't the reason I fled. If I could have stayed with him, I would have. Even against my better judgement, I trust that vulgar vamp with more than my life.

Dato and Lorcan haven't yet earned the same. And, if they stand in my way again, our bridges can never be rebuilt.

For the second time, Dato's winged shadow sweeps over me. 'Do you think it wise to play favourites, mortal?'

'Please, let me go. Let me save my brother,' I beg, trying to sound teary. I'm too tired to shed any more tears. Even if I wasn't, I refuse to. This is me fighting, not crying. If I must perform the role of damsel in distress to make them feel sorry for me, then I'll do it with a secret smile—internally triumphant.

Rounding the next turn, I see him: Lorcan. But it's not him; a huge wolf-like figure stands menacingly in the middle of my chosen path. The mist swirls around him, providing an ominous backdrop. Not that he needs it.

With sharp teeth bared, he snarls. The dark brown fur lining his heavily muscled torso bristles. If he wasn't wearing his signature joggers, I would question whether it was him. The only thing he's missing is a tail. The rest of him is positively wolfish.

Another shudder crawls down my frozen frame. He's fucking terrifying like this. I thought I was intimidated by his size and presence before; this beast is straight out of my nightmares.

However, after the shot of fear comes an unexpected chaser; I have to clench my thighs together to ease the pounding.

Beast-form Lorcan's nose twitches. He sniffs the air and then says, 'Your body seems to disagree with your choices, songbird.' His voice is so gruff I'm surprised I can understand him. He must have caught the scent of my arousal. 'You think your *favourite* is going to help you now?'

Slowly, he shakes his head, tutting, and I swallow thickly.

Adrenaline has my legs shaking. My breaths are coming too fast as I wait for his next move.

Eyes gleaming gold through the mist, Lorcan growls one word... 'Run.'

CHAPTER 36

Next Move

Drinking two bottles of wine and three glasses of whiskey wasn't the sleeping aid I had hoped for. Instead, my hangover arrived prematurely, preventing me from the rest my depleted body needed.

There are seven hours left.

Still bone tired, I leave my bedchamber and move with purpose towards the Harvest Hall.

On the way, I'm intercepted by Marguerite. With her hands on her hips, she looks up at me through narrowed eyes. 'The child is upset again. What did you say to him?' she demands, and I bristle at her chiding tone.

If Marguerite were anyone else, I'd throw her in the dungeon for the night. Unfortunately, I can't revert to that punishment with her; the woman practically raised me.

Being a keeper demon, I was made by the Underworld, not born to it like harpyiai are. Like mortals, they have a mother and a father, whereas the Shadows shape keeper demons from their father's power. My father had to relinquish a fair chunk of his power for me to be made. And the DiMinos line always produces one heir—male. It's the opposite rule for Raven's family line. Their first child is always a daughter, tied to the DiMinos heir through our shared curse. Although never in the way Raven and I are connected—twin souls—one born, one made, at the same moment.

There must be a reason for it.

'Well?' Marguerite prompts expectantly. She knows she can get away with being this direct with me.

Folding my arms in defence, I answer flatly, 'I told him the truth. And he's not a child; he's an insufferable teenager who needs to learn that no world revolves around him.'

'Julius, he's a fifteen-year-old boy who was taken in the middle of the night from his home to a place worse than his nightmares. He also has a right to be worried for his sister,' she counters, placing a hand on my elbow. The touch instantly calms my nerves, and my tense shoulders slacken.

'What would you have me do? Let them go? You, of all people, know I don't have that luxury.'

'I know,' Marguerite says softly, rubbing her thumb over my arm to soothe me. 'But that doesn't mean you can't show them kindness. They're mortal. They're scared. Be aware of that. Be understanding.'

'Kindness doesn't come as naturally to demons as it does mortals.'

Nodding in acceptance of this fact, Marguerite replies, 'I understand that. But it doesn't stop you trying, mon chéri.'

Exhaling my frustration, I withdraw from her, not in the mood to discuss such matters when I have more important things to concentrate on, like charging my power so I'm strong enough to make my next move.

'I will consider your suggestion. But, for now, I must recharge.' I stride past her, then rotate my head to add, 'Check on the kid. Make sure he's all right.'

'I was going to,' she tells me. 'Right after I checked on you.'

My immortal heart swells a little at her concern for me. 'I'll be fine. I just need to recharge.'

Not waiting for a reply, I continue down the hallway, my pace unsteady.

After responsibly withdrawing energy from a soul I haven't used in a while, I take a detour before leaving the Harvest Hall. With my power replenished, I'm surer on my feet—the exhaustion expunged from my limbs.

I come to a section of the hall I rarely visit. It's where all my staff's souls are kept safe. I usually refrain from touching the souls of those who serve me. That's the one good thing my father ever taught me: do not abuse those who will one day reclaim their power. It will only come back to bite you. It's a shame he never extended that courtesy to me. But then he knew I would only obtain my power when he was gone.

When I open the metal gate which separates this section from the main hall, power buzzes in my chest. The bartered souls of my commanders are centre stage—Dato, Lorcan, and *Hex*.

Because I've never withdrawn power from them, their souls are still bright white and throbbing with their luminous energy. Hex's, in particular, has been here the longest. He pledged a century of service, and he's about halfway through. When his time is up, he can reclaim his soul and leave Galbrek if he wishes.

After his betrayal, he doesn't deserve a soul untouched.

With this thought burning hot inside my mind, I step onto the podium displaying his contained soul.

Despite not needing it, I withdraw more power from the bright orb; I don't restrict my intake.

I want his soul to shatter. I want to cause its corruption.

My eyes widen as Hex's energy charges through my veins. And, sucking in an ecstasy-filled breath, I let my head roll back.

If Hex hopes to steal what's mine, I'll use up what's not yet his.

At present, I don't give a fuck what this does to my reputation as a keeper demon. Hex's betrayal has already tarnished my pride. When other demons discover he disobeyed a direct order for a mortal girl's pussy, the DiMinos name will be dragged through the mud regardless.

Satisfaction rolls in waves as I take and take from my rival, unrelenting. My body is brimming with more power than I know what to do with. I've never felt so unstoppable.

What *does* stop me is a sudden pounding of my heart—wild and painful.

I lift my hands from the dimming orb, stumble back off the podium, and then rub at my tightening chest.

Raven: I sense her again.

She's terrified; adrenaline is pumping through her blood. The hammering of her heart is causing shockwaves, which pummel my own.

I breathe through the shock to my system and quickly bridle my power.

Despite the pain, I'm glad to sense her alive and well, frightened though she may be. She must be running from something. My legs are shaking from the strain she's sharing with me.

Has my wilful little starling given Dato, Lorcan, and Hex the slip? With them around, she shouldn't be in any danger.

Then I remember the window, seeing her in Hex's clutches with the other two nowhere in sight. Did Hex steal her away from them?

At the time, I was too enraged to question why they were alone together. Knowing Hex, I doubt he would have done anything to harm his friends. He cares for Lorcan and Dato. He wouldn't have hurt them even for his own selfish pleasure, making me think they were likely busy dealing with another foe.

With my anxiety overlapping, I search within myself to find Raven's well of emotions. With my overflow of power, I should be able to tap into it.

Fear is what I find. But also... anticipation? Desire?

The sinking weight in my gut forces bile into my oesophagus, causing me to choke in disbelief.

My starling isn't running away from danger. She's welcoming it.

She wants to be caught.

Shadows pass over my eyes as my endless rage is awoken again. My overflowing power drips off my fingers, sizzling on the stone floor in pools of midnight sulphur.

Whoever is chasing what's mine is about to discover what it's like to be prey.

It's time to make my move.

CHAPTER 37

Punishment

RAVEN

Pain shoots through my legs as my feet pound against the uneven terrain. My lungs are overworked; every harsh gulp of air is laced with invisible fire.

The three demons chasing me have hung back, making their presence known in more sinister ways, like before. I'm being hunted by their shadows, which is far scarier than if I saw them in front of me.

In their presence, I've found comfort. With their absence, my anxiety is at an all-time high. The threat of them is worse.

The anticipation alone is killing me.

Maybe I'm more afraid of my wanting to get caught than actually getting caught.

Dato's shadow swoops, cutting the air above with a swish. Shrieking, I duck. But when I look up, he's nowhere in sight.

The sound of Hex's low chuckle sneaks up behind me, but spinning to find him, I can't.

'Your favourite can't wait to hear you scream his name when I have your face down in the dirt,' Lorcan threatens, yet his tone is a smoky caress. 'But he won't save you from me. So, you better start saying *my* name as a prayer. Because when I catch you, it won't just be Hex who will show his teeth.'

A shiver tingles through every layer of my skin as I push on, sneaking paranoid glances over my shoulder. It's not only my heart pounding; the pulsing heat between my legs makes it harder to use them effectively.

My foot snags on a displaced stone at one sharp turn, and I come crashing down to my knees, skimming them. Red blood swells to dampen my torn-up leggings, and I curse, knowing this will probably stir Hex into a frenzy. Wincing, I try to rub the pain out of my knees before I stand.

When I move on, I can hardly walk, let alone run. I'm so fucking tired. *Just catch me already*! I shout inside my head, limping along like a wounded puppy. Pride is a forgotten sin.

'Are you bleeding, darling?' Hex asks from somewhere unknowable. 'Do you want me to lick it better?' His voice contains false sympathy. 'It will be the last time I'll use my tongue to take care of you. From now on, all you'll be getting is the pinch of my fangs.'

'You can stop tormenting me now. I'm fed up with the threats. Get to it already. I don't have time for this,' I assert, stopping and straightening to hold my head high. 'If you want me, come and claim me.'

For a long minute, my challenge hangs in the air. The nightmarish world around me goes still, and an eerie silence stalls even my breath.

Out of nowhere, I'm grabbed under my arms and lifted off my feet. A winged demon (who I assume is Dato) carries me the rest of the way down the path while I kick and scream at him to put me down. He doesn't fly away with me. He doesn't even lift me higher than the maze wall. I imagine it's for my safety. If I fight him to the point where he drops me, I can't go splat at this height.

I use my short nails to dig into his arms, which are secured tightly under my bust. 'Dato! Let me go!'

With a devious snicker, he finally listens, dropping my weight without warning. I feebly try to stop my momentum by pinwheeling my arms, but a second later, I'm on my scratched-up hands and knees again. Tears of frustration leak from my eyes, and I groan loudly.

'We don't want your moans. We want you screaming until your voice is lost,' Hex tells me with no hint of compassion. God, he must be *really* pissed off with me for ditching him. 'But, by all means, keep weeping on the ground like the coward you are. This isn't the cupboard under the stairs, darling. Still, you're just as trapped.'

The scorned vamp's insult cuts deep, pain filling my chest as I bleed from the heart. He knows how to hurt me without laying a single finger on my skin. He's making me regret ever confiding in him.

I squeeze my eyes shut and force the rest of my tears out. 'Enough! I'm sorry, okay? I'm sorry I ran off. I should have stayed to help. I should have trusted you, Hex. I nearly did. I wanted to. But now you're proving to me that I was right to trust in my instincts first and foremost.'

After that, Hex goes quiet again. They all do.

I stand up on shaky legs and slowly drag my feet to the end of the path, which opens out into a clearing.

Wait. This isn't the typical clearing I've come across before. There's a narrow stream which leads down a gentle decline. A stream that most likely joins the river Melas.

Hot and sticky, I stagger over to peer down the hill. As soon as I spot the black river below, I want to jump up and down in triumph. Yet my bruised knees and seizing muscles refuse to cooperate with that whim. So, instead, I breathe a sigh of relief and sag down to sit on the soft grass by the connecting stream.

And wait.

The cool air dries the perspiration clinging to my clothes and sheening my skin.

Only a minute passes before they show their faces. Hex and Lorcan stalk out of the maze to stand opposite me, expressionless. A moment later, Dato drops from the sky to land beside them.

Lorcan has transformed back into his human-like form. To my amazement, disappointment blunts the thrill of getting caught. His beast form was oddly attractive.

'Are you ready for your punishment, songbird?' Lorcan enquires, crossing his heavily tattooed arms over his tanned chest.

With defiant eyes, I hold their gazes and nod once.

Dato smirks. 'Oh, mortal, you're really not.'

Despite my fear, a sharper thrill zings straight to my clit at his warning.

Eyes onyx, Hex says, 'I bet your pussy is as wet and swollen as your tear-stained face. Isn't it?'

My cheeks fill with as much heat as my core. I close my eyes as if not seeing them will make this humiliation easier to stomach.

'Show us, deal-breaker,' Hex asserts, gravel in his tone. 'Show us how wet we've made you.'

I hesitate despite knowing they're not so wicked as to force me to do anything sexual against my will. I still have a choice here. Maybe not regarding which direction I travel, but when it comes to my body, they won't seek to use it without my consent.

'You better decide quickly because your time is nearly up,' Lorcan urges, raising his scarred eyebrow in challenge.

They know I'd rather not admit to wanting this out loud, but my actions will dictate how this punishment goes down. If I refuse Hex's request, they'll take that as a no. But if I go along with this... show them how much I want it—*them*—then I'll receive the sort of punishment I've been selfishly craving from the start.

As soon as I make my mind up, I hook my thumbs in the waistband of my leggings and slowly drag them down, shifting my hips to get them under my arse. The dark grey, blood-stained material rolls to my ankles, and then I kick them away as soon as my feet are free. My jacket covers the tops of my bare thighs, shielding what they want from view.

'Open those legs wide,' Dato instructs me, his lips wet with saliva after running his tongue over them numerous times.

All three of them focus in on my legs as I spread them, my thighs trembling with nervous excitement.

They each react differently to the sight of my glistening centre. Dato shuts his eyes as though fighting temptation. Hex licks his lips, aching for another taste of me, despite swearing he would only use his fangs from now on. I don't believe that for a second, not with the way he's biting his tongue to save it from my skin. As for Lorcan, his eyes are blazing gold, his jaw so tense, he could snap a bone.

'Slide two fingers inside yourself, then hold them up,' Lorcan directs, the low growl behind his words pooling more warmth where he wants me to touch.

I bite my bottom lip and reach down to run two fingers lightly over my clit before I slip them inside me. My fingers are dripping when I raise them in front of me for the demons to see.

'Fuck,' Hex breathes, looking skyward for strength as he adjusts himself in his trousers.

Now, it's Lorcan who licks his lips while Dato rubs his mouth, his attention still caught between my legs. Out of the three of them, Dato appears to be the most resistant. He's clearly still at war with himself, stuck between his loyalty to the Demon King, and the desire to claim my body along with his more eager friends.

'Top off. Now,' Lorcan commands through gritted teeth.

Without missing a beat, I shimmy my arms out of my jacket, pull my top over my head, and then toss it to the side.

Completely bare, I lean my weight back on my hands, my legs still wide open, and give them a confrontational look, daring them to approach.

But they don't.

Instead, without discussing it (which likely means they planned all of this on the way here), they move as one towards the stream. They hop across it, then casually perch down on a stone shelf.

'What are you doing all the way over there? Are you running from *me* now?' I boldly tease, snapping my legs shut.

Hex huffs a derisive laugh. 'Be careful there. You more than deserve to be left wanting.'

'Do you want me to come to you? Is that it? You want me to come crawling back?' I question, sneering.

'That's exactly what we want you to do,' Dato answers, a sly smile on his face.

My forehead furrows in confusion, not fully understanding.

'Get on your hands and knees,' Dato clarifies, pointing to the muddy bank beside me. 'Come crawling back to us. We want you begging for your punishment.'

I release a shaky breath, clit untouched yet twinging with pleasure. 'My knees are sore,' I complain, knowing it's pointless because they can already see the nasty grazes which still bead with blood, and yet they're asking me to use them, nonetheless.

Dato shrugs. 'And they're about to be sorer.'

Resisting another retort, I blow out the pent-up air from my lungs and comply. I shift my weight onto my hands and knees, wincing at the sting as my tender skin sinks into the softer soil of the damp bank.

'Crawl through that mud to us. We want to see you nice and dirty,' Lorcan encourages, using his index finger to gesture for me to come like I'm a bitch in heat.

They watch me raptly as I slowly make my way across the shallow stream to them, my hands and knees sliding in the almost black mud. The equally dark water cleans most of the muck away, but as soon as I make it to the other side and claw my way up the opposite bank, my naked skin is covered in black splodges. With my creamy complexion, I look like a Dalmatian.

'Such a filthy girl,' Hex drawls, more playfully than before. Is he softening?

Reaching the grass, I wipe my hands on the sparse grey blades to clean some of the mud off my fingers.

'You don't need your hands for what comes next,' Lorcan remarks, the gold of his irises swirling with mischief. 'Come here.'

A spark settles in my lower belly and catches alight. I crawl over to where they lounge on their stone thrones.

'Sit on your heels, right there.' Dato points to a patch of grass in the centre by their feet.

I do as I'm told, resting my bare bum on my muddy heels, palms flat on my thighs. I peer up at them through my lashes, subservient yet seductive. They may exert their power over me, but I still have control. The power in their hands is what I gave them.

I can take it back anytime with a single word.

As if he can read my mind, Hex prompts, 'What's your safe word, darling? Say it.'

After swallowing, I manage to answer with confidence, 'Birdie.'

'Good girl,' he praises with a small nod.

'Wh—what's my punishment?' I ask, the trepidation only heightening the desire coursing through my veins.

All three of their smiles are a salacious promise. Even Dato eyes my body like he's going to devour me.

'Closer,' Dato beckons, his usually smooth voice husky.

I shuffle up until my knees are touching Dato and Hex's boots. They look down their noses at me. Then Lorcan grabs my plaited hair and yanks my head back, but I don't cry out like I've done before.

'You owe each of us an apology,' Lorcan pronounces, tightening his grasp until I wince.

'I've already said I'm sorry,' I remind him, the heaviness between my legs is pressing.

Lorcan leans forward to rub his thumb over my bottom lip. 'We don't want your words; we just want that pretty mouth to make it up to us.'

My throat works as I watch Lorcan recline back and pull his very long, very thick cock out of his joggers. With my wide eyes on it, it jerks to attention.

Hex is quick to follow Lorcan's lead. He unlaces his trousers and offers me the same view. I'm already semi-acquainted with his, so it's no surprise. Curious, I peek over at Dato, who's cupping his erection through his black, armoured trousers.

'Tell me how much you want it first,' Dato says, still cautious. What doesn't seem as hesitant is his tail; it excitedly flutters against my thigh before it lightly loops around my waist, the feathers at the tip caressing the curve of my breast.

Enjoying the sensation, my eyelids fall closed, and I shiver with want. When I open them again, I admit, 'I want you, Dato. I want you to take your cock out and punish me with it.'

My consent is all the fuel he needed. He unbuttons his trousers with shaky fingers and reveals his length to me. It's as impressive as the other two; it's smooth, straight, and achingly hard. He's a similar size to Hex—big but workable. Lorcan is where I'm struggling. My jaw locks just at the sight of it.

'Get to work on that apology,' Hex says, stroking himself. But when I go to touch him, he snatches my hand mid-air. 'Your mouth only.'

Anticipation is a writhing delight inside me. I place my hands on Hex's knees, then lean over with my mouth open, ready to take him.

Hex grips the base of his cock and slides it inside, groaning at the warm welcome I give him as I swirl my tongue against the underside. 'That's it. Keep doing that. It feels so fucking good.'

Taking control, I bob my head up and down, withdrawing to the tip, then slowly pushing down to take most of him—as much as humanly possible. When he hits the back of my throat, I struggle against my gag reflex by stealing a moment to breathe through my nose.

I'm very aware of Dato and Lorcan watching me, waiting for their turn. They're both stroking themselves in the meantime.

Hex grabs a handful of hair at the top of my head to force me down further. When my lips near the base, I gag, and he quickly tugs my head back up. Mouth now empty, I gasp, but as soon as my lungs are full, he drives me down again.

'Did you think I'd be gentle after your behaviour today? First, you tried to kill me, then left me after I gave in to you.'

Unapologetically, Hex continues to push me to my limits, fucking my face, and all I can do is try to endure it, his breathy grunts worth the burning in my throat and the ache in my jaw. Tears cloud my vision, and I peer up at him through them, whimpering—begging without words for his forgiveness.

For mercy.

After a particularly brutal thrust, he gives me a chance to use my safe word, waiting for a beat for me to admit defeat, his dark eyes surveying my flushed, tear-soaked face.

I don't. Even though he's thrown me in at the deep end, this, by far, is the most intense and extreme sexual experience I've ever had in my life, and I'm not ready for it to stop.

'You think you can handle more?' Hex taunts, lifting my chin. He kindly wipes my cheeks free of tears, and my mouth of saliva. 'Lorcan can give it to you.'

Without waiting for me to move, Lorcan drags me to him by the arm and settles me between his legs. 'Open wide.'

I suck in a readying breath and have to practically unhinge my jaw for Lorcan to fit inside my mouth. Shockingly, he's not as rough as Hex. He must know, with his size, he can't be. He lets me dictate the pace, and I try not to disappoint him. I use all the tricks I learnt from magazines growing up: hollowing my cheeks as I suck, running the tip of my tongue along the thick ridge to stimulate him, and rubbing the head against my lips as if I'm using it to apply lipstick.

I'm rewarded with low grunts and snarling moans as Lorcan enjoys what I do to him. His fingers thread through my hair, caressing, not pulling. Instead of pushing, he lightly guides my head down while his hips thrust up on each stroke.

'Your ex is a fucking fool for denying you,' Lorcan says on a groan. 'Denying *himself*,' he corrects. 'You're fucking perfect. So incredible. My beautiful songbird.'

I shine at the compliments, smiling as I lick the salty precum off the tip. Who would have thought Lorcan was a praise dom?

When I use my teeth to apply a little pressure around the head, the werewolf's hips buck. 'Fucking mazes,' he rasps, tipping his head back. 'I'm going to come if you keep doing that.'

'Isn't that the point?' I say before another teasing lick.

'You've still got Dato to warm up first,' Lorcan tells me, taking his cock in his hands to shield it from my tormenting tongue.

'Crawl to me, mortal,' Dato orders, using two fingers to tempt me over.

As seductively as I can, covered in mud and lips puffy, I slink towards the harpy like a prowling leopard, my predatory gaze locked on his. He sits up straighter, cock twitching without me even touching it. To the side of him, his tail is thumping against the stone, making him extra endearing. His draped wings tense up each side of him.

On the way, Hex spanks my arse. Tingles are left after the initial shock to my skin. My desire for more slickens the tops of my thighs, and my clit throbs with the need to be touched.

Reaching Dato, I don't pause to allow him time to reconsider his lapse in loyalty. I take him as far into my mouth as I can, and a breath rushes out of him, along with a curse.

Dato's fingers don't tangle in my hair like the others. He wedges a hand between us to fondle my breast, allowing me some pleasure as I work his shaft with my mouth, using the same tricks I performed on Hex and Lorcan.

'Ah, fuck... shit. You're too fucking good at that, Raven,' he grinds out through whispered moans. It's only the second time he's used my actual name when speaking to me. It makes my heart skip a beat.

I like that each of them has their own pet name for me. But, unlike Hex and Lorcan, and even the Demon King, Dato's is a tool to maintain distance. When he uses my given name, it's more intimate, like he's letting me get past his armour.

Lost to the pleasure I deliver, Dato's tail whips around, slapping against my lower back like a whip. With my mouth full of his cock, I yelp, savouring another tingling sting.

Hex bends to sneak a hand between my legs. His two fingers circle my clit, gathering moisture. 'You like a bit of pain with your pleasure, don't you, darling?' He brings those two fingers to his mouth and licks them clean, then hums his appreciation at my taste. 'Turn around and press your face to the grass, arse in the air. Let us admire what's now ours.'

I give Dato one last savouring lick before I release him. As soon as I do, his tense posture relaxes. I had him so close, right on the edge of that precipice.

Facing the stream, I keep my legs braced hip-width apart as I lower my head to the ground. Behind me, I hear all three of them groan at seeing my most delicate parts on display.

I thought I'd be more mortified than this. But, mostly, this twisted part of me is revelling in the torture, thoroughly enjoying the effect I'm having on them, even though some would think I'm degrading myself to please them—a vile debasement I should be ashamed of.

The problem is I *want* to please them. They say this is my punishment, but for me, it's my reclamation. I'm finding a sense of freedom in the act that is wholly unexpected. It's totally against society's narrow and patriarchal rules regarding what women can enjoy when it comes to their own bodies.

It seems, down here, in the Underworld, there are no such rules or double standards.

I've chosen this. I've chosen *myself* for once. Not out of duty or loyalty or fear in whatever form I'm used to; it's completely out of pure want.

I *want* them. All three of them. And I will have them. If only the once.

The Demon King's beautiful face flashes in my mind, and my heart skips again. If I'm honest with myself, I want him, too. But I know he's not the kind of guy who can share; he wants me all for himself.

Well, that doesn't work for me.

From this point on, the only person who can claim me is me.

But, lucky for these demons, I'm more than willing to share the goods.

CHAPTER 38

Raw

RAVEN

'**B**e a good girl and rub your clit,' Lorcan's deep voice is pitched impossibly low. 'Play with that pussy while we watch.'

Aching for them to touch me, I touch myself, bent over, right side of my face pressed to the ground, arse up. I've done this melting heart position in yoga before, so it's not a stretch.

Hex is the first to stand. He leads Lorcan and Dato over to loom behind me. 'Don't move. Don't speak unless you need to use your safe word. And most importantly, do *not* make yourself come. Do you understand?'

I nod, cheek rubbing against the prickling grass. Apprehension mingles with excitement as I wait for them to make their next move. Are they going to take turns fucking me? The thought alone has my insides writhing in delighted desperation.

The first slap is a surprise delivery from Hex. My right arse cheek burns after contact, and I can't stop the jolt of every muscle in my body or the yelp that follows.

'I said, don't move,' Hex reprimands, smoothing over the hurt with a soft, tingling caress.

For the next smack, I brace myself. Dato serves, but it's not as hard. And he chooses the other cheek to mitigate the damage. To soften the blow, he knocks my hand away to touch me where I need some tenderness. I moan, the pleasure and pain joining hand in hand.

When Dato's ministrations fall away, I replace them with my own again. And, guessing who's up next, I can't stop the tremor that quakes through me.

So far, Hex has shown the most vitriol. He's made me pay for my escape attempt. The same as when we fought earlier; he bit my thigh and made it painful in retaliation for hurting his feelings.

Twenty minutes ago, I was the most afraid of Lorcan. He's been the demon to threaten me more often, the one to punish me with pain and humiliation. But when he had the chance to abuse my mouth, he didn't. He was gentle and praising. The big guy is secretly a softie beneath that tough, wolfish exterior.

Still, Lorcan's spanking is prolonged but lighter with each strike. He doesn't settle for one palm clap like the other two. I count ten. Five on each cheek. During this, I grit my teeth, absorbing the pain and converting it to pleasure with the tight circling of my clit.

'That tight little arse will be covered in our handprints and red raw by the time we're through with you,' Lorcan tells me, trailing his fingers over the skin he's set alight with his worshipping blows.

'Now, say thank you,' Hex requires from me, a smile in his voice. It appears he's finally forgiven me.

Pride rearing, it takes me an extended beat before I can comply. 'Thank you.' The words taste a little bitter on my tongue, but I'd take that over further spanking. If Hex decides to deliver another one of his slaps, I'll be forced to use my safe word.

'Look at you, deal-breaker, doing such a good job taking your punishment and thanking us for it,' Hex praises, dipping two fingers inside me.

At my moan, he withdraws them, then lightly pats that sensitive area with his whole palm. I jolt again, hissing a breath. Pleasure coils deep in my belly, begging to be unwound.

'Do you think you deserve a reward now?' Hex asks, using his fingertips to stimulate me. 'Do you think you've earned our forgiveness?'

'Yes,' I whimper, burning with the need—pulsating—clenching—dying. 'Please. Yes.'

'Are we really going to fuck her?' Dato whispers to Lorcan. 'What about Julius?'

'What Hex pointed out earlier is enough to muddy the waters. You said Julius' exact words were, 'if *one* of you dares to fuck her'. If we all do it, then technically, it's not breaking the rules,' Lorcan counters, obviously happy to wishful think on the matter if it means he can have me even once before this day is done.

'Raven, if you want us to stop at any point, don't be afraid to say it. Okay?' Dato's voice is soft yet insistent. He's making sure I know that I'm the one in control here. I'm grateful for him. Every group needs at least one responsible adult.

'Okay,' I confirm, switching sides because my neck aches. Plus, I can see Dato better with the left side of my face pressed to the ground.

Behind me, Dato drops to one knee. He starts by rubbing the tip of his cock up and down, from my entrance to my hood and back again, over and over, wetting the end with my desire. 'Do you want this?' he asks again, needing to check one last time.

'Yes... Please.' Pride be damned. I don't care how desperate I sound.

'Good, because there's been no one I've wanted more,' he divulges, continuing to withhold himself in this final way, teetering on the edge of giving me all of him.

Wits returning through the cloud of lust, I say abruptly, 'Wait!'

'What?' Dato lurches away. He must think I've changed my mind.

I push onto my hands to view them over my shoulder. 'Don't you need some form of protection? I don't particularly want to end up pregnant with the antichrist.'

Hex bursts out laughing, and Dato stares at me, confusion written on his face, while Lorcan bites on a smile.

'You don't have to worry about spawning the son of Satan with us. Demons can't reproduce with mortals unless there's a deal made with the Shadows,' Hex reassures me, bending to tuck a loose strand of hair behind my ear. 'Also, just so you know, we can't contract sexually transmitted diseases, either.'

Relief loosening my chest, I nod. 'I need to know one more thing,' I say, unsure how they'll take this next question.

'What is it, deal-breaker?'

I look past Hex to make eye contact with Dato and Lorcan. 'Will you force me to go in the wrong direction now that I know the right one?'

My question has all three of them exchanging unreadable glances.

Seeming sure of himself, Hex states, 'We made a deal, and I promise to stick to it. I won't stand in your way.'

'I won't help you reach the castle, but I won't use force to stop you,' Dato promises a moment later, tossing me the barest hint of a smile. His tail, on the other hand, lavishes me with affectionate strokes.

It's like my heart doubles in size. And more hopeful than I've been since I started this quest, I turn my attention to Lorcan, who's frowning in thought, hands on his hips. 'Are you going to be the one who stops me, beastie boy?'

With a small shake of his head, Lorcan gives me my answer without flourish. And, as soon as I have it, tears spring to my eyes.

'Thank you,' I whisper, choked up.

'You're unlikely to make it to the castle by midnight. But it's possible,' Hex says, rotating my face to his as he crouches beside me. 'Now, dry those tears, shut the fuck up, and take all three of us like the good girl that you are. Then, we'll get you cleaned up and let you continue in whatever fucking direction you want. Got it?'

With a grateful smile, I use the clean part of my forearm to swipe across my watery eyes. 'Got it.'

Dato returns to his previous position and doesn't waste any time. He pushes his cock inside me with a groan, filling the tight space inch by inch, and I stretch to accommodate him. Then, holding my hips while his tail snakes beneath them, he proceeds to grind his pelvis against my sensitive centre as feathers tickle my hardened nipples.

'Raven.' Dato says my name like a prayer. 'Oh, fuck. Raven.' His wings spread, silken black and blue feathers rustling in the breeze.

'Oh, God,' I cry, building fast; the extreme foreplay beforehand has set up the imminent explosion.

'There is no God; there is only us,' Lorcan proclaims, a growl scratching his throat.

An intense pang of pleasure reverberates to my very wound-tight core. 'Dato, I'm so close.'

Hearing this, Dato quickens his pace, his tail trailing down to flutter rapidly against my clit.

'Come for him, darling. Let go,' Hex urges, tilting my face again to kiss me while Dato continues to fuck, and Lorcan stands by, watching, his cock firmly in hand.

That glorious coil in my stomach releases like a spring. Hex swallows my cries of ecstasy, his lips sealed over mine, his tongue exploring my mouth.

A handful of seconds later, Dato pulses inside me, finding his release. He stutters out a breath, his hips spasming as he withdraws from me. The evidence of his orgasm trickles down my thigh.

'I can't believe I did that,' Dato says, breathless, shocked by his betrayal. Even if they've found a loophole, he still went against the wishes of his king—his friend.

Lorcan pushes Dato aside to slot himself into position. 'Get over it. It's my turn now.' He grabs my arse with both hands. 'I won't be as gentle as the harpy, songbird. When lycanthropes fuck, they fuck hard.'

'Go on, then. What are you waiting for?' I challenge, moving my hips from side to side to tempt him, even though my nerve endings are still buzzing from the orgasm Dato gave me.

With a wolfish grin spreading across his ruggedly beautiful, bearded face, Lorcan catches my plait and tugs, roughly tipping my head back. 'I'm waiting for you to beg for it.'

'Please, fuck me already. I haven't got all day,' I retort, pushing my luck in the hopes of tasting his wrath.

Growling, Lorcan slams into me, pulling more aggressively on my hair. What comes out of my mouth is practically a scream, but I take all of him without complaint. Thank fuck for the extra lubrication Dato supplied; I doubt it would be as smooth a glide without it.

I tremble while Lorcan relentlessly pounds into me, his fingers digging into my skin, my plait a leash. My arms are close to giving way. My teeth ache from grinding them together as the intense pressure slowly eases, making way for a second orgasm.

'Is this fast enough for you?' Lorcan jibes, increasing his speed.

Unable to form words or coherent thoughts, I let my primal groan answer for me.

'Hex. Dato. Touch. Her,' he instructs them, panting between words.

Dato lowers to his knees on the opposite side to Hex, then reaches past my belly button to play with my clit, while Hex kisses my neck and rolls my nipples between his fingers. I wait for the bite that doesn't come. I guess the vamp is saving that for his turn.

The frantic, unabating friction, combined with the multiple points of stimulation, causes my next orgasm to come crashing into me like a tidal wave. This time, there's no denying the validity of my scream. Lorcan follows me into oblivion shortly after, grunting as he slows, his warmth pouring into me.

'You took him so beautifully,' Hex whispers in my ear as he gives my nipples one last tweak. 'I'm proud of you.' He kisses away a stray tear hovering on my cheekbone.

Fuck. Lorcan is not the only one willing to lavish me with praise. I may have a few new kinks after this, and I highly doubt any mortal man will ever compare.

How can any woman's body handle this amount of pleasure? My heart is beating so fast, I'm afraid it might count as a heart attack.

When I start spasming, Dato ceases his assisting torment, and Lorcan pulls himself out of me, swearing on a heaving exhale.

'You were so fucking tight,' Lorcan murmurs, stroking up my spine after he drops my plait.

My head immediately droops without the tension, my neck burning, and my throat thick with the spit I had trouble swallowing down.

'She's probably not anymore. That monster dick could poke a cyclops' eye out,' Hex jokes, standing to his full height.

'You don't need the black waters to bring your envy to the surface, just the sight of my superior cock,' Lorcan quips, pulling his joggers back over his hips, concealing his absolute weapon.

Hex shrugs. 'I can't argue with that.'

Dato, being the nice one, checks on me. 'How are you holding up?'

Catching my breath, I rasp out, 'I'm okay. I think.'

'Only Hex left to go, then we'll take you down to the river to wash off.' He undoes my plait for me, then shakes my raven waves out until they fall over both shoulders, the tips sweeping the ground.

Without warning, I'm flipped on my back by Hex, Dato's kind face spinning into dark grey skies.

Hex hovers over me, his wicked smirk back on his face. 'Having fun?'

A lazy smile drags up the corners of my mouth. 'Hmm,' I hum, wrapping my arms around my vamp's neck.

'Wonderful. Now, let's get you cleaned up.'

After planting a quick kiss on the tip of my nose, Hex hauls me up from my lying position, and I automatically hook my legs over his hips as he stands.

He walks away with me naked in his arms, heading towards the slight decline leading to the river below. Glancing back, I catch Lorcan and Dato sharing a bewildered expression. They're equally as confused as to what's happening. Or better yet, what's *not* happening.

'Hex, what are you doing?' I question, searching his handsome face for clues. Is he still angry with me?

'I'm taking you down to the river to wash all that mud and cum off you,' he replies with mirth, focusing on the rocky path down the slope. 'Don't get me wrong, it's very becoming on you. I like you dirty. But you'll feel stronger once you bathe in the black waters.'

'But... what about...' I start, giving up on the sentence when he meets my questioning gaze.

'What about what? I'm saving you time,' he says softly before he switches gears, zooming us the rest of the way down at super speed.

In that little flash of time, it's not only my stomach that falls.

CHAPTER 39

Counting Down

Sleep has evaded me for the third hour in a row. I've spent that time staring up at the ceiling in my dimly lit bedroom suite—prison—counting down the time before the guardianship of my very soul is won or lost.

At the double rap on my door, I snap up in bed. 'Who is it?' My tone is unwelcoming. The last person I want to see right now is the Demon King.

'It's Marguerite.'

'Come in.'

The soulless servant enters the room carrying a mug of something hot, steam trailing. 'I brought you hot chocolate.' She passes it to me.

The heat from the mug transfers to my icy hands, making my skin tingle. I take a sip; the taste of chocolate and cinnamon is strong, exactly how I like it. 'Thank you.'

'The King wanted me to check on you again,' Marguerite says, perching at the end of the bed. 'He didn't mean to upset you at lunch.'

'Bullshit,' I mutter before taking another sip.

Marguerite sighs. 'He's not as bad as you believe him to be. His choices were limited.'

'At least he *had* a choice, unlike Raven and me,' I retort, holding the mug close to my chest for comfort.

'He did give your sister a choice,' she reminds me. 'A terrible one, but one nonetheless.' At the roll of my eyes, she continues, 'Look, garçon, I'm not claiming to know your sister, but I'm sure she could find happiness in this life. I have. And, knowing Julius, he would give her almost anything to make sure she felt comfortable here.'

I slam my near-empty mug down on the side table. 'Would he give her freedom? Would he let her keep her soul? Because that would be the bare minimum to expect when you say you care for someone. You wouldn't take away the two things integral to their life—their happiness.'

Marguerite lowers her gaze and smooths a hand over the crinkled bedsheet around her. 'Love isn't always selfless. It can be a rainbow of sins. But, right at the heart of it, there's redemption to be found.'

I deflate, too tired to ponder the intricacies of love right now. 'Where's Julius?'

'He's recharging his power in the Harvest Hall. I'm guessing he wants to be on top form when midnight comes.'

'You mean when he steals mine and my sister's souls so he can lock them up and suck their energy out whenever he pleases while we waste away,' I sum up in a snarky tone, leaning back against the headboard with my arms a firm barrier over my chest.

Marguerite places a hand on my shin. 'You won't be losing your soul until your natural life ends. Your sister... well, hers can't be taken immediately, but the King will have time to work on it once she's living here with him.'

'What do you mean? Why would he have to wait if he wins it?' I question, sitting forward again.

Marguerite's lips press into a hard line as if she's keeping a secret on the tip of her tongue. 'Some things are worth more when given freely.'

She stands, taking my mug with her as she approaches the door.

'Would he ever hurt her?'

My question stops Marguerite in her tracks—her back to me, her hand resting on the door handle. 'He'd sooner become a monster than do that.'

Then Marguerite walks out into the hallway before I can ask her why.

But I already know the answer. I just refuse to believe it.

CHAPTER 40

Favoured Sin

LORCAN

By the time Dato and I make it to the bank of the river Melas, Hex already has Raven in the middle of it, both submerged up to their pressed-together chests. The vrykolaka has also stripped off his clothes to join her in bathing.

Raven clings to Hex like he's her life preserver. Seeing the two of them so close, relaxing in each other's arms after the pounding I gave her, does stir up a fair amount of jealousy. The black waters can't be my excuse since no drop has touched my skin. And if I'm being honest, her admitting Hex was her favourite certainly aggravated me. The hours they spent alone together this afternoon, when Dato and I were busy fighting to protect her, have obviously tipped the scales in his favour.

It shouldn't bother me. It's not like I'm vying for her heart. All I wanted was to fuck her, and now I've done that. My instinct to claim her body has been thoroughly sated.

So, why am I still restless?

There's this ache in my chest that won't ease. Before today, my heart lay dormant; it was an empty vessel that only pumped for the thrill of the hunt.

What started the ache was realising the cunning little songbird had flown our nest of protection. Knowing she was travelling the maze without anyone to keep her safe from the dangers that awaited filled me with this gnawing anxiety that ate away at my sanity.

I've never cared for another's life more than hers. I've even caught myself worrying for her soul these past few hours.

This unassuming mortal is turning out to be the real danger here.

'If she tells Julius what we all did up there, we're dead, you know that, right?' Dato says as he comes to stand beside me. He's watching Raven and Hex frolicking with the same tight expression I have. With a huff, he drops her clothes on top of Hex's pile.

I wave the threat away like it's nothing to worry our heads over. 'Julius pretends to be this big bad king, but he'll forgive us eventually. Anyway, she'll be all his after midnight. Why would it matter to him that we had a quick dip before she was officially claimed?'

'Lorc, she's not some random mortal who came looking to strike a deal. He needs her to break his curse. We may not know the specifics, but we know she's important to him. More so than we anticipated,' Dato chides, his wings jittery behind him. 'He called on the Shadows to perform a skip to secure her. Hex thinks he tried to kill him simply for kissing her.'

'How could Julius care so much about someone he only met briefly yesterday?' I question, still sceptical.

Dato arches an eyebrow. 'I can taste the envy radiating off you in waves, Lorc.' He nods to Hex, who's helping Raven wash the mud off her skin. 'I think we've all learnt how easy it is to come to care for someone so quickly.'

Unconvinced, I shrug a shoulder. 'I still think Julius hasn't told us the truth about her. He must have been keeping tabs, at least. I've always wondered why he showed zero interest in the females throwing themselves at his feet all these years.'

After a minute of pensive silence, Dato queries, 'Do you think she's going to make it? To the castle, I mean.'

'She has a couple of hours left. If no one in the city stands in her way, then I don't see why not. She's heading in the right direction and won't be slowed down by any dangers with us by her side.'

Dato swivels to face me. 'What if someone tries to stop her when she reaches Galbrek? What would you do?'

With an affronted look, I bounce the question right back at him. 'What would *you* do?'

'I don't know yet,' he admits, shaking his head, his uncertain eyes wandering back to Raven, clearly conflicted.

I raise my eyebrows high. 'Looks like I'm not the only one coveting what's not mine.'

Dato's eyebrows fall in the opposite direction. 'It's not yet midnight. She still belongs to herself.'

I snort a humourless laugh. 'If we help her in any way, we'll definitely be dead by morning.'

'As you said, Julius likes to pretend.'

Hearing this from Dato is astonishing. He's Julius' closest friend despite Julius only referring to him as an ally. Before today, I would have never thought the harpy capable of defying his king. Sure, in the past, I've seen the resentment in Dato's eyes when the females he was interested in paid him no attention because they were clamouring to impress the young, pretty, blonde keeper king. Still, it's a shock to find out Dato is thinking about risking his brotherly bond over one girl he's known less than twenty-four hours.

'What about his curse? We don't know why he's after her soul. It could be vital to breaking it,' I mention, being fair to Julius by at least trying to challenge this line of thinking.

Turning away, Dato mutters, 'It's not like he'll need it soon. DiMinos kings don't disappear until their forties. He has time to figure it out.'

My disbelief has me chuckling. 'You really *are* considering denying him the mortal, aren't you?'

'Aren't you?' Dato throws back, his tone more combative. 'Look over at Hex and tell me he hasn't already decided the same. He's fucking obsessed with her. He was the one who convinced us to let her walk her own path. At this point, we might as well help her. We've already rebelled against Julius' order.' When I open my mouth to counter, he snaps, 'Don't give me that shit about technicalities. *'If more than one of us fucks her'*... It was weak at best. Come on. We took her because we couldn't fucking help ourselves. And we'll fight for her soul because we can't fucking help ourselves.'

I laugh because it sounds about right. 'What is it about her?'

Sagging with defeat, Dato sighs. 'I don't know. She has this energy about her. It's like she's switched on a light in this dark place.'

I clap him on the shoulder. 'Wow, you should write that shit down, birdman. Mortal women love a poet. You might give Hex a run for his money.'

'Fucking vrykolakas. They get all their prey hooked on their venom. We never stood a chance,' he jokes, an undercurrent of his familiar bitterness hiding behind the humour.

'Well, I, for one, am not ready to quit.' Alpha instinct rising to the challenge, I drop my joggers and start wading into the river. 'She's still unclaimed, and I'll be damned if I let a vrykolaka steal my prey without a fight.'

My determined approach catches Raven's eye; she lifts her face from the crook of Hex's neck, where she was busy pressing kisses. It's then I realise I haven't tasted her mouth yet. I can describe what her pussy tastes like, but not her tongue.

That needs to be rectified. *Immediately*.

So, when I reach her, I shove Hex's face aside and claim her lips for my own. Her little gasp of shock has my cock thickening. Hex's aggrieved snarl hits my ears, but he lets her unwrap her arms and legs from him.

With my hands squeezing her likely sore arse, I lift her and squish her against me so that I can deepen the kiss. She sighs into my mouth, melting into me as our tongues slide over each other. Her long legs wind around my waist, her hands reaching behind my head to untie the bun at my nape.

My hair is now wild and loose. She runs her fingers through it while I groan my appreciation, cock hard and rubbing against her slick centre.

Even though I would happily fuck her again in a heartbeat, I refrain from pursuing the act. She's running out of time, and after that conversation with Dato, we're as prepared as Hex is to escort her right up to the castle doors.

After one final flick of my tongue, I allow Raven air. I take immense pleasure from seeing the flush of her cheeks and the desire shining in her half-lidded gaze.

'Wow, what was that for?' she enquires, licking her lips to taste me again.

'I had to show the vrykolaka how it's done,' I answer in good humour, elbowing Hex beside me. Despite his ire at me stealing her attention, he smirks.

Raven smiles knowingly. 'I'm guessing envy and lust are your favoured sins, too.'

'Don't forget pride. I couldn't be an alpha without heaps of that.'

She laughs, and the sound does funny things to my heart.

'Dato, take your fucking clothes off and get in here!' Raven shouts, waving him over.

In response, Dato shakes his head, but a reluctant smile tugs at the corners of his mouth. His tail is looping around in agitation. By the looks of it, he's still trying to deny himself what he wants.

'Listen to the songbird,' I tell him. 'Give her what she wants before I come and drag you in myself.'

Dato rolls his eyes but then starts undressing while throwing paranoid glances around as though expecting danger. He's not used to dropping his armour.

Naked, he lifts his wings high and wades in, making his way to us.

'Before you get any ideas, mortal, lust isn't my favoured sin. Usually, all I feel is a little drowsy after bathing in the black waters,' he says dryly when in earshot.

'Sorry, no time for napping, I'm afraid,' Raven responds, reaching for him.

Grudgingly, I let her go, and the harpy tries to conceal his joy in her wanting him.

However, once Raven is in Dato's arms, a glint of mischief lights up her eyes, and she does something completely unexpected. She wraps her arms tightly around his neck and lurches back with all her might until they both hit the water, sinking beneath it.

Spluttering, Dato flounders back up to standing, his wings flapping, soaked.

Raven's head bobs back up from the black depths. And, after she wipes the water from her heavy black lashes, giggles hiccup out of her mouth when she sees the harpy wet and dishevelled. 'That should wake you up.'

For a fraught moment, Dato stares at her, wrath darkening his gaze, but then his lips tic up, and, with a loud swish, he swipes a hand across the water's surface, splashing her.

Raven splashes him back, and before we know it, we're all laughing and raining water down on each other until we're breathless and soaked.

In those precious minutes, the decision is made for me; I can't allow my songbird's shining light to be dimmed so easily.

That's why I will help her get to the castle before midnight.

CHAPTER 41

Pure

RAVEN

Once dry, I dress back in the clothes Dato dutifully carried down the slope for me.

'If I'm reading the sky correctly, we have roughly four hours until midnight. Galbrek is about a three-hour walk from here. With us beside you, demons in the city won't dare mess with you. I'm confident we can get you to the castle in time,' Lorcan assures me, securing his chestnut hair back into a loose bun.

'I can't thank you guys enough for agreeing to help me complete this,' I manage to get out, welling up again.

It's only been a few minutes since they all voiced their intent to escort me to the castle, and I can hardly believe it. They've done a complete one-eighty in only a matter of hours. For most of those hours, I was running away from them.

Did they change their minds because I let them fuck me? Or am I growing on them in a more meaningful way?

I've already acknowledged my developing affection for Hex. It's becoming increasingly clear our bond is mutually obsessive. But to find out both Lorcan and Dato also care enough to want to save my soul is a surprise. In all fairness, when I saw them near death earlier, it affected me far more than if they meant nothing to me.

It can't be love, at least not yet. I've known them less than a full day, and they haven't opened up to me like Hex has. The intimate details of their lives are still a mystery to me, but I'm coming to understand their hearts. Isn't that the most important thing? It's a foundation if nothing else.

Raven, why are you thinking of laying foundations with demons who can't leave the Underworld when you're desperate to return home? I ask myself, strangely conflicted, a hollowing disappointment stealing space in my chest.

Anyway, it's not the right time to dwell on these unwelcome emotions when I have a deal to be won and a brother to save. I can figure out the rest as soon as I complete this quest. Maybe I can visit from time to time if that's even possible. Would the Demon King allow that if he can't have me all to himself like he wanted? If he can't claim my soul?

'Hey, Hex, are you okay?' Dato asks, looking past me, worry lines prominent.

I follow his gaze.

With jerky movements, Hex is struggling to lace up his shirt. And because his fingers are shaking too much, he abandons the task, letting his collar gape.

'I'm fine. Just tired,' Hex mumbles, brushing off Dato's concern.

'You need to feed,' Lorcan tells Hex, tying his shirt for him. 'You gave us too much blood earlier, and that Velociraptor you hunted on the way here wouldn't have been enough to sustain you for long.'

Hex's eyes dart to me, then back to Lorcan before he says, 'I'll find something along the way.'

Why isn't he taking from me? He hasn't shied away before. He's eagerly stolen my blood without asking, taking me by surprise to satisfy his hunting instincts. And his sexual ones.

I hear myself saying, 'Drink from me,' before I realise I've made the decision.

Hex's gaze slams into me. 'You're offering?'

'Yeah, it's no big deal. It's not like you haven't bitten me a million times today.' But it is the first time I've freely given him my blood—encouraged even.

Looking sheepish, Hex rubs his mouth, his fangs likely itching to pop out at the mere thought. 'All right.' He moves towards me, his legs noticeably unsteady.

His touch is hesitant, almost shy, as he sweeps my hair over my shoulder to expose my neck.

For reasons I don't fully understand, I'm suddenly breathless, the pulse point in my throat fluttering.

Hex leans in, and then his nose runs up the curve of my neck, inhaling my scent. Right when I think he's about to bite down, he withdraws to glance over his shoulder at Lorcan and Dato. 'Can you give us a few minutes?'

Lorcan and Dato exchange a knowing look before they nod.

'We'll clear the path ahead. Catch up when you're ready,' Dato says, spreading his wings.

They both hurry to exit; Dato launches into the sky while Lorcan runs the wide path beneath him, keeping close to the river.

'What was that all about?' I ask Hex, curious as to why he's suddenly acting like the gentleman I know him not to be.

With a soft smile, Hex peers down at me. His palm slides to the nape of my neck, orienting my head, so all I see is him. 'With vrykolakas, there's two types of feeding. There's the blood we harvest, and then there's sacrificed blood.'

'Is there a difference?'

He nods, his thumb and fingers working the tendons in my neck as we speak. 'There's a big difference.'

Eyes closing, I hum a moan, enjoying the massage. The pressure he's rubbing away falls to build low in my abdomen. 'Does this have something to do with me offering you my blood?'

'Yes,' he answers, voice smoky. 'When we take from our victims, their blood is corrupted by fear. But when it's sacrificed, willingly, without condition or selfish expectation... it—it runs pure.'

I open my eyes to find Hex studying my face, something akin to awe on his. 'Does it taste better?' The unfiltered question tumbles out as I try to grapple with the short-circuiting of my brain, the depth of his admiration causing havoc.

Hex narrows the distance between us, and when his lips skim my jaw, I melt. 'I wouldn't know. No mortal has ever offered me their blood before, outside of a deal.'

'Well, now you can find out,' I say, heart pounding. My hands glide up his chest to rest on his shoulders. A tremor vibrates through him.

After one final lingering look, Hex kisses me—deeply. It's a frantic sort of kiss. One that you'd give up breathing for.

With his tongue inside my mouth, he lifts me up only to lay me down again beneath a low-hanging tree. Its black leaves trail down, providing us swaying shade, which we use to hide away, just the two of us.

In the very short breathing space between our desperate, wet kisses, I start talking, the intimate energy of this moment sparking doubt. 'Did you—', *kiss*, '—come looking for me—', *kiss*, '—because of the order?'—*kiss*.

Eyebrows pinched and lips swollen, Hex lifts his head to regard me. 'That wasn't the only reason. We were worried about you. The thought of you hurt made us feel physically ill.'

I snort a short, sardonic laugh. 'The three of you seemed to take great pleasure in hurting me only an hour ago.'

Hex pins me with a look. 'Come on, are you really going to pretend you didn't enjoy every single second of your punishment?'

When he dips down, intending to continue our soul-awakening kiss, I burst out with, 'I did actually come across some danger along the way.'

Hex's scowl deepens. 'What danger?'

'I stumbled across these two gorgeous women dancing around this old water fountain. At first, they seemed nice, like they wanted to help me. But then they started getting a bit touchy-feely... one got naked. It went south from there. And not in the good way, if you know what I mean,' I sum up terribly, still somewhat nervous.

Blinking in astonishment, Hex rears back. 'Myth and mercy. You met the Ladies In Waiting and lived to tell the tale? How?' Not giving me room to speak, he adds, 'Even I'd struggle against them.' His palm flattens against my breastbone as though he needs to check that my heart is still beating. 'I'm assuming you didn't drink what they offered, seeing as your heart hasn't been eaten out of your chest.'

'I didn't. In the back of my mind, I remembered what you told me,' I reply, and his lips twitch up. 'But something strange happened during the scuffle.'

His head tips in interest. 'What happened?'

'This light started pouring out of my mouth,' I divulge, an uncertain laugh in my voice. 'I literally turned into a human torch for a second. After it faded, they backed off and gave me directions.'

Hex stares at me for a lengthy beat, his eyes a little wild, mouth parted. 'Please tell me you're making this up.'

I half sit up, using my elbows to support my weight. 'What? Of course not. Why would I?'

Hex shifts his weight off me, eyebrows drawn together. 'Fuck. You... They... *Fuck*!'

Dread has my belly flopping. 'What is it? Tell me.'

Hex scrubs a hand over his face, then sighs. 'Those 'ladies' you encountered were sirens. Well, technically, they're the spirits of cursed goddesses.'

'Goddesses?!' I parrot back, stunned. 'I thought gods and goddesses didn't exist.'

'They don't anymore, but they once did. A long time ago,' Hex says, his eyes losing focus as he stares at nothing in particular. 'Arkhe, or Olympus—as mortals more commonly knew it—wasn't some heavenly place in the sky. It was the first layer of the Underworld. Over a thousand years ago, Arkhe was destroyed during a brutal war between gods and demons.' His gaze clears again as it settles back on me. 'Those two sirens—Thexis and Pysin—appear as spectres when the Veil between worlds is weakest. There must be excess energy in the air causing disruption because they're a rare find. Unlike regular sirens, they're not only looking for hearts to devour; they're cursed to forever search for their lost queen, Persephene.'

My eyes narrow at the familiar name. 'Don't you mean Persephone?'

'The Greeks were never very good at getting the details right.' His tone is a tad bitter. 'If you ever make it back to the mortal lands, do me a favour: never search for images of vrykolakas.'

When I have my phone in my hand again, it's the first thing I'm googling.

'Are some of the myths true, then?'

'No. Never verbatim. Most not even close. But some hold elements of the truth.' Hex slides a hand through his damp hair. 'Persephene was stolen from Arkhe by the first demon king—Hadrexus. He wanted her mind, body, and soul. But she was killed on their joining day.'

'How did she die?' I pry, trying to recall how the Greek myth of Hades and Persephone ended.

'Nobody knows for sure.'

When Hex falls into a thoughtful silence, I give in to the urge to loop the conversation back to me. 'What do you reckon that light was inside of me?'

In his onyx eyes, panic flares. 'Erm... I'm not the right person to ask,' he mumbles, acting suspiciously cagey.

When Hex goes to stand, I pull him back to me. 'Do you know what it is?'

A heavy exhale hurries past his lips, and finally, he faces my scrutiny to respond with, 'I have an idea, but I'm bound. I can't speak on it.'

'Did the Demon King order you to keep me in the dark?' I demand, my hand locking around his wrist so he can't escape.

A muscle wavers in his jaw. 'Not Julius, but he'll have an easier time explaining. You should wait to ask him.'

'I don't want to talk to the Demon King. I want to talk to you,' I whine, pushing for an answer.

My child-like tone seems to amuse Hex. 'You *are* talking to me.' When I throw him a vexed look, he carries on. 'Please, darling, don't worry about it now. You still have a couple of hours to reach the castle. Focus on saving your soul first. That's the most important thing right now.' His thumb comes up to trace my mouth, his attention fixed there.

The fluttering inside me spawns new butterflies in my belly. 'You really don't want the Demon King to claim me, do you?'

Hex slowly shakes his head, his gleaming eyes lifting to penetrate mine.

'Why?' I need him to say it. I need to hear his reason more than I've ever needed anything.

In the electrified moment that follows, Hex holds the world in his glittering gaze. A world full of hope and imagination but also fear and sadness. 'You know why.'

It's not enough, but it's enough for now.

This time, it's me who closes the distance. I crush my lips to his, my arms locking behind his neck to bring him down on top of me.

Burning with the need to be as close to him as possible, I wrap my legs around his waist and grind my body against his while our mouths fit the shape of each other, over and over, until even my teeth ache.

Hex's hands don't linger long on any one section of my body. He's everywhere: pressing, pinching, caressing, grabbing, scratching, lighting my skin on fire. We're moaning and panting into each other's mouths, sharing more than this spectacular kiss. He's so solid against my centre that the slightest friction propels me to that leg-shaking edge.

Holding his face, I direct his mouth down to my neck. 'Drink from me, Hex,' I urge, breath as heavy as the pleasure building in my core. 'I want a part of me inside you when a part of you is inside me.'

My request obliterates the rest of his restraint. With a passionate purr of longing, his fangs penetrate my skin at the base of my throat. There's a flash of pain before his venom numbs the area, dripping through the punctures to dominate my veins. But he only supplies enough to dull the sting; the pleasure he's providing is all skill.

His warm lips seal over the bite when his fangs retract, and then he starts sucking. The manifestation of his tongue ghosts over my clit as he flicks it back and forth on my neck while he feeds from me. The rough noises coming from his throat vibrate under my flushed skin, further heightening my arousal.

'Hex.' I breathe his name like a plea, and he seems to know exactly what I need from him without elaborating.

With both hands, he reaches down between my legs. Then, there's a tugging sensation before the sound of tearing. His fingers are sliding inside me a second later, and I mewl, that hard-to-reach spot discovered easily. Stroking it, he gets me ready for him, but I'm already so wet and sensitised that I'm trembling with the need to be filled.

'I need you, Hex. Please,' I beg, on the cusp of shattering.

It only takes my vamp a moment of fumbling before he's pushing his impressive length inside me. We both gasp at the tight fit and the exquisite burn.

After the first thrust, we lose ourselves to the rhythm. Every other second, his hips crash against the backs of my thighs, which I notice are still covered by dark grey material.

For fuck's sake. He must have ripped a hole in the crouch of my leggings, but honestly, I wouldn't have wanted to wait another second.

Hex's blood-wet mouth drags up my throat, lightly nipping. 'Raven,' he whispers against my skin. 'If I had one last wish in this world, it would be to imprint this moment onto my soul for all eternity, even if I never live to reclaim it.'

The intensity of his gaze and the passion behind his words have overwhelming emotion charging through me at the same speed and ferocity as my orgasm.

Coming hard, I sob as my muscles seize and spasm beneath him. Tears leak from the far corners of my eyes to dampen the hair at my temples. Warmth radiates as I linger in contrasting bliss.

Several long, achingly beautiful seconds pass before Hex comes with an obscenely sexy groan, savouring the last few pumps as we both quiver until the tension in our bodies abates.

Hex collapses on top of me, his weight a comfort more than a burden. He uses an elbow to shift, slowly pulling out of me while providing enough room to refill my overworked lungs.

'By the blood, that was fucking incredible,' Hex breathes, blinking down at me, his thumb stroking my cheekbone. 'It's never felt like that before.'

On the comedown, nerves return in full force, unsettling me. 'What hasn't?'

'Feeding, fucking,' he answers, wonder expanding his pupils until there's no reddish ring left. 'It was pure ecstasy. I can't think of how else to describe it.'

'So, it *did* make a difference?'

Nodding, Hex explains, 'Your blood was like... like sunshine on frost. Firelight in the desolate dark. To the soulless: the heady taste of hope and love.'

When the last word falls from his lips, I falter. 'Sounds nice,' I mutter, shying away.

A few minutes ago, I thought that was the feeling I wanted voiced. Now, hearing it out loud, I'm not so sure I can trust the conclusion without any logic or reason to back it up.

'Raven.' My name sounds more like a confession. He says it like I should know by his tone alone how sincere he is.

'It's weird to hear you use my real name. My darling deal-breaker was actually starting to grow on me,' I say, hiding behind humour.

'Raven,' Hex repeats in a similar tone, except it has an insistent edge.

Avoiding the vamp's searching gaze, I peer down at my body. 'Did you make a hole in my leggings just big enough to fuck me?'

Not answering my attempt at distraction, Hex slots his fingers under my chin and forces my eyes to meet his. 'That feeling... it was real. And I know you felt it, too. Your blood doesn't lie as easily as you do.'

In denial, I shake my head. 'Hex, stop. It's not that. It can't be. You're on a high from the endorphins. That's all.'

'My darling deal-breaker,' Hex murmurs, lowering to touch his nose to mine, lips hovering a hair's breadth away from where I still tingle at the memory of his kiss. 'I'm falling in love with you.'

CHAPTER 42

Stay

RAVEN

'So, you're really going to ignore what I just said?' Hex persists, refusing to give me a moment of privacy while I wipe away what he left behind after his orgasm.

I didn't want to waste time undressing again for a second dip in the river, so a handful of damp leaves would have to do as a substitute. The hole he ripped in my leggings isn't noticeable when I have my top and jacket on to cover my crotch.

I stand from a crouch, then test the situation downstairs by jumping up and down on the spot. When nothing runs down my thighs, I start toward Galbrek, away from the lovelorn vamp.

Hex follows, his footfalls heavier than normal. 'Raven, answer me.'

Without turning to him, I say, 'I'm not ignoring; I'm processing.'

A beat passes. The only sounds between us are the whirl of the sunless breeze and the crunch of dried twigs under hurried feet.

'Are you doubting me because of the 'coward' remark I made when we were tormenting you?' he asks out of nowhere. 'I shouldn't have used your childhood trauma to get a rise out of you. My anger was no excuse. You trusted me enough to divulge that, and then I went and used it against you. I'm sorry.' His voice is full of remorse, as though he's been waiting for the opportunity to bring it up and apologise properly.

'That was shitty of you,' I agree, hiding a smile. 'Are all demons spiteful little arseholes with massive egos?'

'They're common traits.'

'Not exactly lovable,' I comment more dryly, needing an excuse to brush off this formidable feeling still pulsing through my chest. If I keep telling both of us that love isn't possible, this euphoric high will hopefully dull.

It's the first time I've ever wished for my depression to return. But surely, it's better to be numb than feel too much? Especially when my charming vamp can't keep me. He made that clear inside the tree when we hid from the cyclopes. I'm a mortal, and he's a fucking soulless demon. We're meant to live in different worlds, and there's also Julius' wrath to consider. These feelings have nowhere to grow, no light to bloom. They're better off dug up now before they root too deep.

'Maybe not loveable, but certainly fuckable,' Hex remarks in good humour, catching up with me. 'I seem to remember you close to begging for my cock after you'd already taken two loads.' He pinches my arse at that, and I swerve away with a yelp.

I punch him on the arm, knowing he'd barely feel the force of it. 'That's what I wanted to ask you... Why didn't you take your turn on me? Why did you wait until we were alone?'

In a rare show, his cheeks colour. Is my vamp blushing?

'Because...' Hex starts, shyer than I'm used to. This side of him is too endearing. It makes me forget he's not mortal. 'Because I wanted my first time with you to be more than a punishment. More than a game or a deal. I wanted it to be personal. Between us.' He catches my elbow and spins me to face him. 'I'm fucking obsessed with you, Raven. I'm obsessed with every little detail. All I've chosen to learn about you in a single day is more than I've ever cared to know about anyone. And I'm obsessed with discovering more in the time we'll have to negotiate and fight for. I don't care if you doubt it.' He snags my chin and angles my face to make sure our eyes connect when he says, 'I am falling for you. I've already taken that leap, and there's no going back now. From the moment you tried to outsmart me when defining the terms of our deal to when you slapped me for making you orgasm harder than you've ever done before—'

'I never said that,' I interject, despite it being true. Well, at the time, it was, anyway. Since then, they have kept getting better and better.

His hand slides down to grip my throat. 'If you tell me that dickhead ex of yours did better, I'll steal my soul back just so I can travel through the fucking Veil to track him down, chop his hands off, then gift them to you. Perhaps you'll like to use them again.'

'That's a very strange threat, but I appreciate the thought. Very imaginative.'

'Anyway, before you rudely interrupted me, I boldly declared how much I fucking care about you... Where did I leave off? Oh, yes... From the moment you started acting like your bratty little self, I felt it: the first jolt that shook my heart awake.' He releases my throat to capture the nape of my neck, almost shaking me in his earnestness. 'My darling deal-breaker, if you don't stay for Julius, stay for me. I'm not asking for your soul. Live a mortal life unclaimed for all I care. I only want you to live it with me.'

At his impassioned request, my knees weaken. His arm hooks around my waist to steady me, and I exhale shakily.

Live my life with him? No strings attached? No one has ever said a sentence half as heartfelt to me. Not even my own mother and brother.

'Can't you come with me?' I ask, hopeful. 'You said living in my world wasn't impossible for your kind.'

Solemnly, Hex shakes his head. 'Without a soul, I can't pass through the Veil, and I still have fifty years of service before I can claim it back,' he reminds me, pressing his forehead against mine as he sighs. 'The only way for us to be together is if you stay. I know it's a lot to ask. And if Julius poses a threat, we'll run. I know a layer of the Underworld where he won't be welcome.'

I close my eyes, unable to handle the intensity of his stare. 'Hex, I don't know what to say.' At my tone, his grip tightens in my hair as if he thinks I will slip through his fingers. 'We've only known each other a day. This is... too much.'

Hex cups my face in his hands. 'Too much? If anything, it's not been enough.'

'I can't stay here. This is the fucking Underworld! And what about my brother? I can't abandon him again. I need to take him home. I need to be his sister,' I maintain, trying not to let myself get choked by emotion again.

'And I need *you*, deal-breaker,' Hex implores, his expression one of anguish. 'I haven't felt my heart in over a century, but it beats when I'm with you.'

Tears blur my vision of him. 'Hex, *please*. You know what you're asking of me is impossible. I can't live in the Underworld. If I don't leave when I have the chance, the Demon King will keep on with his tricks until my soul is his. I can't risk it.'

Hex's tense muscles slacken before he releases me, then he rotates away, head lowered. 'I understand. It was foolish of me to even ask—selfish.' His tone is flat and devoid of his usual richness.

I stand before him, demanding his attention when I say, 'I'm glad you did. No one in all my life has ever made me feel as wanted as you have, Hex.' Warm, salty water streams down my cheeks, and I muffle a sob with my sleeve.

Before I crack into pieces, Hex holds me together, my head to his chest. 'I'm not the only one who can't get enough of you, darling. You have four very greedy demons dying to keep you for themselves.'

Through my quelling tears, a tight laugh breaks to the surface. 'Well, you, Dato, and Lorcan did a good job sharing me earlier.'

At the reminder, Hex joins in with my mood change, his chuckle shaking me. 'Your body is one thing. Your heart and soul are where we'll fight.'

'My soul is, and will always be, mine,' I state, tipping my chin up defiantly.

Hex's grin is full of pride. 'And what about your heart?' he queries, his handsome features falling into uncertainty again.

Listening to the erratic thrumming of said heart, I go for honesty. 'Right now?' I blow out a breath, yielding to this all-consuming feeling. I reach up to stroke his pink-tinted cheek, our eyes locked. 'It's in your hands, vamp. Be gentle with it.'

A delighted smile spreads across Hex's face, his dark eyes glittering. 'Always... I can't promise the same for your body, though.' With both hands, he squeezes my arse for emphasis.

I roll my eyes and bat his hands away. 'You had to go and ruin it.'

But my smile says it all.

CHAPTER 43

The Weight of Two Hearts

JULIUS

Too many emotions are clogging coherent thought—muddling and leaving me scrambling. These foreign, eclipsing emotions overshadow my own; they're oppressive phantoms which haunt any patience and civility I have left in this demonic shell, chasing them away with their cruel, mocking laughter.

There's only one possible reason: Raven is experiencing something profound—life-changing. And if I were a better demon, I'd be happy for her. However, knowing she's likely still with Hex makes me wonder if these feelings have been whipped up in reaction to him.

Only an hour ago, I suffered through yet more lust; two consecutive waves of pleasure hit me through our bond. And I accepted it without turning into a murderous monster. I fisted myself in tandem, imagining my starling moaning my name the two times we came together, separated by physical matter alone.

But then there was another wave a short while later, after a burst of unexplained joy and relief. I've been walking around in circles, deciphering what is causing these bouts of intense emotions. But there was a strong underlying current I immediately recognised.

Love.

That third helping of pleasure brought with it something new. This full feeling in my chest—this immense ache followed by a soothing warmth. And, while I rode the high with her at the time, the second I realised she wasn't feeling that way about me, I came crashing down, my heavy heart taking the brunt of the fall, breaking it apart.

My starling: the girl who's meant to be mine—my soul's twin—is falling in love with the demon I sent to see her fail.

One thin thread of my sanity remains, which clings to the uncertainty I'm sensing beneath it all: she's still unsure. Which means I may be able to steal her heart before Hex taints it with his poisonous charm.

With that underserving bloodsucker out of the picture, I can show her that uncertainty was her soul battling against her naïve heart. We're fated. We were made for each other. Curse or no curse. Once she's bound to me, she'll learn. She'll understand why I had to claim her in this way. And when she gets to know me, she'll love me. She already does, deep down. Her conscious mind only needs time to adjust—to catch up with our past.

Clutching my chest, I stagger over to my throne, black smoke seeping from my eyes and fingertips, leaving droplets of sulphur in my tracks.

The Shadows are closing in, drawn to the overstimulation of my unstable power. My head tells me to calm down and let Raven come to me. There are only a few hours left, after all. But my heart craves revenge. All that idle power I overharvested is pulsing beneath my skin, eager to answer the call to act out of malice—out of unrequited love and jealousy.

I don't think I can hold it off any longer. I don't think I can wait when a few more hours could solidify her feelings for the vrykolaka.

Perhaps it's not unwise to act rashly sometimes. Not when so much is at stake.

Dropping down like lead, I struggle to regain control over the wild energy clawing out of me. I gulp air and straighten in my seat. But when I look up, the corners of my throne room are filled with thick black clouds of smoke, crawling to the centre, and merging to form one cohesive force.

I pale under their shadow, gripping the arms of my throne, trying desperately not to succumb to the dark temptation to use them for my benefit.

I already owe the Shadows a debt I have yet to pay. If I continue manipulating them with my power, I will begin to rely on them, slowly corrupting myself until the Shadows themselves claim me as their own.

But, right now, with the weight of two hearts dragging me down, I can't seem to fight the descent.

With Hex and Raven in my mind's eye, and the agony of heartbreak blackening my lost soul, I erupt.

And the Shadows rush in to aid me.

To overthrow me.

CHAPTER 44

The Eye of the Storm

RAVEN

Thankfully, my body seems to have fully adjusted to Hex's super speed. After the first five-minute whirl, he slows to let my stomach settle, but the usual nausea barely registers.

With me on the vamp's back, clinging like a baby koala, I try to lighten the conversation but fail. It's not long before we return to the subject of love.

'When I was younger, I doubted I'd ever let anyone care for me in the way you claim to. What I knew of love, I learnt from my mum. Her version of it made me feel empty inside. It's not been like that with you, though,' I express, nuzzling his neck, finding nothing but warmth and comfort where I expected hostility and resentment.

Hex dips his head to kiss my forearm, my limbs wound around him. 'When I first saw you in that pit, I had to remind myself that you weren't her. You look so much alike. If it's any consolation, you're nothing like your mother. You could never make anyone feel empty, no matter how hard you tried,' he tells me, off-hand and casual.

And immediately, my muscles lock, eyes widening at the slip of information.

Hex must sense the change because he stalls briefly, realising his mistake. Shoulders tense, he continues walking, his steps stunted.

'Wait. Wait... Did you know my mother?' I demand, except my voice is too weak and shaky for it to hold its weight.

When the vamp doesn't respond, I push against him to dismount. He drops my legs but strides ahead, eager to create distance.

'Hex! Did you know her? Answer me!' This time, my tone alone is command enough.

He finally faces me, expression unreadable. 'Yes. I knew her. But I can't tell you any more than that. I'm bound.'

I stomp up to him, my anger surging. 'This whole time, you let me talk about her and didn't tell me?' I shove him, but he hardly sways an inch. 'I thought you said you couldn't pass through the Veil. How did you know her if you haven't been in my world for the last century?'

Hex purses his lips, remaining silent.

'The least you can do is tell me when and how,' I urge, the initial rush of anger passing.

If some magic binds him, he might be physically unable to speak on the details. Nevertheless, nothing is stopping me from coaxing as much as I can out of him to test the boundaries.

'You're right; I haven't been to the mortal lands in over a century,' he hints, eyes flashing.

'So... you must have met her here in the Underworld.' My hand lifts to cover my gaping mouth, then falls to my pounding heart. 'Fuck. I'm not the first, am I?'

Hex blinks softly, slowly, a non-committal nod to the truth.

'My mum... was she... was she the woman you told me about? The one who completed the maze?' I question, mind lighting up with newfound understanding.

Jaw clenching, Hex exhales through his nose. 'Only Julius can answer your questions.'

'What about Dato or Lorcan? Do they know?'

Hex shakes his head. 'They weren't around at the time. They came after.'

'But what about—'

In a blur, Hex's hand flattens against my mouth before I finish my question. And when I resist, he drags me behind a tree.

Fighting against the impulse to bite him, I go still, knowing there must be a good reason for him to hide us.

Hex's hand drops from my mouth, but he holds his finger to his lips, instructing me to stay quiet. I frown at him, sending a question through the tightening of my eyes.

'Raptors,' he whispers, and chills slither across my skin.

Despite Hex not specifying the type, I have an inkling it's not the smaller variety we've come across in the maze thus far. The Velociraptors have kept their distance from us, and I haven't seen a Deinonychus since the one that chased me was scared off by my vamp's presence.

If Hex is hiding, that can only mean what he hears coming is bigger and not as easily intimidated.

With care, Hex pushes me up against the trunk of the tree. 'Stay here. I'll go and lead them away. Do *not* come after me.'

My eyes twirl dramatically at his stern tone. 'Can't I just hop on your back so we can zoom past them?'

'No. From the sound of things, it's a large pack. And they're blocking our path ahead,' he explains, holding my shoulders still.

At the news, my heart plummets and gets flipped over by my rolling stomach. 'Shit.'

'Stay hidden. Stay quiet. I'll be back in a flash,' Hex promises, leaning in to press a kiss to my forehead.

A second later, he's lost in a fading streak of movement. I peek around the trunk, expecting to see some sinister shapes in the distance, but the darkness prohibits my inferior sight.

For long, agonising minutes, I wait. My nails are bitten to the wick as nerves get the better of me.

What if they catch him? What if they tear him to shreds, and I'm not there to give him my blood? He could die. Like Dato and Lorcan nearly did, protecting me from those cyclopes.

Thunder claps overhead, making me jump. I look up; the sky is swirling with a darkening mist. In this low light, it's hard to tell the difference between the usual heavy grey clouds and what I suspect is something far more sinister. This storm resembles the beginnings of the one we experienced by the Well of Eternal Winter; the mist is tumbling down in columns, like living shadows.

Shit. This must be magic. This must be Julius interfering once again.

And my gut is telling me that I'm not the intended target.

Hex is.

Following my heart, I race out from behind the tree, heading straight into the eye of the storm.

CHAPTER 45

Consequences

HEX

Leaping to grab the lowest hanging branch, I dodge the jaws of the first Utahraptor as it lunges for me, its insidiously black eyes leaking shadows.

Julius has the pack of five under his command, possessing each in turn. He must be harnessing the Shadows to help him bypass the magical barrier that's preventing him from using his powers to interfere with Raven's quest.

I pull myself up to crouch above the possessed beasts, the branch just thick enough to hold my weight. All five position themselves around the tree, hissing and clicking in excitement. They're nearly double the size of a Deinonychus. They're similar to the raptors depicted in the Spielberg film Raven and Julius love so much. I watched it years ago when Julius was a child.

At least once a week, Julius forced me to accompany him to the cinema room on the lower level of the castle. It wasn't until he was a teen that his father prohibited our friendship. Even young Dato was discouraged from talking to Julius. Asterin wanted his son to focus on his studies into the curse and his role as the future king. It wasn't until Asterin disappeared and Julius became King that we started interacting again. But, by that point, he was already closed off; his childhood innocence expunged.

The red and white feathered raptors circle, flashing their sharp teeth, clawed toes scraping against the ground, upturning dirt.

'Julius, if you can hear me, stop this,' I say through gritted teeth, trying to intimidate the raptors with my display. 'Raven is close by; she could get hurt.'

Either he doesn't hear me, or he's too far gone to care. I've heard once the Shadows invade that space where your soul resides, you can lose all reason.

The biggest raptor jumps, jaws snapping. I kick it back, nearly losing balance. A second raptor tries to reach me, forcing me to spring for the higher branches. These, being more brittle, groan under the pressure and crack.

Before I can come crashing down on top of all five, I dive, rolling in the direction I have the best chance of escaping.

I must lead them away from Raven and hope Dato and Lorcan haven't travelled too far ahead. The three of us together could take on a pack. Me, alone... when they're also powered by the Shadows...

I don't stand much of a chance.

I weave and dodge their attacks using my enhanced speed, racing away from Raven's general direction.

I don't get far.

The unnatural storm rages above, throwing down smoke clouds in the shape of Julius to obstruct my path. Thunder strikes the tree to my left, lighting up this unsystematic battlefield.

I don't have time to duck for cover because the raptors are gaining ground. I loop back, and they give chase, nipping at my heels as my super speed wanes.

I didn't consume enough of Raven's blood. At the time, I was more interested in fucking her and confessing my feelings. In truth, I didn't expect Julius to be foolish enough to call on the Shadows a second time; we severely underestimated the Demon King's possessiveness.

Demons are territorial by nature, but when it comes to sex, most are open to anything, including sharing partners. This overreaction doesn't make much sense, unless he knows what Raven and I have is progressing beyond the physical.

I'm a threat to him. A threat he's willing to corrupt his soul to wipe out.

One raptor darts in front of me, and I collide with it.

After wrapping my arms around its neck, I slam it to the ground, and then we roll down the bank of the river Melas towards the water.

We cause a splash, and I wrestle with the beast, straddling its back and forcing its head under the obsidian waves as the rest of the pack watches on from the bank.

Usually, raptors don't like to enter the river, preferring to drink while perched on the drier ground. But, possessed, who knows what they'll do?

The raptor beneath me thrashes and manages to slash me with its front talons.

It catches my shirt sleeve, the material ripped from my arm. The torn skin underneath bleeds from my bicep to my wrist. To save time, I snap the raptor's neck, then wade to the other side of the bank.

The black waters are enticing the last sin I need to deal with right now—sloth. My body must be drained. As my head spins, I wash the blood from my arm, yet it still seeps more to replace.

I'm caught off-guard by the next thunderstrike. This one cracks down only a metre from me, its electric zap hitting the water's edge, sending its deadly current through anything wet, the water a conductor. I roar with pain as every fibre of my body lights up with the flash of it.

The torture only lasts a few seconds, but by the end, I'm a gasping heap in the shallows, my veins smouldering ash, my skin still burning from that internal fire.

In the aftermath of the strike, a silver lining emerges: one of the four raptors also had its feet in the river and now lies dead near the bank opposite, its feathered skin half charred. Unlike me, raptors aren't immortal beings. I don't die that easily.

When the final three raptors start wading towards me, shadowy eyes dead yet shrewd, I force myself to stand and stumble up the stonier slope away from them.

'Lorcan! Dato!' I yell through a painfully dry throat, praying they'll hear me over the baying storm.

More shadow figures of Julius tumble from the rolling sky, crackling with lightening-hot magic. I hurry to avoid them, unsure what will happen if they catch me.

The raptors are also hot on my heels. The three remaining are nearly as fast as I am, my speed hampered by blood loss and the shocking jolt of electricity.

Running is the only option. I can't fight all three, and I also can't climb a tree fast enough with my arm injured as it is. I hope that Dato and Lorcan have circled back, sensing the storm has brought danger to us. All I need to do is keep up my pace for a little longer.

A hiss on my left, too close to my ear, and a flurry of white teeth.

'Hey! Over here!' Raven shouts, and what's left of my blood runs cold.

It's not only me who whips around at the sound of her voice: all three raptors turn to focus on the brave girl standing out in the open, on the opposite bank of the river, her waving hands a distraction.

When they seem to take the bait—their attention diverting to a prettier target—I skid to a halt and then turn back, unwilling to allow Raven to put herself in harm's way to save me.

I leap onto the smallest at the back, looping both arms around its neck and using all the strength I have left to shatter its bones.

'Hex, watch out!' Raven screams in warning.

Teeth clamp down on my shoulder. The raptor drags me off the corpse of the one I killed and shakes me while the second raptor crouches, ready to pounce.

Sensing this, I reach behind to grab the raptor that has me in its jaws by the head and heave it forward. I roll its weight over my shoulder and hurl it at the second raptor, a sizeable chunk of my skin ripping off with it.

I dip my chin, finding my clavicle bone exposed, the tissue around it still in the first raptor's mouth.

Head swimming and pain profound, my back hits a tree.

The two raptors close in. The one with my blood around its snout tilts its head, its lips peeling back in a snarl, almost as if Julius is behind its soulless eyes, taunting me in my final moments.

'Raven, run! Find Dato and Lorcan. They'll keep you safe,' I call out, not knowing her whereabouts; she's disappeared from view.

Both raptors stalk straight for me, savouring the taste of my fear in the thinning air.

I try one last plea. 'Julius, *please*. Are we not friends?'

The raptor, with my skin still between its teeth, hisses.

I guess that's a no.

No matter. I refuse to go down without a fight. I haven't lived this long to be taken out by a fucking oversized bird.

When the first raptor lurches forward, I swerve to the side, its snout hitting the tree trunk. Less than a beat later, the second raptor leaps for me, its claws leading the charge.

All at once, a scream rips through the darkness behind me as a bright ball of light zooms past my head and hits the raptor square in the chest, sending it reeling back.

Spinning to fall on my knees, Raven catches my eye, her skin glowing pure white, two small spheres of luminous energy pulsing in her palms.

By the fucking blood!

I was right.

It's *Her*.

The first raptor stumbles, its eyes clearing momentarily before the Shadows rush back in to swell its pupils. Cautiously, it backs off, head tilted in confusion.

Hopefully, Julius can see Raven now. If he knows she's in the midst of this, surely he won't risk her life just to end mine?

I get my answer when the first raptor retreats, bounding away from us.

A moment later, the chaotic storm starts to settle. The Shadows return to the sky. The clashes of thunder die out.

Raven rushes over to me, the light coming from inside her fading to reveal those pretty, steely-blue eyes I love staring into. 'Hex! Oh, my God. Are you okay? Can you stand?' She hauls me to my feet, insisting on being my crutch.

'I'll be fine. All we need... to do... is find... Dato and Lorcan,' I splutter, my blood streaming down her cream top, leaving soaking, scarlet trails.

'You need to drink from me,' she says, bringing her wrist to my mouth. 'Come on, bite me.'

Weakly, I shake my head. 'I'd need a lot, darling, and I refuse to weaken you. Dato and Lorcan will help me.'

'Hex, I said bite me!' Raven repeats vehemently, her tone fierce—re-solved—jaw set. At my hesitation, she adds, 'If you don't bite me, I'll bite myself and force my blood down your fucking throat.' Her loving threat brings a smile to my trembling lips.

But, right as I'm about to submit to her request, we're pounced upon.

One second, we're upright, and the next, Raven is being pressed down on top of me as I sink into the mud, the weight of the second raptor on her back, its eyes clear. Julius isn't controlling it anymore.

Warm blood spews from Raven's mouth onto my face. It's only then I notice the tip of the raptor's large toe claw poking through the skin of her neck.

My chest feels like it's collapsing in on me. I scream her name in horror and look up, wild eyes taking in the raptor as it dips its head down, preparing to tear into her flesh.

Trying to shield, I fold Raven into my body, one arm around her shoulders, the other squashed between our bodies. I can't roll to take her place because the raptor still has us pinned, its claw embedded in her throat.

There's nothing I can do.

'No,' I sob, closing my eyes, defeat heavier and more crushing than this raptor on top of us. I can't watch this.

There's a snarl before the deadly weight is suddenly torn away from us. The first raptor—still under Julius' control—has the second raptor by the throat.

But I don't dare watch what happens next because right at that second, Raven's blood spills from the ripped wound on her neck into my open mouth. I quickly roll her onto her back, then use my hands to plug the hole at the base of her throat, applying pressure.

Raven lies still, her lips tinged blue, her skin chalky white, eyes glassy.

'Come on, deal-breaker. Stay with me. Don't you dare die,' I force out, voice rough as I frantically try to stop the bleeding.

To the left of me, there's a thud.

Inclining my head, I see both raptors lying dead, a demon-shaped shadow flickering above until it abruptly vanishes.

The consequences of its wrath bleeding out before me.

CHAPTER 46

Priority

JULIUS

The shock doesn't discard me like the Shadows do. Although I wish it would.

Instead, it stays trapped inside, stealing my breath, freezing my limbs, punching a hole straight through my ribcage as the darkness recedes, leaving me cold and alone in my throne room.

I killed her.

Raven would never have been attacked if I hadn't led those raptors straight to her.

I thought I had them under control.

They were only supposed to kill Hex. But she got in the way—she put herself between them. She fucking saved that worthless vrykolaka and will end up dead in his place.

Watching her bleeding out in Hex's arms... her life draining away because I couldn't control my temper...

Fuck! I can't just sit here and wait for her soul to vacate—abandon her.

I can't abandon her.

I can't let her die.

At this point, I couldn't care less about the curse or the fucking prophecy. All I want is to keep that beautiful heart of hers beating.

My feet had already moved to the window before my brain had time to catch up.

Sensing my connection to her dimming at a drastic speed, my power bursts from me, shattering the window until it provides a clear path to freedom—to her.

My wings manifest, itching to spread, and I dive out of the window without any doubt in my mind, the terms of our deal a long-forgotten priority.

I'm coming for you, starling.

CHAPTER 47

My Heart

RAVEN

The metallic tang on my tongue is hot and thick, sliding down my oesophagus while I choke and sputter. This blood is sweeter than my own, as smooth and soothing as honey. It numbs the pain.

Hex's voice is muffled, like I'm underwater, and he's the surface I'm striving to reach. 'Please work. Please work.'

I think I'm dying.

I'm so cold.

'Come on. For the love of souls, work faster!' His groan breaks with impatience.

There's a constant pressure against my neck. It hurts less than it did before. But I still can't breathe through all the liquid clogging my lungs, throat, and nose. It's everywhere. Everywhere except my veins.

'Please hold on. A few more minutes. It will work. It has to work,' Hex utters close to my ear, his voice clearer, if not thicker. 'Don't let him take your soul. He doesn't deserve it. Keep holding onto it, deal-breaker. You keep holding on to it. All right?'

A pinch to my nose closes that airway. Lips seal over mine, and then air pushes into my gurgling lungs. After that, there's rhythmic pressure on my chest, up and down, up and down, pumping my heart for me.

Another life-saving breath, then more of that honied blood.

Slowly, my awareness returns, along with the strength and capability to breathe on my own.

'Good girl, keep fighting.' Hex sounds weaker the stronger I grow.

Cold skin presses against my lips, forcing them back open. Moaning, I try to close my mouth and twist my head. He's giving me too much.

'Just a little more.'

'No,' I say, raspy and barely above a whisper. I lift a numb hand to bat his away from my face. 'I don't want to turn into a vampire.'

Hex's chuckle is my biggest comfort. 'Then don't die.' He catches my flailing hand and kisses it.

His lips are ice.

Only ten seconds later, my eyelids are light enough to lift. When I open them, the state of my vamp makes me gasp.

He's covered in blood; it's smeared all over his face, in his hair. It's oozing from his open shoulder wound, the cream of his bone uncovered. The skin that's intact and visible beneath all that red is deathly pale. He's shaking as though his body is fighting a losing battle.

Seeing him so weak brings tears to my eyes and fear to my heart. 'Hex,' I weep, a sob threatening to break free.

He's sacrificed so much to save me. Any doubt I had before of his feelings vanishes. He *is* falling in love with me. Or perhaps the past tense is more accurate now.

Hex's expression relaxes somewhat as he wipes the blood away from my neck. 'It's nearly healed. I almost lost you for a minute there.'

'Are the raptors gone?' I ask, panic still clawing at my chest.

He nods, and suddenly, his supporting arm gives out; he collapses on top of me. Quickly, I guide him onto his back so he can rest. His eyelids stay closed for too long before they flutter open and then close again.

I lightly slap his cheek to rouse him. 'Hex. Hex, can you hear me?'

'I can hear you,' he manages, eyes still shut. 'I just need to sleep for a while.'

'No. No. No sleep,' I dissuade, shaking him awake. 'We need to find Dato and Lorcan.'

After I push to my knees, I grab his good arm and tug him up to a sitting position. His head lolls to the side, his neck not strong enough to hold the weight of it.

'Come on, Hex. Now it's your turn to fight. Stand up with me,' I order, holding back tears so I can be useful to him in his time of need.

The thought of my vamp shutting his eyes and never waking up again has my stomach churning with a frightening amount of dread.

Hex was right: what we've found in each other is not too much—it's not nearly enough. We need to fight for more time together. That fight starts with our lives, and then, my soul. If we can make it through all that, I'm sure we can work out the logistics tomorrow.

Hex can't die now; I won't let him.

I haul him to his feet with a strenuous groan, carrying most of his weight. The muscles in my back tighten at the strain—aching, but my well-being is no longer my top concern.

'See. You're stronger than you know,' Hex says, locking his knees so they don't buckle.

'That's because you gave me too much blood!' I snap, irrationally angry at him for putting me first. No one has ever done that before. No one has been that selfless for me.

'Only you would be angry at me for saving your life,' he remarks, his laugh a stuttered breath.

I try to walk, supporting him, but it's a struggle. The tears I've been fighting fall in frustration. 'Why would you do that? Why would you give me so much when you needed it?'

Tenderly, Hex rotates my face to his, pausing my attempts to drag him forward. 'I would have given you every last drop if I had to. Because, if you'd died, the last worthwhile piece of me would die with you. And I can no longer live in a world without your light.' He brushes his lips against mine, then draws back to hold my gaze like it's the most precious sight he'd cherish through any dark days we may face. 'You have my heart, deal-breaker. It's yours.'

Before I can melt into a puddle of tears, Hex kisses me with trembling lips, and I let myself freefall, resigned to try anything to keep him, even if that means I stay lost in this moment forever.

Suddenly, there's a jolt and a crunching sound, then a short gasp against my lips.

Confused, I pull back, assessing Hex's stunned expression.

In that split second, time stops for us. But only for one last heartbeat.

I catch movement behind my vamp's shoulder—a shock of white hair, pearlescent wings bristling, and a pair of narrow silver eyes shaded with vengeful malice.

The Demon King.

When time catches up with us, Hex topples over, and I come crashing down with him on top of me.

Grappling at his body to gain purchase, my fingers slip into a hole in his back, wet and gaping. With it still not registering, I peer up at the Demon King, looming above us, a bloody mass of something pulsing in his hand.

With a vicious sneer, the Demon King growls, 'No, Hex. It's mine. Your heart is *mine*.'

A scream rips from my newly healed throat without enough air to sustain it. In disbelief, I roll Hex onto his back, begging him to open his eyes through ragged sobs. I'm shaking him desperately, frantically, unable to accept what's just happened.

Hex can't be dead. He's immortal. He can't die. There's still a chance I can save him.

Hyperventilating, I slide the thin skin of my wrist between my teeth and tear at it, the physical pain not comparing to the turmoil of seeing Hex lifeless—*heartless*—before me.

I force my blood—his borrowed blood—into his mouth. 'Please, no.'

'That won't work, love. Without a heart, vrykolakas can't heal,' the Demon King says with no hint of sympathy or remorse, his arms looping around my waist with the intent to pull me off Hex.

Like a wild cat, I react by bucking and scratching while screaming at him to let me go.

'I'm not going to hurt you, starling. I'm sorry for what happened with the raptors. I'm sorry for not having complete control of the situation. I'll make it up to you,' he promises, dragging me away from my vamp.

'You killed him! You killed him!' I repeat, over and over, the truth finally hitting me.

'He betrayed me.'

'But he saved me,' I fire back, my face hot and wet. 'He was saving me from *you*.'

The Demon King spins me around to face him before crushing me against his chest, my arms trapped at my sides. 'Then I made the right choice in ending his life. Now, you're all mine.' His eyes are hard, darker than I remember—truly soulless.

With ferocity, I spit in his face. 'I'll never be yours. Not after this.'

Even stunned by my venom, the Demon King smirks, my spit shining on his cheek. 'Only time will tell. Let's see how long that fire in you lasts before it's dying to be stoked again.' His voice is a seductive purr, implying that I'll eventually come begging for his touch.

Sick to my stomach, I struggle against him. 'The only thing you've ever stoked in me is my hatred, demon. I'll fucking kill you before I ever let you have me in any way.'

The Demon King's jaw clamps shut, muscles straining, as he finally hears the truth of my words and the determination behind them.

Through the fuzziness of my anger and grief, I remember when and where we are. 'You left your castle. I've won our deal.' It all comes out in one rush of shocked breath. Mine and Robin's souls are ours to keep. But, despite the good news relieving some worry, the ache in my heart doesn't dissipate.

Hex is dead because of me—because he helped me. Because he dared to love what his king tried to claim for himself.

'You have to let me and my brother go,' I pronounce, lifting my chin, feigning the triumph I should be feeling now.

But I don't.

All I want to do is crumble beside Hex's body until my tears dry to dust at the hope of love again lost.

Silver irises flickering to black, the Demon King replies in a low tone, 'You may have won your soul, starling, but your freedom was never part of the deal. From the start, I warned you...' He lowers his face so our noses brush, and I recoil. 'I was never going to let you go.'

Before I can react, the Demon King's powerful wings sweep us into the air, and we shoot upwards fast. The wind whips my hair back, the shock of its force leaving me unable to breathe—to think.

'I'm sure some time in my dungeons will warm you up to the idea of bargaining with me again since it only took you a few hours to offer your body to my commanders.' His bitterness underlines the threat.

'No!' I shriek, panic surging. He's planning to lock me up until I agree to hand over my soul. I can't let that happen. Not after everything I've been through to get here. Hex told me to fight for myself, and I will continue to do just that.

Thinking of Hex has a tingling warmth spreading rapidly through me, rising to the surface. 'Playing your game, demon, I fought for my soul and won. In the face of danger and strife, I claimed myself. And I will not allow you to have any power over me.'

Faltering, the Demon King squints down at me, but then his eyes widen in surprise. Blood drains from his face as it starts to glow.

No, he's not glowing.

I am.

Light bursts from my mouth in a silent scream, and we freeze mid-air. Magic dances around us as we float, suspended in a moment I finally take control of.

'Raven, no!' the Demon King pleads, a second before I explode.

CHAPTER 48

Catch Up

'The storm is clearing,' I shout down to Lorcan from the tumultuous sky. 'Try it now.'

We've been stuck behind the shadow barrier since the storm started. Julius is undoubtedly causing this chaos; the Shadows must have lured him into using them for fuck knows what. But whatever is happening inside the eye of it can't be good.

Worry is its own hurricane inside me, twisting my insides into tight knots. Would Julius kill Hex for defying him? And would he kill the mortal for denying him? If Raven were a regular mortal, maybe.

On the rare occasion in the past, we've made sure the few mortals who chose to venture into the maze met a swift end. The fact that Julius ordered us to protect her makes me question whether he'd hurt her now. But Julius has always been unpredictable. His mercurial moods can give me whiplash. He can joke with us one minute, then fly into a rage at the slightest perceived disrespect the next.

Julius murdering Raven to secure her soul is what I had expected at first. However, upon meeting her, I quickly came to understand his desire to claim more than just that fiery energy residing deep in her being. Not only is the shell encasing it beautiful, but everything about her shines brighter than anything the Underworld has ever seen. To lose even a hair on her head would be a travesty.

And Hex is practically our big brother. He's been around, getting us all into trouble since Julius and I were kids. Lorcan and Hex are closer friends, spending most of their free time drinking and hunting together. If Julius' wrath claimed Hex, we'd all be at a loss, even Julius. Though he'd never admit it.

In his lycanthrope form, Lorcan tackles the Shadows again, groaning in his efforts to push past the barrier they've created to prevent us from entering.

Testing them myself, I flex my wings in a powerful thrust, sending air surging forward in the hopes of dispersing the impenetrable cloud of dark, smoky swirls from my flight path.

'They're giving way,' Lorcan yells, continuing to push, his clawed hands sinking through.

With my wings keeping me suspended in the calming air, I shove against the Shadows. The solid mass that climbed to an infinite point—I wouldn't dare try to reach—finally gives way under our combined pressure.

As expected, Lorcan makes it to the other side first but doesn't bother waiting for me. He knows I'm faster than him when I take to the skies.

Luckily, I carve out a big enough path through the volatile mass for my wings to fit.

Once I'm through, I soar ahead, catching up with Lorcan and surpassing him.

From high above, the maze glows iridescent. Faintly, but enough to navigate at night. I've flown over the maze thousands of times; I know it like the back of my hand. My sharp eyesight also helps me in times like these when I'm searching for something in particular.

It's not long before I spot three figures amidst a pack of dead raptors not too far from the river Melas. The first is lying down, face turned up, eyes closed—Hex. He's covered in blood and unmoving.

Oh, fuck. Am I too late?

The second is smaller and slighter, distinctly feminine—Raven. She's bloody, too, and being dragged away from the lifeless vrykolaka by the third: large white wings, silvery-blonde hair, dark emerald suit—the Demon King himself.

Fear, sudden and surprising, infiltrates my heart, threatening to hack it to pieces. Hex is likely dead, and Raven could be next.

I must save her. There's no doubt in my mind. Even if the danger I'm saving her from is my king—my friend.

Flying faster than I ever have before, I shoot towards them, still too far away to attract their attention.

With Raven squeezed tight against him (unwillingly, from the looks of it), Julius launches straight up into the air with a powerful swoosh of his wings. At first, Raven clings to him, terrified for her life, but then something strange happens.

The mortal starts to glow, and Julius blanches when he notices, his wings wavering.

Only a heartbeat later, Raven's muscles go taught, and light explodes from her, engulfing them both. The beams of bright white are shocking in contrast to the murky, coal-black sky, chasing any shadow that remained to the corners in which they belong.

Upon realising I've slowed to watch, I shake off this stupor and flatten my arms to my sides so there's less resistance to speed.

If I was told yesterday that I'd be risking even one of my feathers for a mortal, I wouldn't have believed it. Now, I'm flying headfirst into a blazing ball of light energy without regard for my safety.

When the light peters out, I spot Raven; a speck of dust in the rippling wind. She's falling, and she's falling fast.

Julius has also been blown away, his wings smoking. He looks dazed. But, when he lifts his hands to discover them empty, Raven's name tears from his throat with as much panic as is currently seizing my heart while watching her hurtling towards the ground beneath him.

Swooping, I tuck my wings close to my body, letting gravity and force propel me down at lightning speed. My eyes want to close against the berating wind, but I keep them open and locked on my target.

With only metres to spare, I catch her, but the momentum doesn't save us from the ground.

Before we take the hit, I cocoon us in my wings; they absorb the brunt of the crash. Pain lashes at me from all sides as we skid across the hard dirt, my fragile mortal a tight ball in my arms.

With my broken wings bloodied and a trail of feathers in our wake, I uncurl once we're stationary, a maze wall being the obstacle that finally stopped our battering roll.

Julius lands with a hard thud a moment later, still calling her name, eyes wide and bloodshot. His wings don't seem to be in as bad a shape as mine. But they're singed at the tips, with clumps of feathers missing. 'Is she unharmed?' he enquires, rushing over.

'Stay back, Julius! I won't let you hurt her,' I shout his way, cradling a still unconscious Raven to my chest.

His mouth parted, Julius blinks at me as if I've punched him in the gut. 'I—I wasn't... that's the last thing I want to do.'

'Is he dead? Hex? Did you kill him?' I question, delayed emotions threatening to overwhelm me.

A flicker of something like guilt passes over his expression before he wipes it away with his hand. 'I had to. He betrayed me. Raven admitted he was planning to keep her soul from me.'

Fed up with this whole situation, I burst out with, 'We all made that decision. Me, Hex, Lorcan. We all decided to help her get to the castle because you, *Julius...*' His name is a curse on my tongue. 'You, Demon King, do not deserve her light.'

Nostrils flaring, jaw hard as stone, Julius orders, 'Give her to me.'

'No,' I defy, shifting a broken wing to function as a fragile barrier.

Julius' top lip curls into a snarl. 'I'm not above killing you too, harpy.'

'If you threaten him, you threaten me, King,' Lorcan snarls back, leaping between us, the coarse hair on his body standing on end.

'Are you both willing to die for her?' Julius asks, though he doesn't seem all that surprised. He knows how much Raven is worth.

'As much as you're willing to kill your closest friends for her,' I retort, my gaze falling onto Hex's bloodied body again, throat closing.

'Hex is dead?' Lorcan whispers in shock, eyes finding him, too. A whine escapes his snout before his attention sharpens back on Julius.

'Friends?' Julius snorts a dry laugh. 'You're barely my allies, as you're proving by withholding my prize.'

'I'm no one's prize. I won my soul the moment you left your castle before the clock ran out.' Raven's voice is weak yet full of conviction. She pushes up to sit in my lap, my arms still around her. 'You've lost, demon. You've lost us all.'

'I can't lose,' Julius counteracts, more measured than when he addressed Lorcan and me. 'If I lose, the Underworld loses, and every demon dies.'

'What are you talking about?' Lorcan, without turning his back on Julius, helps Raven and me to our feet while continuing to shield us behind his huge, wolfish frame.

Rubbing his face, Julius exhales his defeat. 'The curse. If I don't break it, we're all doomed. Raven is the key. I'm sure of it.'

'I don't understand. The curse is the DiMinos' cross to bear,' I say, thinking he must be exaggerating his need for Raven, so we hand her over without a fight.

'That light you saw explode from her, Dato... that's the kind of energy only an Arkhian can muster,' Julius hints, clearly not keen on giving too much away in Raven's presence.

An Arkhian? That can't be.

'Fucking mazes, you mean... she's of the Lost Light?' Lorcan's follow-up question is more of a gasp.

Julius nods, face solemn.

'Hey! Stop speaking in code. I'm right here. I deserve to know what's going on with me,' Raven speaks up, rightly aggrieved.

'I will explain everything if you come to the castle with me. I won't hurt you. I swear it,' Julius bargains, holding out his hand to tempt her to him.

Raven takes a step behind me while shaking her head. Her arms wrap around herself. 'I can't trust you. You killed Hex without a second thought, like he meant nothing.'

Julius looks skyward in exasperation before he bellows, 'Why the fuck do you care so much?! You've only known them a day. For the love of souls, this is ridiculous.' He rakes a rough hand through his wild hair, pulling at the roots. 'You're meant for me, Raven. You're my soul's twin. That's our curse *and* our salvation. We've been bound to each other since we took our first breath together. One born. One made. Fates forever entwined. There's even a fucking prophecy about us. I need to re-join our souls to put an end to the curse. But the kicker is that you must willingly offer it to me with love's innocence. This deal was an excuse to get you here for an extended period. This is not at all what I wanted. You weren't supposed to choose the maze. You were supposed to choose *me*!'

I've never seen Julius this vulnerable before. And here he is: his polished veneer crumbling. He's no longer the stoic, controlled king whose only emotion is anger. His eyes shine in the darkness, face pained, hurt laid bare.

But Raven doesn't soften. 'And you thought kidnapping my brother and forcing me into a deal for my soul was the best way to get me to fall in love with you?' Her laugh is humourless, almost cruel. 'You're pathetic. You're weak-willed. You're full of hatred and spite. No amount of time would have been enough for me to fall for you. What I said before still and will always stand: if I had a choice, no part of me would ever be yours to claim. I offer you nothing but my pity, demon.'

Faced with her vitriol, Julius wilts, losing hope, and as if the ground mirrors his mood, it starts to quake.

Then, a deafening roar, loud enough to crack the Underworld in two, erupts like the boom of a volcano.

CHAPTER 49

The Real Evil

RAVEN

As a fresh wave of horror douses my anger, I ask, 'What the fuck was that?'

The Demon King's face loses all colour. His eyes are wild as they dart around in heightened paranoia. 'No. Not now. It's too soon.'

'What's too soon? What's going on, Julius?' Dato questions, placing a protective arm around my waist, his tail joining it.

'No. No. I followed the rules,' the Demon King mutters, quickly losing his bearings as the rumble of the earth continues. 'Unless...' His silver eyes alight on me, and fear flickers in them. 'Your power woke him. It must be calling to him as it does me.'

'Wait, who?' Lorcan demands, needing clarification. 'Who woke up?'

The Demon King lurches towards me, shoving Dato aside, but Lorcan grabs the Demon King's arm to stop him from touching me.

'We need to get her to the castle. Now! She's in danger. We all are. This maze is no longer safe for us to roam,' the Demon King claims, ripping his arm out of Lorcan's clawed grasp.

'What danger are we facing, Julius? Explain.' Lorcan grabs hold of my wrist instead, not giving the Demon King a chance to fly off with me again.

'Get your paws off her before I sever your head, wolf. She's mine to protect,' the Demon King threatens, struggling to contain his growing frustration.

Untold power pulsing at the tips of my fingers, I lift them to show their glow. 'I can protect myself, thanks.'

With a panicked expression, the Demon King snatches my hands to rub the light out of my fingertips. His unexpected touch sends shockwaves through me. 'Trap that power deep inside of you, starling. Or you'll lead him right to us.'

I tear my hands out of his clutches. 'Don't touch me!'

'I'm trying to protect you!' he shouts back, concern etched between his eyebrows.

I glare at him, set on never trusting any word from his mouth, even if my gut tells me to listen to his warnings. 'Explain, then maybe I'll listen.'

A resigned sigh rushes out of the Demon King, and he steps back to give me space. The ground is still trembling, a low buzz of foreboding ringing in the air.

'The monster behind that roar is my father. He's been roused from an enchanted sleep.'

Looking befuddled, Dato cuts in. 'Your father?'

'Hang on, I thought Asterin was dead,' Lorcan interjects at the same time.

The Demon King is scanning our surroundings when he answers them both. 'No. I was supposed to kill him, but I... I couldn't.' He pauses, gaze dropping to the ground in apparent shame. 'Instead, I bartered part of my soul for an incantation from the Sorceress Medena, which would force him into a deep sleep. I hid him in a sealed-off, underground cave within the maze. He wasn't supposed to wake until I was ready.'

'Until you were ready to kill him?' I ask, hating that my sympathy for this demon is rising to cause my heart more suffering.

The Demon King nods once, face sombre. 'I thought I had more time. I thought I could break the curse first. I had hoped that with the curse broken, he'd be cured, and then I wouldn't have to go through with it.'

'The curse infected him?' The slashed lines on Dato's forehead are severe. 'With what?'

'With malicious magic,' the Demon King utters ominously, and the night darkens around us, closing in. 'You think I'm the one to fear here? Asterin is the real evil I'm trying to prevent. And if I can't stop him, he will destroy everything in his path. That's why my ancestors created this maze; it's not only to keep other demons out but to keep the monster we all turn into inside for as long as possible. Every DiMinos king succumbs to the infection if they can't convince the first daughter of one particular line of women—' His eyes find mine. '—to love him enough to pledge her soul as a sacrifice.'

Sacrifice my soul? For him? That's fucking laughable.

Another roar splits the air, and every hair on my body stands on end, chills tumbling down my spine in rolling waves.

We all share unsettled looks.

'He won't stop until we're all dead. Until every layer of the Underworld is wiped out,' the Demon King continues, inching closer to me, and against my better judgement, I let him.

When he's within touching distance, he peers down at me, expression smoother. 'Come with me to the castle, and I swear to protect you—protect Robin. To the Veil with it, I'll even protect these treacherous bastards,' he says, sliding Lorcan and Dato a disdainful glance. He offers his hand, giving me the choice.

'I don't want to be protected. I want to be free from you. I want to take my brother home. And I want you to let Dato and Lorcan off the hook when it comes to all their perceived crimes against you. Offer me those things, and I will come with you to the castle,' I counter, setting out my terms, determined to stick to them.

The Demon King's fists clench at his sides as he inhales deeply, as though it's taking everything in him not to force me into this by more nefarious means. 'Fine. I agree to your terms. I will allow you and your brother to go free as soon as the threat of my father is under control, and I have the power to restore you to your world. Until then, you will live with me in my castle.'

'Julius, you can restore them to the mortal lands right now. Don't mislead her,' Dato challenges, still showing loyalty to me.

The Demon King shakes his head. 'I can't. Not anymore. The Shadows have taken my power as payment. If I had any left, don't you think I would have killed you and blinked her back to the castle by now?'

'Oh, shit. You're powerless?' Lorcan's elongated snout crinkles. 'But, if you can't blink us back to the castle, how do you expect us to get there?'

'Well, I had planned to fly Raven there,' the Demon King answers, pointing to his singed wings. 'That might prove tricky now.'

'I'm not leaving with you. Not unless Dato and Lorcan come, too,' I state, sliding a hand into Dato's and the other into Lorcan's.

Once they twist their heads in my direction, their expressions soften. It's a little odd to see the fierce face of a wolf filled with affection, but it's not as unnerving as when Lorcan's angry, even in his human-like form.

'Without magic or wings, the only option is to make a run for Galbrek and hope my father hasn't caught our scent already,' the Demon King suggests, clearly not happy with the idea of travelling by foot with the threat of his monstrous father impending.

'I'm taking Hex's body back with us,' Lorcan announces, his voice gruff. 'I'm not leaving him for the beasts to devour.'

None of us can stop our attention from flitting over to where Hex still lies. A burning pressure returns, throbbing behind my eyes. The pieces of my broken heart fall away to unsettle my stomach.

Broad shoulders heavy, Lorcan trudges over to Hex and picks him up with more gentleness than I ever thought him capable.

Dato squeezes my hand, eyes glistening with unshed tears. I return the gesture, my focus fixing on the Demon King, hoping my hatred could pierce through his cold, black heart, destroying it as he did to my vamp's.

The Demon King stares right back, face unreadable, but I catch the hard swallow before he looks away—looks anywhere but at me or the body in Lorcan's arms.

'Let's get moving.' The Demon King urges us forward, but I round on him.

'One week. You have one week to subdue your father in whatever way you can. After that, you either find someone who can magic Robin and me back to my world, or you take us to the Veil so we can pass through ourselves. With our souls intact, that should be possible.'

The Demon King's jaw works for a beat before he jerks his head in a reluctant nod. 'I guess one week is fair,' he says, despite his expression conveying the opposite. 'I accept your terms.'

For too long a moment, we hold each other's gaze. And, from somewhere intangible inside me, my new well of power swirls with the longing I've always felt in the depths of my dreams.

The Demon King promised to explain everything to me when we reached the castle. But something tells me, deep down, I already know what I am.

What *we* are to each other.

And for that reason, I'm not looking forward to claiming the promise of truth.

'Julius, just so we're aware, what monster are we trying to avoid?' Lorcan queries, falling behind to tail us as we start towards Galbrek. I'm beyond grateful that I don't have to watch him carrying Hex all the way there.

The Demon King takes the lead, and with my concentration forced on his back, the tremors shaking his feathers are not hard to miss.

'The Minotaur,' he finally answers. The tremble in his voice is also a clue to his growing fear. 'My father is the Minotaur.'

Stay Connected

If you want to discuss all things *Dangers Unclaimed*, here's the link to the official Facebook group:

f facebook.com/groups/856301105968707/

And here are the links to my author socials:

♪ tiktok.com/@amberbayleyauthor

◎ https://instagram.com/amberbayleyauthor

The Untold Dangers series will continue with *Dangers Unbound*, releasing Autumn 2024...

My next book, *The Haven Ten: Recollection*, is the second book in The Haven Ten series—a sci-fi romance with a thrilling twist. The first book is available here:

https://mybook.to/IVBgF

Author's Note

If you know me... no, you don't.

Seriously, *Dangers Unclaimed* is the spiciest story I've ever written. I had so much fun working on it. This book combines all my favourite things: Greek mythology, morally grey characters, a sex-positive, pansexual woman discovering and acting on her wants and desires, 80's movie vibes, and dinosaurs.

If you'd told me before I joined BookTok that I'd release a book like this, I wouldn't have believed you, but I absolutely would have hoped you weren't joking.

Acknowledgements

I want to start by thanking spicy BookTok for broadening my horizons. My depraved little mind has been thriving.

Thank you to all my readers for your support. It's tough as an indie author to market your own books, and when people take a chance on work that isn't backed by a big publishing house, it goes a long way to legitimise and destigmatise self-publishing.

Special thanks to my beta readers: Vicky Seymour-Hunt, Taryn Jones, Emilia Higginson, Kimberly, and Laura Bayley. Your feedback really helped me polish the second draft.

And thank you to my copy-editor, Kelly George, for your quick turnaround time and thorough clean-up of my sometimes wordy prose.

Thank you to Holly Ballard, my gorgeous proof-reader, for your eagle-eyed help.

To my favourite bookish people and dear friends, Joyce Dunne, Vicky Seymour-Hunt, and Morgan Koogle, thanks again for being the best support system a girl can ask for. I love you guys so much.

I also want to thank the awesome people who have shown support of my debut novel 'The Haven Ten' on their socials: Carley Lightfoot, Holly Rose, Laura A. Robinson, Holly Ballard, Sophie Claypole, Taryn Jones, Jessica Wootten, Meghan Walsh, Katrina, Lizzie, Haley, and everyone who has read, shared posts, and left reviews. It's been a joy to watch your videos and read your honest and sometimes hilarious reviews. I'm looking at you, Carley.

As for my support system outside of the bookish social sphere; I want to thank the friends and family who are always cheering me on by either reading drafts or buying my books despite not being massive readers. These lovely people include: Laura Bayley, Holly Sugden, Daniel Brooks, Stephanie Poole, Scott and Jodie Meaker, Joy and Chris Wood, and Jade Parkes.

And to my infinitely patient and supportive partner: Russell Wood. Thank you for always knowing how to pick me up on the days my ADHD brain brings me to my knees. You've been a little scared to read this book... I don't blame you for being intimidated ;p. But I know I have your unwavering support in whatever I write, no matter how many inhumanly large, fictional dicks there are in it. I love you endlessly.

About the Author

Amber Bayley started writing screenplays in her teenage years, when she dreamed of becoming an actress and filmmaker, but writing books held a special storytelling magic.

Amber spends her time on the southeast coast of England, living with her partner, a mini dachshund called Hazel, and two needy cats, Rosie and Cleo.

When Amber isn't being a hyper-focused hermit—spending all of her free time reading and writing books—she's teaching herself digital art and travelling the world, one mini-break at a time.

9 781739 499846